SalishSeaPress

Also by Shann Cathro Weston:

Coauthor, editor, *Naturescaping: A Place for Wildlife*
Coauthor, *The Stream Scene—Watersheds, Wildlife and People*

Poems published in *Earth Matters*
  "Stories of the Vaux's Swifts"
  "Dandelion Gifts"
  "Salmon Ceremony"

CURVE OF THE MOON

By Shann Cathro Weston

Published by Salish Sea Press

SalishSeaPress

Curve of the Moon

This is a work of fiction. All the characters and events portrayed in this book are fictional, and any resemblance to real people or incidents is purely coincidental.

Copyright © 2011 by Shann Cathro Weston

First Edition
Salish Sea Press
P.O. Box 1387
Friday Harbor, WA 98250
Cover design and interior layout by Chris Teren
Cover Art: Willow Rose
ISBN: 978-0-6154-1557-4

Library of Congress Control Number: 2010916297

This book is dedicated to Steve, Mariya and Elena. You are my heart.

And to the sacred landscapes I have been privileged to savor.

ACKNOWLEDGMENTS

First and foremost, I acknowledge the creative muse that wants what it wants. For its own reasons, this book had to be born. Secondly, to all the fiction authors who ever wrote a story to take us into another world. When my imagination grew tired, I turned to the river of your mind, put my raft in and floated on your currents.

The landscapes in this book have been my Holy Ground. I have roamed them with my soul and my footsteps, and they have nourished every breath.

Gratitude and appreciation to the music, poetry and art that grace my life.

Gratitude and appreciation to my husband, Steve. Though you did not understand the need to write this or why it took so long, you always supported me. You let it take the time you might have liked to go elsewhere. That was an act of sheer generosity. Thank you.

Gratitude and appreciation to my editors, Robin Meyer, Emily Reed, Adam Stater, and Kim Norton. I cannot even begin to say what an editor brings to writing. It is a bighearted skill and a lot of work. Thank you.

Gratitude and appreciation to Mariya Porten, Julia Loyd, Weyshawn Koons and Cady Davies for your kindly delivered corrections and edits.

Gratitude and appreciation to my friends, especially Jim and Lisa Lawrence, Liza Michaelson, Kari Koski, Christina Sesby and daughters Mariya and Elena who stood by me with unconditional support.

Gratitude and appreciation to everyone who applauded this undertaking just to see creativity at work and who understood that a writer who aspires to be an author needs encouragement at any age and any level.

Chapter 1

Aidan MacLaine spoke the ancient Gaelic words aloud as he drove north to Wester Ross. The whimsical nature of the language never failed to delight him—at once subtle and light, then demanding a deep rumble in the throat with rolling R's that seemed to be made of the hills themselves. The last time he was in the Northern Highlands, he'd taken the trouble to learn just enough to appreciate it.

Now, the intimate translation of landscape poured unbidden through his mind. The delicate russet of bracken fern that sparkled with dew, "raineach". Shining in the distance, the gray mountain regally bore its own name: "Craig Liath". A spill of rough rocks would be marked "garbh", and those who dared travel cross-country should know it. Aidan smiled slightly, remembering how he'd learned that word the hard way.

His fingers played on the steering wheel, composing as he

drove—strong, haunting notes like the mountain Slioch, turning lively as the towns of Kinlochewe and Gairloch.

Three weeks of freedom. Even with the pain and the recurrent numbness in his back—or maybe because of it, he needed room to feel and breathe. Once he'd started thinking about the Highlands, he couldn't stop. Mountains. Wild spaces. He could hear their siren call in his sleep.

This is the right thing to do, he thought again. *There was no way I could justify this to anyone at home. Just couldn't tell them much.* He'd made them settle with vague and brief. In three weeks, he would be in Seattle. *Then I will face the doctor and whatever he has to say. I seem to have failed at trying to will this thing away.*

Six months ago, when he received the letter from Kieran inviting him to come visit the proud new owner of The Big Misty Lodge, he had laughed out loud with pleasure. Years ago, on their first encounter, Kieran had confessed with guilt, but no remorse, how he loved the Scottish Highlands more than beauties of his native Ireland. He'd found his paradise.

Busy, distracted by pain, Aidan had dismissed the invitation. *Been there, done that. When I could scale peaks with the best of them. But now . . . why would a man with a fragile back go to a mountain climbing lodge?* He wrote his congratulations—someday, he would come see how the dream was unfolding.

When the long folded invitation fell out of his pocket in a Glasgow pub, Aidan re-read Kieran's colorful descriptions of The Big Misty, flooded by a sudden wave of anticipation. Perhaps he would rent a car and point it toward the place, consider going further on the drive. It felt like something was waiting for him there. Something important.

By the next morning, he'd left Glasgow behind and traveled through Glencoe with its brooding mountains and haunted history. The place was as beautiful as he remembered, sparking memories. Young and eager for mountains, he'd traveled north—savoring its great swings of light and season, the stark vastness in these mountains that would roll on into the Torridons and then to the Fisherfields, the great wilderness of the Highlands. *How have I gone so long without seeing it again?* Restless energy danced through him. *That's it. I have to go. Now.*

Upon his arrival in Fort William, the idea of seeing Kieran and his lodge had taken hold. When he heard Kieran's cheery welcome on the phone, he realized his deep yearning had found its summons.

"Will you be wanting the scenic route then, Aidan? As usual? Not sure that's the best plan now, with the western storm coming in."

Aidan enjoyed the sound of his old friend's Irish accent, pictured the dimple ready to accompany his broad grin. "I'll choose the route, Kieran. And you could probably predict it. I'll keep an eye on the weather. Promise. But I do require directions to find your hidden little road."

"That's exactly the point, Aidan. It can be treacherous in wicked weather. Two rivers to cross. You've got to time it perfectly."

But of course Aidan would ignore the warnings. Kieran knew he would, though he sighed heavily as he set to giving meticulous instructions.

"You're a stubborn man, Aidan."

"Not trying to be. I just don't want to give up the whole piece of it. Now I must go and not dally. I'll be there by whisky hour."

Within an hour, Aidan was en route, shaking his head over the bright red Land Rover he'd traded out for the mini. Driving north along Loch Lothy, he passed bleak ruins and deserted castles tangled together with the nearly impenetrable history of the Highlands and western Islands. A past full of whispers recognized its own, imploring him to recognize places he had never seen. *Grandfather always said clan blood passed from generation to generation and had its own memory*. He felt the truth of that now.

The lonely emptiness of the northern Highlands had once held many farmsteads before the Famine and the Clearances. The rocks that appeared to grow out of the soil once served as fences or sheltered families in stone croft homes. But after years of abandonment, the print of the human hand was gone. Only ghosts remained.

Sighing, letting go of a sadness that wasn't his, he switched focus—cut left on the slower road that led to Isle of Skye to pass through the rock and sky majesty of the Great Shiel. Slightly beyond, he left the main route, and not without a second glance at Skye's distant Cullins and a tremor of regret. *If I had the time and the health, I would do it all. Just explore the mountains again.*

During a short break in the pretty village of Shieldaig, at the mouth of Loch Torridon, he studied the sky carefully while he filled his tank. Dark clouds were massing on the western horizon. *A couple of hours of good weather, if I'm lucky.*

But he didn't rush—trusting he would be lucky. The peace of Glen Torridon filled him as he drove the single-track road through the close mountains. Loch Maree was as beautiful as ever, but growing agitated and gloomy with the afternoon. The white curls on the waves reminded him of how fierce the weather could be this far north. He didn't stop again.

After the tiny town of Laide, he wryly recalled Kieran's elaborate Irish directions. "You'll pass MacPherson's Pub immediately clear of the angler's shop—tasty food if you wish, and a decent glass of stout—keep on past the holiday cottages, they've been closed the week past, and go on past the Little Gruinard River 'til you arrive at a broad field, more a floodplain, really—that's where you slow up. Look for the large pine on the right. The gate's partially hidden behind it."

The combination Kieran gave him opened the gate like a doorway into a secret realm. Now, with the heft of the legendary mountain An Teallach more felt than seen, at the entrance of the Fisherfield wilderness, he knew only that he was happy to be there. He nudged the Rover cautiously beside the edge of Loch Na Sealga on the road Kieran had described accurately as "clinging like a soaked shirt". Crossed the first river carefully. The water was fast and rising. *It will be impassable in a few hours.* Kieran's warnings were unnervingly accurate. The timing was tight and he had nearly blown it.

Turning into the narrow valley, he drove with the windows open, tasting the rain on the freshening wind, shifting periodically to relieve the pressure on his spine. It was numb again. *At least it's better than the pain. Anyway, a few weeks of healthy mountain air can't hurt.* Right now, he only had to keep the car on the road and arrive in one piece at Kieran's lodge.

Kate rested briefly on the flank of craggy Rhuadh Stac Mor—the sound of blood pounding in her ears from the climb. *This is how beauty lures me into danger,* she thought. The threat of a dark storm had come out of nowhere, as usual. Fionn Loch's sweet shimmer had abruptly turned to lead, and she could no longer see the looming hulk of Slioch, as it disappeared behind fast moving clouds.

When the first glass shards of icy rain fell, she realized she was pushing it. *It's past time to return.* After getting stranded in the Fisherfields more than once, she'd learned to appreciate the local warning . . . 'When the rain comes hard, go home fast.'

Early that day, she'd crossed an innocent looking stream draining the high mountain loch. She'd circled Fuar Loch Mor on her map—written her best translation of the name below it with a question mark. *Big Spring Lake?* She had to get over its outlet before the height of the squall.

Fed by rain, the water would grow minute by minute until it roared over the stones she had used to cross just a few hours back.

This would be a very bad place to spend the night. Not to mention that Kieran would be frantic. Pulling her hat down further on her head, she began her descent.

An unfamiliar sound suddenly lifted above the wind. Through narrowed eyes, Kate studied a scarlet red Land Rover making the hard right turn from the rough track along Loch Na Sealga and disappear behind the surrounding hills. Like a red stag during hunting season, she halted, listening hard for a long minute.

Odd. Kieran usually insisted on personally bringing visitors up. The Big Misty, her home for the past eight months, was the only destination at the end of ten miles of hazardous road. Someone was driving in slowly, inexorably. Surely Kieran would have mentioned it if he was expecting someone. A quiver of fear shot through her.

For a few panicked heartbeats, she wondered if the straining vehicle could be carrying the one person in the world she most feared. But it was too soon, he was locked away and her life was still her own.

Shake it off, Kate, she told herself sternly. *Can't worry about the future here.* Especially with the temperature falling suddenly as a landslide, and a full hour yet on the sharp slope before she was safely home. She reined in her straying mind, and breathed in deliberate concentration, resuming her race against the storm.

Kieran's paradise was a recreational beacon for mountaineers and ramblers who pined for the thrill of dramatic mountains in an elemental wilderness. Among those who cherished Scottish mountains and hill walking, the word 'Fisherfield' made the blood race. In six hours, they could leave behind the urban noise and bustle of Edinburgh or Glasgow and arrive in a climber's playground— with nine Munros, Scotland's biggest mountains, and many other challenges within a day's hike of each other.

Slioch and An Teallach, the most celebrated and photographed peaks, stood watch over a panoramic high country, with names that sang the landscape—Mullach Coire Mhic Fhearchair, Ruadh Stac Mor, A'Mhaighdean, and Sgurr Fiona. The Gaelic names swirled on the tongue, adding to the mystery.

The Big Misty was well named. Mountains, to every direction, with habitually hidden summits—as if their desolate thoughts could not be revealed in the ordinary brightness of day. The lodge had been carefully placed. A south-facing perspective granted abundant light while its altitude above two remote lochs provided space from the rocky slopes. The Big Misty was as improbable as its location—an elegant stone lodge that welcomed and indulged its patrons in sheer luxury when they returned, inevitably chilled and hungry, from their mountaineering activities.

Kieran O'Connell checked out the clock as he polished the top of the bar. He had two out and weather coming in. *Kate should come in soon. She will be barely ahead of the fiercest rain, but she will be wet. I can count on that.* The thought made him smile. The woman enjoyed being in the thick of the elements, no matter what the weather gods were up to. But it was glorious when Kate finally came home, looking like a beautiful wild animal. He shook his head. *Just get here in one piece.*

Early on, when his attentions had been soundly rebuffed, he'd wondered if he could stay friends with the tantalizing woman who'd come to work for him. They had both wanted it to go well— so he succeeded. Kieran made it his job to tame Kate just enough to keep her on, accepting her desire to be in the high places. *But she drove him crazy sometimes, the way she took it right to the edge, so to speak.* And never mind the very worst weather the Fisherfields could dish up.

As for Aidan. He sighed, and not for the first time. Why did he let himself be talked into allowing the man to drive? It was lunacy, and he knew better. It was simply that Aidan had a way with words, and that resonant voice. Somehow you trusted him, believed he could do it. *Well, he better arrive soon or I'll have to send out a search party.*

Right, I need to settle down now. Kieran hummed softly to himself. His lodge was full, and so were the three comfortable cottages he'd converted from rustic bothy camps. He had thirty people to keep well fed and cozy. *Ah, the place was blooming.* As if on cue, hikers and climbers began to enter, banging mud off their boots, hanging up their heavy outerwear.

It was Kieran's favorite interlude of the year—the summer rush over, the change in the season sharp and full of contrasts— chilly days twinned with fire-warmed evenings. For this lovely reason, he supposed, artists and writers—people who craved the solitude and energy of wild places—joined the vigorous trekkers. Since his own tastes ran to word play rather than hours battling a long climb, he welcomed them as colleagues.

For a few minutes, he was lost in a pleasant reverie. Longer evenings encouraged that fortuitous combination of drinks and stories and people he knew only as Irish Magic—though he never could predict exactly how it arrived. Songs would spontaneously appear, and get passed around the room like bread at suppertime. And if Kate decided to sing . . . it just didn't get any better than that.

"How is it out there?" he called to incoming hikers.

"Weather's coming in fast, Kieran. Glad to be here." He always had a few that slid straight into the bar before even changing clothes. The pair in front of him were brothers from Edinburgh who delighted in racing each other up the peaks, keeping track of their fastest times. "Two pints, please," ordered Phil, looking around expectantly. Kieran knew what they were waiting for.

"Where's Kate?" Jake asked the obvious.

"That is a question only she can answer at this minute," Kieran replied darkly. He poured the first half of the rich brown stout and left it alone to settle. "I am giving her exactly ten more minutes before I send you two up to find her."

They grinned at him. "Not to worry, Kieran, she'll be here."

He huffed a bit, as he turned back to his other worry. Aidan MacLaine. *Delighted he's coming, provided he gets there.* Giving his mind something to do other than fret, he summoned the memory of meeting Aidan. To say he was gifted as a poet was comparable to calling the surrounding crags hills. The man had an uncanny talent for bringing words to life and generating emotional energy with his reading. His listeners was captured by the quiet intensity of voice and eyes and moved by the sheer beauty of his poems.

The first time he'd experienced Aidan's reading, Kieran lingered until the other poets and the audience had clapped and clamored for more and gotten their books signed. When Aidan picked up his coat to leave, he'd stepped forward and extended his hand. "Now, my man, you must be thirsty. I have just the place." Aidan didn't argue. People rarely did with Kieran. They'd talked into the early morning in the pub, like old friends resuming a lengthy and substantial conversation.

The sound of a car engine stopped any more rumination. *Thank the Lord. That would be our poet. The same one who ignored everything I said about the difficult roads. He does, at least, have perfect timing before the rain and the dark.*

Chapter 2

Aidan felt the magnetic draw of The Big Misty. He threaded his way over the last half-mile of road that had no right to be where it was and knew it, grateful that all the bad things that could have happened, didn't.

The place appeared to grow out of the mountains, with a view swiftly overtaken by swirls of storm-blown mist. "Not a place for casual tourism," Kieran had told him. His lodge attracted those who were haunted by mountains—people whose hiking and climbing gear always stood ready, escaping as often as they could to high places.

And me, thought Aidan as he pulled into the parking lot. *I need the mountains for a feeling I can't explain, even to myself. I just need them—because they are bigger and wilder than me.* Half amazed to have arrived safely, he turned the car off and took a breather before rolling up the window, enjoying the sweet perfume of heather that surrounded him.

When the lodge door swung open, Kieran broke into a wide grin, answered by Aidan's characteristic half smile. "Right on cue. The master poet arrives just as the fire is to be lit."

Crossing the space between them with a buoyant stride, Kieran placed both hands on top of Aidan's shoulders. They gave each other a brief affectionate squeeze. "Welcome, my friend! I won't ask how the trip was because I don't want to hear. If you can worry backwards, that's exactly what I would be doing." He stood aside and scanned his friend. "Ah, Aidan, you give new meaning to the phrase 'a whim and a prayer.'"

Aidan chuckled appreciatively. "Before I take my coat off, you might as well have some work out of me for the cost of trouble. Where's your woodpile?"

"Nonsense. You get your bag. You did bring a bag, didn't you? I wouldn't doubt that you arrived without a shred of extra clothing."

"I very nearly did."

"Of course you did. And I would gladly give you some of my own togs . . . but," he stopped, contemplating Aidan carefully. "Well, you're a bit slimmer than I remember, unless that's only because I've gained a few."

"Just your overactive imagination playing tricks again, Kieran."

But it wasn't, and they both took it in, the difference between Kieran's sturdy form, with an obvious weakness for good food and ale, and Aidan's tall lean frame.

Suddenly keen to distract Kieran's keen examination, not ready to go inside, Aidan turned toward the entrance. "I'll collect my bag, Kieran. Don't worry. I have enough to keep me more or less clothed. More importantly, I have some poetry to share with you."

Distracted, Kieran nodded, observing the big clock over

the fireplace pointedly. Jake hopped down from the barstool. "I'll take a look for her."

"Yes. Please. The mountain goat is due now. Oh, never mind, I can't help myself."

Jake acknowledged Aidan casually as he threw his coat back on. Kieran walked with them to the doorway and peered out, drying his hands on a bar towel. Jake and Kieran stared so intently that Aidan joined them in their examination of the rocky slope.

The air was full of rain. Invisible mountains skulked behind swollen, gray clouds. Aidan leaned against the rough-edged lichens on the stone wall. The hard cold helped him ignore the tingling in his back. As the first line of showers descended from the ridgeline toward the lodge, he saw her at the same instant Jake exclaimed, "There she is!" He pointed at a human form moving, with both speed and grace, down the slope.

"Once again I am favored!" exclaimed Kieran, immediately turning inside, Jake close behind him. "Now, I'll just go recover a bit, so I can seem calm when she arrives."

"Who is she?" Aidan called after him.

"You'll meet her soon, my boy, soon enough."

Aidan pulled his collar up against the wind and, walking to the car, glanced up again. This hill trekker evidently had no necessity for a path and, with the weather closing in, would be more than a bit damp when she finally got to shelter. He could see clearly it was a woman and one who did not fear being alone in the approaching storm. A blast of icy breeze flared, cutting short his inclination to keep watching. He pulled a small bag out of the car, gathered some books, and checked the ridge once more. She was progressing swiftly. But, as Kieran had said, he'd meet her shortly. *Speaking of Kieran, it was past time for some relaxation.*

Within minutes of the first match, the hearth fire drew in the occupants of The Big Misty as they entered the high-ceiled Great Hall seeking warmth, good company, and various spirits.

The big space was full of nooks to suit every taste, but the heart of it was Kieran's bar, overlooking a comfortable scatter of tables, stools, and chairs. As the fire snapped, the lingering notes of an Irish ballad on a single flute floated through the convivial space.

Kieran had single malt Scotch whisky waiting, ushering Aidan into the highly favored seats by the fire. It was one of the things he cherished best about owning the lodge—leaving the bar to the staff and relaxing with a special guest.

He held out two tulip-shaped tumblers, half-filled with an amber liquid. "I need this more than you do, Professor MacLaine." He grinned, nudging Aidan as he handed him the glass. "It's Talisker. Ten years old. A bit young for us—but one of your favorites, as I recall. Figured you might enjoy a bit of seawater essence after the long journey. Remind you of home. Shall I add a drop of water?"

Aidan motioned no, swirling the whisky, relishing the spicy bouquet from Skye. The fragrance symbolized all the miles he'd driven, the Scottish land in a bottle. He took an exploratory sip, the smoky aroma of peat and the subtle tang of fruit mingling. Nodded approvingly at Kieran who raised his glass in a toasting motion and sampled his own reverential mouthful. They'd discovered this about each other early—how they shared a highly refined taste for the subtle flavors of Scotland's small distilleries.

The first glass was quite simply communion, Kieran mused as they drank, *in the church of friendship.* Smiling at his own fancy, Kieran checked the time again, winked at Aidan, and sprang up to attend the bar. "Okay, you're steadied, now observe our walker when she comes in. She's a gorgeous sight."

Kate nudged open the heavy oak door and leaned in to hang her up wet coat and exchange muddy boots for shoes. Then she pulled the brass latch and stepped inside.

Later, Aidan would re-create those first few minutes over and over. The way his heart skipped a beat. How his chair was turned just so, ensuring she wouldn't notice him immediately. The hot flow of time suddenly crystallized like cooled honey. In the space that followed, Aidan studied every detail of the woman he had seen hiking briskly from the mountains.

Kieran frowned at her wet clothes and hair, sighing as he tossed her a towel. "It's me that will catch the hell of it, you know, Miss Kate. When the cold finally overtakes you and you turn sick. And do you care? Do you ever care?"

"I care, of course, Kieran. I would never want to make you worry." Kate's voice, richly textured, was filled with teasing affection. A silky smile was given freely to Kieran and the ten patrons of the pub. Sitting up straighter, interested and anticipating, Jake and Phil and their tablemates inspected her as practiced horsemen admiring a fine filly.

"Welcome home!" Phil called out.

"About time! Kieran nearly had a heart attack," added Jake.

Clucking a soothing sound at Kieran's lowered eyebrows, Kate briefly acknowledged the table of climbers. She stood for a moment, toweling off her copper burnished hair, which cascaded to shoulder length in damp ringlets.

"Take that wretched sheep skin off," Kieran directed quietly. Kate pulled off her thick wool sweater, revealing a moist undershirt that clung tightly to the soft swell of her breasts, steam rising from her warmed body.

"Curves in all the right places," Phil stated in a loud undertone, as he did every evening.

Tossing the wet sweater under her arm, and ignoring the palpable absorption of male concentration, she walked to the bar and wrapped an arm around Kieran's neck, kissing him on the cheek.

"I'm ready to work. What would you like me to do?"

Shaking his head, Kieran snatched the dripping sweater from her and protectively draped a hooded sweatshirt on her shoulders. "Put it on and zip it up before their eyes fall out of their sockets," he muttered.

More loudly, he added, "Please take this teapot and sit by the fire. If you manage to keep our new visitor busy, I'll count that as enough work for a bit. I've ordered up some food for all of us." Kate spun around and abruptly noticed Aidan.

He'd risen while she'd been distracted. "Hello, Kate." He paused as shocked recognition flashed across her face. The air between them rippled with eleven years of memory. The winds of Montana funneled out, carrying a scent of fireweed and with it, the memory of an improbable, soul-changing event.

Kate had been twenty-seven, in love with her eight-year old son and thrilled to be out in the world. The striking woman in front of him had flowered from that bud. Aidan's throat tightened as she pondered him, wondering what she saw.

"Aidan." She breathed his name, as if by saying it out loud she might dissolve a phantom.

Kieran spoke loudly, deliberately slicing into the prolonged stillness between them. "Sure, you've met . . . why didn't I piece that together? What could be more natural? You're both North Americans, in this little piece of Scotland. Of course you would know each other." He mocked them gently, trying to bring them both back to the present.

"We met each other at a conference. A number of years ago." Aidan did not take his eyes off Kate. No description would ever do justice to that week.

"Well then, catch up over your tea before it cools off. I'll come and join you as soon as Chris gets here." Abruptly, Kieran realized they had already dismissed him. Shaking his head, not used to being ignored, he left them alone. *T'was the seductive, unerring linking of souls,* he would think later. *Warming toward each other in the cold air of the world.*

Her wary instincts ached to run back into the mountains, far from the man sitting in front of her. Kate swallowed hard, trying to ignore her racing pulse. *Aidan. Oh my god. You cannot possibly be here.* Silence pooled between them, thick and uncomfortable.

Ignoring the desire to flee, Kate drew up a chair, determined to have some sort of conversation. She noticed that Aidan sat down carefully, as though his balance was a bit off.

"Your hair is longer," she began. She had to start somewhere, not caring that the topic was mundane. "Very artsy, the 'just-over-the-collar look'" she added.

Aidan laughed dryly. A pang of delicious remembrance bloomed in Kate's memory. "The gray adds a bit of distinction, too, don't you think?" he teased. His brown eyes carried hints of gold.

She remembered this well. *More precisely she'd never forgotten it.* That gentle gaze had been her measure for everything else that happened since. *Okay Kate, you are not going there now.*

"It's hardly gray. Just a smattering of silver, along the sides," she responded, deliberately flippant. At forty-two, Aidan's age showed itself in salt and pepper sprinkling at the temples and in the creased lines of concentration above the bridge of his nose. His face bore the reflection of someone who found the world intoxicating—serious enough to focus intensely and sufficiently amusing to collect laugh lines.

"Ah, Kate, ever the keen observer, with an enthusiasm for accuracy."

"You are thinner," she added.

"Yes. And probably paler than I should be. I've been . . . a bit under the weather." His smile faded. Kate decided not to ask the obvious. *He's battling something.* She sipped the hot milky tea, watching him covertly. *But I see strength. It's like the mountains, the core essence.* Whatever he was struggling with did not obscure this most vital characteristic.

"Quite the handsome lad, aye Kate?" queried Kieran, having edged over to check on this awkward reunion. "It's that

Emily Bronte appeal—you know, Heathcliff and all that."

"Really? I can't agree. Not so dark." Kate couldn't resist Kieran's tease, but kept her attention on Aidan. He returned her gaze, unhurried—measuring how the years had passed.

"No, I wouldn't wish to be Heathcliff," Aidan responded after a thoughtful pause. "Too sad, too angry. Rob Roy maybe, after all was said and done." His mouth curved slightly, toying with the irony of the situation. "Come and join us. Is your man here yet?"

"He is and I will." Kieran disappeared behind the door, talking to his assistant, Chris, a hefty young Aussie well capable of running the bar. Kate poured more hot water for both of them.

Still a sea-weather beauty, Aidan observed. *Laughter and pain shifting like sun and clouds across her face.* As he remembered, she wore no make-up. "I have no idea what to do with it," she'd laughingly told him in Montana.

"You don't need it," he'd responded, tracing a finger down her cheek. He struggled to bring himself to the present. *Say something, Aidan, anything.* "I'm happy to see you, Kate."

She poked at the flames, adding wood. "Strange, isn't it? To see each other again." Kate let the question stand as a statement. "I wouldn't have come looking for you," she added, her voice tensing, "not after our agreement."

Yes, the agreement. The heartrending agreement to leave it behind us, after that week. "I longed to see you," he said quietly. "Dreamed of it everyday. I always thought I would try to find you again."

"Why didn't you?" she asked, turning toward him reluctantly.

He said nothing, staring down into his empty cup. *Because I couldn't, Kate*, he thought. *My daughter needed every part of me until a few years ago. By then, I knew there was a problem with my back, and getting worse.*

"Circumstances intervened," he said finally. Better she would have the memory of Montana than hear the whole complicated truth now.

"Circumstances?"

A shadow crossed between them and stayed. "Let's not rush the conversation, Kate." His voice gentled. "Neither one of us really understands what the other had to deal with."

She could not argue with this—couldn't deny that she saw Aidan's pain and weariness. He was hiding it, trying to hold steady when it hit him. Drawing a deep breath, she also recalled what she'd told herself on the mountain. There was only so much time before things changed.

Watching the play of emotions, Aidan wished for a bit of ease. "If the stories want to be told, they will be, Kate. Let's just agree to that. For now."

Chapter 3

Kieran reappeared with three glasses in one hand, a bottle of wine in the other, immediately assessing their self-conscious struggle. "Free at last," he sang in a clear tenor, "and ready to join you." He made quick work of opening the cork, pouring the wine with a flourish. "We'll start with a full-bodied South African Merlot. So," he passed a well-filled glass to each, "you must have been united by my charm—old friends who had the good taste to find me, and there the other one was."

Kieran's grin was contagious, igniting sudden dimples— the bright energy of his disposition irresistibly appealing. He understood that he had a gift for putting people at ease, and it was clearly the occasion to use his talent. Keeping his voice undemanding and humorous, intuitively understanding that rejoinder was not necessary and maybe not possible, Kieran filled the silence between them with stories of his regulars, seasons in the mountains, and his own escapades with women.

Chris, bustling in and out without fanfare, brought appetizers of delicate autumn mushrooms and sharp local cheddar. Warmed by the glow of wine and food, easy conversation gradually emerged, as Aidan and Kate followed Kieran's enticing prompts.

"And now," Kieran began, hoping the mood had eased, "will you please tell me how you two are familiar with each other?"

What did Kieran already know? "The conference was in Montana," Aidan replied tentatively. There was no hint from Kate of how he should proceed with this. "On a ranch pushed up snug against the Rocky Mountain Front," he continued.

Kieran folded his arms over his belly and leaned into his chair. He was going to get more than that, if just by his hopeful posture.

"Okay, you expect a story, of course you do. The Irish always ask for a *seanachaoi*." Aidan struggled to shift his mood, make it light.

Kate smiled at the mention of one of Kieran's favorite words. 'Shan-o-key?' she'd questioned him uncertainly when she'd first heard him use it.

"Irish for storyteller," Kieran had replied with a faraway tone.

Aidan couldn't resist a satirical side note as Kieran agreed encouragingly. "I learned pretty quickly that it isn't what you do, or have done, that counts with our Irishman. It's how you tell the tale." He made the mistake of looking at Kate, her cobalt eyes dark and impossible to read. "But, my friend, the story needs time. Let's give it air."

Kieran allowed the arrival of dinner to change the energy, his puzzled manner making it clear that he anticipated more details. Chris delivered plates of stir-fried vegetables and thin-sliced curried beef, surveying the table briefly. "Everyone fine here?" The food's savory aroma filled the space between them.

"Heavenly, absolutely heavenly. We're grand, thanks, Chris." Kieran lifted his goblet in a toast. "To deep friends, high mountains and delectable wine." Three glasses tapped each other. The invisible current between Aidan and Kate was so palpably strong that Kieran stopped mid-drink to stare at them. Hastily recovering, he tossed down an extra large measure of his wine and began industriously eating his meal.

Aidan and Kate ate slowly, barely tasting the food, trying to redirect their wayward thoughts. After several pleasurable mouthfuls, Kieran ventured a question toward Kate. "It was after this trip that you began to paint?" Frowning, she waved her hand, sweeping aside any answer, the set of her face unexpectedly guarded.

"I didn't know you painted," Aidan risked, despite her edgy demeanor. At the conference, he'd quickly noticed and admired her artist's eye, forever absorbed in colors and shapes. She had a brand new Nikon and no idea how to work it. He'd offered to teach her. Their heads and hands together, the camera offered the intimacy they both craved as he'd showed her different ways to frame and shadow the landscape.

In the secret spaces of the Rockies, he'd witnessed her talent and passion, shared her enthusiasm for mountains and fell . . . for *that was the true word, surely. I fell away from any pretense that my own life was whole. Meeting Kate gave me a new definition altogether for love.*

"I painted for awhile." Kate could not bear to witness the roll of memories. "But I don't anymore." Her tone was unnaturally sharp. Aidan bit back his questions, perplexed. Clearly, this topic was loaded. Of course she would have painted, her awakened artistry would demand it. But the very word appeared to wound her.

Kieran poured some more wine. "Excellent curry, isn't it? Julie's special recipe." His voice purred warmly on the last sentence. Clearly the subject had to change, and fast. "Sorry. We were talking about Aidan. Your daughter would have been . . . how old?"

Aidan lingered for a moment on the round taste of merlot. "Sheila was twelve. Old enough for me to be able to travel for a few days."

No matter that your daughter wasn't yours by blood, Kate thought. Aidan would never say that. Sheila could call him if the need arose, and he'd carefully kept his phone close. She'd understood her mother could fail her. Probably would fail her. Aidan was just there for back up. He knew this. But protecting Sheila didn't require her permission or her blessing. It was simply his role.

"Her mother was . . . fragile," Aidan continued, choosing his words delicately. "I didn't like to leave Sheila, but, by then, she had some friends and neighbors for support. I seized the opportunity and went, yearning for some part of myself that I'd lost along the way."

"It was advertised as a conference designed to change the world," mused Kate.

"Yes," Aidan agreed, contemplating the fire. "To quote the brochure: 'One week for the icy breath of glacial snowfields to meet the passionate fire of writers and wilderness advocates. Become the voice of bears and mountains, rivers and trout, eagles and elk.'"

Kate's lips curved and Aidan chuckled. "Yeah, kind of memorized it, didn't I? A little overblown, I might have thought. But it laid on my counter and beckoned until I cleared the schedule and took leave of everything else that was happening in my life."

"And . . ." prompted Kieran. "Was it all that?"

Under Montana's luminous summer skies, with its achingly blue-sky days and star-strung nights, Kate Stoker had met Aidan MacLaine. "Yes," Aidan replied softly, fixed on the fire, breathing out a wave of pain. "It was all that."

Kieran's open face clouded, taking in the information, both told and untold, suppressing his questions. Casting an oblique look at Kate, he lifted an inquisitive eyebrow. She sighed.

"Okay, I'll tell—at least a little—and then we're done with the past, Kieran. You have to promise to leave it alone."

As he clearly had no choice, Kieran reluctantly agreed with a nod.

She could see Aidan's pain wrestling with memory. To distract him, she directed an update. "Jordan's working in Rwanda. Twenty-years old and out to save the world."

Aidan met her gaze. Throughout the evening, the pain in his hips and back had been building. Unable to quell its power, he fisted his hand out of their view, forcing himself to sit still. "Good for Jordan," he replied. He would not move until he was sure she was finished with whatever she was willing to say. *Stay with it, MacLaine.*

Taking it slowly, Kate began. "I held onto that brochure for ten months," she said ruefully. "Waiting for my life to begin, while Ian worked the court system, hunting for cracks. When his appeal failed, I got a reprieve." Kate's diaphragm tightened on the memory. *I will never again refer to Ian as my husband, ex or otherwise.*

"May I assume he's in prison now?" Aidan asked.

An indecipherable emotion flashed before she answered. "Yes. He'll be out soon. I hear he's exhibited A+ behavior." *But when he gets out . . .* she could not say the words out loud . . . *he'll come hunting for the one who turned him into the police.*

Before they could read her mind, she let the sweet grass and sage of Montana fill her mouth, breathing out the poisoned taste of Ian. Pulled her knees into the chair, one hand balancing her wine, the other pushing back a stray lock of hair, trying to unwind.

"We'd lived with our folks outside Bozeman for a few years," she continued halfheartedly. "I was forever outside. Couldn't get enough of it. When Ian got locked up, Tracy, my sister, found the brochure. Brought it to me and insisted that I go. That's how I got to the conference."

"And, that's it, guys. Nothing more to be said tonight." Kate gave them a small smile, then turned her attention to the fire. What she saw in Aidan's eyes scared her almost as much as her fear of Ian. She couldn't take his tenderness and caring. There was too much before her and such danger in Ian's imminent freedom. Any warm feeling would make her weak and possibly endanger Aidan. Reaching deep, she summoned the strength of character to let her silence stand final.

Aidan shifted his weight, easing the worst of the pain, grateful that it was becoming numb. *Time to turn Kieran back on.* He encouraged his friend to tell more stories, appreciating that he would rise to the challenge.

Without missing a beat, crossing his legs on a small stool and indulging in an after-dinner pipe, Kieran began recounting a humorous tale of an overweight hiker who "believed the ratio between walking and eating was about ten minutes effort to three hours of devouring meals." When he saw them start to relax, he told another about the couple who came on their honeymoon and left on their divorce, talking and blowing smoke rings until they laughed, releasing the tension.

"He's skillful at comfort talk," Kate remarked when Kieran withdrew to check in at the kitchen.

Aidan shrugged. "I could probably use some of that talent." A half smile tugged at the side of his mouth. "After all these years, Kate, here we are."

She had to know, blurting out the question that she'd wondered about since they'd last been together. "What happened to Kathleen?"

The first night in Montana, they had lain in the tall grass, tracking the wheeling constellations across what Aidan called the 'firmament' and confessed their bad marriages. Aidan had described his as "turbulent as a full-blown tropical gale, and about as nourishing as stale crackers."

"Kathleen died," he replied gently. "Took her own life. I finally brought her to the right doctor after Montana. It somehow helped to have a diagnosis. I knew she was bipolar, but it was important to understand the extent of her sickness. Sheila needed to grasp what was happening to her mother."

He exhaled a sigh. "But it didn't help Kathleen. On the last day she was with us, she had a big episode. Raged at both of us and huffed off in a brutal mood. She just disappeared. There was no word from her at all." Pensively, he summed up the immensity of what they had faced. "Sheila was sixteen. We searched, following any trail we could, for two months."

His back was numb through to his hips. *I'll have to move soon. But I want to tell her this story.* He could see Kate was on the verge of asking him what was going on with him. Better to stay in the past.

Before she said anything, he hurried forth. "At the end of all the leads, we tracked down a small trailer in eastern Nevada, about as far out into the dry scrublands as the thing could be hauled. We found Kathleen's clothes lying casually on the furniture. Food on the counters. As if she'd just stepped out for a walk, intending to return. We hung out for a few weeks cleaning the place, wearing holes in the horizon hunting for her." He waited a beat, letting her take in the story.

"When summer ended, Sheila had to return to school. We were out of options, so we left it in the hands of the police. A year later, they informed us that Kathleen was dead. She'd walked farther into the desert than anyone ever imagined with no preparation and a desire to die. The desert obliged her."

We've both been followed by shadows, Kate thought, thinking of how firmly Jordan had closed his mind and spirit to his father. "Did Sheila ever let go of the grief?"

Aidan surprised her with an unexpected smile. "She did.

We had a very hard year after we got the news. Sheila worried about Kathleen's illness. Whether or not she would carry it into the world. She agreed to go to the same doctor—and because she was afraid, she asked me to come with her."

"Little by little, the two of us became real family. She didn't care to know her biological father—one of her mother's many one-night stands. After a couple years of extensive soul searching and work with various therapists, it was finally evident that her mental health was fine. On her 19th birthday, she called me Dad for the first time."

His voice faltered momentarily, recalling the intense joy that had flooded through him. *When Sheila really acknowledged me as her father.* "She's twenty-three now," he continued, "in grad school at the University of Washington in Seattle. Got a talent for languages, speaking and translating."

Once again, quiet hovered between them. This was a gentle hush, the reckoning of how life changes—punctuated every so often with a sweet triumph, a celebration of patience and love. Impulsively, Kate reached out her hand, slightly flinching as Aidan enfolded it with his own. "I'm glad for you."

"Thanks. There has been only one thing missing." Aidan regarded her evenly, his implication unmistakable, holding on for an extra minute before slowly releasing her fingers.

Kate shook her head, unconsciously saying no. She looked toward the bar, calling for Kieran to join them. So the past was connected to this moment. There had been such profound wondering—dreaming about and longing for this man. The turmoil in her heart was so loud she was certain Aidan could hear it. "I can't imagine why Kieran is taking so long. Shall we have coffee?"

Aidan's brief smile was poignant. "You might remember, Kate, if you think about it."

Struggling not to give in to the intimacy of the memory,

she murmured, "Earl Grey, of course." Unnerved, Kate walked quickly into the kitchen.

Once alone, Aidan could no longer ignore the numbness and burning. The Great Hall was nearly deserted, tired patrons gone, the fire burned to embers. With some effort, he straightened cautiously, keeping hold of the back of the chair.

Kieran, emerging from the kitchen, holding a glass and a bar towel, pretended not to notice. Whatever the situation was, his friend would choose when to talk about it. He busied himself noisily, his back to Aidan. When he turned around, Aidan was by the big window, studying the lashing rain that swirled down from the mountains.

Kate joined them, holding two coffees with one hand and tea with the other. She glanced questioningly at Kieran. He leaned over to her, speaking delicately. "We'll just watch the storm for a few minutes." They stood together, grateful for the intense energy of the squall that demanded their attention.

After some minutes of small talk, Kieran switched to stage voice. "I shall now show you to your room, Professor MacLaine."

"I think that's a good idea," Aidan agreed, stealing a look at Kate, lingering, as if memorizing every detail.

Kate found it impossible to turn aside. This pair of male eyes touched the core of her in a way none of the others ever could. She remembered it, as a slow heat built, and drifted, like the scent of flowers, into every part of her body. Abruptly, she was afraid Aidan wouldn't be there in the morning—that he would melt into the haze of memory.

As if in response, the wind picked up speed and the downpour thundered reassuringly. If nothing else, the storm would keep them all in one place tomorrow.

"Goodnight, Addy," said Kate. Her use of the conference nickname came from some unguarded corner. She was half horrified to hear herself use it—the familiarity undercutting, threatening to erode the carefully built border between them.

Aidan set down his cup, giving her the opportunity to withdraw the memory of seven extraordinary days, jewels in the commonplace of their lives. When he looked up, he said nothing, offered a brief smile as his faith in that recollection, and followed Kieran.

Her gaze followed him out of the lounge, remembering the last time she'd watched his retreating form, her throat aching to call him back.

Chapter 4

The next morning lashed out from murky clouds so full they leaned into the ground and gave birth to cascades. Rain ran in spontaneous rivers all around The Big Misty, the sound of growing waterfalls booming in the mist. Kieran secretly welcomed these days, when all of the outdoor types were trapped indoors, even Kate. He kept the fire well stocked and the piped music at the right level, ordering various snacks to be prepared and served freely on the house. Remembering Aidan's affection for Earl Grey tea, he called for a pot to be brewed and taken upstairs.

Detestable stuff, that tea, Kieran thought, sipping his coffee, *but it makes him happy.* Kate would be up and in the greenhouse in this kind of weather. Best to leave her to her work, especially after the confusing dialogue last night. Whatever had happened in Montana, it was something those two had held close and deep inside for a long time.

Aidan had gotten as far as the desk located in a small alcove halfway to the Great Hall when he met Chris, carrying the tray of tea.

"Shall I leave it here?" Chris asked. *This guest seemed a bit shaky.*

"Yes, thanks." Aidan sank into the chair, as the big man departed with his swift capable stride. Kieran always made the drink so strong that he usually couldn't drink more than one—but on this day, he might welcome an extra push.

Before he saw anyone, he had to write. That much he knew. The night had been long and restless. His whole being was electric with a kind of joy. But damn it, he'd spent eleven years trying to erase the feel of her tender touch on his skin. He'd failed completely.

As before, there were obstacles. There was something about the situation with Ian that made Kate edgy. *Scared edgy.* And this issue with his back could get a lot worse. His primary doctor made a point not to diagnose, but hadn't disguised his concern as he wrote out a referral to the best neurologist in Seattle.

Complications aside, it was as if Kathleen's final words were playing out. They were scarred into his spirit. "I curse you. Don't think you will ever find another woman. I won't allow it!" She'd spat at him and stalked off, slamming the door. He never saw her again.

Pulling out a worn notebook, he leaned forward on the table in front of him and let the words tumble out—hoping for a turn of phrase that would explain his own heart to him.

Finally, spent, he halted the pen's movement. They would come looking for him if he didn't start moving. He would rather walk to them, allowing himself a few precious minutes to work out the pain in his legs and coax feeling into his lower back. Moving slowly, he put the writing away and sipped the last of the cold tea.

"So there you are, MacLaine, at last!" boomed Kieran as Aidan rounded the corner into the bar. "Breakfast in fifteen minutes. I hope you are ready for a poet's work. When the weather is miserable, they always come to us, you know. I've arranged a reading." Kieran's grin was broad as he worked. "Perhaps we could persuade you to play the piano later in the afternoon as well."

"Slow down, my friend, slow down." Aidan held up his hand. "Allow me get the lay of the place, and then, I'm yours. You'll be able to tell me where to be and what to do, and I will happily do so."

"Fine," agreed Kieran easily. "It's my firm intent to fatten you up so I don't feel so lonely. Stay and keep me company while the rain falls and when the sun arrives, step outside and remember why you traveled all this way."

"Fair deal." Aidan quickly checked out the Great Hall. Some twenty people were holed up in the place, many of them as near to Kieran's balmy presence as they could get.

"Why don't you take a tour of the greenhouse? We're quite proud of what we can grow up here." Aidan followed the direction of Kieran's nod.

"Okay." There was no pretending why he would want to go. Why he had to go. Without another word, Aidan walked toward the door.

The warm moist atmosphere hit him like a sultry summer afternoon. Aidan stood inside the entrance, taking cover near a leafy wall of strung tomatoes. Kate was at the far end, in a spaghetti-strap tee shirt and jeans, carefully clipping salad greens for the evening menu. She didn't see him. His breath caught in his throat, and his disobedient eyes stared barefacedly at the luscious curves of the woman before him. Working steadily, utterly focused, Kate leaned over to pick up another tool. The spill of her breasts against the thin fabric was unexpectedly intimate. The warm ache of desire rose through his body, escorted by the peppery fragrance of greenhouse roses.

He edged out, staggered by the depth of his longing. *Not yet*, he thought, *not now . . . maybe never.*

Kathleen's curse howled in his ears. Her ghostly hands were on his skin, shoving shards of glass into his hips. Aidan stumbled out to the porch, directing the cold wind to revive him, struggling for composure. The throbbing lanced deeper through his spine as he leaned up against the coarse stone wall for support.

"Aidan?" Kate had glimpsed his retreat and followed, her arms wrapped around each other against the chill. "Are you okay?"

He was glad that the pain was quickly receding. Not ready to say what he was feeling. "Yes. Just a bit lightheaded. Must be the after-effects of all that food and wine last night."

Kate's eyebrows arched. Not like Aidan to lie so directly.

"I'm fine, Kate," he continued tersely. "I was just checking the place out before breakfast. And speaking of that, Kieran is expecting me." Before she could respond, he willed himself to walk without faltering back to the Lodge.

No, I'm not fine, Kate. I'm totally confounded. I've found you again and it's as impossible as before.

In the lounge, Aidan agreed distractedly to Kieran's excited plans for the reading. He could only pick at the substantial Scottish breakfast laid before him, pushing eggs and sausage around his plate in an abstracted manner. His dreams had been held at ransom for eleven years. Unexpectedly she was here, and he had no idea how to proceed.

Pushing away from barely touched food, Aidan interrupted Kieran's enthusiastic monologue of recent poets. "Sorry, Kieran. I'm not ready to talk yet. First the piano." Aidan gestured in the direction of the baby grand in the music room. *There is only one cure for what I'm feeling.*

Kieran smirked. "You haven't heard a word I've said, anyway. Go on with you, everyone will enjoy it."

Aidan was born to create music. He played as though great forces of nature and soul were being channeled through him. With no need for written scores of any kind, the piano gave voice to the human experience of mountains and weather—at times melodic and sweet—rising to peaks of exhilarating energy. All the music he'd composed on the drive exploded into sound.

It's exquisite, thought Kieran. *Exactly as I remembered. He has the hands of a lover with that instrument.* He watched as his housebound clientele stopped in their tracks and settled as though at a concert.

Out in the greenhouse, Kate could not escape the rippling sound. Aidan had played for her on late Montana nights, after most conference participants had called it a day. He'd restrained the power she heard now, mostly playing quiet lullabies. She'd thought then that it was superb but what she heard now was way beyond that. It rejoiced in everything wild and beautiful. Everything she loved.

The last notes climaxed, resounding in echoing waves. Someone cheered softly and applause broke out spontaneously. Anticipating the rush at the bar, Kieran polished glasses with satisfaction. Aidan bowed from the bench, not yet trusting himself to stand easily.

Kieran shuffled people off into various activities, leaving the customers to Chris. There was renewal on Aidan's face. He meant to take advantage of it.

"You'll eventually tell me what's happening with you?" Kieran stood close and spoke quietly as Aidan rose, pausing for a long moment with his hand on the piano.

Aidan nodded.

"And you are okay for now?"

"Good enough. It's nothing that will kill me today."

"Thank the Lord. I am all ears when you are ready to speak. Hungry?" Kieran asked hopefully.

A slow smile curved. "We just ate," Aidan protested.

"You, my boy, ate exactly nothing." Kate was occupied for a bit longer, Kieran informed him, checking his reaction with a swift side scan.

Chris brought in a fragrant stew, brimming with chunks of savory beef and fresh vegetables, which made Aidan's mouth water, despite the overly generous portions. Relaxing into the easy mood, he enjoyed the food and the company, surprising himself and Kieran by finishing the whole bowl.

"More?" asked Kieran, his forest-green eyes twinkling with delight.

"Not on your life. That's a late breakfast and an early lunch more than my usual. But it was great. Thank you."

Kieran laced his fingers behind his neck. *A perfect time for conversation. Give the food a chance to digest.* "Ever miss being a professor?

"No. Why do you ask?" Aidan replied, startled at the question.

Kieran shrugged. "Don't know. Sometimes I wonder— what am I doing? I'm an educated man. Should I have entered a profession where poetry was the main meal, not a side dish?"

Aidan smiled, then threw his head back and laughed. "Oh, don't get your nose bent out of shape, O'Connell. Let me tell you how being a university English professor worked for me. I was a tormented academic who valued the English language and couldn't tow the line sufficiently to warrant the decent students. So freshmen and sophomores in required classes tortured me with very unique interpretations of what the poets, playwrights, and authors were trying to communicate. They were amazingly skilled at slaughtering words and sentences."

Kieran grinned broadly. "So, other than that, how was the

play, Mrs. Lincoln?"

"I believe you learned that saying from me." A smile still tugged at Aidan's mouth. "To be clear, I was fond of the students. I enjoyed teaching. But there were so many other parts of being a professor that I didn't, ever, really understand. University politics confused me and the hours of endless editing and grading wore me out. Luckily, there were usually a few who kept the fires stoked—students who were, in essence, colleagues taking pleasure in the play of language on the tongue."

"Thank you. You have answered my question quite thoroughly. I feel considerably better."

"It could be different for you, Kieran. But I don't think so. I believe you are better off doing exactly what you are doing. Poetry belongs in the mountains."

"Indeed it does, Professor MacLaine." Kieran pulled out a dog-eared notebook. He cast a satisfied appraisal across his lounge. "So, let's talk poetry," he grinned. The blustery afternoon passed quickly as they sat with their heads bent, preparing for the evening's reading.

Twilight was transforming into its blue hues when Kate slipped in and gave some fresh herbs to Max, the cook, a stout Englishman with a handlebar mustache and a magical talent for food preparation. Aidan's attention strayed to the kitchen repeatedly, while Kieran pretended not to notice. Max loved all pleasurable things, and he found everything about Kate agreeable. He told her jokes to make her linger and offered her tastes of his concoctions for the night's meal.

Finally, she managed a teasing goodbye to him and brought her bowl of fresh salad over to Aidan and Kieran. Joining them with her greens, she breathed out an amused sigh. "I escaped."

"At last," Kieran's gap-toothed grin beamed at her. "I was afraid I would have to send out a mountain rescue team—just to haul you bodily out of the greenhouse—and then perhaps a pit bull terrier to drag you from the kitchen away from our crazy cook."

Kate laughed, determined to break through the intensity of Aidan's attentiveness. He was noticeably uneasy. They had to be able to be with each other easily in this close environment. *If we can't, one of us will have to leave.*

The threat of Ian sharpened Kate's awareness of life, and how precious it was. She deeply wanted to be able to sit in the presence of these exceptional men. But for them all to feel at ease, Aidan had to relax.

When we were in Montana, she called out to him soundlessly, *we had no future. We were free to love every minute . . . and each other. We couldn't give into grieving over what was to come, the inevitable parting. Remember that. We can do it again.*

Kate invited banter, speaking directly to Aidan. "And what are you poets doing, speaking of crazy?"

Blinking, he received the message. *Lighten up MacLaine. She's asking you to give up your disquiet.*

Studiously ignoring the silent interactions between them, Kieran began reading the comical "Ode to the Wily Mountaineer" that he and Aidan had just completed.

Kate smiled, her eyes slanting toward Aidan. *Play, damn it. Drop whatever you are thinking and let this sweet occasion be easy.*

Kieran paused, waiting. Aidan had written the end of the ode but, at the moment, he appeared to be rather preoccupied. After a few seconds of silence, Aidan took over the story, reading with an understated sardonic tone that soon had both Kieran and Kate chuckling.

When he was finished, Aidan ventured a glance at Kate. Her response was wordless but clear. *Thank you.*

"How do you survive, munching that rabbit chow?" Kieran complained, gesturing at her leafy salad.

"Oh, Kieran. We couldn't have both of us eating like you, or there'd be no food for the guests."

Kieran chortled ruefully. "Probably true. If I would shift my mind to women instead of food, I'd be better off."

"I never figured that you had to decide between the two, Kieran O'Connell. You seem to have a magnetic draw for both," Aidan noted wryly. Kieran blushed, and his glance flitted to the assistant cook laying out dinnerware. Julie was generous in size and attitude, a bubbly woman with a loud, spontaneous giggle. She caught his attention and winked at him. When Kieran's bearing turned sublime, Aidan and Kate laughed together, irresistibly. It was easy. *Too easy.*

Suddenly, Kate stood up, flustered and ready to leave. "So, before I return to my labors, give me a time frame for your concert tonight."

Kieran snorted. "It's a reading, girl. The concert happened while you were in there talking to your plants."

"I could hear it. The plants and I could all hear it." She risked a loitering look at Aidan. The memory of Kate in the greenhouse pulsed heat into Aidan's face and the rest of his body. For several heartbeats, a charged electric exchange passed between them.

His eyebrows furrowed, Kieran suddenly found his notes very interesting. Aidan cleared his throat, working hard to stop his wandering thoughts. "The piano needed some exercise."

"Well, you gave it that," Kate replied, determined to shake her agitation. "I don't suppose it's ever been played so . . . muscularly. Wild horses come to mind." Before leaving, she queried over her shoulder: "Will you both be reading tonight?"

"Yes, both of us and a few unlucky secret writers we found in various corners, trying to go unnoticed with their notebooks," Kieran responded, his tone purposefully jovial.

Kate pulled her attention from Aidan. "I'll be there, later." She made a motion toward the long winding hall. Kieran had referred to the adjoining studio earlier without offering to give

Aidan a tour. "For now, I have some cleaning up to do."

Kieran appraised her, both wary and hopeful, teetering on the verge of making a comment. Tensing, Kate's posture flashed a warning. He surrendered immediately, gazing casually up at the ceiling as she turned toward the hallway.

"Seven o'clock." Kieran yelled after her. "And don't worry about your dish, I'll take it to the kitchen myself."

"That's why I left it for you." Kate's final rejoinder was meant to invoke amusement—but the angle of her bearing betrayed her.

She doesn't want to deal with whatever's down there, thought Aidan. *But she can't keep herself away.* He slanted an unspoken question at Kieran, who studied her as one who has often mused over a perplexing problem, unable to solve it.

"You ask her, Aidan. I am not at liberty to say anything, obviously. If she wishes to tell you, she will, and it would do her good. Surely, you can inquire at least, though I can't say how she'll respond." Kieran held Kate's dish, facing the kitchen, uncertain what to do next.

"Are you waiting to be dismissed?" Aidan asked with ironic humor. "Go on, Julie's waiting. Thanks for the encouragement to talk to Kate. I will, and no, you don't have to say anything more on the subject. I'll see you later tonight."

Julie poked her head out of the kitchen, brightly surveying both men, but settling on Kieran. *The man is luscious,* she thought. *Utterly delicious.* "Want to check out the appetizers for tonight?" A Glasgow accent played strongly on her cheerful tone. Her strawberry blonde hair was swept up into a bun, except for one stray strand lightly dusted with flour.

There was no question that she was welcoming Kieran into her world. Her demeanor carried the unmistakable possibility of further invitation.

Kieran cursed under his breath, "Jesus, Mary and Joseph."

"Answer her, you fool," muttered Aidan.

"I would love to, Julie my dear." Kieran's poise was never truly lost. Dimples flashed. "Unfortunately, Aidan must attend to his writing, so it will just be me." He gave a wicked wink in Aidan's direction and followed Julie through the swinging door.

Chapter 5

A feeling of excitement nestled into The Big Misty as evening arrived. Kieran's customers loved his energy, and couldn't wait to hear his poems. Aidan's transcendent piano compositions and concerts had changed the very air. Everyone knew they were in for something special.

The wild weather had finally worn itself out. The moon's dazzling globe burst from behind the clouds, flooding the night with brilliant light. An incandescent glow slid from the tops of the once-hidden mountains into the windows, heralding the beauty to come. Change was coming.

The clearing would bring colder air and real frost, transforming the Highland greens into shades of burnt umber, plum and rust red. At once dusky and radiant, it was a contrast that fit the mood of the year, caught between summer and winter. Reading poetry was the perfect way to usher in such a season.

Patrons and staff assembled in the Great Hall, their chatter growing gradually hushed. Julie was seated near the front, her generous body gathered in a pose of anticipation. Chris, and Mary, his long-time companion, worked among the crowd, serving food and drink as Kieran's welcome rang out.

Aidan waited off to one side. He had to hope he could walk easily to the front when it was his turn. The sharp stabbing sensations were absent at least. A buzz of numbness threatened— but unless it deteriorated, he knew from experience he could deal with it.

Kate watched him from across the room, fighting a reckless urge to stand beside him. Aidan kept his focus on the reading, but he was extremely aware of her presence and her intense scrutiny.

Kieran's readings were funny, poignant and compelling. More storyteller than poet, weaving in myth and history, his observations of the state of the world and his celebration of the beauty of women were buoyant and sharp with word play. Colorful descriptions of mountaineer antics made the crowd roar with appreciation.

His last poem was about food—describing his favorite dishes intimately, caressing the words about the various inventions of the kitchen until both Julie and Max blushed, laughing helplessly.

Thomas, a regular at the Lodge and a great favorite, kept the atmosphere light with stories of his own escapades in the mountains. Thomas was from the deep American South—a fact, he said, he could not elucidate to them. Why he would live in a place lacking peaks was beyond him to explain. It was, however, why he had return to The Big Misty over and over again to "get his fix". His comfortable accent was fun to listen to and the self-effacing poems were both comic and perceptive.

Several more readers took the stage, including Chris— whose broad Aussie accent rolled with a memory of his home mountains and a yearning for the dry winds and blue-jade colors. Clearly there was more than a little homesickness at play. As the room filled with images of the great spaces of Australia, Kieran made a mental note. *Might be prudent to look for a replacement.*

When Chris was finished, Kieran returned to the microphone. It was time to introduce Aidan, and he meant to make it worthy. "You have all had the privilege of hearing this man play piano. You recognized it wasn't music you talked over. You quit what you were doing and you listened. I will venture you felt things inside. Big feelings. And suddenly you had tears in your eyes and an ache in your heart. Or maybe you were filled with joy so strong it gave you chills. You might have looked to see if the mountains and waterfalls themselves had entered the lodge. Am I correct?"

Murmuring, the audience affirmed this. "So," he continued, dimpled grin irresistibly spreading, "now that you understand what I mean, I will give you the name for it. By every right it should be an Irish expression, because it embodies the powerful energy that comes up through the earth and is magically delivered. The Irish, as you may know, have a certain tradition of such things." With an impish nod, he winked at Julie.

"When I traveled in Spain and first heard Flamenco, I was introduced to the term 'duende'. It has nearly no translation in regular English," he continued fluidly.

Irish is right. Kieran's on a roll, thought Aidan, half amused, admiring the lift of words, and the generous acknowledgment. *He is in his element here.* His arms folded and leaning against the wall, Aidan waited. *No stopping him 'til he's done.*

"I use the word 'duende' to describe this poet, my dear friend Aidan," Kieran pronounced with satisfaction. "Though having duende is uncommon, we instantly recognize the quality when someone expresses it. It is an element so real everything else feels counterfeit next to it. Tonight you will get to experience it in your own inner geography, because he will create a space large enough to make that happen."

Signaling the end of his proclamation, Kieran angled an

arm expressively toward Aidan. "It's all yours."

Aidan was grateful the pain and stiffness were temporarily at bay, allowing him to move to the front with his characteristic grace. Kate, watching, felt as if the evening parted with the whole group of poets on one side and only Aidan on the other. She had observed this effect at fire-lit readings in Montana. *Not that he tries to make it happen. It's the willing surrender of the world, wanting his voice.*

Aidan began by thanking the writers and saluting the participants, the warmth in his eyes briefly connecting with each person. He especially recognized Kieran for organizing the event and for hosting him, smiling at his friend who sat magnetically inclined toward Julie just short of actually touching her.

"There are two languages in the world. Poetry and every other. The language of the soul and the language of everything else. In my country, it is easy to forget there are both." Aidan's tone was both gentle and compelling. "It is easy to think that there is only one way to talk—and only about commerce and politics, work and war. But the soul speaks in silence and in poetry. If you don't listen, it also speaks in unexpected action. So, perhaps you book that trip to Brazil or dump the job because you crave its magic more than your own dependability." He smiled slightly as a slight titter rose up from the audience.

"I won't tell you that will never happen. But maybe you just desire the simple freedom you've never had because you've always worked so hard. Poetry can at least give you a clue of what your soul wants. It lays bare the truth of what is really happening."

Aidan stopped, a pause that filled the room like a prayer. He began reading without preamble, speaking into the hush, reading as though he were listening to an inner voice, using uncomplicated phrases and ordinary moments to translate the secret tongue of the spirit.

"A flutter in the heart serves notice
of all in me that longs to stay present."

He reached deeply for the life of the artist, in all its forms, urging them to unbind that spirit "for beauty is essential to balance what is sad and ugly in the world." Kate leaned into the cool wall, trying to blink back a sudden burning.

"You can't explain what it is to be a writer. Not even to yourself," Aidan said, his tone half sardonic but easy. "Your words get wrapped like soft-bodied fruit around the real thing, the hard pit of life's determination that you should write." A small poem sailed forth for illustration.

"The work of the world will never be done
Chase the day down to its end
To the black pool of night
And whatever dreams or haunts it may bring.
No matter what, the irrepressible morning arrives.

Trying to be a poet in this world is hard,
The spider web of more pressing things is thick and tangled.
The way to writing is dangerous, a precipice
With beautiful, deadly spaces on either side
Waiting to take your life."

Aidan's poems chronicled their lives, evoking the shared and inevitable procession of events . . . at once universal and yet so utterly, newly discovered. The entire assembly grew motionless listening, remembering unchangeable and heartbreaking moments, the sweet promise of love, tender and poignant transitions of children born and grown.

"I would not wish away the grief inside the pride.
I am grateful to have known and deeply loved
What has been given to the pulse of the world."

He didn't leave them there long, transforming the audience's disposition, and soon they were laughing at his ironic descriptions of life with a teenage daughter and the writings of his students.

Aidan changed the mood once more, returning again to the luminous splendor of the Fisherfields and praising the sweet comforts of The Big Misty. He smiled again at the audience members, reminding them "you've made your own choices and sacrifices to journey to this cathedral. And we are all here together for no good reason except to be alive and in the presence of something wild and holy."

He gestured outside to the moon-soaked peaks and toasted the mountain gods, apologizing to them, "for even here, I carry the salt veins of the ocean." Trailing his last poem, the mirage of his island home unexpectedly materialized, shimmering in "the slow sweep of rain on still gray water."

At the end of the reading, the audience shook themselves as though they were coming out of a spell. Applause thundered as Kate slipped out. *So glad I got one more chance to hear him. Whatever happens next, I am grateful for that.*

Chapter 6

The next morning broke vivid and clear. Aidan was anxious to see the peaks in the sunlight. He didn't believe he could really keep up with Kate in his present condition, but perhaps, just possibly, she would give him some time in the middle of her beloved mountains.

Kate had exactly the same thing in mind. When he rounded the corner into the lounge, she was already dressed for hiking, reaching for his tea and pulling a warmed roll from the oven. "Hi there, mountain goat." He endured the twist of heart, incautiously happy to be alone with her.

"Hi yourself." Kate smiled, offering him the steaming tea. "That was an amazing reading last night, Aidan. Really incredible. I had to leave you to your fans."

"I'm glad you were there," he responded candidly. *I felt you more than saw you,* he thought. "Going out today?"

"Yes." She quickly flipped her luxuriant hair into a simple ponytail, pushing a roll toward him. Her clean smell mingled with the aroma of coffee, tea and bread. Aidan decided not to think about which one was making his mouth water. "Kieran is out collecting new visitors, and I have a proposal for you."

Kate leaned forward on the bar's oak surface, holding him earnestly with eyes that reflected the vibrant blue of the morning sky. Brilliant layers of daylight slanted in the windows, lighting up her face. Aidan held on tightly to the hot cup, grateful that the capricious pain was absent for now.

"We can use your car to drive most of the way to the very best place. There's a special waterfall . . . it's worth seeing." When his expression clouded, she added, "It's not far. And I have a picnic. Let's sneak out before Kieran gets his hands on you."

There was a brief silence. He wanted to be with her more than he feared it. "How can I resist?" he said finally. "A beautiful woman wants to take me into the hills. Kieran would forgive me, I think."

The frost on Aidan's car gave testament to the chilly attitude of winter, hiding closely behind the deceptive autumn warmth. The sunshine was radiant, bouncing off the flanks of the mountains. They followed the only road out, turning off just before it reached the loch.

Following her direction, Aidan steered the car onto a narrow rutted track, glancing sideways at Kate. "I feel as if we're running away," he said. A sudden joy flooded through him. He was in the Fisherfield Wilderness in Scotland and Kate Stoker was next to him. It was the most unexpected event he could imagine.

Kate said little but her entire being echoed his elation. They drove on, the edge of earth and shrubs frequently brushing the sides of the car. Kate pointed out the two varieties of heather, "the bell and ling", as they traveled upward.

"Fraoch a' Bhadain," murmured Aidan.

Kate threw him a keen look. "Yes. They say the red flowers are stained with the blood of the old clan warriors."

"And the white are lucky and protect those who wear it," he rejoined playfully. Higher up, the heather gave way to the brilliant orange of deer grass, shining in the sun. "Lus-feidh," whispered Aidan. "So glad to see you again."

The vista of Highland peaks surrounded them, dominated by the hulk of AnTeallach. Dozens of streams carrying last night's cloudburst tumbled off the steep cliffs. The road was stitched together of rocks, snaking upward over the slender iridescent finger of Loch Na Sealga.

"Suddenly, the word 'bhoireann' comes to mind." Aidan's tone was mildly sardonic as the Land Rover lurched along.

"What's it mean?"

"Stony place."

Kate smiled. "Fitting. More poetic than saying Torridonian sandstone. And those are the leg breakers," she continued, pointing toward the scattered boulders and tufts of grassy tussocks. "What's the Gaelic for that?"

"Probably something like 'oh shit!'"

She chuckled then grew pensive. "You know that phrase 'The Holy Ground'?" she asked.

He did. And his lower back was becoming numb. Fighting to keep his mind on the road and on the conversation, he continued. "It was the fishermen's quarter in Cobh, near Cork. Over time, it became synonymous with Ireland itself. The place where the Irish immigrants stepped off Irish soil forever. That was their holy ground, from what I understand."

"Yes, that's the origin. I appreciate the phrase though. I believe the ground can be thought of as holy, especially in certain places. This is one of them."

They drove slowly with their windows down as sun-warmed air slid along their necks and shoulders. *And there are also some moments in life that are holy,* he thought.

"Just around the corner, Aidan. The road ends here," Kate instructed. His body's ominous numbness was leaden. They sat briefly in the parked car, taking in the luminous beauty. When the hush shifted into a sudden bodily awareness of each other, Kate responded by jumping out with her camera. "Give me a minute," she said with intentional flippancy.

Aidan got out slowly, dreading a lack of feeling that would deny him the chance to walk easily with Kate. Unexpectedly, burning sensation flooded in so fast that it nearly took his breath. He gripped the car door and exhaled raggedly. "Transform it, MacLaine," he whispered to himself. By the time Kate walked up, her mountain flower photographed and recorded, Aidan had managed to release the worst of it.

"We've seen a lot of waterfalls, but this one is special. We can reach it in about twenty minutes." She tried to discern Aidan's mixture of unreadable emotions. "Sound good? Are you up for that?"

"I can't wait to see it," Aidan replied, with a slight edge. "Lead on." He couldn't hide the weakness. She and Kieran both had noticed it, of course. But he wanted this, choosing to ignore her questions. They would not second-guess this trip. And he had to hope the pain would stay manageable.

Swinging up her pack, Kate started down the narrow trail without saying anything more. Aidan's first few steps were shaky, but to his relief, normal feeling returned. He quickly caught up to her, welcoming the once-familiar sense of well-being and strength. His life, if just for a little while, felt whole and possible.

She'd listened for the sound of his footsteps, to tell her all was well. Memories rose like the rising of stars. They had walked like this on the eastern edge of the Rocky Mountain Front. Exalting in the honeyed alpine fragrance, they'd admired the indigo-washed mountains, with a view of prairie that stretched tightly on the sphere of the earth. Every day during the conference, they had found some small opening and escaped to be alone with each other.

Aidan could feel the trail shift and transform under his feet. Kate was remembering Montana, and he went willingly, wordlessly with her. He was acutely aware of the way her strong legs moved, and how her jeans hugged the sweet shape of her hips. They rounded the bend and arrived at the source of the rushing water they'd heard along the length of the trail.

The waterfall was spectacular. In a land wealthy with cascading streams, this one was extravagant. Rainbows danced in the vapor from the plunge of streaming water into rock pools and jeweled the vibrant green of ferns and moss. They stood side by side for a discomfited minute in its exquisite grandeur, trying to deny the awakening familiarity of each other. Showered by the spray, not caring, Kate finally risked an oblique look at him.

Aidan stepped back, trying to restrain his overpowering desire to touch her. He was losing the battle. "Kate." The single word hung in the mist, loaded with longing. Thunderheads moved across her face as she recognized what she was seeing. Her muscles tensed and she moved aside, feeling panicky, facing him warily. "Come to me, Kate." He held out his hand.

Breathless, Kate hovered in confusion. *The walls between us have to hold.* She reminded herself that she had to be able to leave anyone and any place behind.

"Come here," Aidan said again, speaking low and urgently. She advanced tentatively toward him, her fingers spread wide— half accepting, half warding him off. Taking a chance, he tugged her into his embrace as though wrenching her from danger. With a soft curse, he pulled her close against him, starved for her touch, the woman smell of her.

Too many times this had been a dream. Now he needed to feel the warm reality of her body. Drawing her chin up toward him, he pressed his lips gently on her receptive mouth.

Again, memories burst inside him, remembering the unconsummated loving they'd shared in the mountains. Not willing to risk a child or to dishonor Kathleen, they had always stopped short. But the feel of Kate was deep in his bones. So many years of yearning had followed those stolen loving moments.

Kate fought for control, battling the landslide of images and emotions. This cherished, passionate kissing had visited her every night since she'd left him in Montana. The tender exploration that promised so much more. Aidan had stepped out of her own nightly reveries into this strong man who held her tightly, unable to disguise his desire for her.

But not now. Ian will be out soon. It will change everything.

Shuddering, she pressed her palms against his chest, pushing herself away. The air between them shivered.

"I can't, Aidan. I have to be free right now . . . and able to move when I need to." Her voice faltered. "We have to let the past be and somehow carry on in each other's company again. With no expectations."

Aidan did not reach for her again. *What was he thinking?* The poison of Kathleen's curse was at work in his life. Kate didn't need his problems to complicate her own. Until he understood what was happening to himself and how far it would progress, he had to confront it alone. Still, his whole being trembled with the shock of the broken contact. He leaned against a boulder, welcoming its cold into the heat of his core.

Kate turned to the waterfall, her tears brimming over, the print of his body beside her alive with grief. For several minutes they stayed apart, silently wrestling with their injured hearts, not daring to speak. Aidan finally moved to stand behind her, breathing in her presence. He kept his hands at his sides.

"It's okay." He was quiet. She spun around and studied his features, seeing the reflection of her own desolation. He put a finger up to her lips. "There's nothing to be said. It's not time. Leave it. Let's have that food you brought."

Yes, the food. Kate pulled out a small tarp to sit on and carefully unwrapped a feast of goat cheese and crisp local apples, a fresh crusty brown bread and smoked salmon. To this, she added a large can of spicy hard cider to share between them, and remarkably, a thermos of hot potato soup.

Aidan blew out an appreciative breath. "Amazing, Kate." *Only this,* he told himself again. *Just this magnificent waterfall, this delicious food and Kate next to me. Nothing more.* Using the rock for support, he slid down beside her.

Flustered but determined, Kate meant to invite him into a relationship with her, on terms that she could handle. "Let's not be silent, Aidan," she pleaded, as she struggled to shed the tension. "We sure talked in Montana. God, those nights we sat up so late after everyone else fell asleep. Did we ever sleep at all?"

Surprise flickered at her challenge. "Maybe Montana was the only time we were really awake."

Kate's swift withdrawal slapped hard. Deliberately, she concentrated on the waterfall, her shoulders stiff.

"Did you keep in contact with anyone?" he asked, more carefully, delicately threading his way.

"Not really." Her voice catching and halting, she struggled to answer his question. "I had my hands full raising Jordan. I made myself believe that special time could never be duplicated, so there was no point in trying to hang on to it." Fighting for control, she struggled to continue. "Did you . . . get in touch with anyone?"

"Yes, some. There were a few exchanges. Brad and Ellie even visited me. But it was the same for me. There was no way to hold onto it." *Because so much of the splendor had been you.*

"What did we talk about that was so remarkable?" she continued, lifting the mug of soup and handing it to him. *We have to eat and talk to try and bring us both back to earth.* "Remind me,

Aidan. I re-played those conversations to myself so often, but they needed you." She could not risk the deep physical contact with him but she desperately wanted connection.

Oh sweet woman, can I do this? Aidan took a mouthful of the hot soup. *Can I pretend I haven't ached for your touch for so many years, and just talk?*

"Aidan?" She could read the battle waging inside him. "What was it we so loved?" The question belled in the air, echoing with longing. "The taste of sweet plums you called it—the play of words."

Unable to resist, he accepted the bread and salmon she'd wrapped together and given him. Tasted and enjoyed the food. Allowed it to ease their talk. The memories were irresistible. They had laughed at their own earnestness with expressions so rich they had become the foundation for their jokes.

"The taste was sweet summer plums, the juice running down your chin. The taste of sunlight in your mouth." His eyes wandered, touching where his hands dared not go.

"Yes!" She rocked, feeling the stroke of his scrutiny, breathing out the heat. "That's what you called it. All those crazy poetic verses you made up while we pointed out stars in the night sky."

"Oh, so they're crazy?" He kept it quizzical and light. They both laughed, relief flooding between them.

She hugged her knees, opening toward him, but shielding herself with words. "We talked about loads of subjects. The re-enchantment of the ordinary, remember? That was one of our favorite topics."

He didn't say anything as they shared the apple cider, passing the bottle between them and drinking from it. *Like friends,* thought Aidan. *Or lovers.* It was important to take her lead.

Speaking slowly, he remembered with her. "It was what we both knew as kids—that astonishing world that adults think is commonplace—the magic of water, animals that talk. A plum tree that holds a whole secret world. We figured maybe it had to do with being small and close to the earth."

He was relieved to see the shadows disappearing. "The re-enchantment of the ordinary was what grown-ups have to do, how we have to fight for the world of imagination and creation."

"And why we both seek mountains to keep ourselves alive," she added.

Aidan watched her, a small smile tugging. That interlude with Kate had been like nothing he'd ever known. Now, utterly still, he wanted simply to accompany her reminiscence. Kate kept talking gently, noting he was listening as he always did, with his whole attention. Both of them cherished the fragile energy of this exchange. It didn't matter what else was happening.

"I remember you saying there is an inner wilderness. An untamed private place," Kate said earnestly. "I had never considered that. I believed wilderness meant the land had to be as wild as possible. But you said if the culture was undomesticated, it gave you . . . " she groped for the word.

"Permission," he finished for her, remembering mountain meadows, the sparkle of rivers slipping out of snowfields. When the earth circled on the radius of their discovery of each other.

"Yes." Blue eyes scanned him, seeing he had stepped again into the past. "Permission to let the imagination run free, you said—hearing the ancient voices, to be specific."

"Which also generates the landscape for poets," he added, smiling again. "Excellent reason to travel in the Celtic lands." Suddenly willing to take a risk, he added, "And you, my keen-eyed witness, are you painting from these photographs you're taking?"

She began to pack up the food. "No." Clearly this was all she wanted to say. Aidan's attentive bearing coaxed a brief and unenthusiastic response. "I used to," she added reluctantly. "Now I only take pictures."

A cooling wind began to play at the top of the waterfall, capturing the moisture and swirling it around them. The rapid chill drew their conversation to an end. Knots of pain dug into Aidan's back, their weedy tendrils edging up his spine, warning him. He asked Kate to take some photographs of the falling water from the other side, understanding she would agree—giving him space to get up and move again.

Chapter 7

Kieran met the Land Rover when they arrived at the lodge, his arms full of firewood. "Ah, the wayward pair returns. I hope you had a wonderful experience because I have a new load of visitors and I require you both." A scowl didn't really fit Kieran's disposition, though he attempted it and tried his best to hide an unruly grin.

All of them were busy with activities over the next several days at The Big Misty, which was full with guests. October had ushered in a new palette of autumn colors, hastening to emerge before the winter snows. On cue, the Highland weather became even more impetuous. A sunny morning could develop into a howling sleet storm within an hour. Aidan didn't ask to accompany Kate again on her daily hikes. He knew she needed to move fast when necessary, racing the lowering clouds and he would not risk slowing her down.

The very air felt restless while she was gone. Over breakfasts and projects, Kieran had slowly gotten Aidan to talk about the bouts of pain he was dealing with. Once he understood that Aidan would leave soon for a medical assessment, he carefully held the present moment as it emerged, without further questions. Each day, they worked until Aidan's edginess became too obvious to ignore. Finally, Kieran would dismiss him, bemused—asking for music—marveling at the aching beauty of the compositions.

When Kate returned from the hills, Aidan had no ability whatsoever to stay apart from her. Nothing about it made sense. He knew all the reasons why it would be better to avoid her, but he couldn't fight the desire for her presence.

This day had been unusually fair, warmed by its memory of summer. When he saw her on the final slope to the lodge, Aidan worked the balkiness out of his body while she greeted guests and Kieran. As soon as he could, he walked carefully toward the Great Hall, mindful that his balance was unsteady, the nerves in his lower back numb.

Kate watched him approach, chewing her lip. She had tried several times to bring up the issue of Aidan's health, but she was far from any satisfactory answer. Whatever was attacking him was capricious, coming and going without warning of any sort. He didn't know what was causing it, and he wasn't keen to talk about it. By mid-October he would be on his way to consult a specialist, in Seattle.

"Ah, Professor MacLaine, you've come for your dreadful tea, I presume?" Kieran poured a cup for Aidan with a dramatized shudder, then coffee for himself and Kate.

"Thanks." Aidan let his shoulder lean against the wall. The three of them relaxed in each other's company, without speaking of it, giving him time to recover.

"It must be special to be a professor," Kate mused. "I barely graduated high school before I got pregnant. Do you have a degree, Kieran?"

"Och, yes, I have the useless thing. Four tiresome years for a piece of paper that says 'Bachelor of Arts in English'. Spent most of my hours chasing women and drinking with friends, but I persisted until I received the bloody certificate. I gave it to my mum since it was mostly for her. Doesn't help much with this kind of work."

Kate's eyebrows arched. "Only people who have diplomas ever say that, Kieran. You had four years of your own life, learning from books and teachers and peers. From where I'm standing, that's pretty special."

He shrugged, abashed. "You're right, as usual." The chastened attitude rapidly gave way to a wicked grin. "But off with you both. I have been invited to the kitchen to learn the secrets of Julie's and Max's sauces." Flashing dimples, Kieran disappeared through the swinging door, welcomed by Julie's cheery giggle. Kate and Aidan exchanged an amused smile.

Aidan felt stronger and ready to move though wary to change the light mood. All day a resolution had been growing. It was time. *Even if it shook her up.* "Will you walk with me awhile, Kate? There's one place I haven't seen yet." He knew from Kieran that the sinuous passageway led to a locked door. And that there was a studio behind it.

"What has Kieran told you?" she asked coolly.

"Only that it was not his to talk about."

"He's right." There was no offer to move. The atmosphere between them snapped with questions, the set of her mouth guarding the answers.

Aidan yielded, wanting to keep her close. "You lead then."

She hesitated, gave herself a moment, arms crossed over her chest. "It was incredible out there today," Kate struggled to calm herself. "I wish," she stared intentionally out the window, "I wish you'd been with me." Heard him release a restricted exhalation, felt her knees go weak. Made a decision that surprised her. "Some of my photographs are there, if you care to see them."

His gaze burned into her keenly, accepting the invitation. "I would love to."

She turned slowly, stepping to one side, willing the vigor of his energy to sweep past her. "Okay, Professor MacLaine," she risked a cautious smile. "Nice title. Fits you. I want to show them to you. I think," she added. They walked side-by-side, winding their way through the lodge and passing guests who greeted them. Kate dug her hands deep into her pockets, afraid her arm would somehow find itself encircling his waist.

Trying to find something to say, she blurted out, "Your doctorate was in English?"

"No. It was on the creative process."

"I don't truly know what that means."

"I think you do," he countered evenly. "I imagine we will see it at play soon."

The corridor led to a locked entrance. Kate pulled a single key out of her pocket, but said nothing. She opened it with a fierce motion, swinging the door open. They stepped into a well-lit studio with south-facing windows. Kate flung her arms out in a careless gesture. "Here they are, Professor, creative . . . whatever you want to call it."

There were ten framed photographs lining the walls. Here were Kate's flowers—golden rowanberries and the vibrating claret of wild roses. Her landscapes featured broody clouds over textured crags, the morning sun filtering through pink-edged valleys. Gusty breezes bounced off the arching curls of the loch's waves. The centerpiece was her royal waterfall, its mist dancing upwards as a new being fashioned of water and air.

I can hear the solitude of the northern Highlands here, thought Aidan. *The echoes of lonesome and windy quiet.* In Kate's Scotland, clearly, nature ruled over humans.

She knew that he would not speak until he was ready. He

didn't disappoint her expectation. Concentrating hard, deepening the lines between his brows, he directed every part of his attention to examine the photos. Kate had hungered to show him the photographs from the first day. They were the one thing that had survived since the loss and death of her paintings.

Now that Aidan was here, studying them with his thorough consideration, there was a hollow anxiety in her chest.

When he was finished, the frown remained. "Why are these so far from everyone? You recognize they're exceptional, Kate. They deserve to be in the Great Hall."

"I don't want them there." Her tone was fragile. "Don't need to be reminded every time I pass them. I wouldn't have put them up at all, but Kieran insisted. I think he figures I will someday relent and let this place be a gallery."

"And these have to do with your paintings." It was a statement more than a question.

"I told you. I don't paint anymore." Her arms crossed in front of her, defensively.

"Why?" His one word question hung starkly between them.

"I don't owe you an explanation."

"That's true. So, don't answer, if you don't want to. The pictures are outstanding, and you know it. They're the kind that bring the world alive."

The burning began its incendiary approach up his spine. This one would build into a wildfire. "Thanks for showing them to me." He let her confused silence pool between them with no further commentary. "Okay. I guess I need to head back."

Fighting tears, she watched him open the door to the Great Hall, and take several steps before responding. "My paintings were stolen." Sharp and hard, her words hit with bullet force.

He stopped, without turning, his palm on the wall next to him. "Do you want to talk about it?"

"No." Her reply was edgy and unsure.

If she didn't say more, he would have no choice but to keep moving. The blaze in his body was growing. "I would like to hear about it, Kate."

Everything in her wanted to deny him. Everything except the part that wanted more to keep him there. She walked slowly to him and drew her finger down the length of his back, adding pleasure to the waves of pain. Standing stock still, he exhaled sharply, his fingers curling into a fist.

"There's a sunset view from here worth taking in." Kate circled an arm around him, lending instinctive support and simultaneously revolving with him. "It's really hurting, isn't it?"

He bit down his own resistance. No use in trying to contradict it—he was glad for her sustaining aid. "Yeah, it's a hard one."

Kate's mouth was dry. *You're playing with danger*, realizing she would not heed her own counsel. "How 'bout we sit down for awhile?" she heard herself saying. "It's a fine place to talk."

He laid his arm lightly around her shoulder, allowing her to lead him past the photographs to the window. The burn deep along his spine was raging. "Okay, girl," his voice was strained as he sank into a chair. "I'll have to wait this one out. If you're ready to talk, I'm not going anywhere for awhile."

Concerned and unconvinced, she remained standing. "Aidan, tell me about this thing. It's more than you're saying."

"There's nothing really to say. I told you, I'll be conferring with a doctor in Seattle. But until then, I'd rather not venture a diagnosis and I can't worry about what I don't know."

Troubled, she continued to mull over what she was observing. "Kate, you'll wear tracks in your forehead from scowling," Aidan chuckled. "There's nothing to be done about it immediately. All I can do is take a break 'til it calms. And it is," he waved away her next volley. "Anyway, weren't you about to talk to me about your paintings? What happened?"

Kate paced, speaking over her shoulder. "I started painting almost as soon as I returned from Montana," she said, letting the story stand unembellished. "For the first few years, I was crazy for all the hours I could carve out," she added. "Ian was gone. I was suddenly free to express all of these amazing images in my head. I couldn't put the paintbrush down."

She scrutinized the photographs as though they belonged to someone else. "I am fond of them. But they are barely preludes to painting," she said, her voice catching. "The painting puts the color in, gives the landscapes dimension and beauty to the close-ups. Painting was what I was meant to do. It's my degree, and those years making art were my years in college."

There was a painful pause. Kate sighed. "I was good. I knew it. I was never more whole than when I was painting and the finished canvases were alive."

If I could easily stand now . . . But can't do it yet. Important to keep her talking, at least. "Where are they, Kate?"

She continued as though she hadn't heard him. "I produced thirty paintings. The sum total of my work, wedged in between working to make ends meet, raising Jordan and," her explanation trailed off . . . *and my memories of you*, she finished in her mind.

"Where are they, Kate?" Aidan repeated gently.

"Ian heard about them, of course—through his spies," she continued dismally. "Getting one of his henchmen to round them up and take them off was child's play. I left the house one day to pick up Jordan and when I came home, they were gone. Just like that. As an extra measure, they made certain to rough up the house."

"And you have no idea where they are?" he asked, appalled.

"I've never seen them again."

The weight of her loss filled him with a heavy aching. Crushing. For her to generate a body of work, know it to be special, then to lose it all. "Have you tried? Did you report it?" He didn't speak his most devastating thought. *Could they have been destroyed?*

Her smile was thin. "You forget how dumb I was, and quite alone. I made a lot of decisions that a real grown-up might not have. So—no, I didn't report it. I haven't tried to do anything. I had faith in Ian to be utterly first-class in being evil. I didn't do anything but grieve once they were taken."

A young woman with no resources. *The paintings that gave her life and inspiration ripped away.* Aidan struggled to make sense of it.

Unexpectedly, she continued speaking. "I . . . I'm not painting any more anyway. It was a miraculous period for me, but it's over."

Incredulity mixed with concern. Aidan caught her as she passed, pacing again, and pulled her down next to him. "Why aren't you painting anymore?" he asked carefully.

Despair shadowed her face. "I gave up. The closer I got to Ian's release, the harder it got. It's become impossible." She sprang up again, walked swiftly to the small utility closet, pulling out eight canvases one by one, and lining them up against the wall. They were unfinished and raw, created with degenerating skill. Black swirls of angry darkness covered some of them, the canvas of others was torn as her frustration had mounted and overflowed.

"Even in jail, he's stolen my life," she gestured helplessly at the spoiled paintings. "Whenever I start a painting, all I can think of is Ian, and how he would react to it. Can't help picturing it— him laughing and belittling. Bullying me. I see him stealing it all over again. The idea paralyzes me, and I can't even hold my brush steady. So I stand there and watch it die. Sometimes I'm so angry I murder it."

Aidan's mind was spinning. There had to be some solution to her impasse, some process to begin the hunt for the stolen canvases. "But . . ."

"No, that's it, Aidan. There's nothing more to do or say. You asked, so I showed them to you." She stacked the ruined canvases in the closet. "I don't understand why I keep these. I keep thinking I might find a clue, some way to start again."

Irrevocable, final, impossible. "Nothing more to say tonight, Kate. Thanks for telling me." He rose from the chair, shaking his head when she offered to help. "It's okay. I'm alright now."

Shoulder to shoulder, they watched the last of the sun's slanting rays slip behind the dark mountains, burnishing their tops russet and crimson. Mutely, full of their own thoughts, they walked gravely from the battlefield of Kate Stoker's creative process.

Chapter 8

For most of the next day, Kate made sure that they went their separate directions. Raw emotions churned through her, carrying a succession of images. Aidan's celebration of beauty and spirit. His surety that she was meant to participate in this inspired life. His passionate reaction to the unforgivable loss of her art. The way he knew her mind before she spoke out the words. *And damn it, the way I feel about him.*

There's no refuge, she thought helplessly, giving up. Rain spattered down in rhythmic squalls between short sun breaks. The greenhouse quickly felt too close. Pining for open space and solitude, she headed for the peaks, walking fast until she found her favorite ledge overlooking Fionn Loch.

Lying on the cool earth, she watched the rain advance, pulling the hood up over her head until it passed. She pushed her shoulders into the wet heather and sharp rocks, coveting the cold, wanting the hardness of rocks. Anything to take her mind off Aidan. This was getting too big, too strong. *Out here, I feel the mystery of existence flying around me—the huge and incomprehensible power of the earth, and my small life within it.*

And that was exactly it. Aidan would always allow such a thought. Welcome it even. He never pretended to limit the cosmos. It was a gift he carried—the inner wilderness he recognized was precious beyond articulation—letting his own heart roam within it, infinite and free.

It was late afternoon when Kate entered the door, so distracted that she barely registered Kieran's greeting. *She's wilder than ever*, he thought, observing her drenched hair and muddy jeans. Her awareness slowly centered on him, ignoring all the other occupants in the lounge.

"Come all the way in," he directed gently. "You are as wet as a river otter. And hardly fit to work, I might add."

There was no repartee from her as she mumbled "sorry".

"Himself is in the same state, if that makes you feel any better."

Despite her agitation, Kate smiled at Kieran's Irish way with words. "He's wet, too?" They chuckled at her attempted humor, Kieran's contagious relief shaking tension from both of them.

"Can't lure him out of the studio," Kieran continued cautiously. "He requested the key." Turning away from Kate's challenging stare, he persisted. "Sorry. I was afraid it would make you mad. But truthfully, the yes just came out of my mouth when he asked. It seemed right." He took her sweater with a shake of his head. "Do you always have to be nearly drowned before you go home?"

"You let him into the studio," she repeated. "Um, yeah. That makes me mad." *What was he doing there?* She did not plan to have him take this on.

"He's been there awhile." There was no point in trying to talk her out of being miffed. He clearly had to send her in to Aidan.

"I was hoping you would bring him some food and drink, and eventually entice him out of there. The guests have been calling for the piano."

"I'll be back," she replied shortly, heading upstairs for a shower and a quick change. In the meantime, Kieran assembled a tray for her—the plates artfully filled with pork cutlets, savory chutney and steamed vegetables. He tucked in a bottle of wine and two glasses, as well as a candle and matches, over her protests.

"We're not on a date," she protested.

"And why not? You should both be so lucky." He shrugged as she glowered at him. "Well, anyway, you'll eat. You have to be hungry, and don't try and deny it."

Her footsteps echoed in her ears as she walked slowly to the place where the man who haunted her dreams waited with what was left of her art. Aidan was gazing out the window when she turned the corner.

Plunking the food down noisily, she sat without speaking until he looked at her. His eyes were unwavering and quiet. *Infuriatingly calm.* "Why are you here?" she demanded, trying to sound stern.

"You have a right to be upset," he answered softly. "But I will to ask you not to be, Kate. I couldn't stay out of here."

She lit the candle, muttering "just for illumination", ignoring the one-sided lift of his lips.

"What is this wonderful smelling feast?" he queried.

"You know Kieran would track you down and force feed you if necessary. It wasn't my idea."

"Of course not."

Wanting temper to strengthen her, alarmed as it drifted away. "Okay, I'm starving and he knew I would be." Capitulating abruptly, she nodded as he held up the wine, questioning. "I still need an explanation."

After the wine was uncorked and poured, he held up his

glass. "Thanks for forgiving me."

"I haven't," but she joined the toast. "Now I'm eating, and you're eating and explaining."

He swallowed a mouthful of wine and a few bites of warm food before he spoke. "I think you deserve to find out if your paintings still exist."

The opening in her snapped shut. "There's no point. I'm not going down that road and neither are you."

"I am, Kate." His face was resolute. "I don't plan to roll over on this, like Kieran does. Frankly, I don't care if it makes you irate because your paintings are at stake and they're more important. And you want to find them. Don't tell me you don't."

He kept eating while she eyed him guardedly. "Why are you doing this?" She could not keep her voice from shaking.

Aidan laid his fork down, deliberating on his wine glass, alternately sipping and swirling the ruby colored merlot. "Let me tell you a story, Kate. Maybe it will explain my motive to you. While Sheila was growing up, the university was a decent place—steady. But I wanted something else," he continued. He hazarded a quick glance at her, hoping that bringing his reasons into the story would calm her.

"I could see the islands and water from my desk and started dreaming about how to best represent a threatened beautiful ecosystem. Kept coming back to art. And then, well, the artists would need a gallery."

Despite herself, she could feel herself unwinding, accepting the offer to enter his world. She nodded once, and kept eating with no further interruption.

"I needed to write, and I longed to play the music that was creating itself inside my head. I would ride the ferry every chance I had to take pictures," he continued. "One day, I woke up with a crystal clear thought. I wanted to live in the center of the landscape that was calling to me. It took me a while to summon the courage to give up the university life, but I haven't regretted it."

Her dinner was finished and his cooled. "I understand how it is to create, Kate," he said simply. "How hard and glorious it is. How it fills your life. I can't imagine losing it and not knowing what happened. I became a gallery owner so I could represent artists. It is the core of my world. Perhaps you could say it's the obsession of someone who spends too much time alone."

Kate watched the dark mist roll down from the mountains. A small muscle in her cheek clenched.

Aidan waited a heartbeat to regain his own equanimity, instantly regretting the implication. "At any rate, I have connections in the art world. Good ones. If your paintings are out in the world, we could identify that very quickly."

"And if they are rotting in someone's basement?"

"Then we have to follow some clues. I am hoping you'll give me some details to go on, and I will follow it from there."

Picking up her wine glass, she sat quietly and mulled it over. The last thing in the world she wanted to do, with Ian returning to the world soon, was to start poking around for the paintings she'd given up for dead. *Sill, she owed them something, didn't she?* Those incredible beings had flowed from her like grace. They deserved to live, even if she wasn't there to take them out into the world. *Aidan could do that.*

She allowed herself a small sip of merlot before answering. "You got me. I do want to know. If you're willing to try to find them, I'm willing to give you what little clues I have." A hesitant smile shined briefly. "Enough for now?"

"For now." Bittersweet aching filled Aidan's chest. He would have this, if nothing else—Kate's acquiescence, allowing him into this treasured part of her life. Indicating the half-full bottle, ignoring the intermittent tingling in his back, he risked a gentle touch on her arm. "Keep me company for awhile?" The waning moon rose leisurely over the peaks, watching over them.

Chapter 9

The night was hard, fevered by his desire for Kate, alternating with numbing pain. Before the first shafts of gray lightened the sky, Kathleen visited Aidan. Afterwards, he would remember it as a dream, or so his daytime logic would say. But in the ghostly light of dawn, she was real.

Kathleen did not speak. She motioned to Aidan, inviting him to look at her directly. Staring, examining, discovering her over again, he saw the vision before him was entirely released from illness. She was serene in a way he had never experienced.

Kathleen's curse was her sickness—he'd accepted that for a long time. But somewhere along the way, he'd allowed the memory of her final bout with it to fester and grow into a dark apprehension that he would forever be alone.

Her image brightened briefly, then vanished. When it vanished, so did his apprehension that had doubted his future. Without further struggle, Kathleen's curse was gone.

Aidan woke with a start. The pain was present, for sure, but he felt strangely energized. What was between Kate and him was suddenly theirs alone. That didn't make it any easier. *No one to blame.* Even so, a newborn sense of possibility stirred. Dressing quickly, he walked in the dark with one eye on the approaching dawn, heading for the Great Hall.

Kate entered just as he sat down. Examined him up and down. He was pale, with a tired edge around his eyes. "You look like you've seen better mornings."

"Nothing the Earl won't chase off," he replied, saluting lightly with his cup, glad to be alone with her again. "Your coffee is ready," he continued as Kate ducked behind the bar.

She took a few moments to pour it, observing him carefully, puzzlement creasing her brow. Despite the obvious fatigue, he seemed oddly peaceful.

"I'm okay, Kate. I would be lying to you if I told you I slept well. But between you and the caffeine, I'll be as good as I can be in a few."

'The pain is better?"

"Mostly numb today. The issues take turns."

"Pain meds don't help?"

"They can sometimes take the edge off. But to do more, I have to swallow so many that the rest of my life doesn't function. So I keep it to a minimum."

"I've been waiting to ask that."

"I know. Am I forgiven yet for last night?"

Kate brought more hot water for his tea. "For pushing me to open up to you? For not letting me off the hook? Yes. I forgive you."

He was surprised at her answer, more astounded to hear himself blurt out exactly what he was thinking. "How do you manage to be so beautiful every morning?"

Her face registered such a mixture of consternation and

appreciation that he laughed, relaxing them both. "Okay, change direction. I'm hoping you have some information for me," he added.

She sat down next to him, balancing her steaming mug, setting down milk for the tea. The coffee's strong flavor grounded her. He clearly was going to be stubborn about this, so she might as well get it over with.

"I've been considering the probable suspects," she began. "Ian had three men at his beck and call. Victor Almerzado was the oldest. Hispanic—though no idea from where, exactly. Smart, tough, continually in trouble. Jerry Sanger—a nice retired cowboy facade. Child molester in his spare time. Ken Hunter had leopard's eyes, stalking everything in sight. Had a habit of appearing so suddenly my mouth would go dry. Never could figure out how he arrived. I think the chances are excellent one of them did the dirty work. They would have easily figured out how to take the paintings while I was working."

"Can you give me any more basic information to start with?"

"I'll write it out for you. Everything. Okay?" She poured more coffee. "Let's not spend the whole morning talking about it."

"Fine."

She stirred the milk in, observing him thoughtfully. The weariness was starting to ebb. His color had returned, and . . . *what was it about the man that was so damn attractive to her*? He'd turned a few heads since he'd arrived. No use pretending she hadn't noticed. *Maybe it was the appeal of those dark expressive eyes.* But it was the way they looked at the world that filled her, made her want more.

A slight smile played at the corner of his mouth. "Whatever you're thinking, don't stop."

She burst out laughing. "I suppose I must have been totally transparent just then."

"I hope so." His rare full grin warmed the room, pushing the night and its ghosts further away.

Better change the subject before I am completely undone. "Want to hear the story of how I found myself here?"

"Of course I would."

"It had to do with you, no surprise. When you talked about the Fisherfields in Montana, it made an impression. I was searching for someplace to go. I think I followed your stories right into Kinlochewe, without knowing what I was trying to find. I stayed for a few days, and had decided to leave when I saw a poster advertising a Ceilidh. I had to ask around before I really understood that it was the perfect opportunity to get my fix of Celtic music, though going alone was scary enough to almost change my mind. I sat there, like a rabbit at a fox party, nursing a Guinness I could barely swallow."

Talk, don't touch. That was what Kate needed. *So make conversation, MacLaine,* he thought urgently. "Until a big Irishman plunked down beside you."

Kate laughed. "He did, and you can imagine it perfectly well."

"I can indeed. 'Jesus, Mary and Joseph', he would have said to himself when he saw you. Waited for a bit to be positive you weren't tangled up with someone. Then he waltzed into your life as if he'd known you forever."

"Same as he did with you."

"Exactly."

"He enjoyed the Ceilidh so thoroughly I forgot all about being shy. I even sang along and entirely astounded myself by having a dance with him. And before I knew what had happened, we'd agreed to meet the day after. He asked me if I would consider working at his lodge. I said yes so quickly it amazed both of us. But I wanted to disappear somewhere. And there is something about Kieran."

"That I know well. Impossible to say no to."

"But trustworthy."

"To the core."

"That was the main thing. I realized he was flirting with me at first, but he skidded to a stop when he discovered I didn't desire that kind of relationship. He could have dumped me then, but he didn't. He just grew to be a very good friend. I've only ever had one other friend," she mused, considering. "I suppose you could say it was the same story with him."

His eyebrows rose slightly, questioning.

"Only an old high school friend. But we've stayed in touch for all these years." She got up and lit the oven. "Now you," she said quizzically. "Tell me something about you I don't know."

"Well," he let the contentment of the moment play in his heart. "That could fill a book, probably. But since we're here, I'll limit it to the Scottish Highlands. I think I climbed every waking minute the first trip. I announced I was investigating MacLaine history and I did. But I also spent more than a few weeks exploring—outer Hebrides mostly, and those awesome Glencoe mountains. The second visit, I slowed up."

"That's when I traveled north to Wester Ross. Followed the scent of peaks like a hound on a fresh trail. The Seven Sisters in the Great Sheil. The Torridons. The Fannichs. The Fisherfields."

Her eyes widened, watching how he looked as the names rolled out, seeing rocky summits reaching to the sky.

"Guess you could say I was seeking God." Her amazement teased out a chuckle. "Don't tell me you're not doing the same out there everyday, Kate. Give it another name if you need to. I had a backpack and a will to roam. I wanted some meaning and a reason for my life."

Kate pulled out a hot roll she'd been warming, buttered it quickly and split it between them. Chewing pensively, she sat, lean legs crossed. Her light undershirt was practically painted over her supple body. Aidan was sure he would lose the battle and pull her into his arms, but his discipline held. He concentrated instead on the taste of the tea and bread, watching the sun crest the peaks in a thin line of tawny amber.

"I guess what I'm seeking is beauty," she replied at length. "I like to walk out onto the yielding earth and just witness it. I can't say I believe in the God I grew up with, but there is an essence of divinity. It's easy to feel it in the mountains. Some kind of nameless intrinsic intelligence. I guess you could call it God."

It was this about Kate—this beauty inside her, the real and uncultivated energy of her spirit that he held dear. *Duende*, he thought. *The discovery of truth and a soulful willingness to express it.* Aidan sipped the smoky tea, relieved that the morning pain was beginning to ebb. "Ever experience it with the sea?"

"Not really. I have, I mean, yes. But I haven't been near the ocean very often."

He swallowed down the invitation that welled up, thinking of his house with its stunning view. *A long, lonely, beautiful vista.* Silencing a sigh, he resumed the conversation.

"I'm not certain exactly what to call what I discovered in those mountain explorations," he continued. "On my best days, I identify it as unconditional love . . . the way the sun shines on everyone, no matter what. When I recognize I'm loved purely for being alive."

"Yeah," her eyes were riveted to his. Aidan looked out the window, shielding both of them from the strength of the bond between them.

"I've had that feeling too, Addy." There it came again— the intimacy, the corresponding jolt in his spirit. Hearing her own words, seeing the effect on him, she sighed apologetically. "I'm sorry. It slipped out."

For an instant, he was at a loss for a response. He tapped his fingers together, fighting for the right thing to say. "It's just that no one calls me that anymore," he finally replied. They talked as the sun's illumination drove the shadows from the mountains, continuing an unhurried conversation, picking their words sparingly.

"I should leave," Kate pronounced when the light was strong and hard. "Can you drop by the greenhouse later? I have some amazing roses coming into flower."

He stayed seated, sporting the barest suggestion of a smile as she gathered the cups. "Okay, so don't answer," she continued after a beat. "You appear to be feeling better. I'm positive Kieran will be here shortly with the intent to feed you."

"No doubt. And yes, the Earl did its job, as usual." Kate observed him cautiously, once again trying to read the change she saw there.

"Off with you, mountain goat," he waved at her flippantly. "I can't imagine I would find any reason whatsoever that would keep me from coming to see your superbly impossible blooms."

After she departed, he let her fragrance wash over him, breathing in the sweet air of destiny. Grateful those years of dreams had met this day. He sat motionless and quiet, listening to his heart shout its love, recognizing that the story of his life had just been re-written.

And Kieran was late, he realized with amusement. There could be only one reason for his habitually prompt friend to be so uncharacteristically tardy. Her name would be Julie.

By the time Kieran roared into the Great Hall, Aidan had the lights on and was serving coffee to the morning patrons. His friend was freshly showered and clearly tired but glowing.

"Welcome to your establishment." Aidan placed a mug of well-sugared coffee on the bar in front of Kieran. "It's a great honor to serve you for a change."

Taking the steaming beverage, Kieran said nothing, but his eyes were dancing. He sampled it with a saucy grin. "Perfect, my man. You're hired."

"Actually, I'll take a trade. I need access to a phone and a computer line for my laptop by this afternoon. Somewhere private."

"Och, Aidan, what are you up to now?" His tone was dreamy and distracted. Kieran's mind was obviously on other subjects.

It was best to tell him. Aidan spoke in a low tone, directly into Kieran's ear. "It has to do with Kate's paintings. The ones that were stolen. She's agreed to allow me try and find them."

Kieran's bearing shifted dramatically into the present. "You are a magician," he exclaimed. "This all happened last night? Of course it did. I figured that you two were in some deep conversation when you didn't come out of there until . . . after I was otherwise occupied. You couldn't have sat there fighting all night."

"Not the whole time," Aidan smiled.

"You appear to have had about as much sleep as me," Kieran chuckled, checking his stock of Earl Gray.

"Probably. But it wasn't as much fun."

"Too bad. I think heaven about sums it up. Yourself?"

"Okay this morning."

They worked together, starting to gather orders for breakfast, serving tea and coffee. "Max will be working with Mary this morning. Julie had the morning off."

"Lucky her. Next opportunity, arrange the same for yourself. Now what about that space?"

"My office is the best. If you can find a place to park your computer. The desk is . . . a bit full. But it has a couple of phone lines so you should be in business. And it's private. Lord knows no one would ever try to find me there. The place is only a warehouse for my papers."

By mid-morning, Aidan had successfully chased off 'himself', using Kieran's own phrasing, to get some sleep. "Alone," he warned, "or it doesn't count." The sunny promise of the morning had steadily disintegrated into a lead-gray sky and a cold wind. *Kate will come down from her mountain early today.*

He watched for her while he played the piano. Timed so that when she entered, he stood at Kieran's usual place, unable to keep away a playful grin. Kate brought the whole outdoors with her, the energy of mountains and fast-flowing streams. Her damp clothes carried the fresh aroma of wind and heather. *What I would do to be able to join her.*

"Where's our Irishman?"

"Sleeping, at least he'd better be."

She wrinkled her nose and laughed. "Oh. He's been that busy, has he? Good for him."

"He's supposed to arrive here shortly." She cast an eye around the bar, nodding at the waves in her direction, uncertain what to do next. *Don't leave, Kate,* he thought, with a flutter of anxiety. *Stay and let me be with you for a while.*

As she read his look, everyone else in the lounge faded from her awareness. Quickly hanging up the rest of her outdoor garments, she grabbed an apron and put it on.

"Obviously it takes both of us to make up for one fast-talking charmer. What can I do?"

"You can help me write the dinner specials," he was aware of the heat in his face and the catch in his throat. She followed him as he went into the back room, and when he stopped, stood closely behind, longing to put her arms around him.

Aidan picked up the markers, trying to concentrate on his task. Her breath hit the back of his neck—shaking him with an earthquake of yearning so strong he almost dropped them. He turned slowly toward her, taking her hand. Grateful she did not pull away, wondering where to go with it, he held her there, their fingers linked.

They could hear Kieran coming down the hall, greeting patrons as he went, clearly in an irresistibly excellent mood. Aidan's gaze swept up her body. Not certain his voice would hold, he whispered the only truth he knew at the moment. "Someday, I will want more than looking." Gently, he released his hold.

Taking the markers from him, she reached up to cup his cheek. Stayed a moment, even as her heart shivered. "That makes two of us."

Kieran was fast approaching. Aidan forced himself to step away from her, searching urgently for a way to break their trance. "I need the details you promised me."

"I have them. I wrote them up on the mountain. But you have to come to the greenhouse to pick them up."

"I'm not sure that's safe," he responded with the hint of a smile.

"Probably not. But you'll have to live dangerously. I really want you to see these roses."

Kieran burst through the door, sweeping aside the intimacy of the scene, shouting, "Where's my barman?" Surprised to find both of them so quiet, his tone immediately turned conspiratorial. "Oops. Have I disturbed you?"

"Yes, we were plotting revisions to the menu," Kate retorted thinly. "Good morning, Sleeping Beauty."

"Och, beauty I'm not, but I am forever grateful to you, Aidan, for letting me off the hook." His green eyes roamed over both of them, doubtfully, aware of the dissipating heat in the room. "I can deal with the customers if you have something to finish," he added pointedly.

Aidan laughed, a sound laced with irony. "Thank you for the offer, my friend. It's not possible for us finish anything in here." Ignoring the lift of Kieran's eyebrows, he shrugged.

"Anyway, I have a piano that's been missing me. And I have an offer later to admire the improbable beauty of roses in the middle of a Highland autumn," he added. Glad for a momentary interlude of strength and health, he walked out through the swinging doors.

When the piano started up, Kate kept her head down and her work apart from people. *If that instrument was a woman,* thought Kieran, *she would be lost in the heat of passion.* No doubt at all.

It felt almost illicit to listen in on the raw feelings and desire of the compositions. But everyone did. As Aidan played, talk simply petered out. People found things to do nearby or they sat unabashedly and took pleasure in the music. Kate left suddenly with no comment to Kieran.

She'll be seeking solitude, he thought. *Of course she would.* She would make a beeline for the greenhouse and be grateful for her bright warm space populated only by plants.

As the piano music came to a standstill, Kate knew Aidan would be on his way. She bent over the plum-colored roses, carefully de-budding the stems so that only one bloom would dominate. When he entered, it did not surprise her that he stayed well apart from her.

Something had been released. It was riveting and half-frightening. The golden highlights in his eyes reflected the multicolored blooms, as he took them from her gently, lingering for a minute. Their conversation was brief. An unspoken agreement pulsed between them to leave it for the night as it was, the questions unanswered.

He left with an armful of vibrantly colored blooms and all the details Kate could remember about the potential art thieves. It was late, he told her briefly, retreating resolutely from her warm green world.

Chapter 10

Freya Johansen was a busy woman. Art was her world, her mate and her family. She owned no pets and had few friends. There was no time to squander on meaningless relationships, even if they were momentarily pleasant. Her passion to represent the arts made her one of the best in the world, and she traveled at the drop of a hat to deliver art or meet with either artist or patron.

Freya never used the word "customer." It was far too crude and really not correct. If the arts were to survive, there had to be people, preferably people with money, who sponsored the creators themselves. The old term "starving artist" was a little too accurate.

There were very few men in her world that had ever stopped her in her tracks. Aidan was one of them. She was proud of how she had adjusted her intense attraction to him into a more productive affiliation. Mentoring implied a special relationship, but nothing that would become messy.

When Aidan entered the art scene as a neophyte, she recognized a discerning eye and a true talent for representation. Without trying, Aidan could introduce artist to patron or vice versa in a way that bonded them firmly. And that was merely the beginning of his talents.

In the early years, there had been times she could hardly think when she listened to Aidan's quiet elegance. *He hardly needs to write poetry*, she'd thought, *he speaks in poems*.

It was a narrow edge but she'd managed not to tip over it. Transmuting any semblance of attraction was necessary to continue their relationship. Over the past few years, they'd met rarely but talked often. Freya was only a year older than Aidan but she'd had many more years in the business. She'd had a lot to teach him and he'd been a willing student.

In return, he brought her contracts and forged connections she could not have managed on her own. As thanks, she made sure he received the true monetary value of his work.

When her caller ID showed Aidan's cell phone, she picked it up with no hesitation. He was one of the very few who didn't have to wait for her to call at her leisure after she'd listened to the message.

"Hi," her smoky voice coiled through the receiver. Satisfaction purred in her chest like a cat wrapped around a heater. *Not exactly phone sex, but titillating nevertheless*.

"Hey there," he responded cordially. *If he felt the same toward her, he hid it well*, she reflected, observing the hard lines of the Chicago skyline. Oh, he was unfailingly friendly and warm. She did not doubt he harbored great affection toward her. Fondness was not the same as ardor, however. Shrugging, she reminded herself that this was how she wanted it.

Freya was used to on-demand men. Her silky coffee-colored skin was a legacy of her chocolate brown mother and her Scandinavian father. The languorous green eyes, full mouth and seductive flare of her hips were sure-fire men attractants. She didn't covet Aidan's attentions, at least not openly. But it was frustrating that he didn't yearn for her, at least a little.

Okay, get over it, Freya, she reminded herself. They were, at least, committed friends and occasional business partners.

Shaking off the last of her vaguely resentful energy, she resolved to enjoy the interlude with him. "What's up? You've been as scarce as a warm day in a Chicago winter. I was starting to believe you'd taken up a new profession."

No point rising to the bait. "Sorry I've been out of touch for the past few months. I'm in Scotland, Freya." He could so easily picture her in the luxurious Gold Coast condo that served as home when she wasn't traveling, its big window views stretching out toward Lake Michigan and downtown Chicago. It felt a million miles from the Highlands and a lodge devoted to the requirements of people who craved open spaces. "I'm way up north, in the mountains," he added before she could ask.

Freya always insisted on give and take so he didn't rush. She enjoyed his descriptions of The Big Misty and its charismatic proprietor. When he introduced Kate into the conversation, she sat up. There was no doubt that this woman was special. *Was he in love with her?* She pictured him falling fast, with no net to catch him. A thrill of jealousy shot through her. It was surprisingly arousing. A kind of vicarious affair.

As Aidan told the story of the stolen paintings, Freya enjoyed the tension in her muscles. This story was not only sexy—it was a thriller as well. He had her full interest.

No one, she agreed, should be robbed of their art and kept in the dark about whether it was alive or not. She imagined the paintings as hostages, real and deeply pained to be separated from the light of day and their creator. It bothered her only a tad that he understood this so perfectly.

"That's quite a tale, Aidan MacLaine," she breathed into

his expectant silence, after he finished. "I suppose you called me because you want my help." She paused. "Naturally. And I am willing to give it, as you knew I would be. Partly because it's you asking and partly because you know that I could not bear the thought of the paintings being either destroyed or hidden. If she's as good as you say she is, they deserve to be found. Or if nothing else, given a decent funeral, if we find out they have been destroyed. At least then she'd have a chance at mourning them. Maybe she could paint again."

"And," she hurried on, before he could respond, "Kate is obviously quite important to you. First I've ever heard that tone. Don't even try to deny it."

"You're right," he agreed quietly. From his terse reply, she realized she would not hear more than that. *He's not ready for it.*

"The details are few and far between," he continued. "But if anyone can be productive with them, it's you. Freya, there's something else you should be aware of."

He quickly explained what he could about Ian. *She had to be warned to be careful.* Too much prodding might have dangerous consequences. It was critical that Freya understood this before she agreed to do it.

When he'd finished, she found herself reaching for a glass of Spanish sherry, Aidan's gift from the Andalusia region. *While I'm at it, I might as well enjoy a cigarette,* she thought. She let him tarry as she gathered her comfort items.

"Ah, Aidan, I realize you hate this, but really, it's hard to beat a cigarette on occasion." Freya leaned out on her porch, enjoying the cool lake moisture and the drift of smoke on the breeze.

"I understand, dear, it's just that most people can't enjoy it once in while. You are unusual—in most ways, come to think of it, and very resistant to addiction. Too bad you can't market it."

"Yeah, it would be a great fundraiser for my causes. Smoke a cigarette for the arts. Once a year—for the fundraiser. Sin and no penalty."

"Um, okay," she sighed into his silence. "I expect you'll require an agreement from me."

"Should you care to accept the case," he mimicked the Mission Impossible voice. "You understand the challenges and the risks. The only reward is some sort of intrinsic satisfaction and making me happy, I guess."

"Well, those, my dear, are some of my most motivating factors. I accept the case, Agent MacLaine. I will get right on it. Keep in touch with me."

"Thanks, Agent Johansson. You are a gem in every sense of the word."

"No need to butter me up. I already said yes. Sleep tight in those . . . umm, what did you call them? 'Autumn-colored peaks,' I believe it was. Good luck with whatever you want to happen with the lady artist. I can tell she's stunning without asking. Just don't forget your old flames." Smiling to herself, she hung the phone up gently.

Chapter 11

Aidan spent most of the next day in Kieran's cramped office researching possibilities and transferring what little he had to Freya. Names and last seen locations. Descriptions. Kate's notes were not exactly full of helpful details. As a young mother, she had been acquainted with these men only in passing. They were Ian's henchmen. She had never wanted to learn much about them.

Lucky his friend and mentor had an obsession with the shady side of life. Freya had a stable of reformed criminals held in reserve for such a purpose. When art went missing, Freya was often contacted and she had a great track record of recovery. She didn't carry out any of the dirty work herself, but she certainly had a mind that understood crooks. Freya had the best in the business.

He sent the details to her and spent the rest of his energy sending out the call to his contacts, in the modest chance that the paintings might be in circulation.

Kieran brought food and drink to the office and leaned up against the desk for a brief conversation. Kate was "out there" again, he reported. The day was overcast but the rain was holding. Did Aidan desire anything else?

The second time, Aidan accepted the tray and put it down, amused at Kieran's distracted dreaminess. "Thank you. I will never go hungry in your house. Nor want for anything. At this instant, I am working and you are required elsewhere, my friend. Don't fuss about me."

When his work was finished, he headed straight up to the alcove, where he often wrote in the mornings, avoiding the Great Hall. He decided not to risk heading down for dinner, concentrating on writing instead. The burning pain in his back was fierce.

The white-lidded, cloudy day spent itself, dissolving into a blue-gray dusk, interlaid with stars. The alcove was perfect, with its large full-of-sky windows. He was reflecting on the luminous palette when Kate arrived.

"Glendronach, a fifteen year-old single malt from the Speyside region of the Highlands," she announced, sitting down, passing him the bottle. "Kieran's newest offering."

Assembling two glasses and a small carafe of water, she mustered up a perplexed demeanor. "Kieran says to take note the 'smoky honey highlights' of this one." She exaggerated the description with Kieran's accent and an impish expression.

Aidan's half smile flickered. "You did that well."

"Thanks," she responded, studying mountains that were slowly disappearing into the night. "Gorgeous. It was cold and windy today. Gray. But it's gorgeous now."

"It is. And the scene outside is fine too."

Her head swiveled, mouth pursed, ready to joust at him. Loitered on Aidan's face, completely shattering her concentration.

"So, let's try it," she recovered, pouring the whisky. They toasted and drank. Kate frowned, trying to sort through the complex flavors.

"Very rich," Aidan said approvingly, amused at Kate's concerted examination. "Sweet," he pronounced, swirling his glass and taking another appreciative taste. "Lush and spicy," he mimicked Kieran better than she, with a faultless emphatic overtone and firm motion of the head.

She burst into laughter. "Are you really describing a whisky, or the way you two prefer your women?"

He just smiled at her over his glass.

"Will you come down for dinner?" She knew what he would say but had to ask.

It would be a risky gamble tonight, with the unabated burning. "I'm not really hungry, Kate. I think I'll stay in."

She nodded slowly, giving another go at Kieran's tone and mannerisms. "Another wee dram then?"

Aidan could not resist a slight grin. Now that she was here, his spirit lightened. Kate gave him something else to think about other than the goddamn pain. "If you'll join me."

She was pouring the drinks as he said it. "Can you taste this stuff Kieran talks about? The seawater tang and sherry and all that? I can sense the peat but frankly, that overwhelms me."

"Try this little trick." Aidan trickled a few drops of water into her glass. "This will make it smoother. Some of us are Scotch drinkers, and fewer of us enjoy picking apart the intricate flavors in single malts. It's a humble group really, and probably rather rare, not to mention obscure, in the general population."

"I prefer wine. A nice solid merlot."

Nodding agreeably but thinking more about what they weren't saying, he gathered courage for an admission. "I'm glad you're here, Kate. I'd have gone the day not seeing you."

"Too dangerous?" she ventured.

"Shark-infested waters."

"For sure," she sighed out the words. "I probably would've

done the same. But when Kieran suggested I bring up the Scotch, I could hardly wait for him to find the one he was going to send to you."

Half afraid, but unable to keep the question from spilling out, Aidan asked what he could no longer ignore. "Maybe if you had enough Glendronach, you could tell me about Ian."

"Maybe."

He hated to watch her tense up. But she wasn't closing down.

"You deserve to hear it. You've earned it, though god knows why you want the gory details." Kate ventured another sip. "Oh, that is much easier on the tongue."

Aidan affirmed this with a tilt of his head, keeping his attention steady.

"I think I can do this. I'll try, anyway. Keep in mind I was eighteen when I met Ian,.."

"Young and ready for anything."

"Exactly. So, he was scary, but I craved excitement. My folks were dead and my sister Tracy married and busy with her young ones. I made up stories to satisfy her and refused to pay attention to the warning signs. 'He's only like that when he drinks,' I would say to myself. It took about three months of me playing 'the cool girl with the bad guy' before I finally figured out it wasn't a game."

She started to take another sip, settled for a brief sniff of the glass. "One night, after he'd been at the bar for hours, he drove to my house and wouldn't take no for an answer. Pounded on the door. Came at me when I opened it. Nothing I could do would make him quit."

Her mouth drew in a thin line. "In fact, the more I struggled and fought, the more excited he got. When he fell asleep that night, I laid awake and admitted to myself what a huge mistake I had made tangling up with him. But I'd put off my sister, my only family, with the big bravado. So, I didn't tell her, or anyone."

Aidan's jaw tightened with anger, imagining a young and foolish Kate, caught up in the aggressive actions of a cruel man.

"Four weeks later, I knew I was pregnant. When Ian found out, he made a show of marrying me. He insisted that my sister Tracy fly out to witness our Justice of the Peace wedding."

She forced the words out. "Tracy kept staring at me as if I were insane. She could tell what kind of character Ian was from the start. We attempted it once—to talk in private—but he was good at riding herd on us." Kate choked out a harsh laugh.

"I didn't have a clue what to do. I wouldn't consider an abortion. Even if Ian had allowed it, which he absolutely wouldn't have. By then, I knew that he would track me down if I ever attempted to leave. I was already caught in his web. Tracy felt it too but she had nothing on him and didn't know how to stop him. He was careful to maintain outward appearances that couldn't be challenged. "

For a minute, Aidan thought she would end the story there. Kate struggled with the next section of the story. "After the wedding, there was the 'honeymoon'. We went up into the central Idaho mountains, where Ian had a cabin. Stayed for ten days while he drank and took me whenever he wanted. I was his property." Aidan touched her arm, trying to ease the pain of the memory.

Swallowing hard, Kate continued. "So began our married period. When I got too big, Ian discarded me. He would leave for days, and when he returned home, he always had money. Spent most of it at the bar."

"Tracy came back for Jordan's birth," she added with a weak smile. "She pleaded with me to leave with her, but the labor had been hard on Jordan and me both. I didn't have the strength to go and I couldn't imagine how we could run off without being followed by Ian—who would have gone berserk if I'd left him." She shifted uncomfortably. "Should I keep going?"

"Yes, though I hate it at the same time."

"Me too. Dumb girl that I was, I made light of the situation, concentrating on the joy of having a baby in my life. And so we did nothing. Ian arrived a week after the birth, from wherever he'd been and sent Tracy packing. Then he took the baby and me to live at his house."

The moon and the cold stars had been her only witness for so many years. She leaned forward to pour more whisky into both glasses. Aidan's grave countenance was wounded by the difficult retelling of her early years.

"Jordan was the center of my universe," she said simply. "My son somehow healed the disaster of Ian's inflictions and miraculously escaped inheriting Ian's vicious nature. For a few years, Ian ignored us. He was constantly distracted, leaving and coming home with money that couldn't legitimately be his. Gave us barely enough to live on. I didn't care, as long as he stayed preoccupied. But of course, he didn't."

They sat for several moments, each holding a small glass with the taste of Scotland, inhaling the fragrance, welcoming the warm slide of whisky to their core.

Kate managed a smile, elusive as nightfall, tired and gentle. "That's all I can do tonight, Aidan. He went to jail. You already know more than anyone. Now, I'm exhausted and you should be."

"I want to hear the rest of the story."

"Okay," she agreed. "But that will be for another night." Her tone was final. Setting the glass down, she gathered up both his hands and kissed them. "When you first arrived," she murmured, "I couldn't imagine being able to do this. Any of it."

She stood up. "Thanks for listening. I'll leave the bottle and the glass for Kieran. He'll peek in on you. Of course he will. Don't expect him to be without food. Goodnight, Aidan."

Within an hour, Kieran arrived at the alcove where Aidan was still trying to gather his heart together. True to Kate's word,

Kieran was loaded with food. "As you said yourself, no one goes to bed hungry in my house," he announced, uncovering a fully loaded compartmented dish. "I asked Julie to fix us up, since I hadn't eaten yet either, and she gave us what she called 'a sampler' of all their goodies."

"Plus you got to talk to her."

"That too," responded Kieran roguishly. Aidan couldn't help but smile at his big grin. "Well, dig in, you must be hungry," Kieran urged, placing fork to the meal. He maintained a companionable ease with a droll report of the events of the day.

"Julie did us well," Aidan relaxed and watched Kieran enjoy the last morsels. When Kieran finally laid his napkin aside, signaling the contented end of an excellent repast, he decided to explore a bit. "Tell me about you and Kate. She told me how you met, you old rascal. How you had your eye on her. But somehow you turned that around."

Kieran stretched expansively, relishing the memory, pouring the single malt. Packed a pipe he knew Aidan would refuse. "Fine fifteen year old, don't you think?" He examined the ocher liquid attentively, downed a hearty mouthful from his glass and beamed with approval. "The very thing," he sighed reverently.

"Are you stalling, my friend?"

"Och, no, there's no reason for it. But a fine tale can't be rushed." Kieran enjoyed another lingering sip. "When I met Kate, I felt my heart melt. I was very keen about her, and interpreted her affection wrongly at first. We do have fun. I foolishly thought I had a chance for a little while," he chuckled mischievously. "But she never let me in any further than friendship-deep. Made it clear, by implication, her far-away air— sometimes directly—that she was not available."

Kieran lit the pipe, drew in, and blew a smoke ring. "It became clear, even to my thick headed brain, that she was waiting for someone. Or someone had so claimed her soul that there was no room for anyone else. Certainly she had no interest at all in a casual dalliance. And many a fella's worked at it, I can tell you."

"When I saw her look at you . . . " he paused. "I saw how she looked at you," Kieran repeated meaningfully, "and the way you looked back. Then I found out why I was never in the running."

Aidan said nothing. The delicate relationship between Kate and him was a tangle of knots. He had no assurance how—or if—they would be fully released.

"But yet, I love her dearly, as a friend," Kieran continued readily ignoring Aidan's unsettled look. Love was a complicated thing indeed. "Anyway, I have all I can do, merely trying to get Julie to take me seriously," he added, with a nervous laugh.

Aidan studied his friend, appreciating the deep veins of feeling, effectively camouflaged by the easy manner and fast humor. "Read to her, Kieran."

"She would never be interested in such a thing."

"Try her. Share it with her. Permit her to sense your nature by reading your poetry. She won't see it otherwise. You keep it too well hidden."

"That scares the hell out of me."

Aidan shrugged. "I sympathize," he smiled ruefully. "But it feels right to me. If you want her, you have to let her discover what you're made of."

Shaking his head, Kieran tucked the pipe into its case and picked up his glass. "Maybe. Not sure I'm up to it. You keep the bottle with you. Might need another wee dram."

In the dark, several hours later, when sleep was hard, Aidan heard his own advice. It was time to tell Kate how he felt. He had to say it out loud. No matter if she already knew.

Chapter 12

For five days, they held to a rhythm that slowed to enjoy the season. Mid October featured a multihued landscape shining with earth colors. There was a feeling of enchantment in the lodge—like the world had gone supernatural—and everyone was caught in the magic of its spell. Every excuse to be outdoors or to stare out the window was given freely and taken shamelessly.

Kate set off every morning but made a point of returning by early afternoon when Aidan brought his feelings to the piano. She made it her business to be working in the vicinity when he played. Aidan felt her presence as the brightness of day. Understood it was her way of telling him more than words would dare express.

His heart refused to lie to the piano and his fingers celebrated Kate's life in the peaks, translating color and mountain, wind and cloud into musical notes.

As Kate trusted the solid earth, Aidan had faith in the

dance between his fingers and the piano keys. Especially when he could not rely on his body to respond as it always had, this delicate interplay of instrument and spirit sustained him.

On the day before Aidan would leave, the changeable weather unexpectedly became fine again, the morning bathed in sunlight. He rose before dawn and made it to the Great Hall before Kate.

When she rounded the corner, he had tea and coffee ready. "Since you can sense every change in these mountains, I figured you'd be up early today."

Smiling, she accepted his comment and the hot mug. "Mountain goats need to take advantage of favorable opportunities." She fiddled with the spoon in the cup, stirring it in a preoccupied manner. "You're leaving in the morning?"

"I'll be back, Kate," he reminded her. "That's the plan. Unless . . . " a small pause spread the words out. Gave her an idea of all the possibilities that ran through his mind. "Unless the doctor visit gives me really bad news or tells me I have to act immediately."

We have reached this point, he thought. When certain things had to be said, they had arrived at the place where they could speak it out out. Even when it was hard.

"We're starting to trust each other," Kate spoke to herself as much as to Aidan.

"I believe you're right."

"Can we escape again?"

"I won't be walking much."

"That doesn't matter."

"In that case, I would love to go with you."

They drove from the sleeping lodge, chuckling over Kieran's distraction with Julie. Kate had another special place to show him. She directed them along a precipitous incline.

"Hope the Rover makes it home," she laughed.

"Don't let her hear your doubt. She's very sensitive. I must tell you, however, that your roads are more like cow paths."

"Granted. But Aidan, that's what makes them special."

The trip was short but opened into another world. It brought them onto the shore of Fionn Loch, with a view that opened into a brilliant expanse of glistening lochs and the creamy saffron of the bog lands, guarded, as usual, with mountains. Aidan let out a soft whistle of admiration. "You are one for finding glorious views, aren't you?"

"They find me," she said, smiling at his open awe.

It was always hard, at first, getting out of the car. No reason to try and hide it anymore. Standing slowly, he waited for the burning to pass, surprised when her arm encircled his waist.

"Take care of yourself, Aidan." Her words tumbled out, in a hurry. "Find out what it is. Do whatever you need to do to be healthy."

He eased against the car for support, pulling her back when she started to withdraw. "Hang around for a moment, Kate. I want you close." There was a flash of resistance, giving way almost immediately as she allowed him to draw her in, leaning her head against his chest. The sun warmed around them, a light breeze sighing. Without knowing where the journey would take them, they simply held each other.

He held the sides of her cheeks, dark eyes searching hers. Tiptoeing, she answered him by reaching up for a kiss, allowing the aching softness of it to fill her. Deep and hungry—trusting the Highland peaks to keep their secret, a feeling of joy expanded into the wild spaces of the Fisherfields.

"Makes me think about how long I've been celibate," he murmured when they paused, making her laugh.

"Me too." She stayed close and stroked his back. "Suppose we remember how?"

"I believe I could manage to recall it," he responded dryly. His skin tingled with the touch of her hands under his shirt. For a few seconds, he actually believed somehow it would happen, both of them yielding to the magic of the mountains—the blissful warmth of the day.

He wasn't surprised when she stopped short from the brink. With a supple pivot, she landed in a side-to-side motion, breaking the sexual energy. With his voice husky and his breath quickened, he spoke into the charged air. "Thanks for thinking about it, at least."

"You have no idea, Aidan MacLaine. What I'd like to do with you."

"I'd love to find out."

Troubled, she turned to him again. "We can't do this lightly. You leave tomorrow. Let's just see how it goes." They stood motionless and close for several minutes, clinging to each other's presence.

Finally, not fully trusting he could say it out loud, Aidan posed the question festering in his mind. "You said Ian would be out soon. How soon?"

She was shocked that he would ask her now. "We should just watch the view, Aidan." Unwilling to taste Ian's name on her tongue, she was not able to wait out his silence. "In three weeks." The answer snapped, brittle in Highland breeze. Abruptly seeking distance, she took a couple of steps away from him.

"I'm sorry." He held out his hand, patting the space between them as if it would help. He risked losing the intimacy and ease they'd just shared yet he couldn't leave tomorrow until he ventured one level deeper. "Do you believe he's a real threat to you?"

Suddenly she was at the beginning, before Aidan had arrived in her life again. It had been a beautiful—crazy—dream. Her gaze turned opaque and impossible to read. She knew where this question was leading. The answer would alert Aidan that something very real and very dangerous loomed before her. *If I say yes, it's real, then all of Aidan's instincts will be to protect and save me.*

And Ian would kill both of them without a thought.

It had been a mistake to let her guard down. Aidan read her too well, she reminded herself shakily. She cleared her throat. "No, I . . . It's only an old fear."

The lie was flat on her tongue. Aidan heard its dissonant echo. Felt the dishonesty bleed from her as from an old wound, re-opened. Understood she would say no more.

"Would you tell me if you ever needed any help?" He understood she would lie again.

"Of course. Thank you."

Only his hand firmly interlocking with hers kept her from moving apart altogether. "I don't suppose there is any chance at all of returning to where we were?" he asked helplessly. Another Gaelic term flashed. *My love.* "Mo gradh."

She spun into his embrace and planted a kiss on his mouth that nearly tore his breath away. Everything she'd longed to say, and had not, trembled on her lips, flooding him with a searing passion that threatened to knock them both flat. Just as suddenly, she rotated again, facing outward to the scenery, keeping his arms closely around her waist, resting her head against his chest.

Say it, MacLaine, just say it. He spoke softly, murmuring into her hair, "I know it will not amaze you that my feelings for you are still alive. Or rather, they never died." He could feel her tears gathering. What he would say would both injure and heal her.

"I think we were meant to find each other again. Our dreams pulled us here." Tightening his grip as she let out a choked sob, he uttered the simplicity of what he knew. "I love you, Kate Stoker."

In answer, she met his eyes, tears falling from her own. Once again, she curled into his chest. Her silence echoed his words as she held him—wishing to make the day stop—so they could stay in this place forever.

Chapter 13

The Land Rover spun rocks more than once but Aidan managed to prod it up the steep slope. When they arrived at The Big Misty, Kieran observed them curiously but refrained from teasing. Both of them were too close to an edge.

In the late afternoon, Aidan's final piano concert rolled through the Great Hall. Kate retreated to the greenhouse. By saying out loud what been secret and hidden, Aidan had shattered her reserve. The opening in her center threatened to expand until it swallowed her whole.

A few weeks ago, she would have called it ridiculous. But now, there was a feeling so vast in her she could hardly contain it. Her head bent to her work, her vision blurring. The piano notes reached for her with his tender passion. She stopped abruptly, no longer pretending to move.

Perched on a stool, surrounded by the nurtured green

world, Kate allowed herself to say it all out loud to herself and the plants. Aidan played every minute out with all his heart, fully engaged. Awake. That was the rare truth of it.

She never knew exactly what he would do because he didn't play from a script—he interacted with life. Common things and everyday events were constantly reframed, transformed in the poetry of his mind.

Oh, the man was stubborn enough. He wasn't perfect. And he had such boundless honor it could get him in trouble. Or keep him from getting into trouble. Like all those 'almost' times in the Montana mountains when he wouldn't bring shame on Kathleen's name.

At least act as if you're working, Kate, she told herself. *I recognize what you covet*, she told her hands, turning them over, smiling a little at their willful desire. *I know.* And it wasn't only them. It was all of her, wanting his touch, craving contact with his skin, hungering for his embrace.

Steady, girl. Think of anything else. This one is too raw and too perilous, on the eve of his leaving. Her gut tightened with aching. Thankfully, as though he were listening, the music changed, turning light and playful, like his gentle irony.

No doubt she was naïve compared to him, but he made that a blessing instead of a liability. He cherished it as fresh and bright. And he always found the deepness underneath, the veins of old wisdom that ran through her soul.

Ian had wanted to own her. *Still did, even locked up.* She was dazed by the force of her need to protect Aidan from Ian. His love and his natural instinct to defend her would drag him into her unsafe life. That could not happen. *Dear beautiful man. That cannot happen.*

There was no point in trying to work. She would take a shower and allow the water to wash off the traces of her muddled afternoon. Then she would help in the Great Hall, and spend this last day in Aidan's presence. *You're gone, aren't you? Just to breathe the same air as him? You're well and truly gone.*

And the nice thing was, as foolish as that sounded, it felt more real and more true as she walked into the Great Hall. Aidan responded to her as though they were dancing, waltzing invisibly under the shadow of the mountains. Round and round, through the chores and the patrons, Kieran's banter and dinner. She could tell by Kieran's narrowed eyes that he was trying to see their hidden revolving silhouettes, trying to discern exactly what was happening under his nose.

By late evening, the Great Hall was once again nearly empty. Kieran invited them both to join him in a late nightcap. His infectious, good-natured energy was too delicious to resist and they relaxed into its sweet gift. *And for some merciful reason,* thought Aidan, *so far anyway . . . the pain is muffled.*

After inspecting the label of his latest whisky closely, Kieran winked at Aidan. "This is to keep you in mind of us—Highland Park, eighteen-year old. From the Orkneys. And you, Kate. Do you have something in that goblet of yours?" Not waiting for an answer, he poured wine for her.

They lifted their drinks and saluted each other. "Sláinte, Aidan," Kieran enjoyed using the old Irish salutation. "We'll be counting the days 'til you return. Now then," he continued smoothly after a satisfied mouthful, "what was that song that we sang for the family reunion that was here in the summer?"

Kate narrowed her eyes at him. "Kieran, you aren't planning to ask me to sing, it's too late!"

"It's always too late, or too early or too something," he retorted, just short of incensed. "I merely desire to give my furry ears the benefit of your lovely sound before I sleep tonight. For sweet dreams. Because Aidan leaves tomorrow. Do you require any more reason than that?"

Aidan's slow smile invited her to respond. He had a love of

singing himself, and had participated in various songs in Montana. But she'd been too shy then, and he hadn't heard her sing.

"Are you up for this, Aidan?" she questioned doubtfully. "You know it will lead into more single malt and a cascade of Kieran's jokes and songs."

"I can't think of anywhere I'd rather be, Kate," Aidan responded. "As long as Kieran doesn't drown you out."

In triumph, Kieran began singing before Kate had a chance to change her mind. His clear tenor filled the song with a nimble flood of words. *Only an Irishman*, thought Aidan.

Kate watched Kieran with mounting amusement. He could make up verses on the spot and he was delaying her entrance until she couldn't stand it any more. "The chorus, for god's sake, Kieran, the chorus now!" she laughed. He winked at her and they entered the chorus in a full harmony. Low pitched and rich toned—she complemented Kieran's sassy daybright singing. Aidan sucked in his breath. Kate's voice was like the rest of her, untamed and free and gorgeous. She led the next few verses on her own, finally relaxed into the present. They sang the chorus again and then the last two verses together.

When they finished, Aidan joined Chris and Mary and the last few patrons in the Great Hall in appreciative applause. "Where have you been hiding that instrument?" Aidan expressed admiringly.

"I told you, MacLaine." Kieran's face was glowing. "She keeps it locked up like precious china. But it is a thing meant to be used."

"Sing another, Kate," called Mary. "Sing that one for Chris and me."

This request is one she can't refuse. Kieran smirked with satisfied delight.

Kate threw up her hands in helpless surrender. "Join me, Kieran O'Connell. And wipe that Cheshire cat look off your mug."

One song led to the next, as Kate had predicted. Warmed and blended, she and Kieran jointly held an exquisite arrangement. At the end of each song, the Great Hall vibrated with its echo until someone called out another for them.

Aidan ignored the building numbness and every thought that threatened to steal away the richness of the moment. *Imprint this night on your soul, MacLaine.* Hold it in a secret box and let it fly free around him when he needed it. As he knew he would.

At last the impromptu concert came to an endpoint. It was late and they had to stop. Their last song was an old ballad, slow and heartrending in its simple story of love and loss. *Let this be our goodbye*, Kate thought. *If I am still here when you come back . . . If not, then remember this. Remember me like this.*

After the final song, Kieran took Kate's hand and thanked her. She hugged him and kissed him full on the mouth. "Thanks for not letting me get away with my resistance."

Nearby, Julie beamed. "That was rare good singing."

"Right, my friends," Kieran said, urgency in his tone, grinning in her direction. "I am closing the place up. Aidan, you will be leaving early?"

"Yes." Aidan felt a hollow opening in his chest. "Evening flight from Glasgow."

"Well, I'll be up, so you have that wretched tea before you depart." Kieran squeezed Aidan's shoulder and embraced Kate. "Goodnight, you two." He dallied easily with them for a moment, then sprang toward Julie eagerly. They walked off hip to hip, his jokes punctuated by her ringing laughter.

Kate smiled at Aidan. "It appears we just got thrown out."

"Apparently. Would you . . . " he faltered, fearing her refusal. "Would you be willing to sit on the porch with me for a few minutes?"

"The cautious side of me says no," Kate replied softly. "But it's drowned out by every everything else that says yes."

Aidan released the knot gathering in his stomach. Getting up would be difficult. The gnawing ache was starting. "Why don't you meet me out there? Maybe grab a coat or a blanket."

Without answering, she went in the direction he indicated. He stood with effort, steadied himself on the mantle of the fireplace as the burning flashed through him. *Call me out, sky and moon. Give me strength to walk out there and sit in the starshine and mountain breath with her tonight.*

She was sitting with a tartan wrap tugged up to her chin when he rounded the corner. His taut bearing told her the old demon was plaguing him. To give him space, she pointed at a lazy W constellation. "There's Cassiopeia."

"And the Pleiades, 'Seven Sisters', according to Greek mythology," Aidan added, observing the wreath of the Milky Way. He used both hands to brace as he slipped in next to her. She pulled the wrap around both of them, allowed his encircling arm. They picked out the three brilliant stars that made up Orion's Belt. "And there," Aidan pointed, "those bright patches are his sword." He treasured her warmth against him. "Ever seen the Southern Cross, Kate?"

"When would I ever have done that?" Impatience touched her tone. As quickly gone. "I would like to see it sometime, though," she added broodingly.

"Someday," Aidan spoke carefully, keeping his tread light, "we'll lie on a warm beach under a brilliant tropical sky in Fiji and find it." He breathed out slowly, trying to give her that faith in the future. "Okay?"

She kissed his shoulder, her voice ragged and faint. "Okay." *Give yourself to that vision Kate. Even if it all comes to an end. Embrace the vision of this man you love and you next to him with all your tomorrows new and clean.* That much she would never let Ian own.

For a long while they were quiet, holding on to their

dreams, feeling the earth spin in its place among the stars.

"Will we see each other in the morning?" he asked.

"No," her voice trembled. "Let's not. I have a pre-dawn date with a particular spring. I want to catch the light of the dawn as it hits the water."

"You'd better catch some sleep then, mo gradh. I'll see you when I return." He emphasized the last line, stroking her cheek. "Goodnight sweet Kate." He kissed her lightly, held on for a few extra heartbeats. "Go. While I have this much control. Don't forget me."

Her blue eyes brimming, she responded with one word. "Never." Gathering herself with every ounce of will she had left, she turned and walked inside.

Chapter 14

The plane banked, beginning the bumpy descent into Seattle, not yet visible under the canopy of rain-swollen clouds. Tired and heartsick, the weight of the travel hours laid heavily on Aidan—scenes from his Highland departure playing over and over in his mind.

He'd left Kate realizing that he wouldn't sleep well, waking up repeatedly until he could make out the first stains of dawn piercing the dark sky. Standing at the bedroom window, he'd watched her moving steadily up the slope until she disappeared into the misty embrace of the mountains. His breath hitched. *Farewell, beloved.* Once more they would meet in their dreams until providence brought them together again.

As the sun was clearing the horizon, he'd met Kieran in the Great Hall. "This will have vanished by the season you plan to return," Kieran had gestured expansively at the landscape. "The colors. The fullness of the light. It will be the start of winter."

Right now, that felt like a lifetime away. The slow, difficult drive through the mountains had led to improbably wide roads with traffic that moved at a shocking speed. It was the whole busy world he'd forgotten existed, roughly awakening a survival instinct strong enough to guide him into the Glasgow airport. In the space of less than a day, he was transported to another world, his soul fragmented, wearing the scent of the Highlands.

As the plane descended below the clouds, he wearily surveyed a familiar Seattle skyline—the slender Space Needle aiming for the sky, ferries traversing the silvered reflections of the city's bustling Elliott Bay.

Sheila waved, stepped out of the crowd with her arms spread as he emerged from the secured part of SeaTac Airport.

"Dad!"

That Aidan was her father had become a truth so real it was the foundation for everything else she believed in. His love for her—and his refusal to give up when she thought she could throw it away—were the cornerstones of her life. She bounded toward him, simultaneously assessing—the way he taught her to do. *His gait is careful, as if expecting trouble.*

They hugged like they always did after an absence, standing close, remembering their entire history—the pain and the victory of it. Aidan's fatigue was eased with the simple joy of their reunion.

"You look fabulous, as always," he announced after standing back to observe her, a smile edged up on one side.

Sheila was striking, as Kathleen had been. She'd inherited her mother's olive complexion and shining black hair. The hazel of her eyes soaked in the rich tone of her green scarf and spun it out, sparkling with emerald highlights.

In some unexpected ways, she also resembled Aidan, as though their years together had created a blood link after all.

Resembling him, she was tall and slender with a similar graceful build and the same intent tendency to inspect the world.

"And you look," she laughed, struggling for the words, "almost healthy." He was not as gaunt as when he'd gone away, she realized. The days in the Highlands had given him a flush of vitality he'd been on the verge of losing.

Aidan knew nothing he could say to her would halt the scrutiny. It was, after all, what he would do. Luckily, for no decent reason but its own, despite all the travel, the numbness was absent, the pain muted.

They chatted on the route home, keeping the topics relaxed, taking it easy. Sheila's apartment was well placed—perched on Seattle's Queen Anne Hill with a sweeping view of Puget Sound and the Olympic Mountains. She savored the idea that her father's favorite panoramas and hers presided over the same mix of water and mountains.

The minute they entered her door, she ushered him toward a favorite window seat, noticing how he studied the snow-covered peaks across the blue gray water as though they reminded him of something. *Or someone.* "You relax for a minute. Tea?"

He swiveled the plush blue chair so he could look to the north toward his own windy home. "Not yet, thanks. Sit for a minute. I need to tell you about The Big Misty." In a few minutes, in poetic phrases only Aidan could handle, he recreated the majesty of the place he'd just left. "I'm heading back as soon as I'm able, Sheila," he concluded.

The hush that followed this announcement was filled with such an extended deliberation that he couldn't help but grin at her. "Okay, Tigress, what are you hunting for?" he finally asked.

"I am trying to see the woman who claimed your heart."

"What makes you think there is a woman?"

"What makes you think I can't tell?" she retorted with an impish smirk.

"You won't believe it."

"Try me."

She would never let up until she understood at least part of the picture. "It was Kate, from the Montana conference. I told you about her. I didn't believe I would ever see her again. Thought she'd surely be remarried."

"Why was she there?"

"Not sure, exactly." The memory of The Big Misty and the Fisherfields was so raw it was hard to continue. "She was working for Kieran . . . " He told her as much of the story as he could. Not surprised when the breezes of the Highlands danced about him. When he finished, a perplexed look clouded Sheila's face. He nodded. "It's complex, isn't it?"

"Why can't you fall in love with normal, ordinary women? Don't tell me, I know. You are not a normal, ordinary man. If you were, you wouldn't have married Kathleen and we wouldn't be sitting here now."

She moved to the kitchen to make tea. "Okay, Dad, you have my permission to revisit and explore this some more."

"Thank you, I appreciate that," he rejoined without irony. "I can't predict how anything will proceed. I just have to go find out. First though, let's talk about this specialist you found."

Their conversation shifted, slowing, fitting around the shape of tea and cookies. Aidan was scheduled for the initial meeting tomorrow with a well-regarded neurologist. They'd already been warned there would be tests, a number of them.

"And while I cook us dinner, you are going to sleep," she announced after they had talked it out, giving him a hand up and steering him firmly toward the guest bedroom.

After he departed, everyone at The Big Misty felt Aidan's absence. The piano sat silent and the splendid melodies echoed only as memories. Kieran found himself polishing the instrument

trying to ease his own sharp sense of loss. As for Kate, she'd grown
too quiet and the teasing play of words with him had vanished.

"You are in danger wasting away entirely," Kieran
announced, appearing in the greenhouse when he couldn't stand it
any more. He held out a bowl of steaming mushroom soup.

Kate nodded, agreeing with him. "Okay, you got me. I
happen to be famished." She held out her hands, accepting his
offering—offered a tentative smile. "Thanks. Have you eaten?"

"Och, Kate, surely you know the answer to that. The world
could stop spinning and I would, of course, find a means to eat.
But I truly aspire to keep you company." Sitting his companionable
body down close to her, he announced, "Aidan called today."

Kate laid aside her spoon, waiting.

"He's busy with the tests. They're trying to figure out what's
been plaguing him." Kieran watched her shoulders tense.

"He misses us," he added lamely.

A smile flashed. "He didn't say that."

"He did, of course. It was just between the lines. As so
many things are."

"I think you're right," she replied broodingly. "It would be
there, between the lines."

He was surprised and encouraged. "Kate, I will tell you
something that certainly cannot surprise you. We need you. You
need us. And I miss you and there's nothing subtle about it."

Kieran was calling her back to life. *This sadness is a dangerous
distraction,* she told herself. She had to become alert again, and
then she could figure out what to do. Finishing the soup, she stood
up resolutely. "I'd better deliver this to Max myself or I'll never hear
the end of it." She mustered a teasing tone. "Of course, you should
come too, to check on things, in case Julie is there."

Chapter 15

In Seattle, after the MRI scans, Aidan met again with neurosurgeon Dr. Will Burke. Will was younger than Aidan by a decade. His physique was lean and sharp and perpetually in motion. He often made his patients and colleagues a little nervous at first. Later, they would appreciate how the odd energy of his body reflected an astute mind. Somehow it was comforting how his high forehead gleamed with perspiration as he focused total concentration on unraveling their medical mysteries.

Aidan own nerves quivered as he waited for his doctor to finish reading the chart—not knowing what to expect. "You had a fall or a car accident," Will stated. It was not a question.

"Car crash, eight years past," Aidan acknowledged. Kathleen had been in one of her worst spells, raving and threatening him as he drove. The weather that day had been icily treacherous and he'd started seeking a place to pull over, recognizing he could not calm her. It was too late. After a steadily increasing rant, she'd pushed at him violently and the car twisted hard to the left, skidding and slamming up against a tree.

When it happened, he was mostly relieved. Sheila had not been in the car. They did not hit an oncoming vehicle. Neither of them was seriously hurt. The accident, in fact, had momentarily subdued her, at the sight of her own blood and his.

Kathleen had worried later about scars on her once blemish-free face. Her broken arm caused her great pain but had healed quickly. Aidan's one big cut was above the hairline, and though it bled freely, it didn't show afterwards.

Initially, he believed they'd escaped without significant harm. Except for one thing. He had been thrown sideways with great force, with the weight of Kathleen's unsecured body on top of him. The doctors told him he was lucky he did not break a hip or his back. There had been a troubling numbness the length of his lower back, but Kathleen had taken so much care and concentration. And he had been anxious to make things as normal as possible to Sheila.

Somehow, he hadn't taken the trouble to deal with the issue. It seemed unimportant, compared to Kathleen's increasing loss of control.

"Normal sensation gradually returned and stayed for several years," explained Aidan. "I really believed it had healed. Then this irregular pattern of pain and the burning started up in the past year. And the lumbar area becomes numb, sometimes all the way through to the hips, same as it did just after we crashed."

Will nodded solemnly. He did not inquire why Aidan had not obtained help immediately. His business was medicine. Whatever had prevented Aidan from seeking advice was testimony he wouldn't disclose easily. Nor did Will wish to hear it. He had been in the business long enough to recognize that people's lives were complicated, even messy. Usually, the less he knew about their personal history, the better he could concentrate on what had to be done.

"Okay," Will said, satisfied he had the relevant information. "Well, these symptoms you are experiencing developed from that event. I want to run a few more tests on the nerves before I can give you a full diagnosis. But I can tell you this. You will have to get it treated."

He did not speak aloud all of his doubts. Only after sufficient testing would he lay out the whole process. If he was going to gamble on it, he wanted decent odds. "You will not be able to wish it away," he continued inexorably. "It will degenerate, minus intervention—potentially it could get so bad you will no longer be able to walk."

Aidan's blood chilled. *Damn this thing.* He listened carefully while the doctor outlined the timetable of assessments and tests. That gave him a couple of days to head home. It was a detail Will didn't need to know.

Leaving the medical office, abruptly crowded by the gray concrete around him, Aidan conceded to his craving for home. He phoned Shelia at her apartment and left a message on her machine, telling her he was leaving for the island and would return the day after next. She would be exasperated with him for taking off so quickly, but he expected she would understand.

Flying was the best option. He knew several pilots of private planes that went to and from of the islands. It took less than an hour for him to locate a flight. He leaned forward, appreciating the lift into the sky and the blue that sliced between and above the clouds. The heaviness dissolved as he left behind the congestion of the city, replaced by evergreen trees and smaller towns.

When islands appeared as ships in the middle of a long reach of salt water, he leaned forward. *Kate would be crazy about this place.* He pushed the notion as quickly out of his thoughts. There was a lot of uncertain ground to cross.

Claire and Ben met him at the island's little airport. He counted them as friends and he genuinely appreciated them as the managers of the gallery. When his plane touched down, both of them waved boisterously, grinning with greeting.

Since the onset of his symptoms, Aidan had been increasingly uncommunicative. He'd gone to Scotland to deliver some paintings and to do a reading. They'd lost contact when he'd totally disappeared after a short note to tell them he was traveling into the Highlands.

Aidan couldn't completely disguise his unsteady walk or flashes of pain when he arrived. Ben bounded forward to take his bags, while Claire hugged him tightly, sustaining him with her own robust frame.

They don't wonder what to do— they leap to it, intuitively assessing what is necessary and who can best do it. He smiled, trying to reassure them.

"Welcome home," Ben exclaimed cheerfully. Standing several inches shorter than Aidan, his 'Island Style' tee shirt stretched over muscular arms and the smallest bit of softness around his middle. Younger than Claire by four years, his sandy hair contrasted with her long chocolate-colored tresses, but they were so alike that people often asked if they were siblings.

Strongly built and brimming with energy, Claire's bighearted personality was obvious in her open face. Both of them were attuned to Aidan, showing no inclination to feel ill at ease. They would go when he was ready.

"How was your flight?" Claire stepped lightly from Aidan, with a deliberately casual manner.

"Beautiful, as always." Aidan paused. He rested briefly while the throbbing slowed. "I'm happy to be home, even if it's only for a couple of days."

"We have a list for you of course. But don't worry, it includes some things that will be fun," Ben laughed.

"Oh, I'm sure." Aidan started to walk slowly out of the tiny lobby. "Knowing you two."

Claire and Ben exchanged concerned glances as Aidan moved ahead of them, but they did not press him for information. Not yet. They would need details before he went away, but for now, it was enough to just have him with them.

The gallery was freshly scrubbed and well tended. Aidan enjoyed the familiar spark of pride and affection at the sight of it. He understood the intensity of their silence, waiting for him. Their faces were bright with questions and fierce with loyalty.

"The place looks fabulous," he began. "And I realize you are dying to ask me where I've been. So thanks for letting me breathe. I will tell you, I promise. Before I leave."

The day passed in a blur of activity. The gallery was, in fact, in need of Aidan's attention. Ben and Claire had done remarkably well without his input, but Aidan's creative talent was what drove the work. They all found pleasure in the synergy of their alliance.

When the afternoon started to darken, fatigue finally caught up with Aidan. "I'm officially calling it quits for the day," he said. "Let's go home." He would not listen to their request to join them for dinner. "Tomorrow, if I can take a rain check. Tonight, I just want to relax at the house."

Claire sighed meaningfully. "We both knew you'd say exactly that. So we took the precaution of stocking your own place in case you decided to be pigheaded, which we thought you would be."

Outside, the cool air was moist and heavy with salt vapor. *So different than the mountains.* The velvety dark was hospitable and he was glad to slip into it. They gave him the keys to the car and did not accompany him out.

As his old Volvo smoothly turned over, Aidan silently thanked Ben for getting the vehicle ready. He drove the long way home on winding island roads, savoring the sound of the sea, the smell of wet earth and fallen leaves.

The porch light is on, of course, he thought, when he pulled into his driveway. *They wouldn't do it any other way.*

He entered a warm house, complete with flowers and a bottle of Oregon Zinfandel on the kitchen table. There would be food in the fridge, he knew that much. Pouring himself a glass of wine, he walked in and out of every room, walking the stiffness out, trying to see his life in a new way. His own footsteps sounded noisy in the pervasive hush.

"It's a monk's existence," he said out loud. Oh, it was picturesque and full of creative energy. But it was lonely. *God, it was lonesome.* Kate's face surfaced in his mind and he couldn't push it away.

Aidan sat down heavily, his heart aching for her presence. He'd lived too many years with memories. *I want her in my life. But I have to just wait and see where all this testing goes.* For hours he sat in between waking and dreams in his quiet house.

It was three hours before dawn when he finally moved again. Staggering slightly, working out the numbing twinges, he entered the alcove that held the piano. In the daylight, the window view would open out over a scene of incomparable beauty—restless blue gray water and the snow-capped Olympic Mountains in the distance. But in the shadows, Aidan's mind traveled across time and space to another place. Different mountains. A multi-colored carpet of heather and bracken fern.

His fingers touched the piano gently at first, slowly gathering power like a strong summer storm. With no one to hear and Kate too far distant to scare, he poured his love for her into the music he heard from the depths of his soul.

The phantom he'd loved for eleven years had shape-shifted back into his world. He could hear Fate's faint laughter. When a hazy band of burnt sienna light lit up the horizon, his hands slowed and finally stopped on a deep stillness.

He needed a few hours of rest before he confronted the river of Ben and Claire's enthusiasm. The burning always accompanied him persistently, but true to its capricious nature, it had receded during the night.

Standing carefully, he was rapt before the majesty of the vista spread out before him. Emerging from the ink-black night in stages, the sky and water were the color of steel, the surrounding land cloaked with darkness.

To the west, Vancouver Island and the restive strait of open water were hidden in fog. *Realm of mystery.* Aidan opened the window to let in the salt smell, listening. The sound of orca whales blowing their long exhalations traveled over the water.

The breath of the ocean, he thought. *Mountains and water, tides and currents, they are so much bigger than us. Love is nothing to them, nor music. It is just the earth turning and the moon dancing in the sky.*

Or maybe it was love, of a kind, that of the moon for the earth and the ocean for the rivers that rushed down the slopes of mountains to give it life.

Chapter 16

When Aidan returned to the gallery late in the morning, he drove up slowly, flooded by memories of how he came to own it. For years, he'd contemplated the landscape of water and islands through west-facing windows of the English department. Five years ago, the calling had become impossible to ignore. He'd bought the gallery with Jack, a colleague in the art department.

For three years they had worked together, directing the work in turn, balancing their teaching loads. They had held each other up with easy humor, amazed and humbled by the success of their first foray into private enterprise.

One day, wearing a smile he could not erase, Jack ushered Aidan into his office, and with carefully articulated words, announced that he planned to leave the work. "Actually," he'd said, "I'm moving to Canada." Aidan's lips twitched remembering the blush that spread all the way up into Jack's cheeks, disappearing into the two feathered wings of remaining hair on either side of his balding head.

Improbably, the inveterate bachelor had found another love besides job and art. Jack had somehow found the opportunity to meet and woo a fellow artist, a newly-arrived immigrant from Australia, who'd established her studio and house in Vancouver. It was a feat Aidan had to admire. And it gave him the inspiration to follow his own longing and move to the islands.

Within six months, Aidan bought out Jack's share and converted his position at the university to professor emeritus. With great satisfaction, he moved into the modest house built into grass and rock with space for a piano and windows that opened to mountain and seawater.

When Ben and Claire answered his ad for a gallery manager, he knew at once they would be friends. They were made for island life—both self-sufficient and neighborly. Ben had a talent for fixing things and enjoyed playing music with anyone who was willing.

Claire had long decided that she would rather have dogs than children. She devoted her free hours to a menagerie of pets and orphaned animals, volunteering for both the animal shelter and the local wildlife rescue. A natural communicator, Claire was the main contact with customers and the first connection with artists and patrons. She also was fond of organizing Aidan's schedule, clear that traveling was better for her when it was vicarious, deriving great enjoyment from imagining Aidan in locations she would enjoy hearing about.

Grateful it was Monday and that they were closed, Claire waved her pencil over the calendar with the list of potential bookings beside it. Aidan had always relished the tours, which were so different than his university work. It allowed him to combine his readings with the work of the gallery, delivering or selling pieces. With Aidan's condition worsening, she frowned over it, anticipating his signal.

He laid a hand on hers. "Yes it's confusing," he said gently. "Let's do a few other things first. I have to be sure you've gotten all you need from me on the homefront—that you can do without me for a longer spell."

Claire's eyebrows drew down and her mouth tightened. There was a profound silence, as Ben and Claire weighed the heaviness of Aidan's statement. "Shall we start with tea—or tea for me—anyway?" he continued. "You two coffeehounds have your perpetual pot brewing, I assume. Lay the work out and we'll tackle it one step at a time. Then, we'll talk."

Relieved to have a familiar ritual, Ben and Claire moved immediately on his suggestion and the hours passed quickly with their tasks. By the middle of the afternoon they completed the most detailed work. They had arrived at the moment they'd anticipated and dreaded. The question of Aidan's absence and travel had to be answered.

While Claire and Aidan discussed the last few art pieces, Ben placed the afternoon meal on the cleared worktable. The soup had been simmering all day, its savory aroma filling the gallery with the tang of onion, carrot, beef and potato. Claire's crusty home baked bread was a meal in itself, full of nuts and whole-grained flavors.

"And the beer, Ben. Aidan has to try your most recent creation," Claire called, laughing. Ben's most recent hobby of homebrewing had not always been smooth. His first bottles exploded like geysers when opened, showering him and the surrounding vicinity with frothy liquid.

Recently, after a bit of expert advice, Ben's inventions were a great deal more stable and had started to become quite delicious. They relaxed over the meal, appreciating the beer, filling themselves on the hearty tastes before they had to take the next step.

"Okay," said Aidan at last. "Let's talk." Ben and Claire sat motionless, listening intently to Aidan's somber words. He gave them the briefest of descriptions of the accident. They needed no more to merge it with the history they already knew of Kathleen and her illness.

"Well, that episode has re-emerged from its hibernation. You've observed it yourself," he granted. "So, I have to move this thing to the front burner now. Get it fixed, if it can be. Otherwise . . ." his voice trailed off. "It isn't a pretty picture," he finished uneasily. Ben sat with his head bowed, staring down at his empty glass.

Claire spoke with a gathering energy of determination. "Whatever has to be done. Whatever you need to do." Her voice was calm. "The travel can be put on hold. The customers can wait. You are the only important priority."

Ben got up—picked up the glasses in one hand, set the other on Aidan's shoulder. "I couldn't agree more."

They need a few minutes to take it all in. Aidan stayed seated as Claire put the calendar and lists away and helped Ben clean up. There was enough pain lurking in his back that he had to wait while they were busy. When they were done, they simply sat with him again.

He'd always known he could count on them. Even so, he struggled with the next bit of news. Clearing his throat, he continued. "There's one more thing. Crazy as it may be, I hope to take one more trip before . . . whatever Dr. Burke has in mind. If I can. " Pausing, he drew a steadying breath. "I . . . plan to return to the Highlands. There's an old friend there."

He stopped, feeling awkward. "Okay, before you try to figure out how to form the question, yes, it's a woman."

Their expressions made him want to laugh out loud. *Was it so improbable that he would explore a relationship? They only see me as a solitary being,* he thought. *They assume—maybe everyone assumes—I prefer to be alone.*

He left their silent queries floating, like twirling tufts of dandelion seeds, letting them land as they may. "That's all. There are more questions than there are answers. For all of us. We just have to allow it to sort itself out."

Ben and Claire gravely assessed the truth of this statement. Their world had shifted to a new order and different priorities had instantaneously emerged. With no more conversation, they understood that it was important to keep things moving on an even keel. Delay anything they could. Make the best decisions they could for the gallery.

They threw themselves into this evolving reality with characteristic zest. They finished as the afternoon spilled into twilight, insisting that Aidan return with them to their home for dinner. He did not refuse them and locked up the gallery himself to give them a head start, working out the tightness in his back.

After they finished another delicious meal in their warm kitchen, Claire shooed them out. Ben was eager for Aidan's assessment of the second-hand piano they'd recently installed. He was delighted when Aidan, after testing the quality of the sound, let the melodies fly.

"Nice, Aidan. It sounds great!" Ben pulled out his guitar and accompanied him. Within a few minutes, Claire was beside them, humming and singing along, a dishtowel over her shoulder. It was a contented moment, held tenderly. One they had earned this hard day.

With each song, Aidan's yearning for Kate grew. He ached with memories of the interlude at The Big Misty—its music and poetry. Kieran's good humor. And the woman who filled his soul.

"Time for bed," he announced suddenly. They protested, but weakly, reading the purpose in his bearing. He hugged them both. "You two are the best. Trust your instincts. You'll do the right thing."

Driving slowly from their cozy home, escorted for a short distance down the dirt road by their two golden retrievers, he felt the tug of his life—hard and undeniable—toward an unknown future. Adjusting the rear view mirror, watching the dogs gallop joyfully after his car, he imagined them as emblems of that new and irrepressible direction. *Let it be like them,* he thought, *full of vitality and trust.*

Chapter 17

When he arrived in Seattle, Aidan went directly to the hospital for the second round of tests. He endured the endless tedious appointments by jotting fragments of poetry and musical compositions.

When they were over, he felt well enough to visit Pike's Place Market for a little while. He needed the contrast of bustling people and the vivid colors and smells of the Market to recover from the stale hospital atmosphere. Mercifully, the unpredictable pain was at bay for the better part of an hour, allowing him to wander leisurely, gathering ingredients for a recipe he had in mind to cook for Sheila.

Once in the car, he called her. She'd invited her boyfriend, Andy, to dinner. "It's time he met you," she said mischievously. He could hear the smile she was wearing.

"Then I'd better make you both a meal, so we won't have

take-out again."

"He's a vegetarian, Dad."

"I can handle that. I happen to have some very fine vegetarian recipes, if I can find any ingredients in your empty refrigerator." He didn't tell her he'd already shopped. "Bring some wine. And don't find too many reasons to stay late at work."

At Sheila's apartment, Aidan picked his favorites from her extensive collection of classical music while he cooked. The tests had been tiring and he hurt. Leaning against the counter, satisfied with the rich smell of dinner drifting though the kitchen, he checked the clock. It would be morning in the Highlands. Without a conscious thought, he reached for the sound of Kieran's voice. *And news of Kate.*

"Lord, you sound as if you are next door," Kieran boomed. "You didn't sneak in here and call me from the lobby, did you?"

Aidan relaxed into the familiar teasing. "I must be far indeed from the way you're shouting, Kieran," he said after a stretch of banter. He struggled to stay light. "How's your greenhouse gardener and resident singer?"

"Yes, the she-wolf. I was wondering if you would ask. She was a bit peaked after you vanished. Must've eaten something that disagreed with her." Aidan waited in silence, understanding the unstated implications. It was better said this way.

"She found the mountains endlessly fascinating. And when she returned from them, it was straight to the greenhouse." Kieran huffed a little, remembering how it had been in the first hard days after Aidan left.

"I've managed to tame her a little. She will at least eat and talk with the customers again. On the rare occasion, I can even rouse her to laughter." Kieran grew more serious. "She's growing a bit nervous, though," he added, as though thinking out loud. "Some worry is eating at her. I expect it's to do with that ex-husband of hers."

Wish I was there to talk it through with her. If she would allow me, he reminded himself. "Tell her . . . I miss her. Tell her I will come as soon as I can. If she wants to know."

"Och, she would deny it if she heard me say it. But the sound of your name makes the woman stop still and she's hungry for any word. I merely have to find work to do while I talk to her. She needs the privacy."

"Thanks for telling me." Everything he knew about himself and the world suddenly seemed in question. He sat in the darkening light after they hung up, waiting until the feeling mended around him, struggling to push aside the urgency of his need to be with her.

A half hour later, Sheila and Andy arrived with two bottles of wine, wide smiles and fresh flowers. The fragrance of lilies and ring of their laughter reclaimed the apartment from the essence of Kate.

Andy was a sleekly modern young man, wearing thin classy glasses, a mauve pullover sweater and high-end jeans. His easy laugh pealed out spontaneously as Aidan surveyed him thoroughly before offering a hand.

"God, I know that look! Yes, I'm not good enough for her. But I won't put her in the poorhouse either, and I will never beat her."

Aidan and Sheila grinned at each other. "See-through father attitude. Must be pretty obvious. I'm sorry," apologized Aidan.

"No worries," replied Andy nonchalantly, holding up the wine bottle to Aidan for approval. "Australian Shiraz okay?" he asked, reading the label with a faultless Aussie accent "Lush and complex with a peppery aroma and hints of plum."

Aidan accepted the bottle and popped the cork, pouring three glasses. "Your taste in wine seems to match your taste in women." He smiled bittersweetly, reminded of Kate's playful rendering of Scotch labels, handing the glasses out. Leaning against the counter for support, he studiously ignored Sheila's concerned frown.

Andy took in the scene instantaneously, winking at Sheila, teasing her to snap out of it. He knew what was happening, but for sure, the father would not want to be coddled right now.

Their dark hair was the exact same shade of rich brown, Aidan noted, almost black, but for the red highlights. Sheila was similarly tall so that their shoulders brushed against each other casually. Her clothes matched Andy's in outdoorsy urban, as if they were in a downtown park on Sunday.

The dinner was uncomplicated and hearty. Aidan's skills in the kitchen had been developed over numerous years of catering to Sheila's picky palate and he knew exactly what she favored. True to his experience, she admired the colorful dish enthusiastically. "Wow, Dad—this is beautiful!"

Andy lit candles as he joined in the appreciation. "Penne pasta, Shiitake mushrooms, red peppers, broccoli, Italian parsley," he reeled off. "You know your girl."

"And ricotta salata cheese," added Aidan, a smile tugging, watching Sheila sigh with approval as she sampled a first bite.

"You did this so beautifully. I adore the fennel," she crooned. "And all these other amazing flavors. Fresh thyme?"

"For someone who never cooks, you have remarkably well developed taste buds, my dear," Aidan retorted, nodding. He picked up his glass and led an old style blessing, as he had always done with Sheila—glad to be in her life, directing the conversation toward their work.

The two had side-by-side offices at the University of Washington, they told him, down extended gleaming halls festooned with alluring bulletin boards. Their talk was studded with phrases of Italian, Spanish, French and Portuguese as well as literary quotes, delivered in appropriate accents. They were quick to laugh at their private jokes and often finished the other's sentences. They commiserated with each other about the travail of post-doc work, trying to please stuffy professors, the sleepless nights surrounded by stacks of obscure books and bad coffee.

Sheila and Andy are more akin to friends than lovers, mused Aidan. His early interactions with women had been wide-ranging, short-lived passionate romances and flirtations with classmates. When he'd met Kathleen, he'd reckoned he was ready for a more serious relationship. He'd taken her brooding energy as disappointment in the world, a place far too coarse for her delicate refinement.

Her dark creativity had been attractive and he'd reached out to her. Thinking maybe he could help. Or not thinking. When she'd brought him home, he'd met Sheila for the first time.

Aidan involuntarily glanced at her, drinking wine with her lover-friend, engaged in a humorous game of wit and words. *How confident and happy she is*. But she had been different once.

The memory of Sheila's distressed eyes staring at him from around the corner of the small unkempt house she shared with her mother was still strong. She'd been just five and had faith in no one. From that instant, his heart was entwined with her, no questions. And he'd taught her to trust him by always being there for her.

He'd committed to both of them, from that point on, keeping his unspoken promise even when he met Kate. There was never a question if he would abandon Kathleen. Or betray Sheila's fragile trust that they were a family. She'd had grown up believing that Aidan had loved Kathleen, because she needed to believe that. But it was always Sheila that he'd adored.

"Dad, there you go again, getting distant." Sheila's voice grabbed at Aidan and brought him to the present. "And tired," she added, in a worried tone.

"It's been a long day. In fact, I'll take my leave. If you two won't miss me too greatly." They both grinned. Uncomplicated. Nothing he'd ever experienced.

Sheila tilted her head at her father, seeing his exhaustion. "Andy, would you mind clearing the table?"

Standing immediately, Andy expertly piled plates across one arm, shaking Aidan's hand with the other. "No, don't get up. I've got this. Great to have met you."

"You clearly have a waiter's past," teased Aidan. "An excellent skill for overly educated people. I am pleased to have met you as well. Glad that Sheila has someone who can keep up with her."

"I don't know about that," laughed Andy, scooping up the wine glasses. "She's usually out in front, but I try hard." Catching the hurry up frown on Sheila's face, he tapped his heels together and bowed grandly.

"Okay, I'm out of here. Glad to have finally met the father that Sheila thinks the sun rises and sets on. Goodnight, Missy MacLaine. I plan to ambush you with homework on this very same table when you are ready." He moved quickly toward the kitchen.

Andy will find plenty to keep him busy, Sheila thought. She gave her hand to her father, celebrating the evening with the gentle contact. They walked toward the den she'd converted to a bedroom. "Did they find out anything?" she asked.

"Too early. I have a one-day reprieve, so I'll head up to Bellingham tomorrow. Then one last test and, hopefully, a diagnosis."

"Drive carefully, then. Say hi to Christine. Goodnight, Dad," she pressed her cheek against his shoulder. "I love you."

It always feels like a miracle to hear her say it. "And I love you, my dear. Always and forever."

Chapter 18

Aidan drove north through shifting sun breaks to Western Washington University in Bellingham, heading straight to the office of his oldest friend, Christine Bailey. He knocked on her closed door, chuckling out loud when she opened it petulantly. Clearly she had spoken to one too many students that day. On seeing him, her conduct swiftly shifted to pure glee.

"Get in here, before anyone discovers us."

"Why, are you planning to have your way with me?"

"I never mess around with colleagues." Christine pulled him inside, closed the door and hugged him. "Besides, I'm old enough to be your grandmother."

"That is a great exaggeration and you know it. Mother, maybe."

"Where the hell have you been anyway, Aidan? You look like you've been fighting with the devil and losing."

At 74, Christine Bailey was a force of nature. No one who had seen her in action could deny her vigor. Once the head of the English Department, she had only recently agreed to slow her schedule down and commence teaching "part-time." Of course, everyone knew she would not respect that concept.

The only way Christine's age really showed was in her wealth of accumulated knowledge and organizational memory. The university counted her as one of its most valuable assets. Christine was in the office five days a week, and more often than not, came in on weekends as well to "tidy up."

Her passion for work only wore out when she carelessly stacked a myriad of appointments in a row. Today was one of those occasions.

"Let's go," she grumbled, throwing papers and books in the leather satchel she'd been using for as long as she'd been teaching. "I've already put in my eight hours and then some."

Aidan was amused as ever by her brisk manner. "I'll meet you at your house. First, I must raid your bookshelves and marvel at your overflowing calendar."

Rolling her eyes, she made a face at him that was an exact replica of the adolescent expression of "whatever", ignored his smirk and ducked out the door.

A smile continued to curl the edges of Aidan's lips as he scanned her books and flipped through the months of her calendar. Every box had something written in it. He always enjoyed viewing a glimpse of that volcano energy.

A book under his arm, he stepped out into the hallway, taking a minute to read the scatter of notes on her door. Everyone wanted a piece of Christine. Invitations, comments, appointments and smiley faces adorned the cork board outside her office.

Aidan drove slowly through the streets of south Bellingham, enjoying the beautiful old houses. He sat outside her house for a few extra minutes. *Might as well gather some strength*. Christine would coerce the truth out of him as always.

They had been friends since the morning he had walked in as a fledgling teacher. She had immediately sized him up and decided he was worthy. Their friendship had weathered the passing of both Kathleen and Eliot, her late husband. Christine was the only person who really knew Sheila's history. How she'd struggled to trust her own sanity and how far she'd come to trust Aidan implicitly.

Aidan knew things about Christine that no one else could have guessed. After the pain and trauma of losing Eliot to a premature heart attack, Christine had buried her grief with a mountain of work. Only Aidan discerned that much of the pain was because she and Eliot were not able to have children. After the grieving subsided and she'd resumed her career, she'd confided a doubtful desire for passion to re-enter her world.

But with her schedule, he'd argued, how could anyone find the way in?

She was too old, she'd responded. She had the drive of a young woman but the body had aged.

"You're quite attractive, Christine," he'd countered with a laugh. "And 'aged' is hardly the first word that comes to mind to describe you."

"I appreciate you for saying that. But I know what I know," she'd snapped. It was a conversation they would return to again and again.

"Finally," she said the minute he entered the door. Her cozy house was cluttered with projects she'd brought home. It was a second office. *She did have one concession to beauty though*. In between the stacks of books and papers, and all through the house, there were potted plants of every shape and size. *Her babies*, he thought—though he didn't dare say it out loud.

"Tell me everything," she said, offering him a plate of

cheese and sliced fruit. She made no secret of her curiosity.

"You're already familiar with most of everything," he sat down quickly before she took too much note of the unsteady walk.

It wasn't necessary to explain the car accident. She'd heard it all as it happened. She was acquainted with stories about Kate from his Montana stories. Knew that the memories had both haunted him and kept him alive the years after. Her eyebrows arched in surprise when he told her about meeting Kate again. It didn't have to be spelled out for her—how passion could re-ignite. Dry brush hit by lightening.

"But," Christine said, puzzled when Aidan stopped. "What could be stopping you star-crossed lovers from finally leaping to it? Your kids are grown. The ex-mates are out of the picture. Why isn't this a happy story?"

"That's just it, Christine. Ian is due to re-emerge from jail. Kate seems pretty positive he is hell-bent on getting revenge. She was the one who called the cops. Changed his life for the worse. Supposedly, he's been on best behavior. But Kate is nervous. Big time nervous. She doesn't believe it."

"And so . . . " she grew thoughtful. "She would be on pins and needles. And would not tolerate being hampered if she needed to move fast. Hiding. Is that what she's doing there at The Big Misty?"

"I think so. And there's one more thing. I'm surprised you haven't already gone over it with a fine tooth comb." The numbing sensation was creeping up on him.

"Yes. This thing with the accident. Sheila and I have worried ourselves sick over you. So if you think you've been it keeping it a secret, think again. It's been deteriorating, Sheila told me—and I can see it for myself. And that's what you are doing in Seattle. Finally seeing a proper specialist."

Reluctant to even bring it up, Aidan deliberated out the window. "Your garden is rather exploded, Christine."

"Yes, it is," she replied impatiently. "I simply lose interest in it by late August—exactly when everything really starts to grow. Now quit stalling."

"I'm not sure yet what it will take, 'to get it taken care of', so to say. Maybe it can't be fixed. But I have to allow the doctors their way—or it will deteriorate, as you say."

"Well, you know what my unsolicited advice will be. You've certainly gotten it repeatedly."

"Of course," he smiled. "Go forward. Take one step after the other and begin the journey."

"I should have been a general in the army," she laughed. "When I hear you say it." As the afternoon shadows elongated, Aidan and Christine shifted their conversation.

"Why didn't you take on a lover after Kathleen?" she questioned. "Surely you were starving in that relationship."

"Yeah," Aidan agreed. "I was. We had a primary flush of sexual attraction. And then it died completely between us. After she died—after my head cleared—I might have sought out other women. But I couldn't forget Kate."

"When the numbness and pain began," he continued after a preoccupied silence. "I didn't try to find her again. I figured I had plenty with Sheila, the gallery and my music. I basically buried my physical side unceremoniously. When I saw Kate again, literally almost the minute I saw her, what I thought was dead pulled itself out of its grave and came back to life."

Christine frowned. "You could be describing me, growing old and experiencing myself after Eliot died. I figured I had buried it too. Who expects an old woman to have desire? Or to wish she could dance with a lover again?"

Delight flashed across Aidan's face. "Explain, Bailey."

Christine chewed over his request, struggling with her own emotions. Then she burst out laughing. "You have to promise not to tell anyone. Everyone expects me to be a shining example of decorum."

"I only want to know who you are."

"That's precisely why I love you so absolutely." She sighed expressively, considering her answer. "Oh what the hell. I have a boyfriend, my next door neighbor."

"Sam? I assumed you two mostly fought over whose azaleas were leaning over into whose backyard and what to do with neighborhood squirrels. He's quite a bit . . . " Aidan stopped himself abruptly.

"Younger," she finished coolly. "Yes, we fight, but there is an element of . . . Oh, I can't quite put words to it. Maybe it's all in my head. I don't think so though," she continued, with a dreamy tone. "No, it's not all in my head. Yes, he's thirteen years younger. Is that an issue?"

"Hardly. Anyone would appreciate a head start dealing with you," Aidan laughed with a fresh appreciation for Christine. "And is Sam an acceptable dancer?"

She nodded with a sassy grin. "Excellent. It's a pleasure I didn't have with Eliot. So as much as I loved him, here I am, going on. Still learning and experiencing new things. I was the one who started it with Sam. Had to forget all kinds of reasons why I shouldn't do it. Show my vulnerability and all that—admitting I wanted his physical companionship. Scary. Goddamn scary. But it was too lonely to stay stuck in my fear."

"And I do relish arguing with him," she chuckled. "A lot. We start out kind of fighting and end up at each other's house, sharing a beer or coffee, depending on our mood and what we were doing. We laugh, Aidan. Eliot was so wonderful in many ways, but we never laughed like that." Aidan's expression reflected mixed astonishment and enjoyment.

"It started going deeper overnight," she continued with an impish tone, "I stuck a note on his door. It said 'if you call me tonight, I will be over to play'. And he did. And the rest is . . . " she paused, trying for the right phrase. Gave up. "What we are trying to figure out."

As the afternoon waned, Christine had provided him with more food than he could eat and talked him into considering a poetry class in the 'next academic year'.

"At least contemplate my proposal. I promise older students and only those who really can write and read poetry."

"I'll think about it. You have a distinct talent for talking me into things you want me to do."

She just smiled slyly.

"I need to go, Christine," he said, shaking his head when she offered a glass of beer. Shimmers of pain gathered in his back, warning him that he had the long drive home yet.

They lingered outside sociably for several minutes. "Find out what has to happen to heal that back of yours and mind you keep me in the loop, Aidan MacLaine. Then go get your lady. You'll never forgive yourself if anything happens to her. And you won't have a moment's rest if you don't find out if the relationship can move from dreams to something real."

"You're right, as ever." He lowered his voice, glancing playfully toward Sam's lighted window. "And, you, my dear Bailey—have fun with your neighbor. Maybe, just maybe, you could work a little less and learn to play a little more. You're not too old to learn to do that, are you?"

She answered with a grin that wouldn't stay away. "I don't know. Maybe. But it's possible."

Turning the corner, driving slowly, he glanced out at the side mirror. Christine waved, backlit by the streetlights. But for the gleam of her flowing silver hair, she looked for all the world like a young woman.

Chapter 19

For three endless days after he returned, Aidan's routine revolved around the hospital on the hill. Evenings he would escape to Sheila's world, depleted and quiet, too tired to resist her fussing and grateful when Andy arrived to distract her. Twice, Will brought in another specialist and carried on a lengthy sotto voce dialogue. They told Aidan just enough to keep him at bay.

They had to have some spinal fluid this morning. Disrobing came first, of course. *After you got in that little hospital gown, you were theirs.* You no longer belonged to the world, only to the machines and instruments that measured your vitals as though they summed up your life. But his spirit was in his free imagination, in the fresh wind of the Fisherfields. With the woman who fueled his heart.

Suddenly, he had to hear Kate. The moon hiding behind Seattle's cloudy daylight would be presiding full force in the Highlands.

She answered, as though she'd been expecting him all along. Aidan's pulse jumped at the sound of her. "How's the mountain goat tonight?"

Kate let out a long breath. "Did you hear me thinking about you? I was practically willing the phone to ring."

"How are you?" he managed.

"Okay." There was a small pause, as if she were trying to convince herself. "I'm okay," she repeated. "It's quiet here. We especially miss your music. Where are you?"

He considered the plain hospital room, bristling with tubes and equipment. Not a scene he wanted to explain to her. "I'd rather hear about where you are, sweet woman. Is that moon shining in on you?"

It was. Nearly full and brilliant with white light pouring in through the windows. "It's here, Addy," she whispered. "I'm almost the only one watching it. Kieran and Julie shacked up early. Most of the patrons are gone. Just Chris finishing up, and me watching the moon— wishing."

Trying to will himself across 5000 miles, he asked. "Wishing for what?"

She laughed at that, a sound that carried loss as much as enjoyment. "You want me to say it."

"Guilty. Say it."

Her voice was faint. "Wishing you were here." Aidan gripped the phone as though it might slip from him and take away the sweetness of her presence.

She had more. "Wishing I'd said yes to you. Wishing I was in your arms."

In three simple sentences, Kate tore open his carefully built border of anesthetized feelings about what was happening in his life. And he had nothing to offer her right now. Not until he finished this test and then listened to the judgment of the doctors. Whether he was ready or not. Only then, and everything depended on what they would say, could he celebrate the love and the promise he heard in her tone.

"I have that very much in mind. For you to say yes and for you to be in my arms," he stammered unevenly. There was nothing to say after that. Besides wanting her so hard it wore grooves into his soul—besides that—all he could do was to wait for the medical assessment. And then take action.

There was a lost silence. "Have the doctors found out anything?" She could sense the medicine-laden smell of the hospital.

Clearing his throat, Aidan tried to shake out the hoarseness. "They're working on it. God, they work hard at it. I should hear some news this afternoon."

Kate allowed the vagueness to stand, as though it made sense. After a brief delay, she started telling him about the season. The first snows had fallen, Kieran was perennially singing these days. Chris and Mary were talking about a visit to Australia. Thomas, the southern writer, had returned for one last trip before winter. And Jake and Phil had also returned to tackle the cold mountains for a last challenge before Highland weather turned them toward warmer places.

There was something in her demeanor. It stretched toward him, beyond the words, as if talking to him was a lifeline of some sort.

I don't want to hang up, he thought. *Keep talking to me, about anything.*

The nurse entered, sympathetic but attending to the business ahead. "Give me a minute," he mouthed, his hand over mouthpiece, waving her into the hall for a few minutes.

"Kate, I have to go," he delivered the declaration reluctantly.

Not trusting herself to speak, she held on, wanting to keep him present.

"Kate?' he repeated thickly, surrendering to the inescapable reality of the hospital. "It's test time. Again. As soon as this is wrapped up, I'm coming there. I swear. Okay?" *If I can. If circumstances allow it.*

Her response was noncommittal. For hours after, submitting to a needle that looked far too big—and the ache that spread from its sharp edge throughout his entire body—he brooded over the meaning of her stark words, the hollowness of her voice. Her unstated dread that the future did not have a place for her.

In another place, so far away in spirit it belonged to a different reality, the barren hall of the prison was a nightmare, with doors that went into places you didn't want to know about. Ian Prescott walked slowly, keeping his tight-muscled body calm, head bowed, accompanied by two guards.

Ian had learned to keep his head inclined. This would be the final hearing before freedom was his again. The climax scene. *Play it to the hilt.* He'd even mastered making his voice shake with emotion. There had been countless times to practice it in the endless cycle of days and nights that ran into each other.

Ian's sky-blue eyes could freeze a person in their tracks, like savage dogs with powerful jaws coming straight at the face. In the privacy of his cell, he'd practiced hooding their icy depths until he could muster a fully guileless attitude. *Act remorseful.* He knew it well. It was merely a play, and after all the rehearsals, the actor was ready for the stage.

It was obvious what they required and he would give it to them. He would clearly deserve a second chance in their minds. *The model prisoner.* His thoughts skipped over and over into the rut they'd worn deep. *She'll get hers, she'll get hers.* He lifted a lip in a snarl before he managed to regain control.

After she hung up the phone, sensing Aidan and Ian at the same time, Kate sat alone in the lounge. She turned to the moon, as if the pale light held the core of Aidan's tenderness. A cold ball of panic was forming in her core. The cancerous fear would grow with no rules, destroying everything good around it. *Ian would be released soon, so soon.*

If she waited for Aidan, Ian would find and destroy them both. If she traveled to Aidan, he would find them faster. She had arrived at the point where the chasm lay before her, the hounds of hell howling, distant but clear. And no choice but to jump.

Without being able to predict where or how she would land, she had to leap, whether or not she survived. *At least Aidan would be protected, and Kieran.* Deeply anguished, Kate made plans to leave The Big Misty.

Chapter 20

Back at the hospital, Aidan made it through the last test, though it was the most painful of all. When his strength returned, he was able to move stiffly to Will's office. Not bothering to knock, he entered wearily and sat down. "The verdict, please."

Will sat behind an oak desk and folded his fingers together examining Aidan as though he were a deeply interesting museum exhibit.

"You had some freebie years thinking you were fine after the accident. But you weren't. The effects just took awhile to show up. That little road incident resulted in scar tissue tethered right on the spinal cord. In effect, the nerves in your back are being strangled, one by one."

"So, it's what you thought all along."

"Yep. Trauma-related syringomyelia. But there are a lot of variations. I wanted to check it out thoroughly before I cut and good thing I did."

"Can I assume you found some worthy information?"

"Qualified yes. That's why I did the consultations. Sometimes the thing just can't be fixed. You can't get at it. So, I had to make sure it was worth putting you through . . . what you'll have to go through. The positive news is that we can do this at all, as far as we can see at this point. After the operation, you'll have a reasonable chance at walking out of here with no more pain and the feeling in your back fully restored."

Aidan's deadpan conduct wavered. "And reasonable is . . .?" he asked tersely.

"I don't know," Will responded soberly. "Figure about 75 percent." Reading the question on Aidan's pale face, he added, "The final outcome has a few possibilities, Aidan. If it doesn't go right, you could end up in a wheelchair. Maybe worse."

Will paused, feeling the heaviness of what he was saying. "Obviously doing nothing is not a good choice," he continued. "You've maxed out your time-frame already. If it's allowed to travel its free course, well . . . it's nothing you would wish on yourself."

It was absolutely critical that Aidan understand the whole picture, so he kept going. "The pressure has caused a cyst that will elongate over an undefined period. As it presses on all that scar tissue, it destroys the center of the spinal cord. The fluid builds too much weight, the damage becomes irreversible. If left to grow," Will looked down briefly, "it could start to smother the brainstem. That means life support, Aidan. Let's not even go there yet."

"Okay. I'm in no hurry for that conversation. What's the bad news?" Aidan could not resist a small ironic smile.

"The recuperation will be arduous. Painful and long. Every day will drag down your spirit and weaken your body. It will hurt like hell. At times, you'll find it unendurable. And we'll all be working on blind faith because we won't find out until a few weeks after if you will be able to walk—or what we have."

Motionless, Aidan absorbed Will's words. *There is nothing to say.* The choices had all narrowed to one path and he had to follow it through to the end.

Will stood up, poured a glass of water for both of them. "Okay, my mouth's dry, how about yours?" he teased awkwardly. "You'll enjoy a bit of a reprieve, anyway. Think of it as a vacation before the real work begins. You need to be as strong as possible ahead of submitting to the real thing. Before we move forward on the big operation, we can do a preliminary procedure that will help you be up and walking about."

Aidan's eyes blazed. "Go on."

"It's tricky, so take that manic look away. It will fool you and then dump you if the timing's ignored. I can relieve the current symptoms, but they will return. You will have about two weeks, no more. You can't afford to do anything that would shift the spine and compromise it. You understand?"

"But for during that time, I will be able to move . . . normally?"

"Two weeks, Aidan. Exactly two weeks."

Before he knew it, Aidan was checked in and counting the tedious hours until the next day's operation. He convinced Sheila he would be fine that evening, and that yes, she could visit him as soon as it was over.

This operation gives me the chance to return to the Highlands. He focused his mind on that one sustaining idea. By morning, he was more than ready for whatever came next.

Aidan guessed the whole scene of getting ready for the operation would feel as though it were happening to someone else. It did. He had only the remembrance of counting backwards a few numbers. Then he was waking up, groggy and aching—slowly focusing on Sheila's anxious face.

"Don't you have a thesis to write?" he asked, hearing his

voice sound like gravel and allowing her emotional embrace.

"Don't kid yourself, Dad. You're just one distraction in a world of many," Sheila countered, with a relieved laugh. Humor carried its healing energy into the room as they continued to tease, continuing when Will walked in. From his easy demeanor, they discerned it had gone well.

"You might as well enjoy this day, Aidan," announced Will. Characteristically, the doctor managed to write in his notebook, give instructions to nurses, check his patients and work out their needs all at once, alternately frowning and relaxing as he found solutions.

"Tomorrow, I introduce you to Bella. She will push and prod and cajole you until she deems you able to dance. That's her criterion for being released from this place. At least a slow waltz. Fix it in your mind, 'cause otherwise you'll be here forever."

"I can't wait. As a matter of fact, dancing sounds pretty good."

The next morning at 7 A.M. sharp, Will entered Aidan's room with a diminutive woman at his side. "This fine lady is Bella LaGrover. Originally from Belize. She'll hurt you, but somehow you won't mind. She's the best physical therapist in Seattle."

"Thank you, Dr. Burke, I appreciate it." Bella's soft voice was in contrast to her sturdy frame and her sweet and salty Caribbean accent. Her skin was smooth, the color of caramel. A lighthearted grin lit up her face as she shook Aidan's hand with a grip that caught his attention. "I'll be pleased to be working with you. Get you up on your feet in no time."

"And I," Aidan couldn't help but smile, "will do whatever I need to. Just give me the directions."

"Oh she will, my boy, she will. I leave you two to get acquainted." Eyes flashing mischievously, Will swept out into the hallway.

"I don't know why he has such a look of trouble on him," Bella said mildly. "We just got to work hard and get you back to doing whatever it is you do."

As the first day with Bella wore on, Aidan thought about Will's fleeting smirk, and cursed it some as Bella required stretching and movement that felt as though it was tearing muscle. As Will had predicted, he could not hold it against her and found himself laughing in response to her stories and jokes even as his teeth gritted in pain.

When Sheila arrived that evening, Bella had departed and Aidan was utterly exhausted.

"You will not eat hospital food," she announced matter of factly, as she laid out various containers of Thai take-out. "And Dr. Will said a glass of wine wouldn't hurt you either. He said it would relax you. And that you might be grateful for it after today."

"That would be an understatement. Was he smiling devilishly when he told you this?"

Sheila cocked her head, bit back a smile, then nodded solicitously. "Yes, I believe he was. Mentioned something about a woman named Bella."

Aidan sat up, wincing slightly. "Oh yeah. That one. The hurricane."

"Is she helping you?" They sat together on Aidan's bed, talking easily, sharing wine in plastic cups.

"Yes. Yes, she is. And I appreciate her. A taskmaster with an endless series of distracting stories. Strong as a man, but she has a beautiful woman's touch."

"Will said in a day or so you could go home if Bella said you were ready to dance."

Aidan put down his cup. "Did he now? Well, in that case you better bring some waltz music next visit 'cause I would love to get out of this place."

By the end of the third afternoon with Bella, Aidan was

walking again and rejoicing in his first pain-free steps in months. When the work session completed, he looked at her expectantly as she prepared to leave.

She burst out in a cheerful laugh. "So, Mr. Aidan, you got that waltz music your daughter brought you?"

"I do. I thought you would never ask. Shall we try it out now?"

A flash of pleasure crossed her expressive features. "With some, it's only a tease so they realize I mean business about getting well. But, if you're willing, I would like to have this dance for myself."

Slipping the CD into the player that Sheila had placed by his bedside, Aidan held out his arms and Bella spun gracefully into his embrace. Together, in the waning afternoon light, they gently moved, her small body following his steps easily, circling slowly in a one-two-three motion.

When the music ended, Aidan gently hugged her. "Thank you, Bella. Thank you so much."

Bella's benevolent smile was warm. "No, thank you. That was one fine dance, Mr. Aidan. You go take on the world. Be here when Dr. Burke told you." Blowing a kiss to him, she walked out, nearly colliding with Will as she did. "He's ready," she said over her shoulder.

A few hours later, Aidan celebrated the delicious experience of walking out of the hospital. Sheila listened intently on the car ride home—as he told her his plans to travel to Scotland on gallery business. She had seen Claire and Ben arrive with art wrapped securely for the journey. Watched them talk, low and intent, about work and details of the business. Fragments of the conversation had been audible. She already knew that there was a trip that would begin in Glasgow.

"What then, Dad? So you still mean to go to the Highlands?

To her?" She couldn't keep the tension out of her tone.

Aidan shouldered over, speaking earnestly. "Her name is Kate. Yes. I do mean to go back to her. That's all I know and all you need to know. I hope there will be more, much more to say. But for now, that's enough."

At nightfall, he decided not to call Kate, though he hovered briefly near the telephone. *Better to be a surprise.* He would be there in a few days.

Christine was in the kitchen when he woke up in the morning, humming to herself and preparing breakfast. She was elated to see him and more so because she had surprised him. In answer to his unspoken questions, she spoke rapid fire—hunting at the same time for the perfect pan for her omelet.

"Your sweet daughter and I have long since exchanged house keys, dear. Makes life easier when we visit. And Sam wanted to see that new exhibit at the Museum. He likes to visit his son and pretend that he is alone in the world. Dropped me off here. Might as well take a bit of free sympathy if you can get it, I guess."

"Anyway, I wasn't going to permit you to escape without seeing me again, so here I am. We'll take you to the airport after breakfast." Flourishing the pan she found, Christine grinned and wrapped her arms around him. "Are you breakable or can I give you a real squeeze?" she asked.

Aidan gave her a lopsided grin. "I think I can take whatever you can throw at me, Bailey." He snatched the pan out of her hand, scooping her into his arms.

They ate in the kitchen, enjoying the hazy view of the Olympic Mountains on the skyline. Christine and Sheila gossiped about university business and Aidan was glad to have their attention drawn from him. He liked listening to their pleasant camaraderie, watching as the waters of Puget Sound changed to steel gray.

In contrast, his heart took on a quickened pulse—a sense

of urgency mounting. Once again, Kate's desolate voice rang in his memory. *Something was building.* It probably had Ian's name on it, as all of her pain and fear did. His jaw tightened, despite the ring of laughter from the women.

Christine and Sheila drove him to the airport together. He'd half-heartedly tried to talk them out of the effort, but it was too agreeable to be with them. They insisted on coming into the terminal with him, and on carrying his small bag and the packages of art.

He stood with them at the rear of the extensive security line, marveling at feeling stable and pain free. Smiling gently, he asked, "Gonna try and sneak through with me or are we saying adieu?"

"Me first, Sheila, so you can say goodbye in private." Christine said lightly as he set down his bag. They hugged briefly. "Go find out if she is truly the one." Unexpectedly she wavered. "Don't get your heart broken." She stopped, embarrassed.

Aidan ran his knuckles along her cheek. "But maybe hearts have to be willing to be broken. I seem to remember some wise lady taught me that."

"Your turn, Sheila. I'll be at the coffee place." Flustered, Christine walked off without saying another word.

They both watched her leave before turning to each other. "She's on an edge these days," remarked Sheila.

"For good reason. I suppose you know more about that than me."

Sheila's smile sparked with humor and compassion. "Sam. Yeah. The neighbor who is flipping Christine's world upside down."

His warm eyes held her, filling her with his love.

"Oh, Dad, I hope it all turns out okay for you." She embraced him and held on, resting her cheek in the crook of his neck. "Don't forget what your doctor said. That's the only thing. Don't lose track of time. Don't do anything stupid."

He chuckled. "So many don'ts. Those were supposed to be my lines."

"Come back ready for this god-awful thing you have to go through," Sheila continued in a rush. "I'll be counting the days, Dad. I love you."

"Bye," called Aidan, waving as she pivoted and left him. "Wish me luck," he added softly.

Chapter 21

Aidan rode the train from the Glasgow airport into the center of the city, a single knapsack over his shoulder, the art shipped forward to his hotel—profoundly grateful for the simple ability to walk easily.

The train moved smoothly past miles of row houses, tiny yards, and grimy industrial complexes. *Straight out of a Dickens novel,* he thought. Ignoring this landscape, modern commuters relaxed over newspapers and conversation. Aidan normally delighted in these intervals, enjoying the world and the people he would never meet, leading complex lives he could only guess at.

This morning was different. His stomach steadily tightened with apprehension. *Just nerves,* he thought. Still, he felt edgy, and because of it, he did not rest once he'd found the simple hotel Claire had booked for him. It was graceful and homey. A typical Claire discovery. She had a rare talent for finding the perfect place.

The temptation of the comfortable bed didn't attract him, despite the wearisome hours on the plane.

It seemed suddenly critical that he go to The Big Misty as quickly as possible. After a brief shower, he went about his business, moving his appointments up by a day and moving fast in the elegant core of Glasgow to accomplish them.

On impulse, he bought a European cell phone, to have a number that he could use when he needed it. He'd left his regular phone in a box of clothes at Sheila's, wanting to be free of incoming calls. By sunset, at the hotel, exhausted with jet lag but unable to sleep, his anxiety continued to mount to an almost unbearable level. *I have to find out what's going on.*

The minute he heard Kieran, his heart sank. Distraught and tight with grief, Kieran told him that Kate was gone. She'd left two days before on a trip to the camping cottage. He'd used all his tricks to discourage her.

"The weather is dodgy, I told her, but she would have none of it. There was a fearsome agitation about her. No reasoning helped at all. I asked her to wait until she'd heard the news from you, but that only made it worse. We fought."

Kieran's tone became constricted and apprehensive. "Then she headed off, with no more argument. I expected she would cool off up there, but when she didn't return, I went looking for her myself. Of course, she wasn't at the cabin. I don't think she ever went there. She only used that story to divert me from her real plans."

Aidan stared into the wall, his mind racing. *The foreboding had been real.* The preoccupied quality of their last conversation flooded back like a tidal surge, unstoppable and turbulent. Taking a deep breath, he struggled to think clearly. "Did you find anything? Any clue at all, Kieran?"

"When I got home, I went through every little bit of paper in her room. Everything. She didn't have more than she could fit in a rucksack." Kieran's tone was muted. "I pieced together part of an address. Actually only the name of a place."

So it was this, the smallest fragment of Kate's life. One clue as to where she might have vanished. Memories of trying to track Kathleen with the same sort of barely tangible evidence washed over Aidan. But this was very different. Kathleen had run from her internal demons. Kate was escaping someone real—though he couldn't yet measure the certainty of the menace.

"The name. Kieran, what was it?" he asked urgently.

"Ulva. It's all I have. An island, off the west coast. Inner Hebrides. I haven't said a word to anyone. You're the only person I believe she would be willing to see—apart from her son."

One small trace. That was what he had. "I'll leave in the morning." Stress and weariness wound tightly through Aidan's mind. "Tell people she's gone on holiday, that's all."

"Of course. Just find her . . . " Kieran trailed off. "Tell her I'm sorry," he added awkwardly.

"She knows, Kieran . . . how you feel about her. I'll touch in with you when I find her." *Let the feel of confidence, real or not, lead the way to her.*

The morning dawned, cold and bleak as his mood. The clock in Aidan's room had moved the minutes ahead with relentless ticking, a sound he had listened to for all of the nearly sleepless night. By business opening hours, he was ready, pacing with his coat on, arranging final pick up on the art pieces.

He called Claire to hold the rest of the Glasgow projects. She swallowed her questions, and took notes from his terse directions.

"Does Sheila know where you are?" She could not help asking once he wound down.

His voice softened. "I'm in Scotland. That's sufficient. No sense both of you worrying, Claire. I simply have something that requires my immediate attention. Please be okay with that." There was no need to mention Will's prognosis if he didn't return to have it permanently repaired.

Traffic was light as he left Glasgow, so edgy with lost sleep and anticipation that his hands shook on the steering wheel. The low sky met the sullen earth in a darkening temper—heralding the coming of late autumn, with its rapidly failing light. A thin coating of sleet on the roads made driving tricky. Aidan was relieved when the weak sun finally prevailed over the frozen rain, drying the slickened pavement as he cleared the urban maze.

The countryside had transformed since he'd first arrived on the heels of summer. Moody and turned inward, a constancy of chilly rain mixed and melted together the sober dark greens, grays and browns. The change in seasons featured a straggling series of idle towns and closed tourist attractions. They flashed past him as he drove toward the western sea and whatever providence held in store for him.

The map next to him showed a tiny island called Ulva, lying off the larger Isle of Mull in the Hebrides. Aidan drove in silence, his spirit a combination of despair and determination. He had only one purpose and that was to find Kate.

At the port town of Oban, the energy was busy again. High-bowed herring boats in every color of the rainbow gave the busy harbor a carnival feel, while late-season tourists continued to enjoy the streets.

The ferry was huge, as though it had been designed for a good deal more than the short crossing to Mull. The Caledonian MacBrayne's lower level smelled of rust and diesel, the sound of loading cars echoing in its metallic gut. Aidan climbed to the upper deck, watching the slate-blue water slide by as they sped toward the rust-colored hills of Mull.

He stood outside in the lee of the engine room, gradually unwinding from the long drive. Opening a bag of food he'd bought in Oban, he studied the map he'd bought in the same small store. The cold seaweed-scented wind and the simple meal of cheese, apple and hard-crusted bread roll revived him.

By the time the Caledonian MacBrayne was tied up at dock, he knew exactly where he was going, covering the eighteen miles to the Ulva ferry as quickly as he could on the narrow single-track roads of Mull. He arrived ten minutes before the ferryman quit for the night, hoping that his quick call to an answering machine last night had secured a spot at the island's only year-round B & B. What would happen if this didn't work out, he wasn't sure, but there was nothing else to be done.

The method to signal the ferry was simple and obvious. There was a little sliding door, where those on Mull's shore wishing to ferry to Ulva would display a red square.

"You've got the last run of the day!" called the lean man who responded to the indicator and brought the small boat over within a few minutes.

It was a scene utterly apart from the hustle and concrete of both Seattle and Glasgow. The man relaxed beside the outboard motor as the boat bobbed in its own wake, at ease with the current of the incoming tide.

Aidan called to him. "I'm trusting you might have a communication from Mrs. MacDougal. I phoned ahead, but don't know if she received my message."

"Lila was off island shopping yesterday, but she got your reservation," the driver acknowledged with the briefest of nods. "Not that it was necessary," he snorted. "Not exactly hopping with visitors, is it? I'm to bring you and your things straight up. The name's Brian." Inexplicably, he had an American accent, a detail Aidan found somehow fitting in the odd dreamscape.

The ferry crossing took barely a minute, but when they landed Aidan immediately appreciated they were in a realm quite different—and more remote—than Mull.

Waving aside Aidan's move to pull out his wallet as they stepped off the boat, Brian gestured at an older all-terrain vehicle.

"She paid your fare and extra for me to give you a ride to her place. This is what passes for a car here. It's not far." He gave no further explanation, and did not try to disguise his frank examination of Aidan.

"Thanks, but I've a mind to walk. If you would take my bag there and tell her I've arrived, I would enjoy the exercise."

The ferryman shrugged and grabbed Aidan's bag. "All the same to me. Follow the road leading out. Take the right fork. She'll have the porch lights on. I'm the only house beyond her. You won't get lost."

"Brian," Aidan asked cautiously, "has a single woman, an American, arrived here recently, in the past few days? She would be dark-haired and medium build. Wouldn't hurt your eyes to look at her either."

"No," Brain said flatly, offering no further conversation and mounting the ATV.

Aidan tapped his shoulder. "If such a woman were here, she could be told that it's Aidan MacLaine who's arrived and that he will wait to see her."

Brian's impassive face gave away nothing. "I'll take your things to Lila's," he responded curtly, starting the motor and clattering off. Aidan walked slowly on the track in the gathering darkness.

Every fiber of his being called out to Kate, trying to find her footsteps with his own—trying to sense her presence in the misty quiet of the island. For now, there was nothing else he could do. He just had to abide here and it made no matter how patiently he did it. *Kate would come, if she were here, when she was ready.*

The walk ended at a fairytale cottage complete with white picket fence, tucked into the dark trees on one side, the porch with a wind-washed view of Mull on the other. Dinner was ready and a warm fire snapping in the hearth. There were no other guests.

"I have very few visitors in winter. Most tourists have gone back to the city." Lila moved with energy that belied her use of a cane. "Now, I'll just show you around." She told him she'd been divorced for several years. "Not that I could turn any man's head at my age," she laughed. "Anyway, at sixty-nine, I've decided I enjoy my food too much to keep the best figure. And I have Buck. I named him after Buck in *The Call of the Wild*, you know, because he has an untamed heart."

Lila spoke so many words in the space of a minute that she made Aidan's head spin, but he did pause to address Buck. The dog was everything Lila wasn't—silent and reserved. Buck was some degree border collie, the rest of his parentage unknown. His wavy black coat was thick and glossy. Evidently, Lila not only doted on him, but also fed him the best of food. Buck sauntered forward as Lila mentioned his name and greeted her in a restrained fashion, his tail gently fanning. Then he turned to Aidan and carefully sniffed, lying down when he was finished with his examination.

"You've got your own private entrance," Lila said when she showed him the bedroom. "I do hope you fancy it."

It was, in fact, a very comfortable situation with its own kitchen and a welcoming fireplace. "I like it very much, thank you," he replied gratefully.

She insisted that Aidan join her for dinner. "After you've refreshed yourself, of course. I took the liberty of stocking the place with one of our local whiskies. Help yourself to everything you find in here." Tapping Buck lightly on the neck to follow, she shut the door.

Aidan poured a glass of the amber liquid. It was Oban's own, and he tasted it with gratitude, for the memories it kindled and the easy malt taste that lingered on his tongue. Opening the window, he leaned out as a slack tide calmed the fast-moving water in the narrow inlet between Mull and Ulva.

The threat of rain had never really arrived. Swollen clouds banked on the horizon while straight overhead the black night erupted with stars. *The memory of Montana lives in skies like this,* Aidan thought.

He was doing the one thing that felt right and real by showing Kate that he wouldn't let go of her. The waves slapped gently, sighing on the shore—and again Aidan sent a silent call to her.

The evening slipped by slowly. Sharing Lila's delicious food, he fed the fire as she talked and stroked Buck's head, willing the anxiety of his journey to calm. He would wait—as long as he could—for Kate to find him. When the clock started crowding ten, he took his leave.

"Time for bed, Lila." She nodded agreeably, delicately smothering a restrained yawn, and saw him to his room. Her hand on Buck's head, she waved as he shut the door.

Chapter 22

For three days, Aidan stayed close to Lila's house. On his request, she gave him a list of projects that needed fixing. He worked with Buck at his side, enchanting her by his sincere admiration of her cooking. The weather was damp and windless, the colors muted in the deep silence of Ulva. At dusk, before darkness descended, he walked the narrow roads alone, centering his whole spirit on Kate.

On the fourth evening, he stayed out longer, reluctant to leave the shadows. With rising misgiving, he wondered if it was a mistake to hope Kate would make the first move. When he came through the door, Lila was thoroughly alarmed and nearly ready to call out someone to find him.

"Sorry, Lila. Sorry." He grasped her hands and kissed them. "Time ran away from me. Really, I didn't mean to make you anxious."

Forgiveness was one of Lila's qualities. Relinquishing the worry immediately, she fussed over getting his dinner out and lightened up to enjoy his company. Tonight, she encouraged him to talk, asking questions she knew that he would answer. She'd had no success with nudging him to talk about his purpose in Scotland or details about his life in the States. Instead, she inquired about his walks on Ulva, a practice she'd long ago given up.

Holding her bright eyes steady with his own, he told her of his discovery of secret glades which she had once known intimately. He reminded her of standing stones she had leaned against as a young woman and the lovely evensong heralding of a dark night.

"Now, my dear, I must go to my bed," Aidan said, with the hint of a smile.

Lila stayed seated, her gaze gone misty. "I roved all over Ulva as a girl, Aidan. I knew every part of it. But after I broke my hip, I never went out again. Fear of uneven ground, I guess. Or maybe, I just gave up being young," she sighed. "You brought it all back to me tonight and then some. Beautiful, beautiful words. No, I can't go to sleep yet. I'll sit by the fire and remember my lovely island."

Pausing, Aidan patted her shoulder. "Don't give it up, Lila. Use your resources here. Get out again and explore."

"Let me muse on it," she responded pensively. "Some places are best left with the memories of youthful years. I don't want to visit them as an old woman. Age has crept up on me. But I will consider it. If there are havens that call to me yet, I will consider it." She did not accompany him to his door.

Aidan leaned against the door as he closed it. Questions floated in the stillness. Since he had no answers, he laid on top of the quilt, too tired to remove more than his shoes and drifted into sleep.

When the single knock tapped, he felt the quiet sound more than he heard it. He rose on one elbow, momentarily disoriented. The knock struck once again, softer, the doorknob turning cautiously. In one motion he was on his feet, his heart hammering. The door opened half way, hovered for a minute, and then Kate stepped inside, hesitant and cautious. Neither of them moved.

"I don't know how you found me," her voice trembled.

He moved toward her carefully, trying not to push her. "I've been looking for you my whole life," he responded quietly. "I think it's about time I found you."

Her hand clenched but stayed on the doorknob. "Brian swore he told you nothing. He said an Aidan MacLaine had arrived on the island. That's all."

"It's true, he guarded your secrets well. And I was hoping my name was enough." Without reaching for her, he waited, wanting her to get the whole message from his eyes, so she would see the unbroken hours and years of his life that had worn her name. She tore herself from his deep gaze, taking a half step—unsure of her next move.

Fear was urging her to flee. He could sense it. "Kate, sweet Kate. Don't run. Please don't run away."

"I should," she spoke urgently, as if trying to remind herself.

"I should, too," he whispered. "We should both leave and return to our own lives. Try to forget we ever saw each other again."

She didn't resist when Aidan took the final step and pulled her into his arms. "But I can't do that, Kate. I can't forget. Can you?" She shook her head mutely. He lifted her chin, using the heel of his hand to wipe away the glint of tears.

His eyes are that vibrant brown of spring trees, she thought unexpectedly. *Hinting of summer warmth and growth.* How his beloved face had anchored deep into her soul.

Holding his hands on her cheeks, Aidan drank in the taste and scent of her. Kate welcomed him, her mouth open and soft as his warmth melted the cold of the night, keenly returning his embrace. Finally, with a protracted shuddering breath she stopped, her head resting on his chest.

Ian's cold glare flickered in her mind, and as though he saw it, Aidan's arms tightened. "If you are in danger, I need to know," he murmured. He stroked the length of her back, as if gentling a wild horse. The sweetness of the touch sparked fire, but her stomach tightened again. How could she expose this tender man to the menace chasing her down?

Involuntarily, she made an effort to disengage, but Aidan would have none of it. "No, Kate. Not now. I've come too far to let go of you," he said fiercely, not releasing her. "We can't waste this time, no matter what the future holds for either of us," he added almost inaudibly.

Her face clouded, full of questions. In response, he kissed her again, his lips lingering on hers, trailing his fingers down her throat to her collarbone. Pausing for a long minute, he dropped his hand further, sliding it slowly below her stomach. Desire blazed, the flame building through them.

"Make the questions and fears stay outside," he continued huskily. "God, woman—let us have this one night. Then we'll talk about where to go from here." Tugging off her coat and sweater without asking, he drew her close again.

Kate's expression shifted, as though an inalterable moment had arrived. One she had dreamed of for too many years to deny. She kicked off her boots and faced him, her hands slipping under his shirt, delicately running her fingers along his skin.

Aidan held his breath at her touch, then blew it out slowly, feeling the distance dissolve. An upwelling of bliss followed her touch. When she felt the recent scars, she shot a questioning glance at him.

He caressed her cheek. "Tomorrow."

Murmuring a quiet assent, she opened to him again. Let her touch roam, suddenly impatient for all he could give her. His breathing quickened. Taking her hand, he led her to the bed, pulled her down beside him.

"My love," he whispered. Cursing softly, he gripped the swell of her hips—the need of his body contradicting the softness of his voice. "Mo gradh." There was no way to know if this night would be the only one they would ever have—or one of many, in a lifetime of loving. It didn't change anything.

She unbuttoned his flannel shirt, demanding the satisfaction of skin. Impatiently pulling off his tee shirt, sighing at the feel of his bare chest—Kate put aside past and future—surrendering to the urgency of the present.

Aidan kept pace with her, unclothing her with shaking fingers, kissing her breasts, discovering what she wanted, seeking the center of her silky warmth. The ache of unleashing his love shot through every part of his body and heart. It was as though the moorings of his life were coming undone, one at a time—snapping off from their snugly-tied harbor. The wild sea was entering, potent and breathtaking. Even with the ominous injury in his back, he was filled with a feeling of vitality and strength.

Heat like she'd never known it. Only Aidan could cool the searing craving that opened from the depths of her soul. Teasing open the zipper of his jeans, she welcomed his hardness, matched the rhythm of his movement with her own.

He entered her in the astonished manner of new lovers—lost in the nameless, ancient dance of man and woman, the world stopped around them.

I give my whole life to you. Here. Now. Kate no longer tried to form words, rising to meet him, tender and reckless. She pressed her mouth to his shoulder as the cresting sensations arched through her body, her breath breaking on a moan.

He fought for control while her heat shimmered around him. Fisted his hands, holding the pleasure, even when it built toward pain. Slowed down, tantalizing them both until she pulled him in deeply and held him there. With a groan, his body tightened as he let go—the storm released—exploding thunder and lightening. His seed filled her as they climaxed together, their lips hot against each other, shuddering in the effort to be quiet in Mrs. MacDougal's home.

Afterwards, they lay tangled in each other's arms, the pounding of their hearts easing gently. Aidan cradled his head on his arm, strumming her skin along her neck to her stomach, watching her.

"Afraid I'll disappear?" She hid a small smile.

"Yes." He didn't smile back.

"Oh darling." She drew him close. "I know. Let this night be enough. For now." Gradually, they yielded to sleep's insistence. When they woke a few hours later, the unexpected nearness of their bodies pushed them quickly from their reverie. Surprised all over by the tenderness of skin-to-skin—discovering again how hard and fast desire built. Shaken by its power, they dreamed in each other's arms.

Minutes before dawn, Kate stirred from their cozy nest. "I'll not be here when Lila wakes up." A wicked smile worked its way across her face, and she rose up, nuzzling his mouth, shoulders and neck.

He groaned at the pleasure of her touch, tugging her close again. "You won't be leaving like that. I won't allow it."

"You have to, dear one. But I will meet you at half-past ten. Ask Lila about the trail that leads south. There's an old dam. I'll meet you there." Rolling away from his ready body, she dressed in the pale light. Motionless, Aidan watched her—wanting to make it commonplace, not a vision. When she left, he laid in the warmth of their lovemaking, memorizing the scent of it.

Buck was his support during breakfast, while Lila talked to both of them with words that churned like a fast river past the slow eddy where he daydreamed. The dog sat quietly, his head on Aidan's knee.

When Aidan requested directions to the old dam, Lila scanned the cloudless sky with approval. "It's a fine day for it." Presenting him with some biscuits and a thermos, she regarded him carefully. "And you are in a very fine mood, yourself." Aidan could not resist a slow grin, giving her no answer—fully appreciating that it would drive her crazy.

Flustered, Lila stared for a minute. "Okay, you don't have to tell me why. I am glad you're happy. That's all. I trust you'll be here by dinner? Take Buck with you, he's taken rather a liking to you. And he can keep an eye on you, too. Remind you to come home." Without waiting for his answer, mildly disconcerted, she turned back to the kitchen.

They set out on the narrow hard rock roads of Ulva, Aidan savoring the cool breeze and the hushed atmosphere, Buck following close as a shadow behind him.

Kate leaned against an ancient beech. At the sight of her, he imagined a fairy princess in a magical wood, and blew out a low whistle. A part of him expected her to be gone, and last night become a dream once again. "Sorry I'm a bit late," he said. "Escaping Lila is no mean feat. I brought Buck with me."

She bent to Buck and gently squeezed his ears in salute. "He's a serious sort, isn't he?" she remarked. Straightening, she nestled her arms around Aidan's neck.

"How are you this morning?" she asked, smiling up at him.

"I had the most amazing dream that the woman I've loved for eleven years came to my bed," he replied, stroking her cheek with his fingertips.

"And did she love you well, this vision of yours?"

"She did indeed. The only problem is that she left me wanting more." He smoothed his hand at the small of her back, started the slow slide down her hips.

"First," she stepped aside slightly, her thumb brushing teasingly down his chest. "We walk."

Chapter 23

The cart road was impossibly narrow, a remnant from an era that knew nothing of automobiles. Climbing through the beech-wood forest, they rested awhile at the crest of the hill where the trees dissolved into heather and rocks, and took in the extraordinary view.

"It's tomorrow, so time to tell" Kate deliberately returned to the scars on Aidan's lower back, gently exploring. "You are walking without pain," she ventured. "An operation made the difference, it seems."

"It did," he agreed, inviting no further inquiry.

"I'm so glad. It was awful to see you struggle with it."

Aidan studied the ground, his eyes shadowed.

Kate stopped. Clearly there was more of the story to be told. "Aidan? What else? What aren't you saying?"

Shaking his head, he let the words spill out slow and stark. "The thing is complicated. The doctor was able to temporarily relieve the pressure that was causing the symptoms. There will be another operation to make it permanent."

She frowned, expecting him to say more. "That explanation is hardly sufficient."

He brushed his lips lightly across hers. "Easy, my dear. Details will come in their own time. We have other business. Let's attend to that." They stood in the middle of the cart track, grateful for Ulva's immeasurable peace. Buck sat down, sniffing for interesting smells.

Aidan took her hand and held it against his chest, his fingers interlaced with hers. The air stilled as they resumed walking. There had to be a shift in conversation, and they were both dreading it.

Trying to stave it off as long as she could, Kate mustered a light tone. "You're not as thin as you were," she observed, with an appreciative grin.

His mouth twitched. "Well, I've been on a strict regime of overeating, thanks to my friends and Sheila. They must have gotten word to Lila as well, so she could participate."

"Well, it looks good. You look great, Addy."

At this, he laughed out loud, his face shining. "You have questionable taste, dear one. But I am happy to hear you say it. As for you," he teased, "there must be something wrong with my eyes. I can't seem to tear them away from you."

At the peak of the hill, they sat against sun-warmed rock, and contemplated the splendid scene before them. The basalt layers of Mull shimmered cream and pink over the iridescent water while the mystical island of Iona hugged the horizon.

"That one's Staffa," said Kate. "The one full of seabirds. Doesn't it look like a diving whale?" She pointed at a high hump, its dark fin piercing a sparkling Hebridean Sea.

"Yes it does," smiled Aidan. "And you can hear the Mendelssohn symphony in their cries." His arm circled her waist. "I explored a lot of these islands, though I never made it to Ulva. Always found it seductive—the paradox of standing stones and

Druid caves coexisting with Viking remains and ruined cottages."

"Okay," he broke the easy mood with regret. "We can't put it off any further. I need to

hear about Ian."

His straightforward appeal weighed heavily on them. Kate tensed, sat up abruptly. She couldn't deny this request. "I would do anything to have this be the first day of my life, if it weren't for Jordan," she nestled in, allowing his sweet warmth to anchor her. He understood this—nodding, encouraging.

Kate returned to the view, consciously inhaling the potency of the land, and finally began speaking. "Here goes," she began, unable to stop an involuntary sigh. "You've waited long enough for this. After those few years, Ian's behavior became more and more strange. He would leave guns out after cleaning them. Almost daring Jordan to play with them. He would erupt into angry fits over any little thing, kicking the wall and swearing. Then he would get a certain look . . . like a mean dog ready to attack."

"Oh, I hate talking about this." She dropped her head, sighed again, and continued reluctantly. "Ian never laid a hand on Jordan. Pride of property," she added angrily. "I suppose I was lucky he preferred the game of verbally abusing me more than hitting. But he threatened. And I was not really sure how far he would go." The memory of Ian with a whisky bottle in his fist and a snarl on his face made her stomach quiver.

After a prolonged pause, Aidan swept aside the specter, his voice tight. "Keep on, Kate. It's not going to get any easier for either one of us."

"I know," she agreed faintly. "Ian was obsessed with a man named Mike. I started overhearing fragments of conversations when Ian was on the phone. He got more and more threatening. At the end of their last conversation, he slammed the phone down, yelling 'you'll get yours!' A day later, he came home with his shirt covered in blood. Smirked at me while he yanked it off. Threw it in a plastic bag. He didn't have a mark on him." The memories rolled through her, bitter and choking.

"And he hummed. So completely out of character. He hummed this tuneless sound, washing up and incredibly pleased with himself. Played with the gun as if it were a woman he was flirting with—twirling it, caressing it while he cleaned."

Kate started to stand, agitated by her own story. Aidan settled her against him, trailed his thumb on her cheek. "Kate. Talk it all out."

"He left the house and never said a word," she continued dismally. "I had to find out what he was doing. Jordan was sleeping, so I called the neighbor girl and asked her to come watch him—and I followed Ian."

"Sounds like a big risk."

She shrugged, distraught. "It was a risk—but there wasn't any other choice, not really. I figured he would go to the place he called 'his secret lair'. You could walk to it almost as fast as drive if you took the shortcut through the woods. Ian never walked anywhere, so he didn't know that. I jogged down the trail and, right on cue, I heard his truck pulling into the clearing up ahead. It's easy to hide when a man's distracted with a job. And he did have a chore."

Kate spat the words out. "I saw him burying a body. Shot more times than could have possibly been necessary to kill him. I didn't have to witness the whole thing to see what was happening. I ran back, got the neighbor home. Then I packed Jordan in the car and drove away."

"To the police, I hope." Aidan could see a young woman telling them this crazy story—hoping they took her seriously.

"Yeah. The cards played in my favor. I knew the lieutenant and his wife from Jordan's school. They sheltered me while they investigated my story about the dead man. When they went to the house, Ian was working up another rage because I was gone.

He was already thick in the sauce. The gun was lying on the ground. They told me Ian dove for it when they arrived, but they outnumbered him and outmaneuvered him. Took him down with a flesh wound."

Kate laid her head on Aidan's shoulder while he simply waited. The tale had to be told. He could neither rush it nor stop it.

She continued, sober and pale. "Of course, Ian would find the best lawyer. That would forever be his tactic. They managed to make it masquerade as an act of passion."

"Naturally," Aidan muttered.

"I foolishly entered the courthouse for the ruling. When Ian was sentenced, he glared straight at me as if there was no one else in the room. His entire attitude was murderous." She shuddered. "No mistaking his intent. 'You're next,' he mouthed at me just before they led him away."

Kate kept talking, wanting to be done with it. "I knew then that I would have only so much time free of Ian, and that one day, he would return to kill me. When I got the opportunity to go to Montana, I leaped at it." Her smile was poignant. "And then I met you."

For several moments, there was nothing more to say. *That meeting changed everything.*

"When I returned home, with my heart all re-arranged, it was all I could do to raise Jordan." She would see this story through. "Painted in the mornings, worked afternoons, and dreamt about you at night."

Aidan held her closely—holding his own memories. *Passionate creation. Holding on. Dreaming.*

The gulls of Staffa rose over them, calling. They listened, glad for the raucous call of life and freedom. "What does Jordan think about all of this?" Aidan asked at length.

Briefly, her smile deepened. "If you met him, you'd assume he was an easy going guy with no real issues. But I believe there is a piece of his spirit he keeps secret." She grew serious. "It's not a happy place for him. I talked to him only once about it. He told me, in the shortest of words, that it had to do with being too afraid to stand up to his father. Never mind that he was too young to do anything. I think he decided he somehow failed me."

Aidan frowned, taking it in. "Didn't Jordan ever ask about Ian after he was taken to jail?"

"No." she continued pensively. "If I brought it up, he would change the subject or walk off. So I stopped. It was as though the man who fathered him had died. Ian didn't write, and we never visited. I don't think Jordan understands the threat to me now. Because we didn't discuss it—there's a lot he doesn't know."

"Is it possible Ian could have changed? Or that he would be too tired of jail to get in trouble again?"

"No," she replied wearily. "He wouldn't change. It's the way he is. He could no more do that than a rabid animal could be nice. But as the years passed, I started to relax. Figured it was safe to get on with my life. It was Brian who warned me not to let my guard down."

"Brian? The ferryman?"

"Yes, the same Brian," she responded with a dry chuckle. "Not the real ferryboat driver. I expect you noticed. Brian Sawyer is one of a kind. He literally travels where he wishes to go, and finds employment for as long as he fancies. His method is to discover who is scheduled for a vacation and to step in for awhile as their substitute. I don't believe there is anything that Brian can't do. The quickest study I've ever met."

"Huh. I was so intent on finding you. I noticed his accent of course, but I didn't even ask. Not that he would have told me."

"You're correct, he wouldn't have told you anything. I went to high school with him. We were kind of sweeties for awhile, but it didn't go any further. I've wondered more than once if maybe he's gay and can't quite tackle it. Relationships don't stick with him. But we've stayed friends, all these years."

"You mentioned him. At Kieran's place."

"Yes. My oldest friend, very nearly my only one. Brian didn't hear much about Ian after I got married," she went on. "He was traveling abroad quite a bit, so we kept in touch only enough for him to hear the main news, especially Jordan's birth. After Ian went to jail, he appointed himself to safeguard me—calling to check in, or popping over whenever he was passing through. He knew how afraid I was of Ian."

Kate scanned the wheeling birds meditatively. "A year ago, Brian arrived at my house and sat me down. Told me he'd worked as a cook for a while in the penitentiary where Ian was. Somehow, he'd gotten Ian talking."

Whatever Ian would say couldn't be anything I would want to hear, Aidan thought angrily.

"Ian started bragging, and making allusions to the woman that 'stuck him in the Pen. How she would learn that he never forgot, and never forgave.' Told Brian she was his wife, didn't matter that the divorce was final after he'd been in for a few months. But in Ian's mind, a wife was property. That would never be erased."

Aidan's fingers tightened. "Almost done," Kate exhaled deeply. "When Brian came to me after that conversation, I'd never seen him so worked up. 'Make no mistake about it, Kate,' he'd said. 'He means to find you and hurt you. Go to the police.'"

Her voice cracked briefly. "But I didn't. There was no real proof. I couldn't involve Brian or my sister Tracy or Jordan. Ian wanted me."

"If other people started crowding the picture..." murmured Aidan. He could see where this was leading.

"Ian would just have them picked off, too, one at a time," she finished. "All looking like 'accidents'."

"Trapped." Aidan felt the burden of the single word.

"That's it. Hard as I try, I can't find any way through it."

Kate fought for the courage to continue. "So," she continued resolutely, "when Jordan came of age at eighteen, he yearned to trek in exciting places more than anything. Off he went, with the idea he would be gone for a couple of years, traveling the world and working as he went. I assured him that I would go traveling too. That way, the fact that we were both out of touch for extended periods seemed natural. I think he figured Ian was locked up permanently."

Aidan pulled the thermos of Lila's hot tea out of his backpack and poured it into two small cups, handing her one. "And, to protect him, and everyone else," he responded bleakly, "you disappeared off the map, leaving Ian nothing to find."

Kate sipped the hot tea, feeling the day begin to cool, as the winds shifted across the water. "Yeah. Brian always knew where I was. I made an agreement with him to tell Tracy I was safe. Made him swear not to involve her. She kind of supposed I was—I don't know. Having a mid-life crisis or some such—the way I ran off, and became so difficult to communicate with. Everything had to go through Brian."

Once again, a paradoxical smile appeared briefly. "She assumed we were having some torrid affair, for sure. In any case, she hasn't tried to find me. When Ian goes to her, as he will when he's released, she will have nothing to tell him. But she will call Brian to say he's on the loose. And when Brian calls me, I will know that my life is forfeit." A sudden chill moved through the air.

Kate continued sadly, wishing she could soothe his stricken expression. "And now, what have I done? I've taken the heart of the man that sustained me for so many years—who has only shown me love and friendship—and I've described my ugliest secrets to him. I've exposed him to danger. And I've guaranteed that he won't be the same again."

She took a long breath to keep her voice from trembling. "I've been selfish, my love. I couldn't help myself in the end. I just wanted you so much."

Aidan gathered her up, enfolding her. "There was no way to say no to me, Kate. I needed you more than my own soul. You've exposed the wounds that never should have been a secret. Thank you. Now it's ours, not only yours. And your life is not to be sacrificed."

He held her face. "Look at me. Can you imagine a life with me in it for real? Not only in your dreams?"

She didn't answer immediately. "I can hardly imagine life at all," she added after several minutes, "until Ian is dead." Fighting to regain her independence, she pushed back from him, enclosed her arms around her knees, and rocked lightly.

"Even if he never got out, Aidan, don't you see? He has the contacts to do it one way or another. I am a dead woman. This is all borrowed time. I can't escape him."

There was an aching silence, broken only by the murmuring of the breeze and Buck's soft whine, announcing his presence. The violence of Ian's menace knifed between them.

"No," said Aidan, standing up abruptly, as if to angle his body between that threatening vision and Kate beside him. "He will not take you away. Not now. Not from this moment with me. And not ever."

He laid her head against his chest. "I don't have all the answers, Kate. But you have faced this thing too many years alone. You don't have to assume that this will go Ian's way. He's stolen enough of your memories."

The brief warmth of midday was fading fast. "We should head home. Let's be done with this story now," he continued, taking her hand. Their minds were once again too busy for much talking. They walked, Buck trotting behind them with attentive energy.

At the dam, Kate stopped. "Go home, beloved—to Lila's. I have work I promised to do for Brian." Her mood had shifted from heavy seas to fair winds. "He was so very relieved when I told him who you were."

"You will come back tonight, Kate." It was more a question than a statement. Aidan willed himself to stand still. *Don't ask again.*

"Yes." There it was. In one small word, the turn of her heart, the reversal of the history that had haunted her.

Facing him, she ruffled his hair with delicate tenderness. "Yes," Kate said again, her tone quiet but clear. She melted into the beech trees. The fast-moving forest stream echoed the sound of the pulse beating in his ears.

Half a world away, Ian Prescott walked out into the streaming harsh light of the New Mexico desert. He held a bundle of personal possessions that the world supposed was all he owned. *Ah, but the world really was so stupid.* So easily taken in. The prison guards had actually wished him good luck as they opened the doors, releasing him.

Ian had made a habit of hiding money and weapons before his arrest. He'd used prison hours to arrange a false identity. It was ready for him. All he had to do was to collect it all. *It was ridiculously easy.*

His stance tightened with purpose, ignoring the heady sense of freedom that rushed at him, impatiently commanding it to disappear. He didn't really care about Jordan. The skinny boy had always belonged to Kate. He would be grown and gone anyway.

There was but one aim for him now—avenge the last twelve years. He'd been held captive like an animal. Years of his life that Kate had squandered. *She will be hunted and killed.* If he could do it and not get caught, even better.

But if he did get caught, it didn't really matter. He would make sure he got the death penalty. It would be worth it. Nothing would thwart him. Not the fear of his own demise—nothing. He pulled up Tracy's number. That would be his first stop.

Chapter 24

Lila's home was filled with savory aromas. She'd spent the afternoon cooking, quietly singing to herself—anticipating Aidan's return. "I hope you had a wonderful walk," she exclaimed, greeting Buck first, addressing the question to both of them. Her animated cheeriness was a stark contrast to the emotionally wrenching afternoon.

"I've just presumed you would be liking the catch of the day. I asked that fellow Brian to do the talking with the fishermen, and he delivered the nicest lobster and mussels. I do hope you enjoy seafood. Buck is very fond of it."

There is really no need for an answer, Aidan realized. A companionable nod was plenty, and Lila went on her merry way, filling in the blanks.

"Such a nice garden this year, so you'll be having my own veggies with it. And then, I thought, being American, you might favor comfort food from home, and I made a kind of casserole with pasta."

This statement amused Aidan, despite the roaring aftermath of Kate's story in his mind. Lila bustled in and out, bringing tea and whisky, talking all the while. Aidan patted Buck's head, feeling tired, assessing the next step.

Kieran had to understand Kate was safe. For now.

Excusing himself to wash up, he released Buck to Lila and retreated to his room, glad he'd told Lila to leave it alone. The four walls pulsated with last night's ardent lovemaking. *Kate has stepped out of my dreams and into my life again*. Full of fear and full of passion. His jaw tightened. He would not desert her again.

"I found her," he said shortly when Kieran answered the phone.

"Ah. . . " Kieran's first response was a prolonged exhalation of relieved thankfulness.

"You were right, Kieran," Aidan continued. "She found another isolated hideout. I would still be scouting in the mountains if you had not given me that clue."

"Thank the Lord. I knew you would not rest until you had her in sight." Unexpectedly, Kieran sounded edgy. "I have news for her, Aidan. Regrettable news. Her son called here yesterday, trying to find her. Frankly, he sounded worrisome. Weak. Clearly an effort to talk. He's returning to Shannon, Ireland. As I recall, that's where he started his journey to Africa."

A pause—for Kieran, a weighty pause—hung heavily on the phone line. "The boy said he had a tropical fever. That he'd be checking into a hospital. Said he'd wanted to see his mom. I believe he's sicker than he let on. You know young men."

His brows knit, Aidan pondered this new development. It gave them no time to think, only to act quickly to help Jordan. This meant that Kate would have to come out of hiding. Already, his mind was racing with plans, but Kieran had to be told a fragment of what they were facing.

"I'll tell her, Kieran. Listen, the threat of Ian is very real. I see that now. He might even follow her track to you. Keep what you know to yourself. In the meantime, we'll leave in the morning for Ireland."

After they hung up, Kieran remembered how natural and lovely Kate looked as she crossed the threshold of his oak door at The Big Misty. How he'd timed her arrival and been there, visible and comforting. It seemed long ago, and he missed it deeply. Well, she was with Aidan—and that union was good and real. It kept his faith in love.

Aidan deliberated, his head bowed, for several long minutes. *We have to leave first thing, that's the only step I can forecast.* Lila called him for dinner. Pulling out his phone, asking her to give him a few more minutes, he swiftly made the arrangements. Tomorrow, they would take an early afternoon flight to Shannon, Ireland.

Dinner was punctuated with Lila's good-humored chitchat. Posing questions to the world in general, she would continue the conversation by answering them herself. She took no offense to Aidan's distracted demeanor, and in doing so, allowed him the space to try to hold his heart together.

The food was indeed excellent, and he surprised himself by finishing it all. But he had no will to ponder companionably with Lila. Giving her the unwelcome news that he would be leaving the next morning, he excused himself, giving Buck one last ruffle on the head.

There was nothing to be done but wait for Kate. He stared into the coal fire, his spirit silent and full. It was a solid hour before he heard her nearly silent knock and stood to greet her. Not waiting for an answer, she stepped inside. Once again, he pulled off her sweater and coat and held her tight, kissing her with more tenderness than passion.

Suppressing a sigh, he circled an arm around her and sat

her down next to the fire. Kate tensed, suddenly anticipating bad news. Aidan entwined their fingers. "It's Jordan. He's sick and coming into Ireland today from Africa."

Her stomach flip-flopped as the ground beneath her spun away. "How do you know this?" she managed.

"Jordan called Kieran trying to find you. I called Kieran because he's been worried to death over you."

Sadness layered over anxiousness as she nodded. "I'm glad you called. We left each other harshly," she acquiesced. "Did Kieran say . . . Did he know how bad it was?"

His face was troubled. "Quite, I'd say. Kieran was uneasy about him. A tropical fever is what Jordan called it. That's all I know, except . . . " Kate braced for whatever he had to say. Aidan pushed a handwritten note at her. "These are the numbers of our flight out to Shannon tomorrow."

Conflicting emotions warred as she reflected on these new developments. All her grown life she had confronted obstacles alone. That she would go to Jordan immediately was never in doubt. Aidan's economic script gave the number of two seats on the flight. He meant to be with her.

"Thank you," she said, her voice faltering, saying more than her words.

"What do you have to do to get ready?" he asked, gently feeling his way.

"I have to tell Brian and gather up my things. That won't take long. And I need to lay myself beside you for awhile." He nodded, reassured, a small smile edging the corners of his mouth.

There were so many obstacles they would have to confront. A threat of menace that would hang over every minute, the shivering possibility of heartache threaded through the future. But tonight, they were bounded by the Atlantic waters on a small island off the coast of Scotland.

There was no way to leave earlier—to hurry toward

whatever fate had in store for them. This night was theirs. All the rest was nameless, belonging to another reality—that started tomorrow.

"Leave then. But return to me soon and don't knock. Just come in. I'll be waiting for you." Rising without a word, she kissed the nape of his neck and stepped out.

Sleep had visited and left him with a nearly unbearable longing for her when she returned. Slipping into the bed, the cool of the night trailing her bare flesh, she gladly received the heat of his aroused body pressed against her.

At first light, she was gone again, with a promise to meet him at the Ulva ferry, leaving him once again lying in the print of their lovemaking. Now, the fortunes had to be told, and he had no idea how they ended.

Lila was not her usual talkative self as she sat with him during breakfast. "I wish you'd stay on longer, Aidan MacLaine. I have loads more recipes to try out." She struggled for words, adding, "and Buck will miss you." Finding the teapot suddenly in need of attention, she fussed over it, her face to the wall.

Aidan spoke quietly over her clatter of dishes. "Well, I am glad to have met you both, and I will miss Buck. But I will miss you more, Lila." Her head bowed and her shoulders rose as if to ward off his affection.

"I'll return, if I can. I would be grateful for the chance to walk the roads of Ulva once more. And I would be keen on sampling your fine cooking again, Lila. Maybe I won't be alone next visit. Will that be okay?"

She turned, then, as he knew she would, melancholy burned away by the brightness of her curiosity, her cheeks rosy and warm. "You are not going to say more than that, are you?"

"No," he smiled. "But it's a wish I hold." He hugged her, kissed her on both cheeks. "You get someone to take you out to those favorite places, Lila. They are worth seeing. At any age."

Bending down, he held Buck's head. "You've been a fine friend. Thanks for listening with me."

Hoisting his pack over his shoulder, he waved goodbye to Lila and Buck. He would never forget their house or the loving it sheltered.

At the Ulva ferryboat, Brian checked out Aidan intently as Kate introduced them. "I don't believe you've properly met. This is my oldest and truest friend, Brian Sawyer. And this is Aidan . . . "

"MacLaine." Brian finished for her. "I remember the name, of course, since I carried it to you. And how you responded was pretty damn clear," he added neutrally, nodding at Aidan.

The morning was young when they crossed the channel— sea air heavy with the salt tang of kelp. At the landing, Brian pulled Kate aside, giving her a series of muttered directions and admonitions, which ended in a strong embrace. Holding her arm, he stepped aside and shifted his deliberation to Aidan.

Their stares collided against each other, clashing like drawn swords. After several minutes Brian slowly released her, surrendering to Aidan's unmistakable commitment, doubt giving over to resignation.

"Take care of her, MacLaine." With a lithe leap he was in the boat and, pulling the engine to life, swung out in a wide curve and saluted them before he sped off.

Aidan and Kate walked up the rise above the dock, gazing back on the Isle of Ulva. A place that would forever remain blessed in their memory. Then, resolutely, they followed the single-track road across Mull and boarded the big ferry half-full of chatting locals off to the mainland for shopping and business.

They drove away from Oban, out in the world together— in the open. Everyone could see them now, including Ian. Their words were gentle and sparse, haunted by Jordan's unknown condition, watching the Scottish countryside slide by in the low, slanting light of November.

Chapter 25

The transition from Glasgow to Shannon Airport was rapid, the plane crammed tight with businessmen and women in black suits with the insouciant attitude of frequent travelers. With silence more intimate than conversation, Aidan watched Kate study Ireland's patchwork of astonishing shades of green as she steeled herself for what lay ahead.

They drove out of Shannon in a small car identical to the one they'd rented in Glasgow and distinctly different from the vehicles they knew in the United States. Aidan had become very adept at left-sided driving. "I think my brain is naturally wired like this," he remarked, maneuvering with ease through the hectic roundabouts of Limerick.

After all their traveling, a meal was mandatory. "We'll make it quick," he promised. They could do with the energy for the next difficult steps. Over toast and tea, they collected the names of the hospitals in Limerick. It took only two phone calls to locate Jordan.

"Hi, Mom." Reedy and labored, Jordan's voice was hard to hear over the phone line. "I knew you'd find me."

"I'm on my way, sweetheart. I'll be right there."

There was no point in trying to urge her to eat any more. Aidan gathered directions as they walked briskly into the Irish rain, moving with the instinctive urgency of a parent who is racing toward an injured child. They sped through the Limerick traffic, grateful the morning rush hour had subsided.

He dropped Kate off at the entrance of the hospital, reaching over to squeeze her hand. "I'll come up in a half hour. Give you some privacy."

On Ulva, where the infinite spaciousness was all around, and as far from Limerick as a world could be, Brian's cell phone rang. Only a few people knew his number, and no one called him merely to pass the day. A cold fist of dread balled up in his gut as he answered.

It was Tracy. "Ian is out," she said tersely. "He came to me, looking for Kate. Acted as nice as one could imagine, but I can see it. He means to hurt her."

Or more, thought Brian harshly.

"Thank god you never told me where she was," she continued. "Only now do I appreciate how important that was. He would have found a means to force it out of me." Her voice shook. "I have a mind to call his parole officer."

"Not sure what good that does, since Ian has done nothing but talk to you. I think any move could be dangerous." Brian weighed each word, his mind scrambling. "I don't know what he will do, Tracy, I wouldn't put it past the bastard to try and hurt you, or your family, in addition to Kate. I'll make an anonymous call to the parole officer. Even then he might . . . " With deliberate calm, he continued, trying to let her understand what she was risking.

"Ian could retaliate at you."

"You make the call, I'll take that chance." Tracy answered fiercely. "We have to try and help her."

When Brian hung up the phone, he pondered the appeal of rippling water and island scenery abruptly marred by Ian's dark shadow. A sudden dismal headache pounding, he wondered when he should call Kate. They would be just arriving. *Not yet,* he thought. Give her a few hours first with her son.

Aidan walked slowly through the hospital, sharply reminded of his own borrowed hours and Will's sternly given deadline. Threading his way through the twin smells of illness and an antiseptic army in battle, he found Jordan's room.

There was something fearful festering in Jordan's body. The boy's flushed face was very like Kate's, with the same high cheekbones and striking looks. His dark blue eyes were hers—the color of early evening, with hints of encroaching night. But at this moment, they were glassy and vague.

Drawn and tight with concern, Kate was talking to the nurse. Aidan walked over to Jordan, who stirred weakly and registered some surprise. The man standing before him with an air of grave inspection apparently knew his mother.

"This is Aidan, a friend of mine," Kate stated directly to both Jordan and the nurse who had quizzically started at Aidan's entrance.

The nurse was a petite, young woman, with features as Irish as one could imagine—copper tresses tucked into a bun, skin like cream. After a quick appraisal of Aidan, she relaxed, satisfied, glad this young lad had his people here and flashed an easy smile in their direction as she adjusted the settings on Jordan's IV. "You'll be wanting the doctors. I'll fetch them."

A ponderous exhaustion gripped Jordan. He'd originally felt the fever and cramps hit his body over a month ago, but he'd fought, trying to wait it out. He'd found the job in the Rwandan bush after weeks of travel on his own, often in contaminated conditions that he'd tried, but usually failed, to avoid. If he'd wanted water, he had to take what was available. *It was the water*, he knew it.

In the last week, no longer willing to contain his concern, the foreman of his camp forcibly took action. Ignoring Jordan's protests, he drove the boy to the airport, taking the five-hour journey without hesitation.

Jordan had a bent-eared piece of paper his mother had given him, in case of emergency. He assured his boss as he departed Africa that, since his ticket went through Ireland, he would check in with a doctor there. And his mom was somewhere in Scotland or Ireland, though he couldn't remember which. With the faith of the young in the allegiance of mothers, he knew she would find him.

Oddly, she'd arrived with a man, and in the burning recesses of Jordan's mind, it occurred to him that he had not seen her with anyone, other than his cruel father. For his mother to have friends in her life had to be a good thing.

Aidan watched Jordan's silent surge of approval break the surface, like a fish rising in a calm lake, unbidden and irresistible. He responded with a nod and a slight smile.

The doctor who bustled in and greeted Kate was a short man, with a ruthless buzz cut and a permanently furrowed brow. He acknowledged Aidan briefly, dismissively.

"I'm glad you're here," he spoke directly to Kate. It was a Cambridge accent—sharply articulated—crisply delivered. "He has a great deal more to go through."

He pulled off a bandage, checked the IV, talking as he worked. "I have a specialist in tropical medicine working on this case. At this point, we know more about what it isn't than what it is. Unquestionably, his fever has to break, and I can't predict how bad it will get before that happens." Under his breath, he added, "it's one of those obscure, and often deadly, infections that kill Africans everyday."

Aidan glanced at Kate as she received this news. Saying nothing she waited, arms crossed, holding herself together.

"We don't have to precisely diagnose it," the doctor continued. He'd long ago learned to place a barrier between himself and his patients and, more so, the anxious relatives. Speaking in a neutral tone, he concentrated only on the facts. "What's important is that he works through the peak of the fever with enough strength to recover. After it runs the worst through him, you'll have to decide whether to stay here or leave."

He turned, giving Kate time to absorb his words, writing notes on his clipboard. "Whatever you need," Aidan said softly to Kate, while Jordan studied them over the doctor's ministrations.

"Thank you," she whispered. "I wish to stay here with Jordan," she stated out loud.

"Perfectly understandable," responded the doctor. He didn't look up from his work. "I'll have a cot brought in. Mostly now, we are keeping him hydrated and waiting. I'll have the tropical meds doctor talk to you shortly." He vanished into the hospital maze.

Aidan resumed his place next to Jordan's bedside. The boy was still cognizant, but he was starting to wander into the realm of disjointed reality. Any introduction had to be quick and to the point.

"I'm a friend of your mother's. We first met in Montana eleven years ago. You would have been about six. Do you remember when she went there?"

Jordan mouthed 'yes' without making a sound.

Kate stood silently, as the two people she cared about most in the world met each other.

"We met each other again in Scotland—at Kieran's, the place you called. We've been getting . . . " Aidan hazarded a reassuring smile. "Reacquainted."

"Nice," Jordan mumbled, his mind starting to wander.

He had never really noticed his mother as a woman. *She's kind of beautiful*, he thought. *And not so old as all that.* The arm beside him looked foreign and unnaturally white, sprouting a string of tubes. *Was that his blood, his vein?*

Images of Rwanda tumbled through his head. The clarity of the light and the odd sounds that kept him up at night. A wave of nausea swept over him. The world was beginning a slow, steady spin, forcing him to withdraw.

"We'd best let him rest, Kate. I simply thought he should be aware of who this stranger is." He gave her a gentle hug. "Do you want me stay?" he asked, hesitantly.

"No. I'll stay here. If you would—maybe find a hotel nearby—for yourself—for awhile?"

"Of course. I'll call you when I find a place."

"Thank you." She feathered a brief kiss across his lips. He gathered her in for a moment, then released her to the vigil he knew she would keep.

After Aidan left, she had nothing to do but to witness her son's fleeting lucidity vanish behind a veil of fevered hallucinations and unfathomable descents into unconsciousness. When the first doctor reappeared, Kate was almost startled to see him, trying to recall if he had ever introduced himself.

He was followed by a different nurse, as dark as the other had been fair, with a bead stud in her nose and the expertly applied kohl eyeliner that identified her as East Indian. Neither of them did more than respond to Kate curtly before they began monitoring signs and recording responses. The doctor who followed after them had to be the tropical medicine specialist.

"Call me Johannes," he said in a friendly tone. "I don't have a big use for professional labels. Too much distance between patient and physician." His gaze coolly wandered in the other doctor's direction. "Does she have your name as well, Robert?" His inflection was difficult to discern, but it was not the rolling swirl of the Irish tongue.

"Dr. Robert Salisbury." Robert's brusque reply carried no such invitation or familiarity. Johannes shrugged at Kate as one who must work with a recalcitrant teen.

"Too many years in the military," he spoke so that only Kate could hear. "Do you wish an introduction—to me, at least?" Kate nodded numbly. "Okay, dear. Yes, I think it makes it easier if you know who you are dealing with."

"I grew up in Rhodesia." He sighed, recalling a country he had dearly loved. "It's rather vanished these days. I haven't been there in ages. In fact, I probably won't go back."

Sadness spilled out of his simple phrases. "I took up the study of tropical medicine with the idea that I might return. But life happens, doesn't it? Willy-nilly, with a mind of its own. A wife and two sons later, I am still here and my country is gone. I have been specializing in tropical medicine for ten years. Right here in Limerick."

Johannes Stein was slender, with a shock of prematurely graying hair, and a slightly bent stance. He inclined toward his patients as though they had a magnetic attraction. Over time, his body had adopted the sloping posture as the natural fashion of the world.

"So now, Kate, your young son is seriously ill—make no mistake. I have been tracking him since he was admitted. He has a ways to go, and we cannot say with clarity what the outcome will be." His tone was gentle.

Robert cut in. "We should have results in the next thirty-six hours, though, eh, Stein?"

Kate was starting to recognize that Robert's spare style was trustworthy, if a bit insensitive.

"Yes, I'd say that is the critical period," replied Johannes. "If he makes it through that, he should be home free." Kate felt rooted to the spot. She could not hurry the motion of time any more than she could fashion a positive prognosis out of wanting it to be so.

"Can we do anything for you, dear?" Johannes queried. "I'm afraid we all must watch over him now. There's nothing for it."

Resignation forced her to sit down. She had never been particularly adept at waiting. And it was all that was being asked of her. "No. I don't need anything. I'll just be here, trying not to be in the way."

"We'll remain close," Johannes said as the doctors departed with no further conversation. A profound silence descended, broken only by the clock's loud ticking. *Perhaps it wasn't even so loud*, Kate thought wearily. It was only a sharp reminder of the finite number of minutes passing—with no clear deadline signaling the last breath.

Aidan's phone call was the first sound that broke the quiet. "Are you okay?" he asked. "I'm just a few blocks from the hospital."

Kate told him what she learned from the doctors. "Come tomorrow, Aidan. You might as well rest."

His impulse was to go to her. But the hours in front of Kate were hers to live through. He could do nothing to relieve it.

"Call me, Kate. If there is any development. Any need."

The night passed, punctuated by the cycling of the medical staff, Jordan's labored breathing, and his occasional groans. Kate gazed at his face, flooded by memories, stunned by his pallor. Jordan's dreams disturbed the room. At times it seemed the scent of the Bilbao tree filled the air and a red dust settled over everything in it.

What has he been through, this son of mine? Suddenly, it was as if she hardly knew him. *What had it been like growing up with me?* She had always presumed them close, but here she wondered what flash-flood nightmares ran through the canyons of his mind.

She stroked his forehead and talked to him when he was awake. Jordan lay quietly for several minutes at a time, seeming to listen to her familiar, musical voice. He'd forever loved to hear a story.

Kate told him tales of his own childhood, things he'd perhaps forgotten in the rush of growing up. She remembered the fragments of the little songs he would make up—the funny sayings he'd created. When he slipped again into the current of oblivion, she waited, her hand always on him, in case he craved the sustenance of touch.

Dozing on and off, ignoring the cot they brought in for her—choosing to sit by Jordan's bed, she was startled awake by the one sound she dreaded the most. Her cell phone was buzzing. Only two people had her number, Brian and Aidan. She realized it was Brian before she answered—understood his message would be short and urgent. Ian was out.

Chapter 26

Ian's dealings in the underbelly of the world were accomplished. If one did not have friends, he could buy a close enough approximation. A business associate was enormously more useful, anyway, and far less trouble. Money was the only reciprocation required, and with that, he demanded privacy about his business.

Greenbacks he had in abundance, having recovered his stashes from various places—untraceable cash in watertight containers. *And only my mind holds the map to find it.*

Ian had mastered another fine art before he quit prison. He knew if someone was lying before they spoke. They gave themselves away with tiny gestures, signals they didn't understand or see themselves. *Learning from them was easy, if you worked at it. Learned to hide your own giveaways.*

Apparently, that was a feat beyond nearly everyone. Like

turning a dial on a radio, Ian could fine-tune his own actions to the situation—mimic the correct motions and tone for sincerity. One would swear he was telling the truth.

The minute he saw Tracy he realized that Kate's location was hidden from her. *Of course she would lie to protect her sister. She knows something.* He just had to pay attention.

He'd scarcely left her driveway when he made the calls, directing his men into action. "Watch her movements. Listen to her phone." He could wait. Ian filled his entire being with the smoldering patience he had learned within the four walls of a small cell.

After she hung up the phone with Brian, Kate breathed slowly into the sterilized atmosphere of the hospital. The fear that had been building pulsed out, like smoke on a windless day, drifting in place, filling her mouth with its choking taste. *Ian will find me.* There was no doubt. There had never been any doubt.

He would not hurt Jordan, of that she was certain—if only for the vanity of having a son. And she would not leave until Jordan was well. That reality was written into the heart of mothers.

A single desolate concept grabbed a hold of her soul. *My life is the penalty for putting Ian in jail.* Aidan had almost persuaded her that they could, together, claim a different destiny. But to do that would only expose her beloved as well to Ian's murderous hatred.

Kate moistened Jordan's dry lips, listening to his fever-fed delirium. Quietly, in the Limerick hospital, she reviewed what she knew. Her independent son unexpectedly needed her. Ian's merciless stalking had begun. And the love of her life lay sleeping in a hotel. There was nowhere to go.

She could try to keep Aidan from meeting the same fate. The only right choice was for him to return to his own full life with Sheila and the gallery, his poetry and music. Grief would eventually move toward healing. He would not forget her, but he would live.

He would live, she repeated to herself. And Ian would melt into the gray world he inhabited—satisfied that he was avenged.

The phone rang again. "How's it going?" Aidan's question was gentle.

Kate gripped the arms of the chair, bidding her tone to be cold. "The fever is still building. Really, we are okay here. The doctors have us well in hand." *I can't falter*, she thought desperately. She had to say something to hurt him.

"I think you should head home for awhile, Aidan. There's nothing you can do. I'm just confused with you here. I need my own space now, alone, with my son." She swallowed the raw ache in her throat, ignoring the betrayal roaring in her mind.

Aidan leaned his forehead against the phone, letting her words fall and clatter to the floor. "I don't believe you," he said with no resentment. "If you really want me to, I'll wait here. But I know what day it is too, and I recognize what you are trying to escape from. I won't leave you to undertake it alone. What I feel for you isn't something that can be turned off," he added softly. "Ian will not be allowed to destroy that."

Jordan moaned loudly enough for Aidan to hear. "Stay with him, of course you must. Focus on his welfare, mo gradh. I'm only a call away." He cradled the phone into the receiver without waiting for a response, the weight of love heavy in his heart.

Kate was not surprised when her flimsy resistance crashed around her. All she could do now was focus on Jordan, offering all the support she could. Ian's unseen presence lay in wait. But Aidan wasn't going to allow her to pull away. Grateful, scared, filled with love, she did the one thing she had the power to do—be with her son.

Aidan's phone rang. *Damn it*, he thought, when he heard Brian's voice.

"Did she tell you?" Brian continued, not pausing for

answer. "Of course she didn't. I know how she works. Ian has made his contact with Tracy. He's on the hunt for Kate."

The blunt words hung in the silence. Aidan struggled to open his tight chest as Brian continued relentlessly. "I've called his parole officer. Told him something might be up. He's hasn't been able to contact Ian. Appears Ian's evaporated, into the world as another person, we both suspect. Anyway, they are trying to find him. He will have to be very, very accomplished to move out of the country. Of course," Brian added, with brooding finality, "he is that."

Ian Prescott had indeed disappeared. He walked into his new identity with the confidence of someone unaccustomed to failure. John Hake exited where Ian had entered, his sharp features softened, the poker-straight hair curled at the edges and thinning on top. He had added the last feature painstakingly, calmly pulling out the crown of his scalp without flinching. The color was added after that, a mousy forgettable tan.

He plucked his eyebrows, lifting them in the middle to give him milder features. Contacts changed cold blue to diluted tan. Coke-bottle glasses obscured the power of his stare.

His face underwent the knife for a few extras. 'Not too much,' he'd warned the doctor. It was the opposite of the normal request, adding flesh rather than taking it away, mitigating the angles.

The surgeon was skilled, and well paid. His patient walked out wearing bandages, and the doctor saw to his healing after-hours. After several days, though his skin was red and tender, John Hake was in business.

Following Brian's call, Aidan felt the walls squeeze in closer. Ian would come without notice. Aidan's jaw tensed. Abruptly, he recognized the inevitability of this treacherous hunt—in the same way that Kate had for years. The sound of his own breathing filled the room, as he probed for his own fear. It was there, but it was weaker than what he felt for Kate. Love that poured from his soul like sunlight.

In the hospital, Jordan's condition began to deteriorate. Johannes and Robert revolved around him in turn, monitoring his status and amending life-giving fluids carried by tubes into the boy. Robert told Kate, in no uncertain terms, to keep from interfering with the staff and their ministrations. No matter what was happening.

"Your good intentions and mother's love will frankly impede our ability to give him the best care." His tone was stern. "It won't be easy to witness your son suffering through this."

He ignored Johannes when he entered. "And we may lose him. Temporarily we hope, but no assurances. If you think you can watch that and stay here, you may, I suppose. But it will test you."

Johannes stepped between them. "That's enough warning, Robert."

The older doctor fixed him with a hard look. "Is it, Johannes? I want the boy to receive the best-unfettered treatment. That's my main concern. I've had family members too often swear they'll be able to control themselves. But in the end, when things get dicey, they can't. And then, you have two patients."

"I know, Robert," Johannes began.

"I want you to have one priority, Dr. Salisbury," Kate interrupted tersely. "I appreciate you reminding me to stay invisible and I will." Robert and Kate scowled at each other, both of them fierce in their own role and not willing to give the other quarter.

"Thank you, Robert." Johannes said. It was a declaration, terminating the conversation.

Robert turned sharply and began to walk out. At the doorway, he stopped briefly. "You have my permission to stay. If you can honor what you said." He stalked out peremptorily.

"You have now received a first-rate level of approval from Dr. Robert Salisbury, Kate. That's the best it ever gets. He's such an excellent doctor that we all overlook his lack of bedside manners. He is very concerned about Jordan, as am I. We can't afford to have anything between him and us. Especially if it becomes critical."

"You don't have to soften him or the message, Johannes," Kate replied tersely. She went to Jordan's bed and kissed his forehead. "Honey, I'll be right here. I will be here. The doctors need to be able to help you and I cannot be in their way. Hold on, sweetheart. Fight for your life, and your future. I love you so much."

Eyes glittering with unshed tears, she stepped into the corner and sat down. "Now you, too, fight for him. Don't worry about me."

Johannes nodded. The battle had begun. His mother's teachings always arose in him in these situations. He could feel her presence, as well as the Angel of Death she would tell him was with them—watching in case he was required to guide the spirit to God. Certainly Johannes did not believe such things, but an unbidden tremor ran the length of his spine.

The hours passed like slow-moving clouds across an endless sky. Jordan went from hallucinations to seizures. They racked him without mercy, arching him backward in paroxysms of pain. He would come away from them gasping as a nearly drowned man, the breath whistling in his throat. Dry heaves cracked through him with the force of earthquakes. Johannes and Robert worked shoulder to shoulder intently, with their backs to Kate.

The sickness clattered through the room, a wild African animal, its hooves running across Jordan's chest. As if in response, Jordan began to bleed from his nose and coughed blood up from his lungs. Red stains seeped from unhealed wounds on his skin.

With her control weakening, Kate slipped out without making a sound. Once outside his room, she leaned against the cool wall, seeking its firm support as she fought to maintain balance.

"Kate?" Aidan rose from the seat where he had spent the last several hours.

"I can't tell if he's dying or not." Her voice cracked. Approaching slowly, Aidan laid a hand on her shoulder, steered her into a quiet area and sat her down. Sobs flooded through her like spring-swollen rivers. Aidan made shushing sounds and held onto her—trying to keep her from sinking beneath the load of her grief and worry.

Slowly, Kate pulled the edges of her frayed nerves together. The open weeping gave way to a fear bigger than Ian—the possibility that Jordan might die. "I thought I could be in there. That somehow my presence would help him. But he can't hear me. He's all alone with this thing that's trying to strangle him."

Aidan kept his arms locked around her. He could only offer his deep listening and his own substance for harbor. There was no point in making false statements of hope or even of understanding. Kate was as alone as Jordan, fighting a shadow she could not see or touch, with no weapon. Finally he spoke. "I want to bring you some water, at the least, or coffee. And some food, if you'll have it."

She slowly sat up. His love and concern washed over her, cleansing the air. "No food. Some water would be good."

He brought her a drink and sat as she drank it. Opening a sandwich, he offered it to her. "For fuel, Kate, just for fuel."

Her hands shaking, she dutifully chewed and swallowed, though she had no taste for it. After eating half, she wrapped it up and returned to Aidan. "That's all I can do. Thanks."

In halting sentences, she told him what was happening. Aidan asked a few questions, more to distract her than anything else.

Finally, she surrendered to the next step. Whatever it was. "I think I'll go in again. I hate being there, but I can't to be away from him either."

"I'll be here."

She stroked his cheek. "Thank you." He helped her stand and steady herself and stood aside as she re-entered Jordan's room. It was strangely hushed. Kate wondered briefly if it was the silence of death. But Johannes and Robert worked over him, and she heard the low swishing sounds of Jordan's breath, assisted by a tube that ran into his throat.

"He finally quit retching, so we could help him with the breathing." It was Robert who addressed her, without transferring his attention from his work.

Johannes patted her shoulder. His eyes were tired but she read in them a guarded optimism. "Not a scene a parent wants to experience, was it?" She shook her head. "I believe he's gone through the worst of it. He's in some danger yet, but he's pulled back from the brink."

Kate felt faint, taking in this news. Johannes gave her a brief hug. It was as if the dawn lit in the threatening darkness.

When Robert turned toward her, she knew that there was indeed real hope. He wore a warrior's look—one who had just triumphed in battle. Kate stepped tentatively forward, recognizing she'd received a tacit sanction to do so. The doctors moved aside and there was her son, residual tremors sporadically rolling through his body.

His blood made small scarlet flowers against the white sheets. Jordan's features were not peaceful. Mirages of Rwanda still shimmered through his mind. But they were softening. Kate could feel the winging home of his spirit. She touched his arm. Startled from his delirium, Jordan responded with a brief gesture.

"Return to us, sweetheart," she murmured. "Come back." She sat, holding Jordan's hand.

"Would you mind," she requested, not taking her focus off her son, "telling Aidan? Ask him to come in. He's in the waiting area."

In Oregon, Ian's men reported that Tracy had called a phone owned by a Brian Sawyer. Ian recognized the name, his jaw tightening. *Sawyer. It was that fellow who'd subbed in as a cook.* He'd had a master's touch about him, a technique of opening up conversation and making the speaker think they could freely talk. Unusual sort. *Seem to remember I told him about Kate. But then, it turns out,* Ian's eyes flashed with anger, *the cheat already knew about Kate.*

Of course he'd done a bit of spying on his own, catching a quick minute to shuffle through Brian's mail. There had been one that struck him as odd. It bore a Scottish stamp. The return address was the Isle of Ulva. That's where the hunt would begin. Simple as that. Locate the bastard. Find out why Tracy would have called him.

When Jordan regained consciousness, a long night later, Aidan and Kate were both beside his bed. The tube had been removed from his throat. In whispers and songs, Kate reassured him as he swam toward them—from the storm of his sickness to the solid shore of reality. He recognized his mother immediately. It took him more time to trace the outline of Aidan standing next to her.

Even before he was aware of really thinking, he knew he'd almost died. *Feels like a miracle to be opening my eyes and breathing.*

"Thirsty." His tone was gravelly, barely audible. Kate gave him some water from a bent straw. When he finished, he lay back and felt the rebirth of his life—searching for and finding the one small word that summed up everything he felt at that moment. "Thanks."

Chapter 27

Ian arrived on the shores of Mull as John Hake. He'd breezed unceremoniously through the passport and security checks leaving the States and arriving in Scotland. Two men met him at the ferry landing. They had the tools he sought—the weapons and listening devices. What they didn't have, they could acquire within 24 hours, and anything else he needed. Ian set up shop in the hotel, on the island, but no further than the ferry landing.

This part he would do by remote control, thanks to the Pen for enhancing his skills. He would send out the master thief, Joseph. The short reedy man came well recommended to him. At the first meeting, their hard eyes locked, testing.

Joseph met Ian's studied focus with a small smirk. *So his evaluation is in progress.* He didn't really care what the conclusion was. *Let my work speak for me.* Nothing was secure from Joseph's gifted hands. The owner never had a clue.

After a very short interview, Ian knew he had the right crook. Joseph worked with a partner, but Ian demanded to speak to them separately, conducting a comprehensive interview with each of them.

The second one, Nick, had an impenetrable gaze that betrayed nothing. His motions were economical and neutral. *Another accomplished criminal,* Ian thought with satisfaction. The man was impossible to read. A perfect liar. And perfect for this job.

The plan was easy enough, given perfect timing, a detail they took care with. Joseph and Nick silently examined the character who introduced himself as John Hake while they talked. Strangely, the man leaked.

It was as if the hard core that had been Ian was melting into something new. Dangerous for sure, but not quite sane. It was reckless. Without speaking or looking at each other they understood this. Named their highest price for the job and got it. Knew they would be glad to leave him to take the next step on his own.

Joseph landed a plastic kayak beyond the sheltered waters of the narrow passage between Mull and Ulva. He stashed the boat upside down on an isolated beach and walked the stony roads of Ulva nonchalantly, dressed in the high-tech gear of an avid tourist, complete with binoculars.

Best to approach in this mode—they'd decided, in the open daylight—while the ferryman attended his duties. Arriving at the overlook above the ferry landing, having encountered no one, Joseph slipped into a small blind designed for birders, leaned his bright raincoat against the outside wall and waited.

Late that afternoon, Nick opened the sliding window at the Ulva ferry landing—exposed the red square and waited for the ferry driver to respond. Edgy prickling crawled along Brian's neck as he scanned the bland countenance of his latest passenger.

Nick let the smallest flicker of his awareness confirm that Joseph was indeed in position and ready. "How's the lobster from these waters?" he greeted Brian in a refined Gloucester inflection, without moving from the pier.

"Lobster's great. Are you coming aboard to Ulva?" Brian's American accent confirmed he was the person John Hake wanted.

Nick's expression remained featureless. "I do fancy one to take to the proprietress of the house. A Mrs. Lila MacDougal." He remained rooted.

"Come aboard and I will arrange it from this side," replied Brian impatiently.

"Oh, I would so love to meet the fisherman himself. Would it not be possible to stay here until the boats return? They should be due any minute."

That was true, as Nick's research had already indicated. *No reason to feel so suspicious. Still.* There was some foul rankness—and Brian didn't like the smell of it. He considered the new visitor, but could find nothing to confirm his misgiving.

Brian had laid his pack on the shore, in the ferryman's booth. He preferred not to be apart from it. But Ulva was a sleepy place this season. And Lila would be delighted to have a lobster. Surely it was safe.

Nick's transaction was made as the afternoon was rapidly being converted into a dark moonless nightfall. The boat made the one-minute crossing—a fresh lobster, its claws bound by a rubber band, on the floor between them. At the Ulva landing, Nick thanked Brian and told him he would be leaving in the morning. "Just a short vacation this time." His voice was mellifluous.

As Nick strolled toward Lila's house, Brian could not help

but anxiously ruffle through his pack. It was all there, including his cell phone. *Exactly as I left it.* He could not justify the bad feeling inside him, the lingering trace of something unclean in the air.

Joseph arrived in Ian's hotel room minutes before the downpour finally broke loose. He gave Ian three numbers. Two were saved—a MacLaine and Kate.

There was also a recent call to a Limerick hospital. The man who called himself John Hake sneered with approval. Muttered to himself in the mirror about "having the tools for the next step. The best one of all. The one he'd been waiting for." Joseph backed out, paid and eager to get away.

In Limerick, innocent of his father's preparations for murder, Jordan steadily recovered. Aidan was surprised at how fast his humor returned, in company with his improving strength. Self deprecating and honest, he told them stories of his months, good and bad, in Rwanda. Aidan and Kate allowed themselves to be seduced by his healing, the shock of nearly losing him still fresh.

After the third day of his recovery, at the insistence of both doctors and Jordan himself, Kate gave up her post at the hospital and allowed herself the luxury of returning to the hotel with Aidan.

As they drove, Kate touched Aidan's knee, trying to block the recurrent dread. A heavy weight tightened her diaphragm, bruising her soul. *It's the prescience of evil. I don't know what to think, even less what to do.*

They used room service—not ready to leave their sanctuary. Now that Jordan was recuperating, they had another pressing problem to deal with. *Perhaps two,* Aidan thought. Right on time, the numbness was starting to return.

He had called Sheila's home from a phone booth when he knew she would be at work, carefully worded a message, telling her only that he was okay and would be home soon. She would be frantic with concern over the overdue deadline Will had given him—one that had expired yesterday. He hated to upset her, but there was no way to hurry the things that had yet to pass. They needed total concentration for a bit longer.

Aidan guided the dinner toward celebration, keeping it clear of worry and fear. Toasting Jordan's prospects, he emphasized that Kate was part of her son's future. She was quiet, her heart full of unanswered questions but grateful for Jordan's healing and for Aidan's love.

After they cleared the dishes, Aidan went to the far side of the room, returning with a small box. Kate was abruptly aware of the hesitation in his step—as though he had to summon an inner strength before walking.

He dropped the box in front of her. She knew what it was before she unwrapped the covering. Still, it was a jolt to see the shiny pistol gleaming coldly in front of her.

"In case you need it." Aidan's eyes met hers. Ian would be closing in on them. His hot breath was at their backs. They could not escape it—they both understood that at last. The only solution was to be ready for his arrival.

"I have no idea how to use it."

"I'll show you." He had taken her to the police that afternoon, to fill out a report. *For whatever good it will do.*

The pistol was for self-protection, in the event that Ian eluded any kind of surveillance and attacked her, bent on one mission—the end of her life. Surrendering to that reality, Kate listened dully as Aidan gave a few vital directions.

"Okay. Enough. It's too soon after Jordan's crisis to tackle another menace. Come to bed, then, sweet woman. We've done what we can for now." Fighting for a bit of normalcy, Aidan took the gun and deposited it into the drawer, drawing her into his arms.

She rested for a moment, her head on his shoulder. "You haven't told me about your operation, Addy."

"I know. We need to talk about it. There hasn't been the

opportunity."

"But are you okay? Is the pain coming back?"

"No," he replied truthfully. *It isn't as bad as it had been before,* he thought. *Not yet.*

He kissed her then, slow and ardent. "Let it go."

Time for life to reassert itself—to drop the complications of another day. Wanting to burn away the fears, his body responded as it always did to her scent and touch. Kate's breath quickened with his as they lay down together, shedding clothes impatiently.

Their lovemaking struggled for restraint. Aching with desire, they cherished the harbor of each other, until they could no longer hold back. Afterward, they lay in the sanctuary of their loving, listening to the sounds of Limerick throb below them.

Ian lunged at her, scarred and broken, the knife pointed directly at her chest. There was no escape. She screamed.

"Kate" Aidan's voice was close to her ear and urgent. "Wake up, mo gradh, it's okay."

Her awareness fluttered in two different directions. The deliciously sensual intimacy of the man she had loved all night, torn by the savage realism of her nightmare. She opened her eyes, found his beloved face, relaxed into relief.

"Are you okay? That was some terrifying dream."

She sat part-way up, leaned her head on his shoulder. "I'm sorry, Addy."

He tipped her chin and kissed her. "Tell me."

"It's Ian again. I've been dreaming about him repeatedly."

Aidan lay back, taking her with him. His own nightmares had also started. Ian clawed at his neck, stalked him into corners—until he woke, sweating. "I would like to think it's only our imaginations."

"You're dreaming too? About him?"

"Yes," Aidan admitted reluctantly.

He's near. Ian is near. As soon as she thought it, she recognized it was true. She turned away from Aidan, steadied her breathing on the beat of his heart.

After two more days, Jordan was ready to be discharged from the hospital. Though a bit thin and pale, he'd regained much of his former vivacity. Kate had made arrangements for Tracy to receive him. He was ready to be home and eager to try out college. He'd learned enough about the world to understand the desperate plight of millions of its people.

"I don't know if I'll succeed as a student. Not sure I can hack it, but I at least can learn the basics of how to create a decent sanitation system. That's what nearly killed me, mom," he continued earnestly. "Dirty water. It does it to them all the time and no one pays the slightest bit of attention. If I hadn't come here, to the best of Western hospital care, I would be dead."

Kate bolstered her spirit on Jordan's enthusiasm. If Ian succeeded, Jordan would need a passion to lift him up from the heartache of her death—though, of course, it would appear as an accident. And afterwards, well—Tracy would give him more than ample mothering. *Just as she did for me.*

Both doctors were present for Jordan's discharge. Johannes, beaming, received a hug from each of them. He could not keep the broad smile off as he saw Jordan in his street clothes. *The boy belongs to the world once more.*

Robert insisted on giving him the final check. He wanted one last connection with Jordan, and it was the only way he knew. "You will experience some minor recurrences. But I think you are ready for whatever comes next."

When he was satisfied, Robert offered his hand to Kate. Permitting himself a thin smile, he shared the satisfaction of the victory with her. She held the contact for a few extra seconds.

"Thank you, Dr. Salisbury."

"Mmm. Who knew fresh air could smell so wonderful?" Jordan grinned as they escaped the hospital. The wind was cool and moist, the sky gray with fast moving clouds. They drove to the Shannon airport, chuckling over Jordan's wry commentary as they moved through Limerick. After checking in his battle-scarred backpack, they decided on lunch, pulling out plastic covered chairs—ordering Jordan's choice of fish and chips.

Most of the topic was about Seattle. Jordan pumped Aidan for whatever information he could attain. Aidan relaxed into the conversation, never re-directing his stream of consciousness. He switched topics when Jordan did, allowing the young man to take the lead.

As the hour neared for his flight, Jordan directed a level look at his mother and Aidan. "You guys take your time here in Ireland. Enjoy the place, instead of dealing with me. I'll be fine, if Tracy doesn't overstuff me with food." They all stood up. He hugged Aidan first. "I'm glad you're in my mother's world," he said, full of easy confidence.

Kate's tears threatened to spill, flustering him. "It's okay, Mom, we'll see each other soon."

His youthful casual attitude helped her regain her composure. "Of course," she affirmed. She hugged him tight and then released him—standing close to Aidan. Her voice was unnaturally bright. "Take care of yourself, darling. I love you always."

Jordan studied the despair on her face—not sure what he was reading or what he could do.

The stout man taking tickets had seen numerous such scenes. *Sometimes travelers have to be helped.* "Sir, you must board directly," he announced flatly. With a small shrug, Jordan tossed his small bag over his shoulder, saluted them and walked through the door toward his future.

Kate's heart ached in the hollowness of his sudden absence. Aidan said nothing. He calmly waited, his hand resting on hers.

"I'll be okay," she ventured weakly. Aidan nodded but didn't move. "Let's go," she added after a few minutes.

The rain floated down. They left the airport without speaking, entering into the unknown—marveling at the greenness of the world, the extraordinary ordinariness of the day.

Chapter 28

Aidan drove to the hotel, recognizing they were at a reckoning point, the place to begin the next step. Whatever it was. The pain had returned in unreliable bursts. So far, he'd managed, but they had to address it soon. Time seemed delicate. It had a quality that demanded precision. He had to tell Kate about the impending and overdue operation.

With Jordan gone, the next steps should be clear, but they weren't. Moving again seemed a losing proposition. Returning home with Kate would expose everyone he loved to the threat of Ian. If they stayed, he could lose his strength altogether in the near future—and likely become a liability to Kate's safety and robbed of the life he wanted.

Kate was aware of the conflict inside Aidan with rising anguish. For the past few days, she'd struggled to find some firm footing and clear direction, but everything around her was quicksand.

Once again, she arrived at the same inescapable and terrible conclusion. She couldn't find a way through it. *When Ian appears, Aidan will try and rescue me.* To keep him from becoming the target of the menace that ruled her hours, she had to leave. The thought broke her heart. *But it doesn't change what I have to do.*

"We're quite the talkers today, aren't we?" Pulling up to the hotel, he turned to her. "I think dinner might be in order, don't you?" Kate smiled at him. *Let the blush of love be what he remembers.*

"Why don't you go ahead and I'll park the car," he offered. Nodding, she draped her arms across his shoulders and accepted the kiss he offered, returning it passionately.

"Sweet woman, hope that was an invitation." He searched her eyes. Kate appeared flustered and tense. Without answering, she touched his cheek and stepped out.

A premonition ghosted through the air as she entered the room. When her phone rang, she did not recognize the number. She answered, as though to an inexorable summons.

Ian's voice dripped from the phone like battery acid. "You're dead now." A gloating silence punctuated the threat. The receiver clicked off.

The event she'd dreaded for so long was suddenly coming straight at her with the inescapable command of a tsunami. There was no way to change its direction or get out of its path.

Ian was on his way. He would expect her to be paralyzed, uncertain what to do. *That's how he sees me. There's such a tight window for action.* A small cry escaped Kate, even as her actions toughened with resolve. *If I leave, Ian will hunt me. He'll leave Aidan alone.*

When Aidan returned, she busied herself in the bathroom, so he wouldn't detect her bleak revelation. "Would you mind getting some take-out and having it in the hotel?" she called out. She had to send him away quickly. Then she would melt into the streets of Limerick and far from him.

He could hear the edge in her tone. Feeling drained, he tried to sense why the air felt disturbed. The sound of the shower seemed normal enough. Ducking inside the steamy interior, he asked tentatively, "Are you positive, Kate? It might be better to eat out. We have a lot . . . to go over. A nice dinner might help." What was important was to hear her talk again.

Kate took care to sound steady. "I'm sure. Once I got in, I realized I'd rather relax here. How about the Chinese place—the nice one by the river?"

It would take him nearly an hour to accomplish this. A slow burning lit deep in his lumbar. He wedged a hand against the frame of the doorway, trying to ease it. To send him blithely out was contradictory somehow, but he didn't have the energy to argue against it.

Kate poked her head out, sporting a halo of foamy shampoo. Aidan looked pale. *Oh Addy. I can see the pain is with you again. This is the last thing you need.* "Is that alright? It sounds so appealing. We'll talk over dinner. I promise."

His slight smile signaled surrender, as much to ease her after all they had been through with Jordan. Perhaps it would help settle them for the conversation ahead. "Okay. I'll be back soon."

Kate listened to the sound of his footsteps until she heard them recede down the hallway. She stepped out and quickly toweled off. When she was certain he was gone, she moved with a speed she'd rehearsed often when she couldn't sleep.

Within minutes, she was ready. She held herself stiffly to keep from crying. Allowing herself one indulgence, she buried her face into one of Aidan's shirts. For a moment, she was afraid her knees would buckle and she would collapse, unable to leave him. Shaking it off, she was filled with a singular encompassing feeling. *If you love him, you will leave him safe.*

One more thing. *The pistol.* Shaky and knotted with grief, she jammed it into her bag, easing out the door and into the light rain. She swore softly when the puddle from the approaching cab hit her, and flinching, dropped her bundled things. Feeling panicked, quickly grabbing them, she was consumed with the wish to escape. The taxi sped off. Within seconds she had vanished.

On his return, Aidan could sense her passing. Holding onto the food and wine, leaving the car parked on the street, he stood on the street corner in the rain, breathing out the throbbing in his back. A slow realization surfaced.

He scanned the area, the traffic, not clear exactly what he was seeking. Cars bustled by, wet leaves scattering. A glint of metal next to the curb caught his eye. He stepped up to it and carefully bent to take a better look. It was Kate's cell phone, fallen as she'd hurried into the cab.

How easy it is to disappear, he thought. The phone was cold and wet and dirty. She'd been missing for awhile. Probably left soon after he did. A bolt of pain hit him, causing him to double over with a gasp. The wine bottle fell and shattered on the pavement, and an older man crossed the street and approached with concern.

"Can I assist you, sir?" he inquired, laying a tentative hand on Aidan's shoulder. Everything in Aidan's history wanted to resist the help, to carry forth as though nothing happened. But between the agony in his back and the misery in his soul, he felt as shattered as the glass on the street. *The metaphor,* he thought grimly, *is fitting.*

"Thanks," he replied shakily. "I have . . . a condition. It comes and goes." Allowing the steadying arm under his elbow, Aidan slowly straightened. "I'll be okay. Thank you again." He walked unsteadily into the hotel.

Entering the room with no hope that she would be there, he found the note that he knew would be there.

"So sorry, my love. So sorry. It has to be this way. Please don't try to find me. Take care of yourself. I love you more than I can ever say."

Aidan sat down heavily, staggered by loss, unsure of his next move. *Ian must have contacted her.* He picked up the cell phone, scrolling through its recent activity. It showed an incoming call before he'd gone. *While I was parking the car.* The one unguarded minute. The number was marked 'private' and would not accept a return call.

Kate was gone. The ruinous truth of it pressed to the core of his soul. *And I'm out of time.* Testing his strength, he cautiously rose, surrendering to Kate's irreconcilable decision. There would be no possibility to find her before he had to go under the knife. Without optimism, he would leave the situation to the authorities and return home.

Ignoring the mystified clerk who pointed out that it was dinnertime, he checked out of the hotel and drove north. He stopped at the county seat of Ennis and gave everything he had to the chief of the County Clare guarda. The story would have to be confirmed, but it would give them a head start in finding Ian.

The next stop should be the airport. He turned instead toward the Cliffs of Moher. The darkness was pierced by a three-quarter moon, the rain clearing on a strengthening breeze. It had been his intention to take Kate to these famous crags before they departed Ireland.

Kate fled because she feared for him. He knew that. *I owe her something now.* His own gesture of love would be given to the wild Atlantic Ocean and the Irish night.

Thank you for teaching me what love is, he thought, his eyes tracing the curve of the moon. *Thank you for coming out of my dreams and into my life. With all the reasons why you shouldn't, you did. Even if it couldn't last.* His chest tightened. *Oh god, Kate, take care. I will do everything I can to send protection after you.*

Driving swiftly on narrow roads, he was within a few minutes of the Cliffs when Kate's phone rang. He swerved to the side of the road. It could only be one person. "She's with me, Ian," he growled sharply into the mouthpiece. "I won't let her answer you."

There was an ominous pause. "Then you'll go with her." Ian sneered into the receiver. Aidan jammed the car into gear, pushing hard on the accelerator. Kate had moved so fast that Ian had missed her exit. *Now the bastard is using her phone to track us. Convinced we are together.*

He picked up the phone again. Dialed with his thumb as he drove. Brian answered quickly, his greeting curt. He'd been waiting for word, from either one of them.

Aidan spoke without introduction, breathless and sharp. "Kate is on the run. I am nearly at the Cliffs of Moher, County Clare—tailed by Ian. He thinks Kate is with me. Someone has to know. In case I don't make it." He paused, weighing his chances. "I talked to the police. But they're expecting me to be at the airport."

"Hold on Aidan," Brian responded tensely. There was one tactic—one—that might save him. "Listen. Ian's rage will be the only weapon you have. I caught a glimmer of this—during my stint at the Pen. He can get so obsessed . . . that he loses it. It's worth knowing. Hell—just watch for him to be careless. I'll call the guarda—tell them to drive their asses up there now."

Aidan chewed his lip. *Did Ian ever get sloppy?* In the distance, he saw headlights on the dark horizon. "Brian, I need to floor it. One more thing. My daughter. Sheila MacLaine. She lives in Seattle." Flipping the phone closed, he trusted Brian to do whatever was necessary.

Chapter 29

Aidan drove as close as he could to the famously stark Cliffs, crashing through the parking lot barrier. The car fishtailed into wildly whipping tall grass. He had to get out before Ian's arrival. Pain was gathering like a coiled viper in his back.

His teeth clenched against the burn inside and the turbulent cold outside. Hands fisted on the roof of the car, he leaned forward, harshly forcing his body to stand.

Gusting ferociously, wind exploded around him. He suddenly recalled that the Cliffs had a habit of forcibly concentrating air currents. Nearly every year the unexpected squalls shoved an overly avid sightseer over the edge.

Dicey. But there is nowhere else to go. The only cover was the darkness that trailed the clouds, periodically hiding the moon's glowing orb and the crashing sound of the surf against the rocks.

The headlights were closing in. The yellow eyes of a

predator closing in on its prey, relentless and focused.

Aidan crept into the dark grass, his mouth set tightly against the fragmenting pain and numbness. *It's getting worse and fast.* He had to make distance while he could.

The rim of the precipice was the only place to go. It was also the most treacherous. *But then, I am out of choices.*

Ian laughed out loud at the broken parking barrier and the abandoned car. *Gotcha.* Slamming his hands on the steering wheel, he demanded the careening energy of rage to take him over. *I have them cornered!*

Nick had told him all about the guy, MacLaine, after he'd stayed with Lila. How great he was, yada yada. According to herself.

So perfect. Two lovers gone off to their predictable end. No one would question it. A small rational voice spoke through the haze of his anger. *This jerk probably called for help. Yeah. Better work fast and get the hell out of here.*

Checking his gun and stash of extra ammunition, Ian pulled out a powerful flashlight. Cat and mouse. *All I have to do is work with the moon.*

It was during the transformation to John Hake that Ian began disappearing. The man he saw in the mirror was someone else—pathetic. But he couldn't escape the reflection. He felt himself becoming soft, with lax lines spreading from his mouth—weakness in his character.

Then people began reacting strangely. His eyes were still piercing but weirdly muted. And his fierce manner seemed bizarrely at odds with his manufactured features. In the last few weeks, John Hake had rendered Ian invisible.

He could sense the splintering of his mind. His thoughts were stampeding like a herd of cattle on a stampede he could not control. Their wild seductive wandering excited him—reminding him of the old Ian—reckless and dangerous. They held the ruthless spirit of Ian, hiding behind the man with an indulgent face.

He'd invented John Hake. Damned if the con was going to haunt him. He would let the wild cattle loose. If they trampled over Hake, that didn't matter. *As long as they pulled off the job.*

Aidan shivered, grateful he'd pulled on the dark blue sweater that blended him into the shadowy night. The wind chill was sapping his energy. Tremors of pain shook him. Each time, the burning increased and the recovery took longer.

Brian's implication suddenly became clear. *So Ian was out of practice after all.* And he was trying to do this one all by himself. The spark of anger burned away his fear.

Kate had said once only death would stop Ian. Aidan now knew this in his bones. But he had nothing. *And I don't want to become a murderer.*

An absurd hope began to bloom, like the last valiant flower before a storm. There was a chance, slender as it was, that Ian was so off-center . . . that he would keep making mistakes.

If so, I might survive. Even if I can't imagine how. If luck decided to favor him. If his body did not give out first.

You escaped him, mo gradh. But somehow fate intervened. I kept your phone with me because it was the only link to you. Now Ian thinks he has us both for an easy slaughter.

Surprise was the only option—at the boundary of land and sea. If Ian's careless haste turned the tables against him. There was one faint chance that Ian would meet the fate he planned for Aidan.

The moon went dark behind the fast-moving clouds. Time for both predator and prey to move. Aidan staggered forward, stumbling a bit. The wind was rough and dangerous.

If Ian didn't come forth immediately . . . *I won't have the strength to do any damage at all. It will be over.*

"My life is forfeit." Kate's bleak words echoed back to him. This was the moment when he might be able to erase that sentence and the intimidation that had ruled her for too many years.

Aidan inched beside the rocks carefully, his palms cold and bleeding against the rough surface. Seconds before the moon reappeared, his blind wandering discovered a hidden crevice so large he could stand upright.

The maw of the sea was only four feet away . . . where solid ground abruptly yielded to the dizzying height of space. It was exactly what he needed.

Moonlight flooded the night. Ian scanned the scene, probing and calculating. *That bitch and her boyfriend would have to be near the damn rock overhang.* It was the only place with sufficient shadows to hide them.

His heart hammered with exaltation as he ran in that direction. *This is too easy!* He closed in on the kill, his mouth twitching—the stampeding herd in his brain crashing into each other as they ran.

Aidan watched Ian approach between the cracks of his shelter. The moon's soft light was white, lighting up the features that belonged to John Hake. The man was entirely different than what he'd expected. There was a pulpy smoothness to his countenance, in jarring disharmony with the leopard's bearing of his body.

He was moving too fast with little caution. Out of control. Aidan drew in a deep breath, gathering what strength he could. The time was at hand. The next few minutes would almost certainly end with one of them dead.

Ian neared the rim of the abyss, gulping air. Between the pounding of the surf and his own pulse throbbing in his ears, he could barely hear. When the moon vanished again, he crouched, his pistol cocked and ready, dropping the flashlight.

The sea surged below. *It's hungry,* thought Ian. *I'm going to feed it with two bodies. Kate and her idiot boyfriend.* He moved forward more slowly, damning the noise surrounding him.

The darkness held. Completely invisible, Aidan inched carefully to the front of the cavern. A crazy notion hit him. Since he no longer had his full height and vitality to fight Ian, maybe he could use that.

His own handicap could startle the hunter and cause him to miscalculate. His chest tightened. *Be careful.* Any misjudgment at this point would be critical.

In a fight, Ian would easily knock him down and drag him to the brink of the cliff. But if his own disadvantage attacked him again—he would unexpectedly fall from his full size. And if he had any strength leftover, he could possibly push from a place Ian would not expect—from the ground itself.

A desperate plan and ridiculous odds. *But I have nothing to lose but my own life.* And that appeared imminent anyway.

Aidan could smell Ian's stink of edgy sweat as he approached. When he was close enough to touch, Aidan moved with the conviction of the hopeless. He launched himself straight at Ian, knowing he had to appear as big as possible.

The moon's light erupted over the cloudbank, and for a split second, all Aidan could see was Ian's strangely incongruous façade, feral and fixated.

The pain's snakebite was harsh and absolute, grabbing Aidan's spine and throwing him violently asunder. Ian was temporarily knocked off balance—surprised at the tall man who had so suddenly landed at his feet. There was a heartbeat of shocked motionlessness.

Denying the excruciating burning, Aidan beckoned every shred of concentration and muscle he could. He hit Ian's knees forcefully, causing him to buckle and fall. Rising up partway, he hammered another blow sharply in the middle of Ian's shoulders.

The gun went flying.

Ian twisted and grasped at Aidan, his hands clawing for the throat. "Where the hell is Kate?"

Her name shimmered through the night, heartening and supporting. Aidan pried back the greedy fingers, his answer ready and furious. "I would never tell you."

Ian's livid eyes glittered treacherously from John Hake's soft features. Aidan could see the man was skidding on the black ice of insanity.

"It's over, fucker." Ian pulled away and started to stand up. He would kick this creature to the outer limits of space.

He'll expect me to stand as well, but that's become impossible. There was only one opening in the slow motion of encroaching death and Aidan took it. He launched again, from the ground to Ian's knees, with all his weight and power. It was all he had left.

At the same instant, an unexpected collaborator arrived. The wind hit—a high-speed train, roaring down its own invisible tracks, sweeping away Ian's precarious footing. He reeled on the lip of the cliff, trying to regain his balance. The rock crumbled. Howling a curse, Ian fell, slow motion, backwards toward the raging waves.

Aidan lay on the sea-sprayed rock, breathing hard. *Can't do anything more.* Weariness shuddered though him. It was all he could do to hold onto consciousness. He hoped Ian had sunk below the cold water and would never rise again.

Doesn't matter, he thought again as the wind hit again with vicious energy. Only thing he knew for sure was the scream of pain and that he could not move. *Just hang on 'til someone finds me.*

Several hours later the police found him, barely conscious. They had come without sirens, uncertain what to expect, and fanned out, guns drawn, to the Cliff's edge. When the flashlights converged on the single fallen figure, the lead officer motioned for a backup and cautiously approached. There was an unfired gun lying nearby and a cell phone reflecting moonlight in the grass.

Kneeling, he motioned his men forward. "He's gone over, hasn't he?"

"Yes," whispered Aidan through bruised lips.

"Name's Sean. You talked to me in Ennis." He wasn't convinced Aidan would recognize him in this state. "Appears you had rather a tussle." He called for a blanket, taking his coat off and covering Aidan with it in the meantime. His inexpert fingers warily checked out Aidan's body, disturbed by the strange angle—the way he'd fallen, so precariously close to the sharp lip of the Cliffs.

"Call for an ambulance," he directed. "And scout below for the other one. See what you can find."

A sergeant brought the blanket and a flask of hot tea. "Superb idea," murmured Sean. "If he can manage it." He tucked the blanket in carefully beneath Aidan.

"A bit of tea will do you some good." Working slowly, Sean held the flask awkwardly, succeeding in landing a few drops of the warm beverage into Aidan's mouth. He'd checked Aidan's story far enough to trust his gut. The fellow lying before him was no crook.

"Did he do this to you?"

"Only partly," said Aidan hoarsely. With relief, Sean heard the medics' arrival. He didn't like how Aidan looked. *The man's too still, too perilously close to unconsciousness.*

At least the wind had suddenly calmed, almost as quickly as it had risen. They had been summoned here more than once when the storms had taken their toll.

Sean leaned down, his hand on Aidan's shoulder, trying to encourage him. "Help is coming, lad. Hold on."

Chapter 30

Brian insisted on being present when they called Sheila. "I really want to make the call myself," he argued with the hospital administrator. "He'd asked me to contact her," he pleaded, "if anything happened."

The supervisor had been in the hospital business her whole working career. There was no need to argue with him, she decided. Obviously close to the family. "I'll stand by," she agreed and retreated into the hall to give him privacy.

Sheila was home. She had taken to spending a lot of time in her apartment, dragging work along that she did not have the motivation to do well. Her father would use this phone if he wanted to leave a message but not talk to her. She meant to keep him from trying that again.

Will had called everyday, sometimes twice, with an apprehensive tone, appalled that Aidan would play with his sternly given deadline. They were both growing frantic.

The ringing startled her. She dove at the phone. "Hello?"

The voice on the phone was unfamiliar. He cleared his throat. "Sheila MacLaine?"

"That's right," her heart sinking. *Must be bad news.*

"My name is Brian. I am a friend of your father's and . . . " he interrupted himself, wondering if she knew about Kate. "Your father is in the hospital at Limerick. He's not in danger of dying," he added quickly. "The doctors aren't certain what's going on with him. He's been in a—fight."

"A fight?" Sheila's retort was thin, incredulous. "What are you talking about?"

Brian exhaled tiredly. It was clear from her tone that Aidan's daughter would not permit him to tell anything less than the truth. As quickly as possible, he told her—the story of Kate and Ian, and then of Kate and Aidan. How Aidan came to be on at the edge of the Cliffs of Moher, fighting for his life.

Astounded, Sheila struggled for her voice. "Thank you for telling me. My father has to come home, as quickly as possible," she added anxiously. "He needs an operation immediately. It's past time for it. I will go there and retrieve him. Can he be moved?"

"Not immediately, but soon. Perhaps."

"I'll be there as quickly as I can make travel arrangements."

There was no stopping her. "Right. Okay," he agreed.

"And Brian, thank you, again, for telling me the whole story. Does anyone have any idea where Kate is?" Sheila remembered her father's face when she'd first asked him about the woman in his life. *How alive he'd looked. How totally head over heels he'd been.*

"No," he answered bleakly. "She'd be assuming Ian is still alive and after her. Kate will be underground for as long as she can stand it. I think she imagines she will endanger everyone she loves, and that no one is safe to contact. I'll try to find her," Brian continued, "but she has a knack for hiding."

Sheila had the ticket to Shannon within ten minutes. The plane departed in seven hours. She called Will, tersely filling him in on the situation.

"I'm coming with you," he said unexpectedly. Before she could respond, he was directing orders at his secretary, putting his appointments on hold for several days. "I'll meet you there. And I'll call the hospital in Limerick."

Sheila knew she should get ready. But for several prolonged minutes, she was quiet, considering her father's life. He had forever told her they were family and she'd believed him, because it made her feel better. But this woman was like air to him. Whatever he'd felt for her mom was not love, she recognized with a sharp awareness. *It had been his love for her daughter.*

She sighed, thinking again about Kate and Aidan. How did she look when she thought of Andy? He was her best friend. Well, she didn't light up as her father did, that's for sure. Speaking of Andy though, she had to call him, as well as Christine, and Claire and Ben.

Well south of Limerick, Kate had convinced the farmer that she would work as well as any man. He was skeptical at first, but he let her try. She clearly needed a place to stay. They were a far way from anywhere here in West Cork. And since his sons had gone to college, he could use the help. "Name's William Sheehan. Wife's Nora," he told her as he showed her the humble room where she could stay.

Nora was a small woman, as soft as William was weathered. They named all the children in the pictures on the mantle for Kate. Four children; one in the States, one in Australia, one working in the far north of Donegal, and the youngest, gone off to Dublin for college. Three grandchildren beamed from their frames—a silent family of photographs, standing in for the real thing.

William gave Kate his daughter's boots. "You'll want them for the mud." He led her across a saturated field sculpted by hooves and studded with droppings. The barn leaned a bit, its cavernous hay-filled interior colder and damper than outside. William moved slowly and calmly—told her to watch him and do the same.

"They'll take a bit to get used to you," he warned. "Cows can be jumpy. They have to accept you." The milking apparatus was old fashioned and simple. It was exactly what Kate needed and she took to it easily.

She has a sadness about her, William noted as she concentrated entirely on her work. *The cows feel it too, or at least sense that she's no danger.* An involuntary sigh surfaced, and he wished to erase her sorrow, knowing he couldn't. Not anymore than she could remove the ache in his own life at his children spread so far afield.

Kate showed no interest in ever going into town or contacting anyone from home. Neither Nora nor William asked her about it. They were delighted to have someone to feed, someone else to move inside their tranquil home. Together, they reached an unspoken agreement, to speak only of cows and farm topics over shared meals. After dinner, the three of them read until the long night wrapped them in its healing rest.

At the same Limerick hospital where they had spent so many days with Jordan, Aidan slowly recovered from shock and exhaustion as people revolved through his room. The guarda chief, Sean, was the first person he recognized, his broad face furrowed with concern. He was sitting next to a nervy man who inspected Aidan with closely held interest and spoke with no introduction. "We'll be expecting some details from you."

"When you're able," Sean added, scowling at the Dublin investigator with displeasure. *Did he not observe the patina of weariness and pain on Aidan's face?* Even so, there was some sort of grim satisfaction there as well. *But he's suffered a great loss*, Sean thought. Something precious has been ripped from him. *Had to be the woman—the one he was so anxious to protect before he left Ireland.*

Clearing his throat, he rose. "You keep resting, Mr. MacLaine. You'll remember me, I figure. My name's Sean Flaherty. This is Detective O'Brian. We do need some details, but it can wait until we receive the go-ahead. Your daughter should be arriving in a few hours." Aidan nodded briefly. "She has someone traveling with her. A doctor, I believe. He plans to escort you home, I'm told. For an operation."

Sean ventured a friendly touch on Aidan's shoulder. "See you in a few hours, Mr. MacLaine," he said, glancing at the slender man standing patiently in the hallway. The fellow had arrived with no explanation, and insisted on waiting without taking any kind of break until Aidan regained consciousness.

"You have a visitor who has managed to convince the doctors here that he should visit you first." Tugging lightly on the detective's arm, Sean led them both out, gesturing curtly to Brian as he entered.

Aidan's eyes asked all the questions. Brian responded as though he'd spoken them out loud, intent on giving Aidan a full report. "I don't know where Kate is. She'll be in hiding for a while, I'd say. Having no idea that you somehow miraculously eliminated Ian, she'd be trying to protect you by luring him toward her."

Brian shook his head as he continued. "She'll surface eventually. And I will stay here, doing my best to find her. Tracy has been alerted."

"And Jordan?" asked Aidan.

"He understands his father's missing, believed dead." Brian's jaw clenched. "The boy thinks that his mom is traveling in Ireland, with you, I suppose. He's been asked to call Tracy if Kate calls him. So all we can do is wait. Who else shall I call?"

"Kieran O'Connell," answered Aidan faintly. "The

Big Misty Lodge. His number will be on my phone. Tell him everything."

"I will." After his years of watching over Kate, Brian did not easily trust anyone in relation to her. But Aidan had more than proved himself. Folding his arms, he waited.

Aidan continued, though he could feel a cloud of exhaustion settling quickly. "If . . . when . . . Kate calls you, please see that she understands the medical situation—whatever it is, by then. I might not be able to walk again or worse. If that happens, she's to live her own life. It's been on hold for too long as it is."

Brian gave Aidan a protracted austere stare. "You know as well as I do there's no point in trying to tell Kate what to do." Aidan said nothing. He didn't try to fight the weariness that carried him into sleep.

When he woke up, he was not surprised to see Will and Sheila. Brian was telling the story to the doctor. Will was stern and distracted. Brian spoke with harsh emphasis, adamant that he understand that Aidan and Kate had been hunted. There had been no way to escape it. Aidan retreated toward sleep, understanding Will would struggle, and fail, to comprehend this.

Sheila edged toward Aidan, waiting until his eyes opened again. She remained quiet, wiping at her tears. "Hi," she mouthed secretly. He managed a small smile.

Will's face appeared over Sheila's shoulder, communicating his concern with a glare. The line furrowed between his eyebrows was deeper than ever.

"So," he stated, as though it was all he could think of.

"So . . . hello, Will," Aidan responded quietly.

"We have a lot of work to do, Aidan, a lot of work. If it does us any good at all. Think of it as the price of being a hero. You knew what the consequences could be." Will hadn't meant to lecture, but the pent-up anxiety couldn't be reined in. *Didn't he realize that he had been gambling with his future—and his life?*

"Cut it out," Sheila said, grabbing Will's arm and forcibly directing his attention to her. "You heard what Brian and the police report said. My father is who he is. He could never have abandoned someone he loved in a precarious position alone. No matter what the cost."

She leveled a defiant stare at Will, who met it only briefly. He looked away, the muscles in his jaw knotting. Sheila spoke of a history more complex than he knew. But damn it all, he had to pick up the pieces, and he'd let Aidan, and Sheila for that matter, get under his skin. Even so, he couldn't argue with what she said and paused to let her antagonism pass.

"It's okay, Sheila. Will has a right to be angry with me." Aidan's voice was weak but clear. "I can't explain it to your satisfaction, Dr. Burke. It happened so fast. I won't defend my choices, though. The penalty will just have to play out."

There was an uncomfortable silence. "Whatever they are," Aidan continued softly. "I am sorry for the trouble I have caused you."

"None of that." Will's behavior relaxed somewhat. "I'm your doctor and we will do whatever we need to. Okay, enough said. Here's what you have ahead of you. The guys outside the door, Sean-somebody and the detective are keen to process the criminal report as soon as you feel up to talking to them. The hospital here has to release you into my care, which means your vital signs are adequately stable to make the trip stateside."

Will stopped, fought back a glower. "You are not ready for the big operation, Aidan. You won't be surprised, I'm sure, to discover that you reversed any progress. Depending on the tests I receive today, I hope we can get you into a wheelchair and stabilize the spine enough for you to make the journey home." He made his voice calm, despite the message.

"Is that all?" Aidan's question was laced with irony. Will did not respond, recognizing he could say nothing safe.

Aidan shifted his awareness toward Sheila. "You deserve my apology and you have it, but there is nothing I can say that will take back the worry you went through." Sheila's slender shoulder lifted in a brief shrug, signaling her forgiveness and her unconditional support of her father. The constriction in his chest eased a little.

"Okay, Will. In a few minutes, I will do every thing you want me to do. But now, I need a few minutes alone with my daughter."

Without argument, Will began to walk out of the room. Aidan called after him, "Thank you, Will. The fact that you are here is far above and beyond. Tell Sean to come in after a few minutes, please. We'll get that one out of the way."

He turned his attention again to Sheila. "Now you, my dear, deserve to hear whatever you need to understand."

Blinking tears, not wanting them to stem the flow of communication, she fought the faltering edge of her voice. "I suppose I already know most of it. Where is Kate now, Dad? Do you have any idea? Should we send someone to search for her?"

"No. Brian will find her if anyone does. Kate would have no idea that any of this happened. She meant to bait him toward her."

"But she will surely wish to establish communication at some point? To check on Jordan. And you, for that matter."

"Yes. Yes, she will. When she feels it's safe."

"But that's good, isn't it? Then she will find out what happened and she can come out of hiding permanently. And she can return to you."

A searing sense of longing for Kate flashed through Aidan. "What has Will told you, about the . . . 'consequences', as he calls them?" he asked woodenly.

Her tears could not be bidden away this time. The swell of them broke through her self control, telling Aidan that, as usual, straight shooter Will had spelled it all out.

"And that's why I don't know. I can't say how it will be in the end. If it goes badly, then . . . " his voice dropped, "then I have really failed you and her both."

"Will told me you'd increased your chances of . . . " she stopped, trying to control her emotions. "Of it being bad . . . " she finished brokenly.

He waited, a hushed heartbeat of silence. "Then he probably also told you I increased my chances of living my days in a wheelchair and he won't predict the extent of the paralysis."

Sheila dried her eyes. Set her words out carefully. "But you do have a chance of walking out, free of pain and completely healed too, Dad."

"So, how would you pose that to the woman you loved? I will be going in for a chancy operation. Either in the midst of it or done with it by the time she finds her way back to me. No one is willing to make a prediction yet on the end result. But it could be grim. So how would I say that to her? Wait and see?"

"Will is a very skilled surgeon. You have a great chance with him, or he'd tell us otherwise. Kate will come to be with you as soon as she finds out. How could she not?"

Sheila's question rang through his mind. *How could she not?* The memory of Kate's touch touched his skin. It was only possible to move forward with what he had to do. He hoped he would be with her again. Recognize her. Wrap his arms around her and dance—make love with her—but none of those were guaranteed. *It's out of my control,* he thought. *As perhaps life always is.*

"She will come," he agreed finally. "Only I haven't a clue what shape I will be in when that happens."

The afternoon shadows lengthened, stretched between a difficult past and an uncertain future. "The lab tests showed some good news and some bad," Will said. Aidan heard the words but his mind was playing out the story he had told to the Detective O'Brian and Sean, while Sheila listened intently.

He would not be here today were it not for what had gone wrong in Ian's mind, he'd told them. The man did not look as he'd been described or resemble the prison picture they'd showed him. Ian must have had some sort of work done to change his appearance. But it was the way he'd acted that still disturbed Aidan. And it was exactly what saved him.

Ian had moved like someone demented, haunted by his own hatred and made reckless with his own fury. When Aidan described the fight, Sheila closed her eyes, hurt by the vision of her father, half crippled, using his pain and weakness to trick a savage attacker. Sean and O'Brian wanted as many details as they could attain, pens scribbling furiously as they asked question after question.

Aidan pulled his mind to what Will was saying with effort. "The positive is that we can move you at all and a brace will do rather than an operation." There was always a pause with Will, while he gathered his mind for the bad news. It had the effect of riveting the listener's attention upon him as well, as they waited for the other shoe to drop.

When Aidan's eyes met his, Will continued. "I am fairly convinced you will need to stay in that brace for a full month before you are stabilized and acceptably healthy for the operation. That's the bad news." Risking the warning signals from Sheila, he added, "you've had enough time out flitting about doing damage to yourself."

"We can fly out tomorrow morning. I've made arrangements with the airline," Will hurried on, watching them both weigh the significance of his words. "There isn't really any alternative. We'll have to devise a special sleeping arrangement as well. You'll need a means to rest once you're in the brace and it won't be in a bed. I'm working on that one. I'm giving you a portable device, so you're not stuck in the hospital."

"I appreciate that." Aidan's gaze remained steady. *Surrender. That's all I can do now.*

A day and night can pass so quickly, thought Aidan as the plane banked and began the final approach. Seattle's green was much darker than Ireland. It was the firs, the dark forest color, instead of that brilliant Kelly-green patchwork.

What had he imagined when he'd first gone to Scotland, intending only to travel and sell some art? Did he ever imagine he would be here with haunted memories of the woman he loved? Not knowing where she was and himself with a broken body? *No one ever imagines such a turn,* he supposed. He shifted, trying to get used to the brace binding his entire back.

Sheila laid her hand on top of his. "Okay?" she asked.

"Yeah. Okay enough. Hey, darlin' girl, I've been thinking. How about that thesis?"

"It can wait," she shrugged, trying to dismiss the subject.

"No, it can't. The further you move from it, the harder it will be to get it done. You must keep working on it. And I want to go home, Sheila, to the island."

"But you'll be alone," she protested.

"Hardly. I will be lucky if I have ten minutes to myself. I imagine Ben and Claire would help out." A small smile flickered. "Probably treat me like a hurt dog, and argue about how best to take care and who gets to do it."

She studied her fingers for a minute, considering. "Will told me he figured out the sleeping chair."

"He told me that too. Said he's got the basic makings for it at the hospital. It merely entails a bit of remodeling. Ben could do it in a twinkling. They'll collect me after Thanksgiving. Okay? I want to be home," he repeated earnestly. "I promise to call you every night."

Sheila giggled. "Am I such a worry wart? I must be, because

I would ask you to do exactly that." She linked her arm with his. "It's no secret you're happier with a view of your mountains and water, Dad. Not to mention access to that baby grand. And I think the gallery work would be good for you, too, to keep you occupied. Oh, I really do sound like your mother, don't I?"

Her peal of laughter caused Will to glare over at them from his newspaper. Testy from the lengthy trip, he wondered how, in God's name, she could be finding anything that hilarious.

Chapter 31

Kate worked hard, she made sure of that. She tried to ignore the hurt that spread inside her when Thanksgiving came and went. William and Nora studied her furtively when she wasn't aware, intentionally not catching each other's eye lest their collaboration be too obvious.

They did not need to share with each other what they observed. They recognized the signs of a broken heart. Shadows filtered through the house in the evenings, a tinge of abandonment sighing on the wind. There was nothing to be done. They knew this too. Some things simply had to be endured.

Their books couldn't distract her any more. In the living room after supper, they turned on the scratchy radio, barely catching a reliable signal. The most important thing, William and Nora discovered, was simply to chat, to keep her from retreating too far inward.

If they forgot, she would sometimes pace, peering out at the dark night, her face grief-stricken. They learned to keep up a slow patter, taking turns distracting her with questions. If they ran out of topics, one of them would ask her to read a piece for them or to fetch a cup of tea. They wanted her to feel protected and at least safe, if not happy.

Aidan was on his way to the island. Trying not to think about Kate, he watched the backlit sun give a golden glow to the end of the day. "Their van was the perfect thing," Ben was saying. They had picked up Aidan, the wheelchair, the sleeping chair and had space leftover for the dogs and off-island groceries. All three of them were relieved, leaving Sheila and Will, and the myriad of stipulations they'd all been given.

Aidan was glad to be in their generous company. They had a workmanlike attitude toward his current situation that was easy to be around. Ben and Claire didn't know much about Kate or what had happened to him, but none of that mattered.

The gallery was their world and they were delighted to have Aidan home. So he required a little extra tending, no problem. They had listened patiently to Will's admonitions, which mostly consisted of keeping Aidan from cheating. Ben had swiftly modified the sleeping apparatus and prepared it for its one-month sojourn in Aidan's house.

Sheila had been thankful for their cheerful demeanor. The sight of her strong father in the chair, trapped by the flood of events that had slammed into his life was unnerving. She had mustered a smile and waved goodbye to them, with her arm linked with Andy's.

When they reached the island, Aidan refused Claire's offer to go to their place and declined their half-hearted invitation to stop by the gallery. "Later, guys. I just want to be settled," he told them.

In the end, they had to spend hours at his house anyway, the dogs running in and out as they busied themselves with the details of preparing his home for the wheelchair. Aidan let them do most of the work, giving input when it was requested, staring out the window, ignoring the piano, feeling empty and tired.

Claire sat next to him while Ben adjusted the outdoor entrance. "Are you feeling alright with being alone here?"

"It's what I need," he responded. "I hope you don't think I'm not appreciative. Thank you." There was no way to explain the hole in his heart.

"I can see you're in shock," she said, busily arranging things on the table. It was unnecessary, she knew. But she had to be active. "A lot happened in a short period. You must be exhausted."

Everything about his weary manner confirmed this. It was time to leave. "Good thing we only had one floor to deal with. Call us if you need anything," she said, standing up. "I will be up to check in on you in the morning."

"I'll be fine, Claire. Thank you. I am as comfortable as I can be, and I'm glad to be home."

She kissed the top of his head. "Bye then."

Ben popped in the door, the dogs streaming past him, tails wagging and heading straight for Aidan. "They had to say goodbye. We'll call you in the morning?"

"Oh for god's sake, Ben, let's go. He needs some peace." Claire whistled to the dogs, and taking Ben by the arm, firmly shut the door.

A plummeting silence dropped around him. The tides shifted outside, making waves without wind, pushing sea against rocks. He would not allow himself to call out to Kate, even in his heart. But memories kept tumbling through his mind. The magic of Montana. Kate by the waterfall in the Fisherfields. Laughing banter and powerful singing at The Big Misty with Kieran. Eyes full of love and concern for Jordan. The haunted retelling of life with Ian. Impossibly exquisite moments on Ulva.

She was everywhere inside him. Dreams and reality merged. His body trembled with the memory of it. "Enough, MacLaine," he said out loud. "Stop yourself now." It was time for sleep to bring its respite from thinking and remembering.

In West Cork, Kate could not feel Ian's presence. *He must have been crazy with rage when he did not find her.* He would have immediately returned to pursuing her. *I should be feeling his ugly menace hunting me.*

Instead, her intuition foundered on cold emptiness. She worked with the cows, finding solace in their warm, broad bodies while her spirit ached for Aidan. *Oh beloved, what happened? I can't stay in hiding without knowing you're okay.*

She'd insisted that William take on an apprentice—Peter from next door. Kate figured him to be about twenty-two, though his real age was irrelevant. There had been a problem with the oxygen at birth, William told her. Peter was never quite able to read and write. He couldn't go to school. Or at least his parents thought so.

William and Nora were fond of Peter, and they believed him capable of more than he was given credit for. Peter was eager to be of use and quite capable with simple tasks.

Kate hoped he would continue the work on the farm for many years. She was acutely aware that William was starting to rely on her help. The young man would help ease the loss when she left. *As I will. Even if I can't say when or where I will go.*

The weather had gotten cold. Their exhalations puffed out while they worked. The December grass was frozen in the mornings, crunchy and brown as they walked over it to the barn. Kate's restlessness was becoming unbearable. She had to find out if all was well with Jordan. And she couldn't go on without word about Aidan.

The idea of calling Brian was attractive, but the logistics were complicated. She could not risk a traceable number to William and Nora's house. Her own phone had fallen somewhere, and it was just as well. Aidan and Ian both had her number.

She would have to arrange a ride to town and call from a phone booth. For the first time since she'd been with William and Nora, she showed an interest in accompanying them on one of their bi-weekly shopping excursions. "I'll go with you if I could," she told them.

Their eyebrows rose with curiosity. "Of course, my dear," agreed Nora in her high voice, breaking into a nervous laugh, as she often did to punctuate a sentence. "You must go crazy with us here. Not a very exciting lot, are we? Perhaps we could stay late and socialize a little. We have some friends there. I could arrange a visit."

"Not for me, thanks. Just a quick in and out," Kate's smile was thin. "I only want to make a call." She wouldn't listen to Nora's protestations to use their home phone.

Nora nodded, glancing at William to be positive he agreed—reading the reply sent over his newspaper. "We won't be shopping for another few days, if that's okay."

"Quite fine, no hurry," responded Kate, not really believing what she said. Suddenly, she wished intensely to make the call, to hear Brian. *He would know everything.* He always did.

Aidan's phone rang. Claire phoned twice a day, but this one seemed out of kilter somehow, He'd already talked to her in the morning to assure her that he was fine.

"You up for a visitor?"

His heart skipped a beat. "Who is it?" He heard the edgy quality of his own question.

"Says he's a friend. From Scotland, but he's Irish," Claire replied with a slight laugh. Aidan could imagine her grinning at the man in front of her. *Kieran could disarm the FBI,* he thought.

A masculine voice with a rich Irish accent took over. "That's as opposed to being from America—but Scottish, MacLaine."

Aidan could not help but smile at the sound. "What are you up to, you rascal?"

"Sure, Brian told me it was yourself, who asked him to call with the news that you were home. And I thank you mightily for that. We were closing up the place for the winter when he called, and so I thought, I've always fancied visiting the west coast of America. And good Lord, this is definitely the west coast, isn't it? That's an impressive ferry ride. Right into the teeth of the setting sun. I've rented a car and I've reserved my own accommodations, in case you want to be rid of me. So all you have to do is say okay, and I'll be over."

"Come then. To tell you the truth, I would be happy to have you here. Claire will give you directions. Please ask her also to . . . " Aidan reached for the right words. "Ask her to give you an update about my condition. So you're not surprised."

Kieran was there in ten minutes. He had been ready to walk out the door when he called, trusting Aidan would agree to see him, driving single-mindedly over the scenic roads. Not bothering to knock, he opened the door with his elbow, his arms full of warm dinner for the both of them, courtesy of Claire.

The expansive Irishman deposited the food carefully, venturing a careful look around. Stepping gingerly to one side of the chair, he bent and hugged Aidan, patting him gently on the back. "Jaysus, Aidan, you got yourself in a proper pickle."

"Did Claire tell you nothing?"

"I wouldn't let her. There was nothing to be warned about. I knew you had been badly hurt, from Brian. I will hear the rest of that story from you. When you are ready." His frank scrutiny wandered freely. He chuckled. "Must've built the house around the piano," he commented wryly.

"Just about." Aidan said neutrally.

Kieran regarded him astutely. "I have the feeling it's been pretty quiet here. How long have you been here?"

"Couple of weeks." Aidan pulled his gaze away from the piano, as though the sight of it brought him pain. Kieran chewed his lip pensively.

They sat at the small table and unpacked the latest savory delight from Claire. Aidan shook his head in appreciative disbelief. "I believe she is a chef minus a restaurant and somehow I have been representing all her imaginary customers."

"There are worse things, Aidan, then to be cared for by the likes of her."

"She's taken, Kieran," Aidan warned, with a hint of amusement.

"Of course," replied Kieran mildly. "And probably a herd of suitors in waiting as well. I am only saying there are worse things."

"That I know," Aidan said coolly.

Kieran's unease flickered again. "We must have the elixir of Scotland first, my man. We have a lot of catching up to do." With a flourish, he pulled out a bottle of Laphroaig. "One of the Highland's finest . . . and most expensive, I might add. Thirty years old. This will dance on your tongue a nice long time. Bring the blue peat smoke to mind."

He poured them each a substantial share, adding two drops of water to each with studious concentration. A smile hinted at the edge of Aidan's mouth. "Beautiful, my friend. Thank you." He raised his glass. "To Kate's new life."

Kieran added, "May she understand soon that she's been released from Ian. Thanks to you."

Aidan put his glass aside without drinking. "The tides should have pushed him to shore eventually."

"Well, I choose to believe he's dead. And I suggest you do so as well. The sea doesn't always show its hand." Kieran touched the rim of his glass to Aidan's, waiting until Aidan returned his salute and picked up the glass to drink.

Aidan showed little interest in the meal, but seemed to draw strength from the whisky. Kieran kept his focus purposely on food while Aidan struggled to talk about the past month and a half.

When Aidan withdrew into brooding, Kieran would find a particularly tasty piece, and push it toward Aidan. "You have to try this one out, it's fabulous," he pronounced, smacking his lips, formulating another question.

Kieran heard all Aidan had to say and a great deal he did not. He was a master at hearing the deep echoes inside simple story lines. Aidan was facing an uncertain future and he had no desire for the things he'd always loved—his music and his poetry.

He's been opened up and drained of energy somehow, Kieran thought. Aidan hardly appeared to inhabit his body at all.

When they were finished, Kieran stood on the porch, filling his pipe, facing out to the restless water and the unseen mountains. "Extraordinary place you have here, Aidan. Perfect lair for an artist," he puffed out a slow exhalation.

"Play a melody for me," he continued. "You haven't been playing those ivories, but why not?" Kieran didn't turn around. "Why not do it now? Isn't it the perfect antidote to uncertainty?" The question curled in the air with the smoke that drifted from his pipe. Aidan did not even try to come up with an answer.

Kieran turned and faced him. "You can't disagree, Aidan. Don't give up on this moment, at least." Their eyes locked.

When he couldn't hold the scrutiny any more, Aidan capitulated. He moved toward the piano, shifting from the wheelchair to the bench, experimentally trying the pedals, his fingers resting on the keys. "Damn you for being right and for so calmly confronting me."

Kieran could not hide his grin. Setting down his pipe, and shouldering his way inside, he poured two more glasses of

Laphroaig. Aidan began tentatively, frowning, nearly shuddering as the notes emerged slowly, but Kieran would not let him falter.

With a barman's instinct for encouragement, he kept up a steady banter. "Ah that's fine, Aidan, so fine. There you go. Lovely. That's it, Addy. Good on you. Now lad, keep it up."

Aidan stopped once, with his hands wide on either side of the piano, his head hanging in a gesture of defeat. Kieran said nothing but brought the whisky to him. Aidan accepted the drink and swallowed it in two sips—the slow burn crawling through him for several breathless seconds.

"Go on now," Kieran took Aidan's glass and retreated. "Let it out."

The music burst forth then, too great to be contained in the house. It filled the room and swirled out into the night, dancing with the sea wind, skittering on its waves and rising into the Olympic Mountains. The dam had broken loose. A deep river carried the notes from Aidan's heart to his fingers, flying across the keys.

Kieran clapped Aidan's shoulder in the startling silence after he finished playing—knowing he would be spent. "Grand music, Addy. Thank you." He grinned, dimples flickering in delight. "Off with you to bed. It's fierce late and Claire will be here to massacre me if you don't get some rest."

"You'd be half hoping that's true, O'Connell. And it's you that should be thanked."

"I can go. I have a place arranged."

"Do you want to leave?"

"Not at all."

"Then stay."

Chapter 32

For four days, Kieran and Aidan turned away all visitors. The daily calls satisfied Claire and Sheila, but Christine was anxious to visit. Aidan had never refused her before.

"I can't explain it, but I'll try for you" he pleaded. "I want you to understand. I'd like to see you, dearheart. You must hear that. It's just that we've started something here, and we must complete it."

"And it is?" she retorted, still nettled.

"A kind of healing, I guess. Maybe it's just—Kieran loves Kate too. I don't have to explain it to him. Somehow because of that . . . I'm writing again, Christine. The man just doesn't let up. I suppose I am riding on his energy and enthusiasm. We write and deliberate on the water and the mountains. Kieran smokes or at least he takes a pipe out and makes a show of it. Then he makes every meal seem quite wonderful. When he laughs, he expects me to join in."

"And . . ."

"And I read my poetry to him—at his insistence. I look forward to hearing his verse. At night, I play the piano and he stands and watches the darkness. Truthfully, I am grateful that he stays. He even found a shop to replenish the single malt."

Christine's eyes smarted. She wanted that kind of companion. *Maybe I should take things with Sam out into the open.* "Okay, okay. I'm convinced. It's not that you don't need me or love me. But just now, you really need him."

"Exactly." She could sense Aidan's slow smile. It had been rare enough when he first came home. There were only a few days left before the operation.

Kieran is who he needs. I finally get it. "So . . . call me then whenever you are ready."

In Ireland, it was town day. Kate joined William and Nora, waving goodbye to Peter, who had promised most seriously to get the feeding done. It was a vibrant winter morning, fluffy clouds skittering across a light blue sky, a soft breeze springing up from the wet earth. Kate was quiet, filled with nervous energy—elated and scared to be on her first trip into the open since she fled Limerick.

When she thought of Ian, there was only a strange spaciousness. Thinking of Aidan, on the other hand, had taken on the quality of urgency. She tried to quell the anxious feelings clawing inside her.

They arrived in the market town, so similar to all the others in this part of West Cork. On the last shopping opportunity before Christmas, it was overflowing with customers. There was one narrow main street where the highway traffic slowed to a crawl and people hurried in and out of shops and pubs.

Kate asked them to drop her off at the phone box, telling them she would help with their shopping in a minute. She had only this one call. Her hands were trembling as she pulled out the phone card and punched an interminable series of numbers. *Answer, just answer.* Brian always had his phone. He did not fail her.

"Finally, Kate," he answered before she said anything. "Are you okay?"

The call was longer than she expected. The world fell away when he told her Ian was missing. "Hopefully dead," he added edgily. An aching sob escaped her as Brian described the fight in terse sentences. The phone she'd dropped led Ian right to Aidan. That mistake was the spark that flamed into a life and death struggle.

Abruptly he was clear that Aidan had not really given Kate the full story about the impending operation. *They would have been just a bit busy. Well, they are past the luxury of half-told reality.* He didn't spare the details.

"I haven't talked to Aidan since Limerick. But I've spoken to his daughter, Sheila. She told me about what he is facing."

Kate leaned against the grime-smeared glass walls of the phone booth to keep her head from spinning. *Aidan.* It was the only thought she could hold. He'd wanted to tell her about the operation on the last night.

"He needs to see you," Brian said briskly. "Before he goes under the knife."

"I know that," she responded, unable to keep away the grief. "I know," she repeated brokenly. "I'll leave tomorrow as soon as I can. Can you make arrangements for me? It's hard to do that from here."

"I will," he said, softer. "Gladly. I could even meet you. It will be Christmas Eve, Kate. Let's go home."

She made a quick call to her sister before she allowed herself to relax. Tracy was grateful that Kate was safe. Jordan was doing great, she relayed. He was exploring Northern California and Oregon for a while, checking out colleges along the route, spending Christmas with friends.

"Said he'd rather call every few days than have his own phone. He's asked about you, but I told him you were traveling. Hasn't said a word about Ian. I frankly think he refuses to reflect about him at all."

"He does," Kate countered. "He's made a conscious decision to keep Ian out of his mind. I will tell him everything when I see him again. When he calls again, assure him that everything is fine—and leave it there. Please. Say I've gone to visit Aidan, in the islands north of Seattle. Say I may take awhile. You can give him Brian's phone number if he wants it."

"Okay, will do. Jordan told me you had . . . a man in your life. Brian said he was the one who fought with Ian. Aidan. Tell me I would like him, Kate." Tracy had never known a man in Kate's life other than Ian. "So I feel you're safe."

It's a fair request, thought Kate. Given her history. "You would, Trac," she said softly. "You'd like him a lot."

After the shopping was done, Kate sat between William and Nora on the way home. They could feel the waves of heartache, wonder and concern that radiated from her, patiently attending until she was ready to talk.

I must tell these dear people, thought Kate. *No matter what else is happening, they deserve that from me.*

Before they were home, they had listened to Kate's story with great attention and grave faces. It was the first time in her life that she spoke the truth, all of it, out loud. Her voice trembled when she explained what Brian had told her about the fight—its ultimate triumph and the cost to Aidan.

Hearing the story, imagining how it played out on the turbulent cliffs, William pulled over to the side of the road and sat with his head bowed. He'd heard about a fugitive who was presumed dead, but could not have imagined it would be connected to Kate. When they arrived at their driveway, they waved at Peter, understanding he must be told that Kate would leave immediately.

"I'll tell him," William said brusquely, getting out of the car.

"No, no, no dear," responded Nora when Kate started to apologize. "Never apologize for love. You must go to him, of course you must. There is no reason to wait. Peter is a wonderful help to us, thanks to you for being his fine teacher. You have given us more than you will ever realize. Even this part—remembering love. I would do anything for William. Anything. He's just the same to me as the day we met. I fell in love the moment I saw him and I have never recovered. Keep in touch with us, my dear. Call us once in awhile. If you ever return to Ireland, and bring your man to visit us."

In the dark of his island, Aidan's house twinkled with lights and ornaments. Kieran, Ben and Claire had enjoyed stringing them up together, singing songs and telling jokes. Kieran planned to leave the next morning for a reading scheduled in Seattle the day after Christmas.

"Come with me, Aidan," he urged. "Your writing should be with mine. They've been born together. Proper twins. You can introduce me to Sheila. Then we'll have a few days before the operation, and you'll already be there."

It almost seemed like a good idea. Aidan tried to imagine being up in front of an audience in the chair, confined by the brace. *Might have to get used to it,* he thought. *Or it might be the last reading you ever do.* Still, he hesitated.

Oh god, Kate. There was no logical way to explain what he was feeling. He had to see her before he could read. Every word was hers, though Kieran's eagerness had carried the hours. They'd created together, that was the important thing.

Aidan waited until they were on the porch, sharing a

Christmas Eve dram. "I can't go," he announced.

"And why not?" Kieran's rejoinder was mild, suspecting the reason. "I've got it all worked out, there's absolutely nothing to stop you."

"You, my man, are a gem." Aidan smiled more easily these days. "I can't begin to thank you for the time you've spent here. And it's not because you haven't thought of everything. It's just. . ." Aidan gestured out to the sea, the mountains, and the piano. "I need to be here until I have to leave."

Kieran sighed and threw his eyes upward. "I can't say I'm surprised. You won't leave in case she shows up. If there is to be a reunion, you want it to be here. Of course. I would do the same. You can expect me to haunt you in Seattle, though. And don't for a minute think we won't have more time in each other's company."

Chapter 33

Late morning on Christmas Day, Kieran drove slowly off the ferry, pleasantly full from Claire's over-the-top breakfast, humming snatches of Aidan's music. He slowed for the few pedestrians, hurrying across the road to their cars to catch the same ferry.

A woman wearing a rain jacket made for mountain storms caught his eye. The hood obscured her face, but something was overwhelmingly familiar, filling the car with the delicate fragrance of the Scottish Highlands.

Aidan was right! Kieran fisted his hands, punching the air with joy. *Let her go to him first.* He would not call out. The world was waiting for this, its heart stopping.

On the ride over, Kate remained outside at the rear of the ferry, out of the wind. The islands slipped past as she re-played the past 24 hours. Brian had met her, as he'd promised. She was happy to see him, still holding the memory of the sad faces of William, Nora and Peter as she departed them on the morning of Christmas Eve.

"You'll have to find a different profession," she'd leaned into his arms, profoundly grateful for his enduring friendship.

"Indeed, I have already figured that out, clever detective that I am. I was replaced on Ulva."

"I can't even begin to adequately thank you, for all those years. You'll have far more free hours, cause you're not worrying about me."

"It's more trouble to figure out what I'm supposed to be doing."

"Oh, Brian, find a woman. Or find a man," she'd giggled at his bemused expression. "Well, I don't know, do I? I've never seen you with anyone. I can't really guess who it could be."

"Does it matter?"

"Only that you find someone to care about you. Someone who isn't safe, maybe, such as your best friend from high school who's forever needed your aid and support. Allow me to help you for a change."

"I'll think about it."

Kate smiled, remembering the conversation. He'd been firm about the gun, shaking his head when she gave it to him, wrapped in a brilliant green scarf. Promising her it was only for farm use, he'd taken it and given her back the scarf, insisting she keep it for memories—even hard ones.

In between Christmas stories and the poignancy of being in flight, they'd talked earnestly on the entire plane trip, holding each other long and hard at the airport.

"Where will you be?"

"You'll find out when your phone rings," Brian had replied tartly, handing her a new phone. "Since you lost yours, I figured you should have a new one. To keep in touch with me if nothing else. But old friend, you have places to go." He'd winked, saluted her and left.

And that was it. Kate rented a car at SeaTac, and drove north. The late December sun barely crested the horizon, giving the morning a honeyed glow. She'd never had a home. *Until now. I am going home now.*

It wasn't hard to find the gallery in the small island town. Through the windows, she could see two people working over a big table, despite the holiday. When she knocked, Ben came to the door, surveying her with a puzzled air before he let her in.

She smiled at Claire and Ben, both of whom were staring, trying to ease their anxiety. "Hi. I'm Kate. I'm Aidan's friend from Scotland and Ireland." Nodding, they shook her hand, keenly inspecting her as they chatted. *They're assessing me,* she thought. *Good for them.* She wanted them to be comfortable.

Finally, she asked the question she knew they were expecting to hear. "I would like to surprise Aidan. Can you give me directions to his house?"

That people from near and far would want to visit Aidan made sense. But this one was clearly special. They talked, not probing, allowing all of them to get used to the idea of her being there, giving her a quick introductory tour of the gallery.

Kate knew her desire to go to Aidan was translucent, but she didn't care. She studied the artwork without talking, accepting their intent scrutiny and swallowing the lump in her throat. *The place itself was a work of art. Love and art.* It was gracious and inviting—a celebration of creativity.

Claire and Ben didn't confer, as they usually did. There was no threat from this visitor. Only urgency. Over coffee, Ben drew a map, not wanting her to lose her way. It was suddenly crucial to him that she find Aidan.

It was noon when she drove across the island, exhilarated by distant views of mountains on the far side of the shining water. Pastures rolled out, reminding her of West Cork, the grasses tall and brown, populated with twisted oak trees, cows and sheep. A lake opened on one side—a brace of swans cutting low, gracefully landing one by one.

The sound of the piano was soft, the deeply passionate notes lingering on the breeze. Kate parked the car at the entrance of the driveway and walked in toward the music. The house was located against the rock, facing the infinite sea and mountain landscape. She lingered, listening to the melody of the man she called home. The piano carried her away into deep-hearted memories of Montana and Scotland.

Her breath stilled as she opened the door. Aidan's back was to her, his fingers moving over the keys, a wheelchair next to him.

He could feel the air shift. The hairs on his neck rose as he brought the music to a pause. The brace bound him, not allowing him to turn and face her. For an endless moment he could only hear the loud thump of his heart. "Welcome back, Kate," he whispered.

Pausing just long enough to steady herself, she closed the distance between them in three quick steps, curling her arms around his chest. Aidan rested into her, pushing away all other thoughts for the meantime, feeling his whole being rejoice her return.

With great care, he reached up and caught her hands. Holding her fingers to his lips, kissing them lightly, he pulled her gently down on the piano bench next to him.

Kate's embrace never wavered, ignoring the brace, finding Aidan's mouth. She breathed in his warm scent, satisfying her deep need to hold him. At length, she laid her head against his cheek, in the crook of his neck, tracing the brace along his body. He let her discover the full extent of it, aching from the electric feel of her touch.

After a few minutes, he knew they needed the coolness of the wind. There were things that had to be said.

"Come out on the porch with me, Kate," he said unevenly.

She watched him as he transferred into the wheelchair. It was awkward and he was self-consciously aware of displaying his vulnerability so plainly before her. Observing him gravely, she did not offer to help, knowing that it would only increase his discomfort. Waiting for him to signal the next move, she touched his face with her cupped hand. Again, he broke the contact and wheeled outside.

They sat next to each other, staring out to the shimmering water, the words inside them dying before they were even uttered. "It's beautiful, Aidan." He simply looked at her, remembering how much he'd longed for her to see his view.

Taking his hand, her eyes were disconsolate. "I am so sorry." Her voice broke. "So sorry, my darling. To abandon you to the monster who was hunting me. My god, Aidan, how could you ever forgive me?"

All the restrained grief since leaving him flooded in. "When I think of you fighting with him and then hurt," she choked momentarily. "And not knowing where I'd gone. I gave you all my pain and all my miserable history and you took it and never said a word about your own and what you were facing."

Aidan held her hands, shaking his head, unable to keep back his own heartache. "No, Kate. There was no other way to play it. I made the choice not to tell you. I gambled with the chances, you didn't. You believed you were protecting me. Let it go."

The sound of the sea moved on the rocks. With an impatient groan, he tugged lightly and she curled onto his lap and laid her arms around his neck.

Reluctant to break the connection, recognizing it had to be, Aidan spoke quietly. "Okay, my lady . . . now we talk." Kate started to protest, but his fierce look stopped her. She sighed and stood up. He led her into the kitchen.

"Tell me where you've been," he said, pouring water for tea.

The story of William and Nora and Peter spilled from her, chronicles full of the smell of cows and the cold frost of the barn. "She told me to bring you with me, if I ever returned to Ireland, to visit them." Kate could not help but smile at the bittersweet memory.

Aidan twirled his cup of tea gone cold. Her silence signaled it was his turn. Feeling the weight of it, he began. "I have an operation scheduled in two days, Kate." Finally—at last—it was the occasion to tell the whole story. The accident, his denial. The endless tests. Dire warnings he'd ignored. She sat silently, pale, her pained eyes fixed on his.

"So," he could not hold her gaze. "We just have to see how it turns out. I may not survive the operation. Or I may endure it in some form that could hardly be called living. I could be paralyzed and Will won't say at this point by how much. Or I could walk out. After a rather arduous convalescence."

He stopped, drawn and unsure. "And you, Kate, you own your life again. Go visit Jordan and Tracy. Wait 'til we know what's left after the operation, no commitments."

Kate stared back at him incredulously. "I have found my home for the very first time," she declared firmly. "It is with you, wherever you are." All of her history centered on this truth. "I am not going to leave it. Don't try to make me."

Aidan tightened his grip. "You can't say that. We can't guess what we have in front of us." *She has to understand the naked truth of it.* "I might not be able to move. I might never recognize you."

"You would," assured Kate, thinking of Nora. "Even if you couldn't communicate it, you would always recognize me."

He dropped her hands, turned to the window. "Damn it, Kate. Be real about this," he continued over his shoulder. "Don't you ache for freedom, after all of Ian's efforts to own you? You would go through the ordeal with me, out of obligation. Out of love."

His tone grew hard and urgent. "But Kate, think. It's a maybe, maybe-not deal. If I survive, there's a good chance you'd be stuck with someone who could never keep up with you."

Silence. Kate was always a master at silence. She let the wordless seconds stack up, expressing more than she could say out loud. "When I first met you," she said finally, "I thought of how you were related to the mountains. Strong. Powerful. That's how I do and always will see you."

With infinite care she touched his face. "I love you, Aidan MacLaine. I'm here with every part of my soul. And I am making no plans to go anywhere. That's real. Look at me. Can you read that in my eyes?"

Aidan said nothing for a moment. No one could deny the resolution and the love that radiated from her. "Yes, mo gradh," he whispered, drawing her into his arms. "Despite everything I fear, that is what my heart sees."

The phone rang. Certain it was Claire, he answered.

"Everything okay?" she inquired mischievously.

"What do you figure?" he bantered.

"I think you are a pretty lucky guy, Aidan MacLaine. You've had two visitors that would have broken down my door if I'd refused to give them access to you. Kieran, I might have entertained for an hour. This last one, she wouldn't have accepted even a short delay in seeing you."

Kate, listening, laughed lightly and mouthed, "That's true."

Claire continued hopefully. "Anyway, we're proposing, since it's your last night home, and Christmas night, maybe we could bring dinner up and play some music with you."

Kate stayed nestled in his arms. "I would enjoy that, if you would."

They would have this memory, damn it. It would be a night

for them to celebrate the sweetness of ordinary existence. Some friends, food and music. They may never have it again. But no matter what happened in the future, they would have this.

"Well, I already have my Christmas present," he retorted with intentional playfulness, pushing aside the dark uncertainty of the future, a crooked smile tugging irrepressibly at the edge of his mouth. "But I think Kate should sample that fine cooking of yours and I would enjoy playing some music with both of you."

Relieved, Claire answered eagerly. "Great. Oh that's excellent, Aidan. I was afraid you'd say no. We've been missing you." He hung up the phone watching Kate take a slow walk through the cottage, observing his photographs candidly.

"So outstanding, these . . ." she murmured. She gave each one the kind of respect he'd given to hers. *I want to make this day last forever,* she thought. *Let it be one we will always remember.*

"Read to me." His eloquent language and imagery had danced in her brain, kept her up at night, delighted her with its fierce majesty—this man with such restrained intensity. "Have you been writing? I want to hear it."

Later he would tell her how hard he'd fought to bring back the music and the words. He knew what she was doing. Like Kieran, she wanted him to remember the spirit imprisoned by his injured body and to keep it strong and ready to fight.

"Later, sweet woman." The half smile flickered again. "You have a lot of energy."

"Do I?" Her question was speculative, as she stood beside him. "I should be exhausted. I guess I want to do everything I have been missing. Are you tired?"

He pulled her down beside him. "No. Yes. I am in a different reality altogether. This might be our last day. I am wishing for it to be our first. And I have no way to control it."

Aidan's fingers traced her cheek, down her neck and across her breasts, moving in slow motion. His breathing stopped and started, the need for her building to a nearly unbearable tension. Finally, trembling slightly, he drew back.

The brace came off for showers, there is no reason it can't be taken off now. "If it is the last day, I want to make love to you."

"And if it's the first?" she inquired, stroking his chest, wishing to retrieve the broken contact.

"I want to make love to you."

"That makes two of us, then." There was no possibility regaining the weeks they had lost. But they could do this. They could touch each other again.

He unbuckled the brace and removed it. Shivered as she touched him, caressing him as he had her—muscles tensing.

"Come, sweetheart." Stacking the pillows on the couch, she helped him transfer to a supported position. Leaving words behind, she let her body communicate its profound love and awareness of Aidan.

The lovemaking was delicate, infinitely gentle. Cobalt eyes closed with pleasure, dark eyes watched the yearning in hers. Matched it. When their heartbeats slowed, Aidan held her close. "That was the second Christmas present."

Kate snuggled in closer, mumbled, "umm hmm."

He couldn't help but laugh. "You should sleep. Catch up on what you lost during the flight." Kate relaxed deeply into his arms, yielding to her weariness.

Aidan reflected on her sleeping face. She was part of him in a way he didn't—couldn't—choose to question. The operation would come, with whatever costs. *But no one could take this away.*

A sweet sleep settled over him as well, resting against the pillows, in the hushed darkening of the day, holding her in his arms. They woke slowly as dawn gradually illuminated the violet blue sky. Aidan kissed the side of her neck with lingering sensuality, building a slow heat.

She sat up, laughing. "Oh no, you don't. Let's not wear

ourselves out entirely just yet."

"Why not?"

"Because," her voice grew serious. "Because you need to be strong."

"This will make me strong."

Kate let the flicker of regret register, making sure that he understood it. "Read to me. After we get the brace on." She fumbled with it, suddenly worrying about the fragility in his back. He surrendered to her ministrations without arguing. Allowed her to gently put the brace on, helping her adjust it.

"You know Kieran was here. It's only because of him that there are any writings at all."

Kate nodded. "Good. Good for him."

"Yes. He showed me the meaning of friendship, again. You take the writings with you, Kate. When I'm in the operating room, read them if you want. You'll have a part of me then. No matter what happens."

She would not give into fear. "It scares us both to really feel what's at stake." Her jaw tightened with determination. "But, we can't be afraid. The hesitancy will hurt us. We have no choice. We just have to do it."

Chapter 34

They were sitting on the porch, watching the sky and leaning into each other's warmth when Ben and Claire arrived, accompanied by the ever happy Shadow and Amber. The aroma of Claire's food filled the cottage. It was a full five-course meal, starting with oyster appetizers, a creamy soup from the last of their garden and Ben's spicy winter salad.

After the second bottle of wine they were starting to tease Claire about the real meal when she told them to step out on the porch for a few minutes. No one questioned her.

Kate stood behind Aidan—touching his shoulders lightly, staring into the dark expanse of water. Ben leaned against the rail. An easy peace fell between the three of them as they inhaled the salty damp wind.

When Claire called them inside, they were not surprised to see the table decked out with fresh flowers and candles, roast duck and yams. Each plate was garnished with more fresh greens, as if to celebrate their unlikely existence on Christmas Day. Grinning at their enthusiastic approval, she asked Aidan for a toast.

His gaze gathered them all in. "I am very nearly at a loss for anything to say," he began, ignoring the sound of mock disbelief from Ben. Humor tugged at his lips.

"Okay, you're right. I do have something. It is quite plainly, thank you. A young man reminded me how much those two simple words can hold and mean." He paused, the memory of Jordan's recovery still fresh and powerful.

"This meal is a testament how my dear friends here live on this earth. I am thankful I have the good fortune to share in it."

He gazed over the candlelight at Kate, holding steady for several heartbeats. "There is nothing sufficient to say what I feel for you. Thank you will have to do. And not the least for making it here tonight."

"Amen." Ben's voice rang out after the brief emotional silence, tempting smiles as they relaxed into the meal. An effortless banter played around the table, as they took their time, weaving stories and telling jokes.

After dinner, Ben popped up to clear dishes, not allowing anyone else to help. Claire breezily produced a fragrant blackberry pie "from last summer" as well as coffee and Earl Grey tea.

Kate's painter's eye was busy, studying the golden dogs as they shifted between each beloved person. She found herself watching Aidan's fingers, strong and elegant. *Definitely a pianist's hands,* she thought. *If he loses that . . . No. I will not even think it.*

As if by agreement, no one looked at the clock. They moved onto the last of the Laphroaig and into the living room, the dogs lying contentedly at their feet.

Ben pulled a weather-beaten guitar out of its case. "Guess what I will to ask you to sing," he grinned, his head cocked toward Aidan.

Claire considered her glass of whisky. After a shudder and a petite cough, she neatly divided its contents between the men. She poured a small glass of sweet port instead for herself and Kate. "Sing the Holy Ground, Aidan," she urged, not missing a beat.

There was no need for an answer. Ben began the tune with a soft strumming. Aidan winked at Kate, remembering their drive into the Fisherfields—into her Holy Ground. His voice was like she remembered it, a rich baritone. When he finished, there was a deep sigh of appreciation from his audience.

Claire clapped enthusiastically. "Wow . . . there is something about the way you touch those verses. Makes the melody stand straight up and vibrate. Would you sing one for us, Kate?"

"Not yet," she had to settle after Aidan's song.

"I've got one." Ben spun the mood down another track with a rolling song of the sea, Claire chiming in at the chorus.

"Okay, Kate, it's your turn." Aidan encouraged her. She was ready, singing a cappella—a song she'd learned from Kieran. The Selkie, from the Celtic myths of the seal-humans, came alive in the room.

"Beautiful," sighed Claire. "I've always adored that story. Fabulous pipes you have there."

The night passed, a new moon crossing the sky, pulling tidal energy with it. A harmony of voices spilled out from the small house on the bluff. It was dark but early morning, when Ben and Claire finally gathered their dishes and instruments and dogs.

"We'll be back in a few hours," Ben said with an apologetic gesture, gently closing the door behind them. Tired but not yet ready to rest, Aidan and Kate took a few more minutes on the porch.

"There's the North Star, Kate."

The night sky symbolized all their memories and dreams. "I will be waiting for you." Kate's voice was wistful. "So we can go see the Southern Cross. Remember?"

"Yeah. I remember," he wouldn't give in to fear. Not totally. "On a beach somewhere."

"Fiji. And it's you who has to believe it could be ours."

He didn't answer immediately. "Let's get some rest," he said finally.

They moved together to the couch, leaving the brace on for extra support. There was no effort to re-create the passion of the afternoon. They compromised instead for the sweetness of a light sleep, stirring frequently to awaken briefly—eased by the other's warm presence.

By the next morning, their lives were owned by other people, and by the pressures of the clock.

"How are you?" Kate asked in Will's waiting room.

"It feels surreal," Aidan shrugged. "The smell of hospital is becoming entirely too familiar." His demeanor brightened as a young woman entered, leaving the door open.

Sheila looked at Kate openly. Shifting to her father—his expression told her everything she wished to know. With no reservation, she embraced Kate. "I am so glad you got here before the operation," she whispered.

"Me too." Each feeling a bit self-conscious, they were not willing to allow it to come between them.

Kieran dallied out of sight until Sheila motioned him over. Kate flew into his arms. He welcomed her hug, holding her tight, shushing her apologies. "Hush, hush, none of that. Ah Kate, I've missed you." He wiped her tears away and a few of his own—threw a beaming grin at Aidan.

Will entered, swinging the door open widely. "Oh, sorry. Looks like a family reunion in here." He pondered Kate curiously, the woman whose ex-husband had so murderously attacked Aidan. "You must be Aidan's partner in crime," he continued awkwardly. "So to say. Can we speak alone?"

Kate shot a questioning glance at Aidan.

"There's no escaping it," he said ruefully. "Don't keep her long, Dr. Burke," he added.

"No, I won't. A few words, that's all," Will shot back, guiding her out the door.

The doctor escorted Kate into this office, frankly appraising her. He paced the length of his office, finally unceremoniously blurting out what he had to say.

"The operation is tricky. I've laid awake thinking about it more than once. I have yet to figure out the full extent of the damage he inflicted on himself when he fought with—um—your ex." Will didn't pause, ignoring Kate's frown. "We have already been over the 'do nothing' choice. It's not a feasible option. But there are some significant risks."

Pausing, he blinked at Kate in a tense, distracted manner. *She appears calm,* he thought. *Or maybe merely focused.*

He continued. "For the first few days, Aidan may enter a coma, or an unconsciousness very nearly like it. I fear it will test us, as we try to keep faith that he will wake up. I believe he will, but I can't be definite. When he does, there will be pain. A lot of it. The operation will require me to do some work with the spine and nerves that will be exceptionally excruciating. And I won't be able to help him much with meds until I can see what kind of mobility he'll have."

"Does Aidan know all this?"

"Yes. He knows. What exactly he thinks about it is another story. I expect he's scared. He hates to contemplate the burden it may place on you. But he unquestionably wants it to succeed. Enough to move past his concerns and fears."

"And the operation itself. How safe is it?"

"It's dodgy in places. He's weaker than I'd wish . . . and there's more nerve damage than I'd like. I wish we'd done this thing several months ago."

She blanched for a minute, but there was nothing she could do to change the past. "Me too."

Will nodded broodingly. There was nothing more to say. "Tomorrow morning."

Chapter 35

Kate stayed with Aidan all night, moving when the nurses entered, joining him in the narrow bed after they were gone. In the morning, they lay awake in each other's arms, counting the minutes. Shortly before the scheduled prep time, Kate murmured, "They'll be in for you in a few minutes. Are you okay?"

"Sure," his reply bordered on satirical. "I'm ready, anyway. Get it over with."

The first nurse entered briskly. "Just starting the process," she said lightly as she started an IV. The young woman worked near them efficiently without small talk.

"Remember to rest, Kate," Aidan said, after the nurse went out again. "Don't try to be a hero. When . . . you hear the news, make sure Sheila and Christine are with you."

"I might permit them to have a few hours with you. They'll demand it. But I'm feeling a little greedy right now," Kate teased without acknowledging the implication behind his request.

Aidan drew her into his arms, turned her face up to him—shook his head when her tears threatened to spill over. He kissed her hard and deep. They could hear people approaching.

"See you later." He pushed her gently away.

"I'll be waiting for you." There was nothing left to do but leave. "Go well, my darling," she murmured as she walked out.

Will entered, wearing his surgical blues, followed by Christine, Kieran and Sheila. "Let's take this show on the road. These people insist on saying hello." He was careful not to mention the possibility of saying goodbye.

Kate walked out past them into the featureless hospital landscape. They deserved their contact with Aidan too. Surrendering to the finality of it, remembering Jordan's crisis, she knew time would find every means to move slowly.

When the others returned, they sat together uneasily in the waiting room. "I suppose," Christine ventured, after several wordless minutes had passed, "that no one is planning to leave until we hear." She didn't bother waiting for their agreement. "So, let's make it a bit of a celebration, shall we?"

Shaking her head at their glum faces, she added, "Aidan would like that." This was something she knew how to do—change the energy. *Charge it up*. It was what she could do for him. Her voice amplified with deliberate enthusiasm. "So enough with the gloomy mood. We have the goods on Aidan here. Time to share some yarns."

Kate was the first one to respond. Grateful for Christine's spunky vigor, she encouraged her to reminisce about Aidan as a university professor. Sheila was also eager to hear this. Only Christine really had known him in action there.

Gathering her energy, Christine began Aidan's tale as an academic. Summoning every bit of storytelling ability, she warmed up to her purpose, and the memories flowed.

"The students worshipped him," she said, chuckling

affectionately. "Of course they would. Aidan struggled with being a teacher for all that. He cared deeply about actually teaching, but flat out hated the rest of it. And let me tell you there is a lot more. Used to pass me notes during staff meetings, like a kid himself, with wafts of poetry and ironic comments. He wasn't mean— never caught up in the gossip or politics, just removed. Not at all interested in promoting his own career."

"Oh, I would get so mad when they passed him over for recognition or promotion but he would always say, 'settle down, Christine, I don't care.' He would hide out while grading and when he emerged, he looked as if he'd been fighting grizzlies." She leaned her head back and laughed heartily at the memory, the improbable sound echoing in the halls.

Sheila listened to this story with bittersweet feelings. "I remember those days. It was the only time he had to work to be nice to me. I think he wished the whole world would disappear. He always has to have a creative project bubbling in his head. I learned that early about Dad. Grading was the only period he couldn't access it. Reading of all those papers, and then worse, assigning a grade to a student. It truly was one of his worst experiences. He hated it. But he had too much integrity not to give it his all anyway."

"Thank you," Kieran's dimples glimmered as he grinned. "This all makes sense to me. Seeing how he suddenly showed up in my world as a poet."

With great animation, he recalled their initial meeting. "We traveled together for weeks after. Of course we did. Lord, he was fun to be with. 'Kieran', he'd say, 'what do you think of this?' Out would come some fantastic bit of music or writing. Then, of course, he'd insist on hearing mine. I couldn't imagine how he would have time for anything else. Except, of course, love." He threw a wicked smirk at Kate, who blushed predictably.

Kate struggled to speak up. She wanted to participate—help bring the vibrant memories alive—sure, in some mysterious way, that it helped Aidan. "I'm going to tell you the story of Montana," she began, ignoring the husky sound of her tone.

In words that sometimes trembled, and pauses that fought tears, she gave three people who loved Aidan access to a secret encounter—one that had fed him enough to withstand the hard years that followed.

"And I think," she considered a moment, "no, I'm sure, that week in Montana was a watershed event. It showed him he could teach in other ways and encouraged him to leave behind the university. I believe his dreams and memories kept him company for a lot of years," she wavered briefly.

"Same as they did for me. I don't think either one of us could believe it when we met each other again at The Big Misty. We struggled like crazy for some sort of balance," she added, shaking her head. "I tried to keep Aidan away from the whole horrible story of Ian to protect both of us. And he . . . " her voice cracked slightly. "He was battling his own threat and didn't want me to know."

She gestured at Kieran helplessly. He held up his hands. "Aidan didn't want anyone to penetrate that part of his business," he responded firmly. "We could see something destructive was happening, but we let him be proud. I wouldn't have done it differently," he added defiantly

Sheila stood up restlessly and contemplated the sterile hall toward the direction of the operating room. "You're right, Kieran." She turned slowly and challenged them.

"You couldn't have done it any different because he would never have allowed it. My father is both private and stubborn. You would have run into a brick wall if you'd tried to force anything out of him. And Kate, you had reason to be terrified. He understands, we all do now, that you wanted first and foremost to protect him from that maniac."

"I know this much, Kate," she continued, more quietly. "I have never seen a look on my Dad's face as when he talked about you. It lit up the room. I must admit, it shook me up. I saw it again, even stronger when I first met you, standing next to him. You and he are meant to be with each other. I want my Dad to finally be happy, just for him. Not for me or anyone else. You are the key to that."

There was nothing more to say. It was enough. A small benediction. They lapsed into fidgeting—bringing each other coffee or tea, checking anxiously for the sight of someone who would bring them news.

"Aidan gave me the writing he worked on while he was on the island," Kate said when they gathered again. Kieran straightened up with attention, his eyes intently cheering her on. "He told me to read it while he was under. But we're all here and we all want to hear it. From someone special." She smiled at Kieran. "There's only one proper choice for this. Would you read it to us?"

For a moment, she thought he would say no, so many emotions flitted across his features. Reading Aidan's work aloud was an honor he wasn't sure he was up to. But their hopeful expressions made it impossible to sidestep. "I would be more than happy to do so," he finally replied, with uncharacteristic quiet.

Kieran accepted the papers from Kate, smoothing them out on his knees and shuffling through them. For several minutes, this was the only sound. After he assembled them in an order that appealed to him, he began with no introduction or disclaimer.

For half an hour, he read the poems he had watched his friend struggle to produce. He read in a lyrical poet's cadence, representing Aidan the best he knew how, with his own inspired language.

After he was done, a subdued hush descended. Aidan's 'language of the soul' had joined them, with all of its beauty and muscle. Awed and appreciative, conversation ended. They did the only thing they could do—pass the slow hours—reading, pacing, dozing.

After a solid eight hours, Will finally emerged from the operating room, exhausted and walking stiffly. They rose as one, huddled for comfort. *Always feels like the oxygen has been sucked out of the room when I arrive,* he thought wearily.

"He made it through the operation," he stated in a guarded tone. The silence that followed his announcement was profound as they tried to assess what he meant.

"There was a lot of damage," he added flatly. "He's alive. That's the best news." He felt their eyes boring into him, lifted a shoulder in a helpless gesture. "Sorry, folks. I can't give you a lot more than that. I can't predict the outcome."

"I need to see him." Kate sounded harsh and choked.

"Of course," his tired face was clouded. "He's out, and will be for awhile, but I believe he'll perceive you're there." *Give them something to do. Wouldn't do any harm at this point,* he thought. "Why don't you all go?"

Sheila gave him a quick hug. "Thank you. Thank you for working so hard on him. I'm confident you gave him the best chance you could."

"I did," Will agreed. "Now it's up to him." He acknowledged them in turn as they thanked him, grateful when they turned and entered Aidan's room.

Though they all knew it would be hard, the sight of Aidan's motionless body complicated with tubes and IV's was appalling. Kieran swore under his breath. "I'll be outside," he muttered, leaving without another word. He'd warned them he had a weak stomach for such things, especially when they involved someone he cared about.

"Well, I'll be here." Kate's voice was strained but resolute. She cast an eye at Sheila and Christine as they encircled his bed, their faces solemn and pale. Breathing deeply to steady herself, she smoothed Aidan's hair, gently touching his hand. "We're here, Addy. We'll be here 'til you wake up."

Chapter 36

For an infinite week, Aidan hung on the outside of consciousness. The New Year arrived and departed with no celebration. Once again, Kate slept in a hospital room, watching Aidan—talking to him. Every afternoon, Sheila or Christine arrived, ready to take over. Kate reluctantly left for a few hours, leaving them with him—taking a slow turn through the hospital gardens with Kieran.

No one talked much. There was nothing and everything to say. The winter season fit their mood—dreaming of the past, hoping for the future. At regular intervals, Will fussed in and out, checking vital signs, troubled—looking for change.

After a particularly damp walk, Kate set aside her wet raincoat with a desolate sigh. *January rain was cold and unforgiving,* she thought. It erased every memory of warmer times. She paused, as ever, with Kieran at the entrance to Aidan's room. He would peek in, but no more. Christine got up, shaking the fatigue out of her shoulders, and met them.

This was a bit of a ritual, the three of them standing there at Aidan's threshold, as though they were exchanging news. Except, of course, there was, as Christine said, "no change."

Kate and Kieran nodded. Maybe tomorrow. They could not give up hope.

"Bye then, Kate." He helped her take off her wet coat. "The smell of rain and mud . . . Ah, it's a familiar perfume. You bring the memory of the Highlands into my mind."

"Thank you," she said to both of them, watching them walk down the hall. She turned into the room, swallowing a sigh. She kissed Aidan's forehead and lips. "Hello, dear one," she mused. "Can you smell the rain and wind? Time to wake up."

Dropping in the big chair in the corner, she stared into the dim light. *He's alive*, she reminded herself. *We have to be grateful for that one beautiful fact.* She would not entertain the possibility that he might not wake up. When sleep threatened, she allowed it, needing peace.

"Kate." The single word shivered in the air.

She snapped awake, instantly next to him. "I'm here." Their gaze locked, trying to discern what the other knew. She read the agonizing pain that knifed through him. He searched her eyes for a judgment of his condition. "Must I introduce myself?" Kate finally asked, smiling tenderly, reminding him that this had been one of his major fears.

"No," he said faintly.

She laid her head on his chest, listening to his heart. "Two down, Addy. You are alive. You recognize me." They were quiet, feeling the warmth spread between them. When Aidan did not stir, she sat up and studied him, holding his hands.

"I can't move them," he responded to her unasked question. It was a hollow statement of a feared condition. "I can't move my legs either," he added. His eyes closed as another throbbing surge hit him.

"Will said this could happen when you regained consciousness. We don't know anything yet. Can you feel my hand on yours?"

He stared back mutely, an upwelling of despair on his features. Kate made herself wait, her mouth dry.

"Yes," he finally replied.

Relief eased the tightness in her diaphragm. The loss of sensation would have been a toxic clue of Aidan's bleak future. He deserved the truth of how precarious his situation was.

"You've been in a coma for a week," she began, kissing him on the slender crease between his brows. "So . . . " Kate continued, "let's start with hello, dear one."

"I didn't die," his teeth ground hard against another stabbing explosion. "But my arms and legs did."

His eyes are fathomless, she thought. *Worlds colliding inside him.* She swallowed, wishing she could ease his desolation. "Can you feel this?" She brushed down the length of his body, then feathered her fingers on his feet.

The soft tingle of her touch was intense. His breath wavered as she moved upward to his belly and chest, sweeping down his arms and hands.

Her eyebrows arched, questioning. "Talk to me, Aidan," she said, forcing him to say what she already discerned.

"I felt it all." The concentration lines on his forehead deepened as raw pain lanced through him.

"Okay," she stammered. "Good. That's reassuring, Aidan,"

What he needed most wasn't clear to her. She pulled the chair next to his bed, without breaking her hold on him.

Beads of sweat popped out on his forehead. "Damn it." Excruciating sensations were roaring through him. "There's no point, "he smothered a gasp, "no point in you sitting here witnessing this."

"Are you quite finished?" she replied dryly.

"Go, Kate. Sweet woman, go away. For a while, at least. Let this thing play out."

"I am not going anywhere, Aidan," Kate's frown deepened. "When you get well enough to physically push me out, I might leave you for a few hours."

There was no answer. Feeling the burn of his regard, she met it with her own determined glower. A shuddering spasm knifed through him, cutting short further communication. With her palm on his chest, Kate rang for Will.

Will's expression was unsettled but his tone was firm. He laid a cool hand on his patient's fevered forehead. "I wish I could make it easier, believe me. I hate this part. One step at a time, remember?"

He continued relentlessly. "You survived the operation with all your mental faculties intact. Right now, that might seem more a curse than a blessing. And you definitely have some sensation. That's encouraging, though again, you may not think so. If you felt better now, Aidan, frankly, I'd be worried. At least you're feeling something."

"I still feel you have a fair chance of full mobility," he continued, reading their unspoken question. "But it's a waiting game. We have to keep faith." He stopped for Aidan's response but there was only pain-haunted motionlessness.

"Yeah, not even a word for how bad it hurts, is there? Remember, I can't give you more than minimal meds." Now, observing the burning scream of nerves, there was no way to deny how hard it would be for all of them. Glancing at Kate's distressed face, he added, "We can't hurry the healing. But I should at least be able to help him sleep," he said as he walked out.

"This will take all my concentration, Kate," Aidan ground the words out, unable to say anything else.

She could see the muscles in his cheek clenching. "We won't leave you to undertake this thing alone."

Mercifully, the nurse arrived, syringe in hand. Kate moved out of the room, dialing numbers as she went.

Chapter 37

The next morning, Kate, Sheila and Christine were all there, talking softly. Aidan listened without moving, working to get himself under control.

They'd agreed it was best to approach him individually. "Dad," Sheila said gently, coming forth immediately. "We're here with you."

"Hi," he swallowed hard. Talking was tough. "Been here all along?"

"In and out." Sheila touched his shoulder lightly. "I wish there was some useful way to help you."

"You can't," he struggled to form the sentence—powerless to soothe her, as he had always done. "Thank you for being here, during this time. But sweetheart, no reason to give up your life in this room," he continued. "You mean the world to me, but—" he stopped, unable to finish.

"He means please don't spend all your hours here," Christine was composed. "You, dearest daughter, should go on with what was important for your future."

Sheila bit her lip, looking down. She knew this was exactly what her father would say if he could. "Okay, Dad. I understand. But I'm coming here tomorrow and the next day until you are better."

He nodded, shifting his awareness to Kate.

"Okay, message received. You need to leave too, Kate," Christine said calmly. This had to be done without dawdling.

"I'll go," Kate agreed reluctantly, wincing as another tremor punished him. "For a few hours." Moving to Aidan's side, she lifted his hand and held against her cheek. "I love you. I'm not going to leave you. Don't try to make me. It will tire us both out." She touched her lips to his, and followed Sheila out.

Kieran was waiting for her in the garden. "She finally emerges. She is at last walking with an old friend, whom she's nearly forgotten about." Kate smiled wanly. Kieran steered her forward until she was safely out of range of the view of the hospital.

They sat on a cold bench in the pallid light of mid-January. She laid her head on his shoulder, taking comfort in his easy friendship. In halting sentences, Kate talked candidly, with an aching recognition of how life might be forever changed.

Christine sat beside Aidan describing the winter's progression. When he drifted into a restless sleep, she sat peacefully, remembering Eliot's last few days. But Eliot had no chance of recovery, and everyday had gotten worse instead of better. Christine had never been more aware of the beating of both of their hearts.

Until Eliot's slowed and finally stopped, and he left me—sitting there alone. She'd learned how to sit with little movement then. And now, for her dearest friend, she was glad to be of use.

For several days, there was no change in Aidan's condition

or in the routine they created. Will grew increasingly pensive and avoided conversation with any of them. There was nothing else he could do. If Aidan couldn't pull out of this, he was out of tricks. Everyone understood.

They talked sparingly and about other subjects, trying to distract Aidan and somehow ease the relentless misery. Kate went out every day as she promised, leaving Christine to watch over him—ready for Kieran's comfort and to tell him the latest.

"So, how is he?" Kieran asked cautiously

"In immense pain." The words spilled out. "Full of despair. He wants to be alone with it, but I won't let him." She looked up at the eggshell blue sky.

"And he's right. It's god awful tough to witness. I hate it. And there is nothing at all I can do. We don't talk much. They've got him on a minimum of pain medication to keep from suppressing his natural defenses. Most of his energy goes into dealing with that." It made her feel better to talk about it. They strolled through the twisting paths of the hospital garden.

"These brown winter trees," Kate said more calmly. "So exquisite. The way their grace is pared down. It's space, all that delicious spaciousness between the limbs."

"You are ever the artist."

"I wish." She took his arm, shaking her head. "Anyway, it's a promise. The red vein beneath the bark—swearing that life will return—spring will follow. I just need to hold onto to that."

Kieran sighed expressively. "That sounds exactly like something Aidan himself would say."

When it was time to trade shifts, Kieran walked her to the door and lingered as Kate and Christine embraced. "The only good thing about all this is being in the company of the likes of you," he said. Checking in at Aidan, he withdrew quickly with a bleak scowl.

Kate watched them walk out. Pausing outside Aidan's door,

she gathered her strength. He seemed to be sleeping but she knew better. She placed a finger on his chin. "Hey there," she said softly.

"Not you again." The barest suggestion of a smile skittered on his mouth.

"You were expecting someone else?"

His eyes opened. "There isn't anyone else. Never has been."

"Never will be again, I hope," she added, brushing the hair from his forehead. "How are you?" She could read nothing but pain. "Okay, dumb question." She decided to shift tactics. "Can you see the outside from here?"

His eyebrows lifted, surprised. "Almost," he ventured.

"I want you to be able to see it. The light. I want to feel your presence when I am in the garden." She could see the questions drifting across his mind, but they were buried beneath the layers of loss.

"Oh Addy, don't give up hope. Please don't. You held onto me when I knew I would die by Ian's hand. By some miracle, and by your love and strength, it didn't come to pass. Please allow me to hold onto you now. Let me offer my love to you and we'll see what we have to do. Together."

In answer, his eyes gently traced her face. Kate could feel his touch, even without his fingers. She began a slow massage of his arms, hands and chest, trying to will the ability to move into them.

"What do you do in the garden?" He asked softly.

"I walk with Kieran," she responded. "I tell him about you. He won't come in here," she said, answering his implied question. "It's as if he feels disloyal to you somehow if he's in here."

"Holding the memories outside," Aidan murmured, "so they don't become polluted." He tried to block the hurting and allow the pleasure of her loving hands.

"I suppose. Must be man thing."

A half step from sleep, Aidan could not resist responding. "It's a poet thing."

Kate smiled at that, shaking her head, repeating after him as he dozed. "Of course. It's so obvious. A poet thing."

During the difficult night, his dreams tangled with pain and longing, Aidan felt a familiar tingling in his legs and also in his arms and hands. While Kate slept, he tried flexing his stilled muscles. His heart lurched. There was a fractional response from all of his limbs.

After an edgy sleep, he woke again with a start in the morning, looking instinctively for Kate. Burning energy shimmered in his arms and shoulders. He made another tentative movement with his hands. Stretching his fingers out, he curled them up, his breath catching with the miracle of the movement.

Kate had arrived at the edge of his doorway in time to catch the luminous moment. "Aidan," she ventured, not sure if her voice would hold. "Thank God. At last."

An open smile lit his face. "Come here." It was an invitation. One she had been waiting for. One she had almost given up on.

She sat on his bed, her eyes brimming, swallowing hard—waiting for confirmation. Slowly his arms encircled her, pulling her down, his fingers playing a sweet song of victory on her shoulders. "I believe you healed something."

She sat up, laughing through her tears. "Fine, I'll take the credit," she said, kissing his hands. "Welcome back, music makers."

"My legs are on fire," he said cautiously. She paused, pondering what this might indicate. "I think that might be a good sign. It's excruciating . . . but maybe it's the nerves waking up."

"That's it exactly." Will walked in after observing them for a minute. Deep relief flooded his austere features. "Excuse me for listening in. I have to do a little official testing of what you've already experienced."

When the examination was finished, Aidan was finally

given medication to calm the worst of the pain. He also received a guarded but promising prognosis.

Aidan tried to decipher what else the doctor planned to say. "I can tell by that look there's more than what you've said so far," he added.

Will chewed on his lip. "The best scenario is that it will take awhile. Stops and starts. Frustrating as hell, I would imagine. We'll move you to a rehab facility and you will start the tiring boring process of becoming whole again. Physical therapy every goddamn day. You want finesse and strength—that's going to take some work."

Aidan waited, as Will struggled with the next bit of news. "And, to be honest, you could relapse. Can't say how far. We just have to take it day-by-day and work toward getting well. But I am very heartened to observe this movement, Aidan."

Kate waved away any more conversation. "We'll deal with the other possibility if it comes to pass. For now, I'm going to celebrate."

Early in the afternoon, Christine fluttered into the room, her arms full of cards and little presents. "Your former students have sent a big bouquet of well wishes. I thought you might be up to seeing them. There's a bunch from the staff as well."

Sheila followed behind her, bearing her own load of flowers and cards. "Ben and Claire sent these with me. You have your fans at the gallery as well, Dad." She smiled uncertainly at him, trying to measure his well-being.

He flared his fingers and lifted them slightly, a brief grin shining. Beaming, Sheila dropped her cards on his bed and hugged him tightly, cheering out loud as he embraced her.

They moved him on the first of February. Shafts of translucent sunlight lay over Aidan's bed. A tall weeping willow swayed languorously in the breeze, its naked branches gleaming orange and yellow. Beyond it, a row of stripped down oaks and birches danced together, a stream of mist tangling in their tops. Kate had insisted his window receive the sun.

Aidan's eyes followed Kate when she paced in. The slow pulse of desire was building, intermeshed with flashes of burning pain. But there was nothing to be done about it. Not quite yet. It would be done right, when he was ready. And he was noticing a disquieting inclination on Kate's features. Fatigued, pent up. *She needs to get away.*

That tired face was animated now though. Her smile was warm as she leaned into his bed, slipping her hand under his shirt and kissing him. Full-throated joy flickered between them. Catching her fingers, a soft moan escaped him. He pushed her away gently. "How can I feel such bliss and hurt simultaneously? Sweet woman, I know for sure that certain nerves are working just fine."

"Should we provide some specialized physical therapy?" she asked playfully, taking his hand, running her lips lightly over his knuckles.

He smiled, though the thought was tempting. "No. I want it whole. When I can move easily. I'm willing to wait."

"Well, I don't know if I am."

He had to end this before it went further. "Kate."

The tone was serious enough to cause her to stop and look quizzically at him. "I want you to go somewhere else for awhile." A frown creased her forehead. "Please don't resist it. Think, for a moment, about what you need. This work is slow, and we can't do anything to hurry it up."

Abruptly she stared out the window. She did want to see Jordan and Tracy, and he knew it. *Maybe a short trip.* But he had more to say—she could feel it. He meant to make her stay away longer.

Aidan spoke to her calmly. "You have to start painting again. It's the core of your life."

Kate leaned against the windowsill, overwhelmed with the truth of what he was saying. Aidan would always read and articulate what she needed, even if it was hard. And he was right. Her desire to paint again was roaring inside her, howling with the force of a banshee.

"I've been thinking about it," she agreed. "Honestly, I'm not sure if I can."

"You have to find out. Takes a little solitude to find that bedrock again."

"Maybe it was a fantasy. Maybe I made up being an artist. I have no evidence since the paintings were stolen." She returned to the view, musing. "It seems like years ago when I first showed you . . . what I couldn't do."

"Yes. Yes, it does," he agreed. "I haven't heard anything," he added in answer to her questioning look. "Freya heard the news from Sheila, about the operation, that I made it through. I got that far. But I haven't heard anything from her."

She said nothing, examining the muted colors of the landscape. When she imagined capturing that beauty, the procession of the season—her gut tightened with apprehension—but her heart raced with eagerness.

"You need to paint again, Kate." Aidan watched her shoulders tense, the mix of feelings surging and clashing. "Heal yourself now."

Chapter 38

It was a brief but vivid visit. Jordan had decided on Oregon State University, his conversations lively and full of energy. Kate requested a tour around the campus and an introduction to his professors.

When had he grown so wise and become so handsome and adult? She sat him down and told him the truth about his father—all of it, allowing the ugly reality of Ian to re-emerge briefly.

"I should have put some of these things together. Denial is amazing, I guess. You told me Ian took the paintings. Didn't occur to me to question how." He sat back and thought. "So, I don't really want to hear this. Ian was after you and somehow Aidan stopped him. I guess I am asking. Tell me what happened."

He was sick at heart when he heard about the fight. "Jesus, Mom. You were both dealing with so much. I had no clue. How could I be that stupid?"

"Nothing stupid about it. I was the one with the secrets."

"No wonder you were sad when I left you in Ireland." He looked away, fighting the passion of what he was feeling. "Ian will never own us again. I'll never call him 'father'. You're free of him. We're done with his craziness."

Kate started to reach toward him but thought better of it. "Yes, we are," she agreed.

The shadows fled his face, replaced by a new consideration. "You loved Aidan all the while you were raising me." He said it wonderingly, amazed at what he had discovered.

She was glad to tell him. "Not all the time. There were the first six years, when I merely had a hole in my life. After Montana, Aidan filled that space, in my dreams and memories."

"Then you met him again."

"Yeah." They smiled, marveling more at the face of Lady Luck than at each other.

"And what about your painting?"

"That's what Aidan asked me. And my answer is . . . no idea. I have to start and see how I do. It's unbelievably intimidating—to try again, after years of failure."

"I believe you can do it, Mom," Jordan responded earnestly. "No, more than that. I think you have to. Don't worry about me. I am happy and healthy." He grinned easily at her. "And I'm out to save the world."

"Oh, I know that," she watched his glance follow a willowy brunette up the stairs. "Don't work too hard at it."

Tracy was flushed with joy to see her. For the first time since they'd been kids, she had her sister again. Eliza, Tracy's second grader, brought Kate to school for show and tell. Adam, her fifth grade son, shy and reserved, warmed up to her slowly. *He hardly knows me*, Kate thought with a pang.

She'd taken extra effort to build a relationship, helping him work on a science fair project until they finished it. Tracy's husband,

Sam, was undeniably pleased. He understood how acutely Tracy had missed her sister.

"You'll eventually introduce us to that mysterious man of yours, won't you?" Tracy asked on the day she left.

"Promise. He'll demand it. Adam and Eliza will love him so dearly they'll forget all about me."

Driving up the long stretch of freeway, Kate's spirit was turbulent. The features of her son and niece and nephew mixed with floating raindrops and the dark jade of fir trees. The hunger to paint was growing. She had to place these images on canvas, pass them through her hands, birthing them and herself at the same time.

It made her heart pound to even think it. But she couldn't stop detailing the colors of early spring fringing the freeway—the bare trees shyly unfurling delicate colors of pastel green and the yellow-barked banners of new growth.

Never before had she been so keenly aware of the choice before her. It almost felt like her first day on earth. *I am an artist. I've always been an artist.* Images spoke to her, told her stories, insisting on being made real. The way Aidan spoke through music and poetry. That's what she wanted. *I have to paint again. If I don't, then Ian won.*

It would take weeks for both of them to heal and they each had to do their own work. On her trip, she had questioned Aidan about his progress numerous times. He'd challenged her gently.

"Enough, mo gradh. It still hurts every hour of every day. Hours of physical therapy, like Will said. That's all that's going on with me. Kieran was bored silly so I invited him to work at the gallery with Ben and Claire. Christine and Sheila have me under their wing. They tell me Bella will come when I'm well enough to dance with her again."

"Bella? I think you had a crush on her. That would make you happy."

"Yes, it would make me happy because while she was busy hurting me, I would listen to her sweet voice, and I would understand that I was almost ready to go. What is important in the meantime is what is happening with you, Kate. You find a little place. One that makes you really happy. Set up shop for awhile and remember how to be an artist."

The azure colors of the Queen Anne Victorian in Seattle's Madrona neighborhood blazed in the late afternoon sun. Kate placed the classifieds down on the seat of the car—certain it was the perfect place without going inside. She did check the back, peeking through the fence.

Only Seattle had yards like this, she thought, satisfied. Hidden jewels, they framed views of the Cascade Mountains and the Olympics simultaneously, rising over the tangled and vibrant foliage of eagerly growing plants.

The upstairs bedroom was hers three hours after she called. Susan, her landlady, had a busy life as a banker and was as anxious for a renter as Kate was for a place to land. They trusted each other on sight and dispensed immediately with formalities.

Before she could change her mind, she walked to the frame artist supply shop she'd seen, past city parks and gardens already in full bloom with plants from all over the world. *It's like being in an Impressionist landscape*, she thought, dazzled. Slightly dizzy, cheeks flushed, she plunged into the shop, as though she was diving into cold water, filling a bag with brushes, oils and canvases.

Returning home slowly, she felt faint. *Here is the lush and beautiful world. I hold the materials of art with sweaty palms. I am the bridge between them.* By the time she arrived at the Victorian, the bag was so heavy with promise she could scarcely hold it.

Sitting on the stairs, she dialed Aidan with shaking fingers. "I'm here," she announced.

"Is it perfect?" He heard the tension, but it was too early to ask. She didn't reply—her silence prolonged and loaded. "You said you wanted to find the perfect place," he reminded her.

Shaking her head, she held the art supplies gingerly. "Yes," she answered wryly. Aidan listened carefully to her description of the blue Victorian, surrounded by graceful birches, lilacs soon to come into blossom and the fabulous backyard. He kept her talking for a while, enjoying the stories of family.

When she ran out of steam, she uttered the question they both were avoiding. "When, Aidan?" There was such a deep desire to be with him.

"Give it awhile, Kate. Nothing here has changed. God knows I want to see you . . . but not yet." Not until he was better and she had fully explored her own recovery as an artist. "They did let me walk yesterday," he added.

Her heart leaped. "Walk?"

He laughed shortly. "If you could call it that. Pretty jerky ten steps."

Kate had hungered for those words for so long, she hardly knew what to do with the news. "How can you say nothing has changed? Everything has."

"One of these days, I'm going to dance in there and sweep you off your feet. Let me just reach the point where that even seems feasible." He paused. "How about you, Kate?"

"My painting will be similar to your walking." Her voice caught. *Equally painful.*

"Okay, sweet woman. I hear what's happening. You have to do it. But it won't be easy. We'll talk daily—and we'll hold each other up."

"Brian stopped this afternoon," he continued, changing course. "Expect him to show up tomorrow. I think he has something to tell you."

"He found a lover?" She said it lightly, but when Aidan did not banter with her, she grew quiet. "Wow."

"Let him tell you," Aidan said with a teasing tone. "That's all you're getting from me. But now, you go find something you lost. The inspired act that made you whole."

After saying goodbye, Kate sat quietly, remembering Ireland, and Nora's words, "never apologize for love", her eyes stinging, staring at the paints and brushes.

The next morning dawned bright and warm. In the backyard, Kate situated the easel in front of blooming daffodils. Paint was neatly laid on the table beside her. She picked up a brush, listening to the small sounds that emanated from the colors. Her hand was trembling. *Paint for Aidan. Paint your love for him.* "I'll try," she pleaded to unborn painting. "But I'm scared."

Tentatively she daubed the first colors in. The touch of paint to canvas sent a shock into her arm. She recoiled, dropping the brush. "I can't!" She shoved at the easel, almost toppling it, speaking angrily into the quiet. "I don't need to do this anymore."

Deep grief welled up from her core, startling her. She buckled over, leaning hands on knees, fighting a wave of nausea. *Aidan almost lost this ability. This song of creation.* "I am saying I can't. What the hell am I afraid of?"

Fear is death. Ian was death. "But Ian's gone." She picked up the brush, steadying the easel. *I choose life.*

For five hours, Kate placed careful brushstroke after brushstroke. She was completely startled when she heard Brian's hello.

"I won't approach unless you ask me to." He stood at a distance, allowing her to re-focus.

Amazed at finding herself in her Madrona garden, Kate gestured him close. "It's okay." Brian approached slowly. *Coming up on a deer*, she thought. "Do I appear that spooky?"

"You do, actually." He loitered, taking it easy. She would decide if it was ready.

Warily, she gestured toward the work, allowing his scrutiny. "It's rough, but there's something there, barely able to speak. Hardly able to breathe, but still alive." She smiled tiredly, held out her arms to him. Brian caught her in a hug, and over her shoulder, granted himself a quick look at what she created.

Her first painting was indeed alive. The splash of green evoked the smell of the wet earth—the dance of tender leaves unfurling. It was a pageant of spring.

He puffed out an approving whistle. "If this is what you thought was lost, no wonder you were so devastated. Beautiful work, kiddo. Outstanding."

"That's some high praise, coming from you."

"You better believe it."

"You seem different," she observed.

"Guess why."

"Ooh, that's scary. How presumptuous it will be if I say it out loud."

"Just say it, Kate," he said impatiently.

"You found someone. I mean . . . you are in a relationship where . . . " She stopped. Tried again. "You are . . . in . . . um, a commitment."

Brian interrupted her with a snort of laugher. "Quit your painful groping. You were right to think what you did, all along." Kate fought back the grin that was gathering inside her.

"I needed my lover to be a man," he continued, shrugging. "I had to have enough courage to say that out loud to myself. As soon as I did, Doug entered. Just like that. He tells me not to get too carried away, since he is my first gay love. But I'm free now."

Brian smiled, as Kate's elation bloomed. "I didn't realize I was in prison, but you knew. Once I came out, I couldn't believe I'd spent so much of my life living a lie and being alone."

For the next hour, she peppered Brian with questions, and he obliged, despite the self-conscious subject. For years, he alone had heard her darkest secrets. *Except for Aidan,* he reminded himself. She did keep that one to herself.

But most of it, she had shared with him, and now it was his turn. *What he couldn't say, she would figure out,* he thought, as he sauntered off.

Kate called after him teasingly. "Will I get to meet Doug?"

"Maybe. Probably. Yes. When it's right."

Chapter 39

After the original painting, the second came hard. The first was pent up energy, ready to be released. The second felt like a commitment she wasn't sure she was up to. Standing in the courtyard in the soft gray morning, she was queasy and irresolute. Could she stand up long enough to produce an image on the canvas?

Despair followed floundering. There was nothing joyful about the preliminary applications of color. Kate contemplated the fledgling work, wishing to throw it out—aching to destroy it. Her hand hovered for a moment over the art, threatening. She breathed out a big exhalation and turned aside. *I will let this being exist, even if it's flawed.*

When Aidan heard her tone that afternoon, he asked her to come see him. As he waited in a wheelchair outside the rehabilitation center, her buoyant joy strengthened him as she stepped eagerly toward him.

"Hello, sweet woman," he whispered softly, as she stood a moment in front of him, holding his hands. He tugged her into his lap, drawing her close. She buried her head in the crook of his shoulder, feeding her heart on the certainty of their love.

"I needed that," Kate laughed as she sat next to him. "To say I missed you would be such an understatement it's not even worth saying."

"Well said," Aidan's lips twitched. "Very well said." He turned her hand over, gently touching the bits of color on her fingers and palms. "I hoped this is what you were up to." His voice was quiet, his tone tender.

"It's hard, Addy. So damned hard. I can't really talk about it yet." She didn't like the pallor she saw on his skin. "How are you?"

"I've had a set back," he said briefly. Kate's eyes were somber, listening. "Some of the same symptoms as before the operation. Not as hard, and not all the time, but more than it was. I managed to talk Will out of taking me to the hospital, but there is a question now . . . " Aidan grew quiet.

"A question?"

"Not clear what he's got in mind, exactly. I think he is figuring it out as it happens."

"But . . . " Kate began.

"Will is working on it," Aidan interrupted her evenly. "He will deliver what he has to say, blow by blow, soon enough. What you are doing now is important to me. In some way I can't explain, it helps more to have you doing that than to be here, anxiously waiting."

Kate didn't argue. There was no point. She knew that look.

"When they give me the go ahead to finally leave this place, I am coming to you. And all your free time will vanish," he added cheekily.

As February dissolved into March. Aidan found himself

once again on a battlefield. His health was like an injured bird, bright-eyed one minute, weakly fluttering the next. At night, though he needed it, he held off taking pain medication until after Kate's daily phone call.

"What are you doing?" she asked.

"Watching the light shift on the trees," he responded. "Thinking about spring in the Fisherfields."

"Brian invited me to meet Doug. It's a huge step for him. I'm having lunch with them."

Aidan loved these moments, letting the day go—forgetting the uncertainties surrounding him.

"Jordan wants to call you, is that okay? He said he'd enjoy visiting. But not 'til spring break."

"I'd love to talk to him, Kate. As for visiting, later is better anyway."

The northwest spring was unabashed. *This shameless flowering shows no sign of modesty*, Kate mused. In alternating bursts of enthusiasm and despairing failure, she painted, discovering each color and shape as it took its place on the canvas. Nights, she began the conversation with it, confident that the celebration of beauty was what Aidan required to combat his situation.

This evening, something was off. Aidan was slow to play with her, distracted. "Tell me what Will is saying," she requested.

"Not much. Says some of the damage is degenerative. He went in today with some arthroscopic work."

"Damn it, Aidan. Why are you only now telling me this? Really? I have to come over."

"No, mo gradh. I need to sleep it off in any case. Seems scar tissue was creating the issue. I tried not to listen to the descriptions of 'scraping'. Will was hopeful. For Will."

She didn't dare ask him more. Speaking it out loud felt too discouraging.

As the days passed they talked little of it. Kate reported her elation and despair as painting gradually became easier. Aidan only affirmed that he was working hard. "But Will's detailing has helped. There's progress, Kate."

"Aidan . . ."

"You stay with the daylight and Susan's yard. That's where you belong right now."

"I belong with you."

"You're here. More than you might imagine. You are walking with me through the Fisherfields and looking up at the sky over Ulva."

"You're writing." A wave of pure gladness flooded her.

"Yes. So there's your proof. I am no longer dead to the world after therapy. If they had a piano, I would be playing it."

Kate reflected on the paintings that filled the makeshift studio in Susan's unused dining room. They were developing, maturing. Her will to see them to the finish was growing. "Imagine it, Aidan. Hold onto this vision. I am painting. You are playing music nearby."

Aidan closed his eyes, blocking the view of his dreary room. "About as near to heaven as I can imagine. Tell me about your visit with Brian and Doug today." It seemed too fragile to continue talking about recovery. *As if doing so might destroy it.*

"Well, they're becoming regulars. Susan adores them. She and Doug have developed an interesting friendship. They're quite a pair. She's so short and cheery and well—stout. He is elegant and tall, dangerously gorgeous. Sometimes they look like Count Dracula and some innocent woman traipsing about in the dark recesses of this old house," she laughed. "But he's got a very appealing energy."

"Thanks, great imagery. I'll enjoy thinking about that."

"She and Doug fuss over every inch of the house—re-designing, admiring the architecture and then worrying about the old electrical fixtures. Susan has this enthusiasm for electronics and the house has too few outlets for all the things she plugs in. They called the electrician in to check the old wiring. He told them she should replace it as soon as possible."

"Will she?"

"Yes, she's got it on the calendar. As soon as she's done with the guest bathroom."

"She should move it up." He didn't like the vision of snaking cords he was envisioning. "Kate, tell her to move it up. Okay?"

Her voice was preoccupied, analyzing the paintings. "Okay."

After a beat, he knew he would not hear more. "And you and Brian?"

"We drink too many cups of coffee and I talk to him about painting and you and Jordan while his eyes follow Doug around. If Doug gets too far away, we have to saunter near them as though we happen to be doing something in the same area. Brian tries to be cool. I pretend that he is. But it's obvious he's head over heels. And since he's a total virgin to that feeling, he doesn't know what to do."

"Does anyone?" Aidan bit a smile. "I seem to remember doing the same at The Big Misty."

"Yeah. True. Very true."

Kate used the backyard as her studio when the sun was shining, moving to the shelter of the porch when rain fell softly in the swelling spring. Every day felt precious—like she was carrying them both into the light. She'd grown used to the hitch of her breath as she started and the impulse to give up was still strong. But she couldn't fail, and tell Aidan about it at the end of the day.

They talked little of the daily work. Tired and sick of it, they clung to lighter topics and to wordplay, conjuring the Fisherfields, Montana and other places they had loved and explored.

"Take me into that inner wilderness, Aidan. This the time

for it, when we can't go to the mountains. Make them real."

"We do it together, Kate. Remember 'duende'? That deep soul space that Kieran talked about? When he introduced me at the poetry session?"

"Barely. I was hardly breathing and thinking about you in the most confused and heartsick way."

"Not lusting?"

"That too."

Aidan laughed lightly. "Good. Even in retrospect, knowing it fills me with wonder." He waited long enough to sense her smile.

"Recall your own duende, Kate," he said softly. "Make it real and it will appear naturally with all the landscapes that have fostered you. Paint your aliveness. That's what the creative process is about. You'll never be sure you're going to make it. I don't think it ever becomes easier."

"You just need to do it. Leap and the net will appear. You hope."

"Exactly. Reach for me, now in that world full of wild air. Hold my hand, Kate." As though he was next to her, he led her into his memories and they stepped into another world, imagined and perfect.

As the days passed, Aidan stopped asking Will about progress, and took his anxiety deep inside. Working at movement was the only thing that counted. He used the remaining energy at the end of the day to escape.

His poems roamed into the landscape he held dear—his fingers composed music on the windowsill when he stood in the evening, surveying the greening world. His pulse jumped when Bella arrived.

Her soft features were lit with delight. She gave him an amused stare. "He didn't tell you, did he?"

"That would be a no," he couldn't help but smile at her.

"But you look like an angel, standing there."

"Well, you can expect I am here for a reason."

"To hurt me, I know." A sudden joy flooded through him. "And you would be doing that because I might be ready to dance again?"

"Dr. Burke thinks so. After some hard work, Aidan, you remember. He told me that I better let you have that dance with your lady this time."

Chapter 40

In four weeks, Kate had completed eight paintings. They flowed out of her like a tidewater river, riding on the highs and the lows of the day. Her landscapes were expansive and filled with radiant light. The Highlands blazed with amethyst and lavender, rejoicing in the partnership of rock and lichen. Wild water roared down from incandescent forests and supernatural mountains.

She considered the gathered paintings. They had been born in the depths of her fear. *I can't feel it any more. Instead, I see vibrant beauty and energy.* Aidan had pushed her hard to be alone, to keep moving. He'd kept her from being distracted by his own issues and joined her instead on the invisible and infinite field of creativity. *I am healed*, she thought wonderingly.

That afternoon, she called Aidan. "I admit it, I'm a broken record. But I don't think I can wait any more to see you."

"I like that broken record. I appreciate your allowing me to do it this way. I wanted to be strong enough to come to you without any limitations. And . . . finally, that time has arrived," his voice wavered. "To celebrate both of our victories."

"Arrived?"

"You heard it right," he responded softly.

"Bella gave you the dance?"

"No. She left. Threw a kiss over her shoulder and said Will told her someone else got the first dance."

Kate closed her eyes, tears sliding down her cheeks, not able to speak.

"I'm on my way, mo gradh."

When Aidan's Volvo pulled into the street, Kate started down the steps. Aidan opened the car door, pushed at the air with his palms. "Stay there." He swung his legs out of the car easily, and walked toward her with a slight limp.

"Not quite dancing yet. But getting there." When he reached the porch, they stood smiling at each other.

"Welcome home."

"At last." He pulled her tight for a kiss so hungry and powerful it opened up every nerve in Kate's body.

"Whoo," Kate caught her breath. "Good thing the families are gone," she laughed shakily. The genteel Madrona street was nearly deserted. "What would you like to do first?"

Aidan took a step away, studied her. "Well, I only have two things on my list. See your paintings. Make love to you. Maybe we'll take a rest and some food . . . and make love again."

"Okay," Kate smiled slowly. "Same as my list. Let's go 'round through the back," she said, her arm circling his waist.

Kate had told him about the garden, full of birds and life. She loved standing on the porch in her bare feet, watching shafts of sunshine light the luminous green. With a short, firm shake, the locked door swung open into the kitchen.

"This is the 'gallery,'" she said, leading him into the converted dining room. The memory of showing Aidan her ruined art at The Big Misty flashed by. *My witness.*

Eight new paintings hung on the walls. Aidan studied them in rapt admiration. "You found another holy ground," he said huskily. "They are exquisite."

"They are my love for you on canvas. These are your paintings, Aidan. The ones you helped me create."

"By staring out the window?"

"By your presence and your love—helping me get over myself and do it."

He wove his hands into her hair. "I want to take my time with each and every one," he affirmed. "But first, I need to attend to their creator."

"Is this another part of the creative process, professor?" Kate's skin tingled as his lips swept across hers.

"Indeed it is, sweet woman." Aidan deepened the kiss, reminding her how long they'd been apart. He had dreamed of this too many nights to rush it. Sparks flew as they explored.

"May I show you to my bedroom before we set this place on fire?" she managed.

He held her hand to his chest, his eyes wandering over her. Nodded wordlessly. They climbed the long flight of creaking stairs. Aidan closed the door, leaned against it and pulled Kate into his arms.

He tugged the band from her ponytail, used his fingers to free the luxurious waves. Took her face in his hands and rained kisses over her eyes, the soft hollow of her throat, the bridge of her nose. Found home again in her receptive mouth.

"Can I really be here, after all those days and nights of thinking about it, fantasizing about it. Kate, you filled every waking moment. Every dreaming moment."

His voice was rough and low. "I sometimes despaired of it. Thought it would never arrive. But here you are, sweetheart. Here you are." He fought to hold onto the exquisite beauty of simply being with her.

Moving in a slow dance of passion, their breath increasingly ragged, they peeled off clothes, impatient and famished—seeking the cool bed beneath them.

Her warm skin next to his held the fragrance that had pulled him through from the painful hell that had almost claimed him. This woman, this beautiful, passionate woman, had cherished his heart and life, and by that miracle, he was whole again.

His mouth skimmed along her breasts as he covered her body with his—found his way into her. She arched to him, drawing him deeper, wanting him in the very center of her being. He moved slow and deep, his forehead against hers, their breath mingling, struggling for focus.

"Don't hold back, mo gradh," he whispered. "Take it."

A small cry escaped Kate, as she rippled and dug her fingers into his shoulders. She wrapped her hands around his, opened her eyes wide, her gaze tender.

Her arms reached up for him. She drew him down against her skin, moved her hips to his increasing rhythm—lost in the heat they generated, their bodies linked and mated. *For the rest of time.* A sweeping climax shook Aidan as Kate followed him into the blaze.

After their breathing slowly calmed, Aidan murmured "Are you still alive? Not sure I am." She didn't answer, just tangled deeper, limb-to-limb, heart to heart.

Chapter 41

They stood in the kitchen in the potent sun of a late March morning. Light streamed in, irrepressibly flooding the place with brilliance. After introducing Aidan to Susan, Kate stood at attention as Aidan studied her paintings with meticulous thoroughness.

Susan was enthusiastically pointing out details to Aidan, who, of course, had already observed them. *That half-smile is driving her crazy,* Kate thought mischievously.

"You provided quite a haven here for a recovering artist," said Aidan when he got an opportunity.

"It was a pleasure, in every way. I suppose you'll be planning to steal her off with you."

"I am afraid so. I'll have to beg you to understand."

"Not at all," Susan beamed in Kate's direction. "I know that's what she's been eagerly waiting for."

They drove in the direction of the waterfront, toward the view that Aidan always trusted—the Olympic Mountains gliding under the bottom of receding clouds. It was a short ten blocks to Kate's favorite bakery, a little hole in the wall place downtown. "Great Belgian waffles here," Kate could not keep from grinning, "Today, we are going to do something perfectly ordinary."

Aidan pulled her closer. "Not sure I agree with you. The word ordinary is altogether too ordinary for what I'm feeling."

When the smoke alarms started, there was no one home. The acrid odor of burning electrical wire drifted from the living room, smoldering like a silent specter of destruction. By the time the billowing gray smoke escaped the house, tongues of flames were licking the walls of the dining room. A livid blast of orange flame shot straight up from the middle of the house, capped with roiling black smoke.

Stopping by for a visit, Brian and Doug had just turned the corner. For a frozen instant, they stared in horror at the crimson sparks spiraling up, creating a windstorm of their own. Without a word, Brian dialed 911, pulled the car over abruptly and leapt out of it.

He barked directions—while Doug dialed Susan, then Kate. His message was short and sharp. "Fire at the house. Get home." Within minutes, a squad car peeled in, lights flashing, followed shortly by three fire engines.

A fiery glow lit the afternoon sky as the firefighters pulled hose and sent the streaming water out. Susan drove in slowly, taking in the scene, her heart sinking. She stopped well short of the scene and sat, too stunned to cry or move.

Doug had been waiting for her. He dragged her out of the car, peeled her hands back from her face and hugged her tightly. "I heard them say they didn't think it would engulf the whole structure," he said between shushing sounds. "They should to be able to keep it from spreading." Blinking, she nodded, staring at the house.

As Aidan and Kate swerved in, the efforts of the firefighters were beginning to show. Brian was pacing grimly, apart from Doug and Susan. He watched them double park next to his car and slowly get out. Kate pondered the surreal sight of the house, clouds of smoke coiling from its core. It was a battle site, police and fire fighters moving efficiently around them.

Striding straight toward them, his eyes on Kate, he stood without touching her. "It started in the living room," he began brokenly.

Kate waited for him to say what she already knew.

"Spread into the dining area. They caught it there."

"But everything in the center would be destroyed."

"Yes." It was not necessary to spell it out. She knew the paintings were gone. With a choked moan, Kate entered woodenly into Aidan's encircling arms. Laying her head on his shoulder, she grieved, trying not to imagine the dazzling colors consumed by smoke and heat.

The five of them stood silently, in mixed horror and relief when the fire lay down, leaving a gaping central hole, but most of the house untouched.

The fire chief approached them, his cheeks tinged with soot. "I need to talk to the owner of the house."

"I've got it," Doug said over his shoulder, taking Susan's arm and talking particulars to the chief, firmly steered them away. Kate had her own disaster to face.

Distraught, Brian paced uncertainly for a minute. "God damn it," he muttered. "God damn it," he repeated furiously. "We almost got them out. One more day and we would have got them out."

He stared glumly at the smoldering house. "Take your time." His movements were uncharacteristically disjointed. Shoving his fists in his pockets, he walked gracelessly toward the Doug and Susan.

"Kate," Aidan held her face, anguished. "I don't know where to start. Nothing I can say would make sense right now. All those long hard months. " He rested his cheek against her head, her tears wetting his shirt.

Deep sadness washed through her as she struggled to find her feelings. She was clearly wounded. *But not the same as my grief when I thought I couldn't paint. That was deep, like a canyon I would never climb out of.*

"Where are you?" Aidan asked gently.

"I am standing here in the sun. With you, here, alive." She stated this as a fact, her voice unsteady. "That holds me together." She exhaled slowly, her chest tightened by sorrow. "The beautiful house. There was no other like it in the neighborhood."

She tilted into his arms, dry-eyed and troubled. "And once again, I am an artist with nothing to show for it."

Chapter 42

After the firefighters left and the yellow tape was pulled around the house, they moved into the backyard, escaping neighbors and questions. The green sanctuary was dreamy and tranquil. For several silent minutes, they numbly hung close together taking in the contrast, opposite of the smoking house.

"I'm heading in," Brian stated pointedly, his voice loud and startling in the quiet. "I want to see it."

Aidan nodded, watching Kate's stricken expression. *He's right. We do need to see it. To know for sure.* "Can you do it? We should go in, just for a minute."

Kate didn't answer immediately. The tracks of tears were dry, touched with ash. "Okay," she replied tensely. She made herself stand up and ready. "Yes. I can do it."

As one, they carefully entered the rooms of the house where the overloaded wires melted and burst into flames. Walking slowly through the burned area, they gingerly skirted the holes and smoking walls. There was little left of anything. Nothing of her art.

Kate stared soberly at the area that used to be the dining room. "They really died. Except there is no body."

Susan did not hide her sadness but she rallied somewhat with Doug's muttered enthusiasm for the rebuilding project.

"It's lucky the outer walls held," she said tentatively.

"Yes. It will be the prettiest house in the neighborhood once again with some work," Doug replied purposefully. "And with updated wiring."

"But Kate . . . " Susan had no words to continue. No one knew what to say to Kate.

"Can we go back to the yard?" Kate walked out without waiting for an answer. One by one, they followed her silently.

She stopped by the easel she'd placed outside, gently touching it. "Here I remembered I was an artist. It was one of the hardest things I ever did," she spoke calmly, more to herself than anything else. They stood in silence until she turned and confronted them.

"And I think, that though I lost my evidence, I am still an artist. The fire killed the paintings, but not the will to create them. That is stronger than ever." She regarded each of them—meeting Aidan's gaze for an extra beat.

"I am sad. I know you are too. But don't be devastated," her eyes welled up but determination laced her voice. "I'm not . . . devastated. I will paint again. I will . . . enter the creative process again. That's what I learned . . . during these months. I had a good teacher."

The green plants waved gently in the breeze. The mountains stood watch. Five people huddled closely like survivors in a combat zone, and felt the bright healing resilience of joy.

After a week of cleaning up, Aidan and Kate were ready

to leave. "This one is for you," Kate smiled, handing Susan a luxuriantly colored canvas. It was the one painting that had been safely at the shop—the last to be framed. It featured Susan's vibrant plants, spilling out from the jungle-like porch. Susan's eyes filled as she accepted the painting.

"I want you to visit us," added Kate, patting Susan's shoulder.

"Wild horses couldn't keep me away," Susan replied. "I'll give you some time first to paint some more, okay? We have plenty to keep us busy here for awhile" She glanced at Doug convivially.

"We'll take care of her, Kate," Brian said as he walked out with her. "Doug is already drawing up designs for the whole interior."

"You have a new project."

"I do. And I am . . . dare I say it out loud? Happy."

Kate insisted that Aidan go alone to say goodbye to Sheila and Christine. As was his habit, he took his time alone with each of them. "So, Dad, you'll be on your island soon," Sheila motioned toward the sparkling sea and horizon of mountains. "Think of me savoring the same view."

"I will. It's a favorite thought." He gathered her gently into his arms. "I'll expect you to come up next week, then?"

"I have four days off," she answered, her eyes sparkling. "And Ben and Claire already have me booked for about fourteen different things."

"Good. They'll be fun, no matter what. You deserve to play a little. You'll get to meet Jordan. He's coming at the same time."

"Jordan? Oh, I'll feel like I am meeting my family."

Aidan only smiled at her.

"I am so glad for you, for me—for all of us. I love you so much, Dad."

"And I love you." He kissed her lightly. *Kathleen's severed life lives on in this beautiful young woman. My daughter.* "Always and forever."

Leaving her with a final affectionate squeeze, Aidan walked outside with a steady motion, the returning strength evident in his gait. Christine leaned against the truck, enjoying the sight, laughing at the bear hug he gave her.

As they drove out, Aidan gave a two-handed wave to Sheila. It was a joyous, buoyant move—an expansive, passionate celebration of this event in his life. *This precious and longed for moment.*

A sense of health spread through his body. Where there had been such pain—now the ordinary feeling of aliveness was the most amazing gift, and one he would forever see as miraculous.

"So, how's your love life, Bailey?" He grinned companionably at Christine.

She chuckled saucily. "Tell you what. When you deign to go to Bellingham again, I will introduce you over again to Sam. He deserves better than only being thought of as my neighbor who clips my azaleas."

"I might want to go out dancing," warned Aidan mischievously.

"Oh, we have the best place. Don't you think I haven't already thought of that? Far enough in the country to be away from the university crowd. All cowboy. Practice your slide-slide-step."

"I owe you," he said.

"The hell you do. If you think you do, though, that's great. Come and visit me."

"Soon, my dear girl."

Elated and deliciously flustered, Christine grinned. "I love it when you call me that."

The trip home to the island was radiant. Ben and Claire had borrowed a boat so they wouldn't have to take the ferry. No one talked as the boat cut across the restless blue water. They simply watched the islands come close and when they entered their shelter, relished the sudden flattening of the waves, the splendor of rock and green rising straight up from the sea.

They arrived at port as the April sun burst out of the clouds with a dazzling strong light. Kieran waited on the pier, beaming with delight.

"That's a thing of beauty, a boat coming in full of smiling faces. I have been pacing this place for hours." The waves danced in patterns of riffles and foam. A breeze hugged the water's surface, lifting it up like a dancer's dress, spinning mist into the air.

"I have something to show you both," Kieran's dimpled grin was infectious as he ushered them toward the van.

Kate looked at Aidan questioningly. He tipped toward her and spoke into her ear. "I've figured he was up to some kind of surprise for the past few days, but I really have no idea what it is. Claire is in on it too. Whatever it is, they are both beside themselves. I hope they didn't get us a puppy."

They drove up to the gallery. Though it was after hours, the place was lit up brightly. At the door was a familiar figure. It was Freya.

Kate shot a perplexed look at Aidan. His face was ablaze with emotion. *There could be only one reason why Freya would be here.*

She would have very little of introductions. "Hello, handsome," Freya purred when Aidan walked up to her, kissing him on the mouth. Her sultry voice was wickedly full of fun. She extended her hand to Kate. "Obviously this is your lady. The painter, Kate. I feel I know you."

Kate was so puzzled that Freya giggled like a young girl. "You have no idea, do you? What wonderful secret keepers I am surrounded by! They didn't even tell your man." She gestured grandly toward the interior of the gallery. "Enter, my dear. There are some old friends who are eager to see you."

Aidan made certain he was right behind Kate as she walked in, knowing she would reel exactly as she did, into his arms. Fourteen paintings filled the gallery. They were the chronicles of a young woman's history, her discovery of the world—her hard-won wisdom. Kate stared from the paintings to Freya in stunned silence.

Freya appreciated the sense of triumph before she spoke. It was a lengthy story, but she meant to make the telling very short. "A man named Ken Hunter, currently doing time in the Pen, had them in deep storage. Nebraska. Took quite awhile to hunt him down, three aliases later. But once we did, there they were. I couldn't save them all. Water damage. But I got these."

No one needed to comment on the beauty of the work. Not even Kate. All the normal modest responses by the artist were swallowed by the power that emanated from each landscape and careful detailing. She was as dazzled by them as anyone in the room. Aidan watched Kate touch each painting, seeing it freshly.

Freya leaned against the wall—her shoulder comfortably snuggled against Claire's, an easy smile relaxing on her full lips, wearing an attitude of huge satisfaction. Not trusting his voice, not daring to break the spell of radiant stillness, Aidan slanted a look of pure gratitude in her direction.

Kieran could barely keep from whooping out loud. *Damn these quiet people with all their meaningful looks! These were resurrected lives, hostages set free, beings re-born.*

A sudden urge for Julie ignited. They would whirl each other around, she and he. They would dance and shout with joy. *If she were here . . .* he patted the airline ticket in his coat pocket, reaching for its reassuring bulk. Tomorrow he would be on his way to see her. Heat coiled upward from his groin to his cheeks.

One glance at Kieran was enough to break the spell for Aidan. There was no doubt at all what the lusty Irishman was thinking. He'd seen that look before. He wiped at his eyes with the

back of his hand, letting the contagion of ecstatic celebration fill
him.

There had been so many hazards, so many obstacles. It was
less than a year since he and Kate had met again on a Scottish
mountainside. Who would have imagined all that had happened
and here they were, whole and well and home. *We are home.* He
caught her and planted a wholehearted kiss on her lips. "We've
arrived, mo gradh."

Kate laughed through her tears, hugging him and one by
one, everyone smiling in the room. Everyone jumped when Kieran
popped the champagne and moved forward to receive the sparkling
bubbly, laughing and talking all at once.

The festivity went on until midnight. Freya said very little
about how she had come to obtain the paintings, and would not
consider any payment whatsoever. "I prefer having you owe me,"
she said silkily to Aidan. "And this evening, I am going to retire
to my Bed and Breakfast. I am assuming I will not see you in the
morning, since presumably you two will be busy."

She gave them a lascivious wink. "I leave for Chicago
directly after breakfast. With your man," she added with an Irish
accent, nodding at Kieran.

They stared quizzically at the blushing Irishman. "She
makes it sound so sexy. But actually, we are just sharing a ride to
SeaTac. Och, I have—a date—with Julie."

Kate grinned with sudden delight. "So, you finally moved,
did you?"

"I did indeed. I asked her to travel with me to Australia.
Just on a lark, mind you. And she said yes! She even agreed to
return with me to The Big Misty in the late spring. We're going to
visit Chris and Mary. I had to have something to reflect on while
you and Aidan were so busy and I thought, well, I don't think it's
quite the same thing. But it's a start, by god, it's a start."

"I can't begin to thank you enough," Aidan said. His voice

caught unexpectedly. "Most of all for standing by me when I needed your friendship . . ." His words trailed off. "You'll say hello to Julie for me?"

"I will, of course, and there's no call for a thank you. Sure, I should be thanking you." Kieran's grin grew serious. "There is a wee request, though, Aidan, I'll be asking of you. A favor of my own."

"We'll come, Kieran," Aidan responded, understanding immediately. "You tell us when and we'll go to The Big Misty. I can't think of anything that we would love more."

"Not until most of the tourists have gone home. That's the best time of year anyway, as you both know. A proper good crowd and the best setting for some concerts and readings."

"We will look forward to it. Most especially to seeing you."

"We might have to stop off in West Cork first," Kate winked at Aidan. "There's a few folks I want you to meet."

"And Ulva," rejoined Aidan. "I have a promise there to fulfill."

Kieran swept them up together in a jaunty embrace. He kissed Kate's cheek, then Aidan's, a gap toothed grin spreading broadly on his face. "Don't you two have anything better to do than to be here now?" he asked teasingly.

"We plan to keep Kieran up all night telling stories and singing songs." Ben threw the keys of the Volvo to Aidan.

Claire passed Aidan a wicker basket. "I packed some food up for you."

"You should go ahead and open a restaurant, my dear Claire."

"I like picking my customers too much."

They raised hands in salute as Aidan and Kate drove slowly from the gallery. "Call us!" Ben shouted. "But not before you're ready."

They followed the narrow winding roads, turning the

music up loud and singing along past the dark trees and fields, sitting in the car for a minute outside Aidan's house.

"You must be tired." Kate reached up to trace Aidan's cheek with her fingers.

The sensuous warmth of his eyes had returned. He nodded. "I am. I think I need to be taken to bed immediately."

The full moon shone over the tops of the firs, illuminating the closest clouds like streetlamps. It spread out over the water, spilling its generous radiance across the sea, shining as the lights of the house went out.

Curve of the Moon

SHANN CATHRO WESTON lives in the heart of the Salish Sea, in the San Juan Islands. There, she and her husband raised two daughters while they traveled the world, held many bonfires, and never got tired of the beauty. A poet-naturalist and teacher, Shann had the privilege of watching killer whales for a living for several years. She is passionate about creativity, nature and speaking to people about a Sense of Place.

On the banks of the Shannon River, Shann wrote and delivered an essay that won the grand prize, the Seanachaoi Pub (storyteller in Irish) in a contest sponsored by Guinness. She and her family lived an Irish publican's life for two years, returning frequently to explore the Celtic lands. The Seanachaoi gave her a front seat opportunity to discover the landscape of poets, where celebration of word and song are as important as food and drink.

LaVergne, TN USA
09 January 2011
211701LV00001B/6/P